"GOD ALMIGHTY!" RED SHOUTED. "THE DAM'S BROKE!"

A flood of river-water crashed through a ten-foot cut in the dam's top and roared down over the other side, yellow and roiling.

"She's gonna blow!" Red yelled again.

Suddenly, they saw something dark silhouetted against the night sky. It was Hoppy crossing the rain-slick dam, a dead yearling steer over his shoulders.

"That's it, Hoppy!" Red roared. "Dead cows'll choke that hole."

But then lightning flared, and thunder cracked. The dam-top crumbled and Hoppy, losing his footing, was tottering over the brink toward the raging river below ...

Other Clarence E. Mulford books by Tor

The Coming of Cassidy
Bar-20
Hopalong Cassidy

Clarence E. Mulford

HOPALONG CASSIDY

TOR

A TOM DOHERTY ASSOCIATES BOOK
NEW YORK

This is a work of fiction. All the characters and events portrayed in this book are fictitious, and any resemblance to real people or events is purely coincidental.

HOPALONG CASSIDY

All new material copyright © 1992 by Tom Doherty Associates, Inc.

Cover art by Carl Cassler

A Tor Book
Published by Tom Doherty Associates, Inc.
175 Fifth Avenue
New York, N.Y. 10010

Tor ® is a registered trademark of Tom Doherty Associates, Inc.

ISBN: 0-812-52242-7

First Tor edition: December 1992

Printed in the United States of America

0 9 8 7 6 5 4 3 2

*Affectionately Dedicated
to My Father*

Introduction

IN JUNE, 1991 Bantam published the first of Louis L'Amour's acclaimed Hopalong Cassidy novels, *The Rustlers of West Fork*. Since then, there has been a tremendous ground swell of enthusiasm for Hopalong and his friends. Readers around the country want to know more about these Bar-20 boys—and above all, want more of their books.

Consequently, Tor Books is bringing back the original novels, written by Clarence E. Mulford, the man who created Cassidy and company. It's a good thing too. These are really first-rate books, full of true grit and pulse-pounding action, the kind of books you can't put down.

If you liked Louis L'Amour's Hopalong Cassidy novel—*The Rustlers of West Fork*—you'll *love* this one. This is no imitation, but the real thing.

A lot of western writers—people like Richard S. Wheeler, Earl Murray, Al Dempsey and yours truly—when we get together for a few beers, we sometimes talk about books. We talk about the books that inspired us; the authors who made us love the West and even want to write ourselves. For whatever it's worth, it's a short list. And for a lot of us, the guy at the top is Clarence Mulford.

Clarence, old hoss, wherever you are, here's a Lone Star beer to you.

—Jackson Cain,
author of *Hellbreak Country*
and *Hangman's Whip*

Contents

HOPALONG CASSIDY

CHAPTER I

Antonio's Scheme

THE RAW and mighty West, the greatest stage in all the history of the world for so many deeds of daring which verged on the insane, was seared with grave-lined trails. In many localities the bad-man made history in a terse and business-like way, and also made the first law for the locality—that of the gun.

There were good bad-men and bad bad-men, the killer by necessity and the wanton murderer; and the shifting of these to their proper strata evolved the foundation for the law of to-day. The good bad-man, those in whose souls lived the germs of law and order and justice, gradually became arrayed against the other class, and stood up manfully for their principles, let the odds be what they might; and bitter, indeed, was the struggle, and great the price.

From the gold camps of the Rockies to the shrieking towns of the coast, where wantonness stalked unchecked; from the vast stretches of the cattle ranges to the ever-advancing terminals of the persistent railroads, to the cow towns, boiling and seething in the

loosed passions of men who brooked no restraint in
their revels, no one section of country ever boasted of
such numbers of genuine bad-men of both classes as
the great, semi-arid Southwest. Here was one of the
worst collections of raw humanity ever broadcast in
one locality; it was a word and a shot, a shot and a
laugh or a curse.

In this red setting was stuck a town which we will
call Eagle, the riffle which caught all the dregs of passing humanity. Unmapped, known only to those who
had visited it, reared its flimsy buildings in the face of
God and rioted day and night with no thought of reck-
oning; mad, insane with hellishness unlimited.

Late in the afternoon rode Antonio, "broncho-buster"
for the H2, a man of little courage, much avarice, and
great capacity for hatred. Crafty, filled with cunning of
the coyote kind, shifty-eyed, gloomy, taciturn, and
scowling, he was well fitted for the part he had elected
to play in the range dispute between his ranch and the
Bar-20. He was absolutely without mercy or con-
science; indeed, one might aptly say that his con-
science, if he had ever known one, had been pulled out
by the roots and its place filled with viciousness. Cold-
blooded in his ferocity, easily angered and quick to
commit murder if the risk were small, he embraced
within his husk of soul the putrescence of all that was
evil.

In Eagle he had friends who were only a shade less
evil than himself; but they had what he lacked and
because of it were entitled to a forced respect of small
weight—they had courage, that spontaneous, initiative,
heedless courage which toned the atmosphere of the
whole West to a magnificent crimson. Were it not for
the reason that they had drifted to his social level they
would have spurned his acquaintance and shot him for
a buzzard; but, while they secretly held him in great
contempt for his cowardice, they admired his criminal
cunning, and profited by it. He was too wise to show

himself in the true light to his foreman and the outfit, knowing full well that death would be the response, and so lived a lie until he met his friends of the town, when he threw off his cloak and became himself, and where he plotted against the man who treated him fairly.

Riding into the town, he stopped before a saloon and slouched in to the bar, where the proprietor was placing a new stock of liquors on the shelves.

"Where's Benito, an' th' rest?" he asked.

"Back there," replied the other, nodding toward a rear room.

"Who's in there?"

"Benito, Hall, Archer an' Frisco."

"Where's Shaw?"

"Him an' Clausen an' Cavalry went out 'bout ten minutes ago."

"I want to see 'em when they come in," Antonio remarked, headed towards the door, where he listened, and then went in.

In the small room four men were grouped around a table, drinking and talking, and at his entry they looked up and nodded. He nodded in reply and seated himself apart from them, where he soon became wrapped in thought.

Benito arose and went to the door. *"Mescal, pronto,"* he said to the man outside.

"Damned *pronto*, too," growled Antonio. "A man would die of alkali in this place before he's waited on."

The proprietor brought a bottle and filled the glasses, giving Antonio his drink first, and silently withdrew.

The broncho-buster tossed off the fiery stuff and then turned his shifty eyes on the group. "Where's Shaw?"

"Don't know—back soon," replied Benito.

"Why didn't he wait, when he knowed I was comin' in?"

Hall leaned back from the table and replied, keenly

watching the inquisitor, "Because he don't give a damn."

"You—!" Antonio shouted, half rising, but the others interfered and he sank back again, content to let it pass. But not so Hall, whose Colt was half drawn.

"I'll kill you some day," he gritted, but before anything could come of it Shaw and his companions entered the room and the trouble was quelled.

Soon the group was deep in discussion over the merits of a scheme which Antonio unfolded to them, and the more it was weighed the better it appeared. Finally Shaw leaned back and filled his pipe. "You've got th' brains of th' devil,' 'Tony."

"Eet ees not'ing," replied Antonio.

"Oh, drop that lingo an' talk straight—you ain't on th' H2 now," growled Hall.

"Benito, you know this country like a book," Shaw continued. "Where's a good place for us to work from, or ain't there no choice?"

"Thunder Mesa."

"Well, what of it?"

"On the edge of the desert, high, big. The walls are stone, an' so very smooth. Nobody can get up."

"How can we get up then?"

"There's a trail at one end," replied Antonio, crossing his legs and preparing to roll a cigarette. "It's too steep for cayuses, an' too narrow; but we can crawl up. An' once up, all hell can't follow as long as our cartridges hold out."

"Water?" inquired Frisco.

"At th' bottom of th' trail, an' th' spring is on top," Antonio replied. "Not much, but enough."

"Can you work yore end all right?" asked Shaw.

"Yes," laughed the other. "I am 'that fool, Antonio,' on th' ranch. But they're th' fools. We can steal them blind an' if they find it out—well," here he shrugged his shoulders, "th' Bar-20 can take th' blame. I'll fix that, all right. This trouble about th' line is just what I've been waitin' for, an' I'll help it along. If we can get 'em fightin' we'll run off with th' bone *we* want. That'll be easy."

"But can you get 'em fightin'?" asked Cavalry, so called because he had spent several years in that branch of the Government service, and deserted because of the discipline.

Antonio laughed and ordered more *mescal* and for some time took no part in the discussion which went on about him. He was dreaming of success and plenty and a ranch of his own which he would start in Old Mexico, in a place far removed from the border, and where no questions would be asked. He would be a rich man, according to the standards of that locality, and what he said would be law among the peons. He liked to day-dream, for everything came out just as he wished; there was no discordant note. He was so certain of success, so conceited as not to ask himself if any of the Bar-20 or H2 outfits were not his equal or superior in intelligence. It was only a matter of time, he told himself, for he could easily get the two ranches embroiled in a range war, and once embroiled, his plan would succeed and he would be safe.

"What do you want for your share, 'Tony?" suddenly asked Shaw.

"Half."

"What! *Half?*"

"*Si.*"

"You're loco!" cried the other. "Do you reckon we're going to buck up agin th' biggest an' hardest fightin' outfit in this country an' take all sorts of chances for a measly half, to be divided up among seven of us!" He brought his fist down on the table with a resounding thump. "You an' yore game can go to hell first!" he shouted.

"I like a hog, all right," sneered Clausen, angrily.

"I thought it out an' I got to look after th' worst an' most important part of it, an' take three chances to you fellers' one," replied Antonio, frowning. "I said half, an' it goes."

"Run all th' ends, an' keep it all," exclaimed Hall. "An', by God, we've got a hand in it, now. If you try to hog it we'll drop a word where it'll do th' most good, an' don't you forget it, neither."

"Antonio is right," asserted Benito, excitedly. "It's risky for him."

"Keep yore yaller mouth shut," growled Cavalry. "Who gave you any say in this?"

"Half," said Antonio, shrugging his shoulders.

"Look here, you," cried Shaw, who was, in reality, the leader of the crowd, inasmuch as he controlled all the others with the exception of Benito and Antonio, and these at times by the judicious use of flattery. "We'll admit that you've got a right to th' biggest share, but not to no half. You have a chance to get away, because you can watch 'em, but how about us, out there on th' edge of hell? If they come for us we won't know nothing about it till we're surrounded. Now we want to play square with you, and we'll give you twice as much as any one of th' rest of us. That'll make nine shares an' give you two of 'em. What more do you want, when you've got to have us to run th' game at all?"

Antonio laughed ironically. "Yes. I'm where I can watch, an' get killed first. You can hold th' mesa for a month. I ain't as easy as I look. It's my game, not yourn; an' if you don't like what I ask, stay out."

"We will!" cried Hall, arising, followed by the others. His hand rested on the butt of his revolver and trouble seemed imminent. Benito wavered and then slid nearer to Antonio. "You can run yore game all by yore lonesome, as *long* as you *can*!" Hall shouted. "I know a feller what knows Cassidy, an' I'll spoil yore little play right now. You'll look nice at th' end of a rope, won't you? It's this: share like Shaw said or get out of here, and look out for trouble aplenty to-morrow morning. I've put up with yore gall an' swallered yore insultin' actions just as long as I'm going to, and I've got a powerful notion to fix you right here and now!"

"No fightin', you fools!" cried the proprietor, grabbing his Colt and running to the door of the room. "It's up to you fellers to stick together!"

"I'll be damned if I'll stand—" began Frisco.

"They want too much," interrupted Antonio, angrily, keeping close watch over Hall.

"We want a fair share, an' that's all!" retorted Shaw. "Sit down, all of you. We can wrastle this out without no gunplay."

"You-all been yappin' like a set of fools," said the proprietor. "I've heard every word you-all said. If you got a mite of sense you'll be some tender how you shout about it. It's shore risky enough without tellin' everybody this side of sun-up."

"I mean just what I said," asserted Hall. "It's Shaw's offer, or nothin'. We ain't playing fool."

"Here! Here!" cried Shaw, pushing Hall into a seat. "If you two have got anything to settle, wait till some other time."

"That's more like it," growled the proprietor, shuffling back to the bar.

"Good Lord, 'Tony," cried Shaw in a low voice. "That's fair enough; we've got a right to something, ain't we? Don't let a good thing fall through just because you want th' whole earth. Better have a little than none."

"Well, gimme a third, then."

"I'll give you a slug in th' eye, you hog!" promised Hall, starting to rise again, but Shaw held him back. "Sit down, you fool!" he ordered, angrily. Then he turned to Antonio. "Third don't go; take my offer or leave it."

"Gimme a fourth; that's fair enough."

Shaw thought for a moment and then looked up. "Well, that's more like it. What do you say, fellers?"

"No!" cried Hall. "Two-ninths, or nothin'!"

"A fourth is two-eighths, only a little more," Shaw replied.

"Well, all right," muttered Hall, sullenly.

"That's very good," laughed Benito, glad that things were clearing.

The others gave their consent to the division and Shaw smiled. "Well, that's more like it. Now we'll go into this thing an' sift it out. Keep mum about it—there's twenty men in town that would want to join us if they knowed."

"I'm goin' to be boss; what I say goes," spoke up Antonio. "It's my game an' I'm takin' th' most risky end."

"You ain't got sand enough to be boss of anything," sneered Hall. "Yore sand is chalk."

"You'll say too much someday," retorted Antonio, glaring.

"Oh, not to *you*, I reckon," rejoined Hall, easily.

"Shut up, both of you!" snapped Shaw. "You can be boss, 'Tony," he said, winking at Hall. "You've got more brains for a thing like this than any of us. I don't see how you can figger it out like you do."

Antonio laughed but he remembered one thing, and swore to take payment if the plan leaked out; the proprietor had confessed hearing every word, which was not at all to his liking. If Quinn should tell, well, Quinn would die; he would see to that, he and Benito.

CHAPTER II

Mary Meeker Rides North

MARY MEEKER, daughter of the H2 owner and foreman, found pleasure in riding on little tours of investigation. She had given the southern portions her attention first and found, after the newness had worn off, that she did not care for the level, sandy stretches of half-desert land which lay so flat for miles. The prospect was always the same, always uninteresting and wearying and hot. Now she determined upon a step which she had wished to take for a long time, and her father's request that she should not take it grew less and less of a deterrent factor. He had given so much thought and worry to that mysterious valley, that she at last gave rein to her curiosity and made ready to see for herself. It was green and hilly, like the rugged Montana she had quitted to come down to the desert. There were hills of respectable size, for these she saw daily from the ranch house door, and she loved hills; anything would be better than the limitless sand.

She had known little of restraint; her corner of the world had been filled entirely by men and she had absorbed much of their better traits. Self-reliant as a cow-girl should be, expert with either Colt or Winchester, and at home in the saddle, she feared nothing the desert might hold, except thirst. She was not only expert with weapons, but she did not fear to use them against men, as she had proved on one occasion in wild Montana. So she would ride to the hills which called her so insistently and examine the valley.

One bright morning just before the roundup began she went to the corral and looked at her horse, a cross between Kentucky stock and cow-pony and having in a great degree the speed of the first and the hardiness of the last, and sighed to think that she could not ride it for days to come. Teuton was crippled and she must choose some other animal. She had overheard Doc Riley tell Ed Joyce that the piebald in the smaller corral was well broken, and this was the horse she would take. The truth of the matter was that the piebald was crafty and permitted the saddle to be fixed and himself ridden for varying periods of time before showing what he thought of such things. Doc, unprepared for the piebald's sudden change in demeanor, had taken a tumble, which made him anxious to have his wounded conceit soothed by seeing Ed Joyce receive the same treatment.

Mary found no trouble in mounting and riding the animal and she was glad that she had overheard Doc, for now she had two horses which were thoroughly reliable, although, of course, Teuton was the only really good horse on the range. She rode out of the corral and headed for the White Horse Hills, scarcely twelve miles away. What if her father had warned her not to ride near the lawless punchers who rode the northern range? They were only men and she was sure that to a woman they would prove to be gentlemen.

The southern boundary of the Bar-20 ran along the top of the hills and from them east to the river, and it was being patrolled by three Bar-20 punchers, Hopalong, Johnny, and Red, all on the lookout for straying cattle of both ranches. Neither Hopalong nor Red had ever seen Mary Meeker, but Johnny had upon the occasion of his scout over the H2 range, and he had felt eminently qualified to describe her. He had finished his eulogistic monologue by asserting that as soon as his more unfortunate friends saw her they would lose sleep and sigh often, which prophecy was received in various ways and called forth widely differing comment. Red had snorted outright and Pete swore to learn that a woman was on the range; for Pete had been married, and his wife preferred another man. Hopalong, remembering a former experience of his own, smiled in knowing cynicism when told that he again would fall under the feminine spell.

Red was near the river and Johnny half-way to the hills when Hopalong began the ascent of Long Hill, wondering why it was that Meeker had made no attempt to cross the boundary in force and bring on a crisis; and from Meeker his mind turned to the daughter.

"So there's a woman down here now," he muttered, riding down into an arroyo and up the other bank. "This country is gettin' as bad as Kansas, damned if it ain't. First thing we know it'll be nursin' bottles an' school houses, an' hell loose all th' time instead of once in a while."

He heard hoofbeats and glanced up quickly, alert and ready for trouble, for who would be riding where he was but some H2 puncher?

"What th'—!" he exclaimed under his breath, for riding towards him at an angle was Mary Meeker; and Johnny was wrong in his description of her, but, he thought, the Kid had done as well as his limited vocabulary would allow. She *was* pretty, pretty as—she was more than pretty!

She had seen him at the same time and flashed a quick glance which embraced everything; and she was surprised, for he was not only passably good-looking, barring the red hair, but very different from the men her father had told her made up the outfit of the Bar-20. He removed his sombrero instantly and drew up to let her pass, a smile on his face. Yes, he thought, Johnny had wronged her, for no other woman could have such jet-black hair crowning such a face.

"By God!" he whispered, and went no farther, for that was the summing up of his whole opinion of her.

"He *is* a gentleman," she thought triumphantly, for he had proved that she was right in her surmise regarding the men of the northern ranch. She spurred to pass him and then her piebald took part in the proceedings. The prick of the spur awakened in him a sudden desire to assert his rights, and he promptly pitched to make up for his hitherto gentle behavior. So taken up with what the last minute had brought forth she was unprepared for the vicious bucking and when she opened her eyes her head was propped against Hopalong's knee and her face dripping with the contents of his canteen. "Damn yore ugly skin!" he was saying to the piebald, which stood quietly a short distance away, evidently enjoying the result of his activity. "Just you wait! I'll show you what's due to come yore way purty soon!" He turned again to the woman and saw that her eyes were closed as before. "By God, yore—yore beautiful!"

She moved slightly and color came into her cheeks with a sudden rush and he watched her anxiously. Soon she moved again and then, opening her eyes, struggled to gain her feet. He helped her up and held her until she drew away from him.

"What was it?" she asked.

"That ugly cayuse went an' pitched when you wasn't lookin' for it," he told her. "Are you hurt much?"

"No, just dizzy. I don't want to make you trouble," she replied.

"You ain't makin' me any trouble, not a bit," he assured her earnestly. "But I'd like to make some trouble for that ornery cayuse of yourn. Let me tone him down some."

"No; it was my fault. I should'a been lookin—I never rode him before."

"Well, you've got to take my cayuse to get home on," he said. "He's bad, but he's a regular angel when stacked up agin that bronc. I'll ride the festive piebald, an' we can trade when you get home." Under his breath he said: "Oh, just wait till I get on you, pinto! I'll give you what you need, all right!"

"Thank you, but I can ride him now that I know just what he is," she said, her eyes flashing with determination. "I've never let a bronc get th' best of me in th' long run, an' I ain't goin' to begin now. I came up here to look at th' hills an' th' valley, an' I'm not going back home till I've done it."

"That's the way to talk!" he cried in admiration. "I'll get him for you," he finished, swinging into his saddle. He loosened the lariat at the saddle horn while he rode towards the animal, which showed sudden renewed interest in the proceedings, but it tarried too long. Just as it wheeled and leaped forward the rope settled and the next thing it knew was that the sky had somehow slid under its stomach, for it had been thrown over backward and flat on its back. When it had struggled to its feet it found Hopalong astride it, spurring vigorously on the side farthest from Mary, and for five minutes the air was greatly disturbed. At the end of that time he dismounted and led a penitent pony to its mistress, who vaulted lightly into the saddle and waited for her companion to mount. When he had joined her they rode up the hill together side by side.

Johnny wished to smoke and felt for his tobacco pouch, which he found to be empty. He rode on for a short distance, angry with himself for his neglect, and then remembered that Hopalong had a plentiful supply. He could overtake the man on the hill much quicker

than he could Red, who had said that he was going to
ride south along the river to see if Jumping Bear Creek
was dry. If it were, Meeker could be expected to become active in his aggression. Johnny wheeled and
cantered back along the boundary trail, alertly watching for trespassing cattle.

It was not long before he came within sight of the
thicket which stood a little east of the base of Long Hill,
and he nearly fell from the saddle in astonishment, for
his friend was on the ground, holding a woman's head
on his knee! Johnny didn't care to intrude, and cautiously withdrew to the shelter of the small chaparral,
where he waited impatiently. Wishing to stretch his
legs, he dismounted and picketed his horse and walked
around the thicket until satisfied that he was out of
sight of his friend.

Suddenly he fancied that he heard something suspicious and he crept back around the thicket, keeping
close to its base. When he turned the corner he saw
the head of a man on the other side of the chaparral
which lay a little southwest of his position. It was Antonio, and he was intently watching the two on the
slope of the hill, and entirely unaware that he was being watched in turn.

Johnny carefully drew his Colt and covered Antonio
who he hated instinctively. He had seen the shifty-eyed
broncho-buster on more than one occasion and never
without struggling with himself to keep from shooting.
Now his finger pressed gently against the trigger of the
weapon and he wished for a passable excuse to send
the other into eternity; but Antonio gave him no cause,
only watching eagerly and intently, his face set in such
an expression of malignancy as to cause Johnny's finger to tremble.

Johnny arose slightly until he could see Hopalong
and his companion and he smothered an exclamation.
"Gosh A'mighty!" he whispered, again watching Antonio. "That's Meeker's gal or I'm a liar! Th' son-of-a-gun,

keeping quiet about it all this time. An' no wonder Antonio's on th' trail!"

It was not long before Johnny looked again for Hop-along and saw him riding up the hill with his companion. Then he crept forward, watching Antonio closely, his Colt ready for instant use. Antonio slowly drew down until he was lost to sight of the Bar-20 puncher, who ran slightly forward and gained the side of the other thicket, where he again crept forward, and around the chaparral. When he next caught sight of the broncho-buster the latter was walking towards his horse and his back was turned to Johnny.

"Hey, you!" called the Bar-20 puncher, arising and starting after the other.

Antonio wheeled, leaped to one side and half drew his revolver, but he was covered and he let the weapon slide back into the holster.

"What are you doing?"

Antonio's reply was a scowl and his inquisitor continued without waiting for words from the other.

"Never mind that, I saw what you was doing," Johnny said. "An' I shore knew what you wanted to do, because I came near doing it to you. Now it ain't a whole lot healthy for you to go snooping around this line like you was, for I'll plug you on suspicion next time. Get on that cayuse of yourn an' hit th' trail south— go on, make tracks!"

Antonio mounted and slowly wheeled. "You hab drop, now," he said significantly. "Nex' time, *quien sabe*?"

Johnny dropped his Colt into the holster and removed his hand from the butt. "You're a liar!" he shouted, savagely. "I ain't got th' drop. It's an even break, an' what are you going to do about it?"

Antonio shrugged his shoulders and rode on without replying, quite content to let things stand as they were. He had learned something which he might be able to use to advantage later on and he had strained the situation just a little more.

"Huh! Next time!" snorted Johnny in contempt as he turned to go back to his horse. "It'll allus be 'next' time' with him, 'less he gets a good pot shot at me, which he won't. He ain't got sand enough to put up a square fight. Now for Red; he'll shore be riding this way purty soon, an' that'll never do. Hoppy won't want anybody foolin' around th' hills for a while, lucky devil."

More than an hour had passed before he met Red and he forthwith told him that he had caught Antonio scouting on foot along the line.

"I ain't none surprised, Kid," Red replied, frowning. "You've seen how th' H2 cows are being driven north agin us an' that means we'll be tolerable busy purty soon. Th' Jumping Bear is dry as tinder, an' it won't be long before Meeker'll be driving to get in th' valley."

"Well, I'm some glad of that," Johnny replied, frankly. "It's been peaceful too blamed long down here. Come on, we'll ride east an' see if we can find any cows to turn. Hey! Look there!" he cried, spurring forward.

CHAPTER III

The Roundup

THE TEXAN sky seemed a huge mirror upon which were reflected the white fleecy clouds sailing northward; the warm spring air was full of that magnetism which calls forth from their earthy beds the gramma grass and the flowers; the scant vegetation had taken on new dress and traces of green now showed against the more sombre-colored stems; while in the distance, rippling in glistening patches where, disturbed by the wind, the river sparkled like a tinsel ribbon flung carelessly on the grays and greens of the plain. Birds winged their joyous way and filled the air with song; and far overhead a battalion of tardy geese flew, arrowlike, towards the cool lakes of the north, their faint honking pathetic and continuous. Skulking in the coulees or speeding across the skyline of some distant rise occasionally could be seen a coyote or gray wolf. The cattle, less gregarious than they had been in the colder months, made tentative sorties from the lessening herd, and began to stray off in search of the tender green grass which pushed up recklessly from the closely

cropped, withered tufts. Rattlesnakes slid out and un-
coiled their sinuous lengths in the warm sunlight, and
copperheads raised their burnished armor from their
winter retreats. All nature had felt the magic touch of
the warm winds, and life in its multitudinous forms was
discernible on all sides. The gaunt tragedy of a hard
winter for that southern range had added its chilling
share to the horrors of the past and now the cattle took
heart and lost their weakness in the sunlight, hungry
but contented.

The winter had indeed been hard, one to be remembered for years to come, and many cattle had died because of it; many skeletons, stripped clean by coyotes
and wolves, dotted the arroyos and coulees. The cold
weather had broken suddenly, and several days of rain,
followed by sleet, had drenched the cattle thoroughly.
Then from out of the north came one of those unusual
rages of nature, locally known as a "Norther," freezing
pitilessly; and the cattle, weakened by cold and star-
vation, had dumbly succumbed to this last blow. Their
backs were covered with an icy shroud, and the deadly
cold gripped their vitals with a power not to be re-
sisted. A glittering sheet formed over the grasses as far
as eye could see, and the cattle, unlike the horses, not
knowing enough to stamp through it, nosed in vain at
the sustenance beneath, until weakness compelled them
to lie down in the driving snow, and once down, they
never arose. The storm had raged for the greater part
of a week, and then suddenly one morning the sun
shown down on a velvety plain, blinding in its white-
ness; and when spring had sent the snow mantle roaring through the arroyos and water courses in a turmoil
of yellow water and driftwood, and when the range
riders rode forth to read the losses on the plain, the
remaining cattle were staggering weakly in search of
food. Skeletons in the coulees told the story of the
hopeless fight, how the unfortunate cattle had drifted
before the wind to what shelter they could find and

how, huddled together for warmth, they had died one by one. The valley along Conroy Creek had provided a rough shelter with its scattered groves and these had stopped the cattle drift, so much dreaded by cowmen.

It had grieved Buck Peters and his men to the heart to see so many cattle swept away in one storm, but they had done all that courage and brains could do to save them. So now, when the plain was green again and the warm air made riding a joy, they were to hold the calf roundup. When Buck left his blanket after the first night spent in the roundup camp and rode off to the horse herd, he smiled from suppressed elation, and was glad that he was alive.

Peaceful as the scene appeared there was trouble brewing, and it was in expectation of this that Buck had begun the roundup earlier than usual. The unreasoning stubbornness of one man, and the cunning machinations of a natural rogue, threatened to bring about, from what should have been only a misunderstanding, as pretty a range war as the Southwest had seen. Those immediately involved were only a few when compared to the number which might eventually be brought into the strife, but if this had been pointed out to Jim Meeker he would have replied that he "didn't give a damn."

Jim Meeker was a Montana man who thought to carry out on the H2 range, of which he was foreman, the same system of things which had served where he had come from. This meant trouble right away, for the Bar-20, already short in range, would not stand idly by and see him encroach upon their land for grass and water, more especially when he broke a solemn compact as to range rights which had been made by the former owners of the H2 with the Bar-20. It meant not only the forcible use of Bar-20 range, but also a great hardship upon the herds for which Buck Peters was responsible.

Meeker's obstinacy was covertly prodded by Antonio

for his own personal gains, but this the Bar-20 foreman did not know; if he had known it there might have been much trouble averted.

Buck Peters was probably the only man of all of them who realized just what such a war would mean, to what an extent rustling would flourish while the cowmen fought. His best efforts had been used to avert trouble, so far successfully; but that he would continue to do so was doubtful. He had an outfit which, while meaning to obey him in all things and to turn from any overt act of war, was not of the kind to stand much forcing or personal abuse; their nervous systems were constructed on the hair-trigger plan, and their very loyalty might set the range ablaze with war. However, on this most perfect of mornings Meeker's persistent aggression did not bother him, he was free from worry for the time.

Just north of Big Coulee, in which was a goodly sized water hole, a group of blanket-swathed figures lay about a fire near the chuck wagon, while the sleepy cook prepared breakfast for his own outfit, and for the eight men which the foreman of the C80 and the Double Arrow had insisted upon Buck taking. The sun had not yet risen, but the morning glow showed gray over the plain, and it would not be long before the increasing daylight broke suddenly. The cook fires crackled and blazed steadily, the iron pots hissing under their dancing and noisy lids, while the coffee pots bubbled and sent up an aromatic steam, and the odor of freshly baked biscuits swept forth as the cook uncovered a pan. A pile of tin plates was stacked on the tail-board of the wagon while a large sheet-iron pail contained tin cups. The figures, feet to the fire, looked like huge, grotesque cocoons, for the men had rolled themselves in their blankets, their heads resting on their saddles, and in many cases folded sombreros next to the leather made softer pillows.

Back of the chuck wagon the eastern sky grew rapidly brighter, and suddenly daylight in all its power dissipated the grayish light of the moment before. As the rim of the golden sun arose above the low sand hills to the east the foreman rode into camp. Some distance behind him Harry Jones and two other C80 men drove up the horse herd and enclosed it in a flimsy corral quickly extemporized from lariats; flimsy it was, but it sufficed for cow-ponies that had learned the lesson of the rope.

"All ready, Buck," called Harry before his words were literally true.

With assumed ferocity but real vociferation Buck uttered a shout and watched the effect. The cocoons became animated, stirred and rapidly unrolled, with the exception of one, and the sleepers leaped to their feet and folded the blankets. The exception stirred, subsided, stirred again and then was quiet. Buck and Red stepped forward while the others looked on grinning to see the fun, grasped the free end of the blanket and suddenly straightened up, their hands going high above their heads. Johnny Nelson, squawking, rolled over and over and, with a yell of surprise, sat bolt upright and felt for his gun.

"Huh!" he snorted. "Reckon yo're smart, don't you!"

"Purty near a shore 'nuf pin-wheel, Kid,' laughed Red.

"Don't you care, Johnny; you can finish it tonight," consoled Frenchy McAllister, now one of Buck's outfit.

"Breakfast, Kid, breakfast!" sang out Hopalong as he finished drying his face.

The breakfast was speedily out of the way, and pipes were started for a short smoke as the punchers walked over to the horse herd to make their selections. By exercising patience, profanity, and perseverance they roped their horses and began to saddle up. Ed Porter, of the C80, and Skinny Thompson, Bar-20, cast their ropes with a sweeping, preliminary whirl over their heads, but the others used only a quick flit and twist of the wrist. A few mildly exciting struggles for the mas-

tery took place between riders and mounts, for some
cow-ponies are not always ready to accept their proper
places in the scheme of things.

"Slab-sided jumpin' jack!" yelled Rich Finn, a Double
Arrow puncher, as he fought his horse. "Allus raisin'
th' devil afore I'm all awake!"

"Lemme hold her head, Rich," jeered Billy Williams.

"Her laigs, Billy, not her head," corrected Lanky
Smith, the Bar-20 rope expert, whose own horse had
just become sensible.

"Don't hurt him, bronc; we need him," cautioned
Red.

"Come on, fellers; gettin' late," called Buck.

Away they went, tearing across the plain, Buck in
the lead. After some time had passed the foreman
raised his arm and Pete Wilson stopped and filled his
pipe anew, the west-end man of the cordon. Again
Buck's arm went up and Skinny Thompson dropped
out, and so on until the last man had been placed and
the line completed. At a signal from Buck the whole
line rode forward, gradually converging on a central
point and driving the scattered cattle before it.

Hopalong, on the east end of the line, sharing with
Billy the posts of honor, was now kept busy dashing
here and there, wheeling, stopping, and maneuvering
as certain strong-minded cattle, preferring the freedom
of the range they had just quitted, tried to break
through the cordon. All but branded steers and cows
without calves had their labors in vain, although the
escape of these often set examples for ambitious cows
with calves. Here was where reckless and expert riding
saved the day, for the cow-ponies, trained in the art of
punching cows, entered into the game with zest and
executed quick turns which more than once threatened
a catastrophe to themselves and riders. Range cattle
can run away from their domesticated kin, covering
the ground with an awkward gait that is deceiving; but
the ponies can run faster and turn as quickly.

Hopalong, determined to turn back one stubborn mother cow, pushed too hard, and she wheeled to attack him. Again the nimble pony had reasons to move quickly and Hopalong swore as he felt the horns touch his leg.

"On th' prod, hey! Well, stay on it!" he shouted, well knowing that she would. "Pig-headed old fool—*all right,* Johnny; I'm comin'!" and he raced away to turn a handful of cows which were proving too much for his friend. *"Ki-yi-yeow-eow-eow-eow-eow!"* he yelled, imitating the coyote howl.

The cook had moved his wagon as soon as breakfast was over and journeyed southeast with the cavvieyh; and as the cordon neared its objectives the punchers could see his camp about half a mile from the level pasture where the herd would be held for the cutting-out and branding. Cookie regarded himself as the most important unit of the roundup and acted accordingly, and he was not far wrong.

"Hey, Hoppy!" called Johnny through the dust of the herd, "there's cookie. I was 'most scared he'd get lost."

"Can't you think of anythin' else but grub?" asked Billy Jordan from the rear.

"Can you tell me anything better to think of?"

There were from three to four hundred cattle in the herd when it neared the stopping point, and dust arose in low-hanging clouds above it. Its pattern of differing shades of brown, with yellow and black and white relieving it, constantly shifted like a kaleidoscope as the cattle changed positions; and the rattle of horns on horns and the muffled bellowing could be heard for some distance.

Gradually the cordon surrounded the herd and, when the destination was reached, the punchers rode before the front ranks of cattle and stopped them. There was a sudden tremor, a compactness in the herd, and the cattle in the rear crowded forward against those before; another tremor, and the herd was quiet. Cow-punchers took their places around it, and kept the cattle from breaking out and back to the range, while every second man, told off by the foreman, raced at top speed towards the camp, there to eat a hasty dinner and get a fresh horse from his *remuda*, as his string of from five to seven horses was called. Then he galloped back to the herd and relieved his nearest neighbor. When all had reassembled at the herd the work of cutting-out began.

Lanky Smith, Panhandle Lukins, and two more Bar-20 men rode some distance east of the herd, there to take care of the cow-and-calf cut as it grew by the cutting-out. Hopalong, Red, Johnny, and three others were assigned to the task of getting the mother cows and their calves out of the main herd and into the new one, while the other punchers held the herd and took care of the stray herd when they should be needed. Each of the cutters-out rode after some calf, and the victim, led by its mother, worked its way after her into the very heart of the mass; and in getting the pair out again care must be taken not to unduly excite the other cattle. Wiry, happy, and conceited cow-ponies unerringly and patiently followed mother and calf into the press, nipping the pursued when too slow and gradually forcing them to the outer edge of the herd; and when the mother tried to lead its offspring back into the herd to repeat the performance, she was in almost every case cleverly blocked and driven out on the plain where the other punchers took charge of her and added her to the cow-and-calf cut.

Johnny jammed his sombrero on his head with reckless strength and swore luridly as he wheeled to go back into the herd.

"What's th' matter, Kid?" laughingly asked Skinny as he turned his charges over to another man.

"None of yore damned business!" blazed Johnny. Under his breath he made a resolve. "If I get you two out here again I'll keep you here if I have to shoot you!"

"Are they slippery, Johnny?" jibed Red, whose guess was correct. Johnny refused to heed such asinine remarks and stood on his dignity.

As the cow-and-calf herd grew in size and the main herd dwindled, more punchers were shifted to hold it; and it was not long before the main herd was comprised entirely of cattle without calves, when it was driven off to freedom after being examined for other brands. As soon as the second herd became of any size it was not necessary to drive the cows and the calves to it when they were driven out of the first herd, as they made straight for it. The main herd, driven away, broke up as it would, while the guarded cows stood idly beside their resting offspring awaiting further indignities.

The drive had covered so much ground and taken so much time that approaching darkness warned Buck not to attempt the branding until the morrow, and he divided his force into three shifts. Two of these hastened to the camp, gulped down their supper, and rolling into their blankets, were soon sound asleep. The horse herd was driven off to where the grazing was better, and night soon fell over the plain.

The cook's fires gleamed through the darkness and piles of biscuits were heaped on the tail-board of the wagon, while pots of beef and coffee simmered over the fires, handy for the guards as they rode in during the night to awaken brother punchers, who would take their places while they slept. Soon the cocoons were quiet in the grotesque shadows caused by the fires and a deep silence reigned over the camp. Occasionally some puncher would awaken long enough to look at the sky to see if the weather had changed, and satisfied, return to sleep.

Over the plain sleepy cowboys rode slowly around the herd, glad to be relieved by some other member of the outfit, who always sang as he approached the cattle to reassure them and save a possible stampede. For cattle, if suddenly disturbed at night by anything, even the waving of a slicker in the hands of some careless rider, or a wind-blown paper, will rise in a body—all up at once, frightened and nervous. The sky was clear and the stars bright and when the moon rose it flooded the plain with a silvery light and made fairy patterns in the shadows.

Snatches of song floated down the gentle wind as the riders slowly circled the herd, for the human voice, no matter how discordant, was quieting. A low and plaintive "Don't let this par-ting grieve y-o-u" passed from hearing around the resting cows, soon to be followed by "When-n in thy dream-ing, nights like t-h-e-s-e shall come a-gain—" as another watcher made the circuit. The serene cows, trusting in the prowess and vigilance of these low-voiced centaurs to protect them from danger, dozed and chewed their cuds in peace and quiet, while the natural noises of the night relieved the silence in unobtruding harmony.

Far out on the plain a solitary rider watched the herd from cover and swore because it was guarded so closely. He glanced aloft to see if there was any hope of a storm and finding that there was not, muttered savagely and rode away. It was Antonio, wishing that he could start a stampede and so undo the work of the day and inflict heavy losses on the Bar-20. He did not dare to start a grass fire for at the first flicker of a light he would be charged by one or more of the night riders and if caught, death would be his reward.

While the third shift rode and sang the eastern sky became a dome of light reflected from below and the sunrise, majestic in all its fiery splendor, heralded the birth of another perfect day.

Through the early morning hours the branding continued, and the bleating of cattle told of the hot stamping irons indelibly burning the sign of the Bar-20 on the tender hides of calves. Mother cows fought and plunged and called in reply to the terrified bawling of their offspring, and sympathetically licked the burns when the frightened calves had been allowed to join them. Cowboys were deftly roping calves by their hind legs and dragging them to the fires of the branding men. Two men would hold a calf, one doubling the foreleg back on itself at the knee and the other, planting one booted foot against the calf's under hind leg close to its body, pulled back on the other leg while his companion, who held the foreleg, rested on the animal's head. The third man, drawing the hot iron from the fire, raised and held it suspended for a second over the calf's flank, and then there was an odor and a puff of smoke; and the calf was branded with a mark which neither water nor age would wipe out.

Pete Wilson came riding up dragging a calf at the end of his rope, and turned the captive over to Billy Williams and his two helpers, none of them paying any attention to the cow which followed a short distance behind him. Lanky seized the unfortunate calf and leaned over to secure the belly hold, when someone shouted a warning and he dropped the struggling animal and leaped back and to one side as the mother charged past. Wheeling to return the attack, the cow suddenly flopped over and struck the earth with a thud as Buck's rope went home. He dragged her away and then releasing her, chased her back into the herd.

"*Hi!* Get that little devil!" shouted Billy to Hopalong, pointing to the fleeing calf.

"Why didn't you watch for her," demanded the indignant Lanky of Pete. "Do you think this is a ten-pin alley!"

Hopalong came riding up with the calf, which swiftly became recorded property.

"Bar-20; tally one," sang out the monotonous voice of the tally man. "Why didn't you grab her when she went by, Lanky?" he asked, putting a new point on his pencil.

"Hope th' next one leads yore way!" retorted Lanky, grinning.

"Won't. I ain't abusin' th' kids."

"Bar-20; tally one," droned a voice at the next fire.

All was noise, laughter, dust, and a seeming confusion, but every man knew his work thoroughly and was doing it in a methodical way, and the confusion was confined to the victims and their mothers.

When the herd had been branded and allowed to return to the plain, the outfit moved on into a new territory and the work was repeated until the whole range, with the exception of the valley, had been covered. When the valley was worked it required more time in comparison with the amount of ground covered than had been heretofore spent on any part of the range; for the cattle were far more numerous, and it was no unusual thing to have a herd of great size before the roundup place had been reached. This heavy increase in the numbers of the cattle to be herded made a corresponding increase in the time and labor required for the cutting-out and branding. Five days were required in working the eastern and central parts of the valley and it took three more days to clean up around the White Horse Hills, where the ground was rougher and the riding harder. And at every cutting-out there was a large stray-herd made up of H2 and Three Triangle cattle. The H2 had been formerly the Three Triangle. Buck had been earnest in his instructions regarding the strays, for now was the opportunity to rid his range of Meeker's cattle without especial significance; once over the line it would be a comparatively easy matter to keep them there.

For taking care of this extra herd and also because Buck courted scrutiny during the branding, the foreman accepted the services of three H2 men. This addition to his forces made the work move somewhat more rapidly and when, at the end of each day's cutting-out, the stray herd was complete, it was driven south across the boundary line by Meeker's men. When the last stray-herd started south Buck rode over to the H2 punchers and told them to tell their foreman to let him know when he could assist in the southern roundup and thus return the favor.

As the Bar-20 outfit and the C80 and Double Arrow men rode north towards the ranch house they were met by Lucas, foreman of the C80, who joined them near Medicine Bend.

"Well, got it all over, hey?" he cried as he rode up.

"Yep; bigger job than I thought, too. It gets bigger every year an' that blizzard didn't make much difference in th' work, neither," Buck replied. "I'll help you out when you get ready to drive."

"No you won't; you can help me an' Bartlett more by keeping all yore men watchin' that line," quickly responded Lucas. "We'll work together, me an' Bartlett, an' we'll have all th' men we want. You just show that man Meeker that range grabbin' ain't healthy down here—that's all we want. Did he send you any help in th' valley?"

"Yes, three men," Buck replied. "But we'll break even on that when he works along the boundary."

"Have any trouble with 'em?"

"Not a bit."

"I sent Wood Wright down to Eagle th' other day, an' he says the town is shore there'll be a big range war," remarked Lucas. "He said there's lots of excitement down there an' they act like they wish th' trouble would hurry up an' happen. We've got to watch that town, all right."

"If there's a war th' rustlers'll flock from all over," interposed Rich Finn.

"Huh!" snorted Hopalong. "They'll flock out again if we get a chance to look for 'em. An' that town'll shore get into trouble if it don't live plumb easy. You know what happened th' last time rustlin' got to be th' style, don't you?"

"Well," replied Lucas, "I've fixed it with Cowan to get news to me an' Bartlett if anything sudden comes up. If you need us just let him know an' we'll be with you in two shakes."

"That's good, but I don't reckon I'll need any help, leastwise not for a long time," Buck responded. "But I tell you what you might do, when you can; make up a vigilance committee from yore outfits an' ride range for rustlers. We can take care of all that comes on us, but we won't have no time to bother about th' rest of th' range. An' if you do that it'll shut 'em out of our north range."

"We'll do it," Lucas promised. "Bartlett is going to watch th' trails north to see if he can catch anybody runnin' cattle to th' railroad construction camps. Every suspicious looking stranger is going to be held up an' asked questions; an' if we find any runnin' irons, you know what that means."

"I reckon we can handle th' situation, all right, no matter how hard it gets," laughed the Bar-20 foreman.

"Well, I'll be leavin' you now," Lucas remarked as they reached the Bar-20 bunk house. "We begin to round up next week, an' there's lots to be done by then. Say, can I use yore chuck wagon? Mine is shore done for."

"Why, of course," replied Buck heartily. "Take it now, if you want, or any time you send for it."

"Much obliged; come on, fellers," Lucas cried to his men. "We're going home."

CHAPTER IV

In West Arroyo

HOPALONG WAS heading for Lookout Peak, the highest of the White Horse Hills, by way of West Arroyo, which he entered half an hour after he had forded the creek, and was half way to the line when, rounding a sharp turn, he saw Mary Meeker ahead of him. She was off her horse picking flowers when she heard him and she stood erect, smiling.

"Why, I didn't think I'd see you," she said. "I've been picking flowers—see them? Ain't they pretty?" she asked, holding them out for his inspection.

"They shore are," he replied, not looking at the flowers at all, but into her big, brown eyes. "An' they're some lucky, too," he asserted grinning.

She lowered her head, burying her face in the blossoms and then picked a few petals and let them fall one by one from her fingers. "You didn't look at them at all," she chided.

"Oh, yes, I did," he laughed. "But I see flowers all th' time, and not much of you."

"That's nice—they are so pretty. I just love them."

"Yes. I reckon they are," doubtfully.

She looked up at him, her eyes laughing and her white teeth glistening between their red frames. "Why don't you scold me?" she asked.

"Scold you! What for?"

"Why, for being on yore ranch, for being across th' line an' in th' valley."

"Good Lord! Why, there ain't no lines for you! You can go anywhere."

"In th' valley?" she asked, again hiding her face in the flowers.

"Why, of course. What ever made you think you can't?"

"I'm one of th' H2," she responded. "Paw says I run it. But I'm awful glad you won't care."

"Well, as far as riding where you please is concerned, you run this ranch, too."

"There's a pretty flower," she said, looking at the top of the bank. "That purple one; see it?" she asked, pointing.

"Yes. I'll get it for you," he replied, leaping from the saddle and half way up the bank before she knew it. He slid down again and handed the blossom to her. "There."

"Thank you."

"See any more you wants?"

"No; this is enough. Thank you for getting it for me."

"Oh, that was nothing," he laughed, awkwardly. "That was shore easy."

"I'm gong to give it to you for not scolding me about being over th' line," she said, holding it out to him.

"No; not for that," he said slowly. "Can't you think of some other reason?"

"Don't you want it?"

"Want it!" he exclaimed, eagerly. "Shore I want it. But not for what you said."

"Will you wear it because we're friends?"

"Now yo're talking!"

She looked up and laughed, her cheeks dimpling, and then pinned it to his shirt. It was nice to have a flower pinned on one's shirt by a pretty girl.

"There," she laughed, stepping back to look at it.

"You've pinned it up so high I can't see it. Why not put it lower down?"

She changed it while he grinned at how his scheming had born fruit. He was a hog, he knew that, but he did not care.

"Oh, I reckon *I'm* all right!" he exulted. "Shore you don't see no more you want?"

"Yes; an' I must go now," she replied, going towards her horse. "I'll be late with th' dinner if I don't hurry."

"What! Do you cook for that hungry outfit?"

"No, not for them—just for Paw an' me."

"When are you comin' up again for more flowers?"

"I don't know. You see, I'm going to make cookies some day this week, but I don't know just when. Do you like cookies, an' cake?"

"You bet I do! Why?"

"I'll bring some with me th' next time. Paw says they're th' best he ever ate."

"Bet I'll say so, too," he replied, stepping forward to help her into the saddle, but she sprang into it before he reached her side, and he vaulted on his own horse and joined her.

She suddenly turned and looked him straight in the eyes. "Tell me, honest, has yore ranch any right to keep our cows south of that line?"

"Yes, we have. Our boundaries are fixed. We gave th' Three Triangle about eighty square miles of range so our valley would be free from all cows but our own. That's all th' land between th' line an' th' Jumping Bear, an' it was a big price, too. They never drove a cow over on us."

She looked disappointed and toyed with her quirt.

"Why don't you want to let Paw use th' valley?"

"It ain't big enough for our own cows, an' we can't

share it. As it is, we'll have to drive ten thousand on
leased range next year to give our grass a rest."

"Well—" she stopped and he waited to hear what she
would say, and then asked her when she would be up
again.

"I don't know! I don't know!" she cried.

"Why, what's the matter?"

"Nothing. I'm foolish—that's all," she replied, smiling,
and trying to forget the picture which arose in her
mind, a picture of desperate fighting along the line; of
her father—and him.

"You scared me then," he said.

"Did I? Why, it wasn't anything."

"Are you shore?"

"Please don't ask me any questions," she requested.

"Will you be up here again soon?"

"If th' baking turns out all right."

"Hang the baking! come anyway."

"I'll try; but I'm afraid," she faltered.

"Of what?" he demanded, sitting up very straight.

"Why, that I can't," she replied, hurriedly. "You see,
it's far coming up here."

"That's easy. I'll meet you west of the hills."

"No, no! I'll come up here."

"Look here," he said, slowly and kindly. "If yo're
afraid of bein' seen with me, don't you try it. I want to
see you a whole lot, but I don't want you to have no
trouble with yore father about it. I can wait till everything is all right if you want me to."

She turned and faced him, her cheeks red. "No, it
ain't that, exactly. Don't ask me any more. Don't talk
about it. I'll come, all right, just as soon as I can."

They were on the line now and she held out her
hand.

"Good-bye."

"Good-bye for now. Try to come up an' see me as
soon as you can. If yo're worryin' because Antonio don't

like me, stop it. I've been in too many tight places to get piped out where there's elbow room."

"I asked you not to say nothing more about it," she chided. "I'll come when I can. Good-bye."

"Good-bye," he replied, his sombrero under his arm. He watched her until she became lost to sight and then, suspicious, wheeled, and saw Johnny sitting quietly on his horse several hundred yards away. He called his friend to him by one wide sweep of his arm and Johnny spurred forward.

"Follow me, Johnny," he cried, dashing towards the arroyo. "Take th' other side an' look for Antonio. I'll take this side. Edge off; yo're too close. Three hundred yards is about right."

They raced away at top speed, reckless and grim, Johnny not knowing just what it was all about; but the name Antonio needed no sauce to whet his appetite since the day he had caught him watching his friend on the hill, and he scanned the plain eagerly. When they reached the other end of the arroyo Hopalong called to him: "Sweep east an' back to th' line on a circle. If you catch him, shoot off yo're colt an' hold him for *me*. I'm going west."

When they saw each other again it was on the line, and neither had seen any traces of Antonio, to Johnny's vexation and Hopalong's great satisfaction.

"What's up, Hoppy?" shouted Johnny.

"I reckoned that Antonio might a' followed her so he could tell tales to Meeker," Hopalong called.

Johnny swept up recklessly, jauntily, a swagger almost in the very actions of his horse, which seemed to have caught the spirit of its rider.

"Caught you that time," he laughed—and Johnny, when in a teasing mood, could weave into his laughter an affectionate note which found swift pardon for any words he might utter. "You an' her shore make a good—" and then he saw the flower on his friend's shirt and for the moment was rendered speechless by surprise. But in him the faculty of speech was well developed and he recovered quickly. "Sufferin' coyotes! Would you look at that! What's comin' to us down here, anyway? Are you loco? Do you mean to let th' rest of th' outfit see *that*?"

"Calamity is comin' to th' misguided mavericks that get funny about it!" retorted Hopalong. "I wear what I feels like, an' don't you forget it, neither."

" 'In thy d-a-r-k eyes splendor, where th' l-o-v-e light longs to dwel-l,' " Johnny hummed, grinning. Then his hand went out. "Good luck, Hoppy! Th' best of luck!" he cried. "She's a dandy, all right, but she ain't too good for you."

"Much obliged," Hopalong replied, shaking hands. "But suppose you tell me what all th' good luck is for. To hear you talk anybody'd think all a feller had to do was to ride with a woman to be married to her."

"Well, then take off that wart of a flower an' come on," Johnny responded.

"What? Not to save yo're spotted soul! An' that ain't no wart of a flower, neither."

Johnny burst out laughing, a laugh from the soul of him, welling up in infectious spontaneity, triumphant and hearty. "Oh, oh! You bit that time! Anybody'd think about right in yo're case, as far as *wantin'* to be married is concerned. Why, yo're hittin' th' lovely trail to matrimony as hard as you can."

In spite of himself Hopalong had to laugh at the jibing of his friend, the Kid. He thumped him heartily across the shoulders to show how he felt about it and Johnny's breath was interfered with at a critical moment.

"Oh, just wait till th' crowd sees that blossom! Just wait," Johnny coughed.

"You keep mum about what you saw, d'y' hear?"

"Shore; but it'll be on my mind all th' time, an' I talk in my sleep when anything's on my mind."

"Then that's why I never heard you talk in yo're sleep."

"Aw, g'wan! But they'll see th' flower, won't they?"

"Shore they will; but as long as they don't know how it got there they can't say much."

"They can't, hey!" Johnny exclaimed. "That's a new one on me. It's usually what they don't know about that they talks of most. What they don't know they can guess in this case, all right. Most of 'em are good on readin' signs, an' that's plain as th' devil."

"But don't you tell 'em!" Hopalong warned.

"No. I won't tell 'em, honest," Johnny replied. He could convey the information in a negative way and he grinned hopefully at the fun there would be.

"I mean it, Kid," Hopalong responded, reading the grin. "I don't care about myself; they can joke all they wants with me. But it ain't nowise right to drag her into it, savvy? She don't want to be talked about like that."

"Yo're right; they won't find out nothin' from me," and Johnny saw his fun slip from him. "I'm goin' east; comin' along?"

"No; th' other way. So long."

"Hey!" cried Johnny anxiously, drawing rein, "Frenchy said Buck was going to put some of us up in Number Five so Frenchy an' his four could ride th' line. Did Buck say anything to you about it?"

Line house Number Five was too far from the zone of excitement, if fighting should break out along the line, to please Johnny.

"He was stringin' you, Kid," Hopalong laughed. "He won't take any of th' old outfit away from here."

"Oh, I knowed that; but I thought I'd ask, that's all," and Johnny cantered away, whistling happily.

Hopalong looked after him and smiled, for Johnny had laughed and fought and teased himself into the heart of every man of the outfit: "He's shore a good Kid; an' how he likes a fight!"

CHAPTER V

Hopalong Asserts Himself

PARALLELING WEST Arroyo and two miles east of it was another arroyo, through which Hopalong was riding the day following his meeting with Mary. Coming to a place where he could look over the bank he saw a herd of H2 and Three Triangle cows grazing not far away, and Antonio was in charge of them. Hopalong did not know how long they had been in the valley, nor how they had crossed the line, but their presence was enough. It angered him, for here was open and, it appeared, authorized defiance. Not content to let his herds run as they wished, Meeker was actually sending them into the valley under guard, presumably to find out what would be done about it, The H2 foreman would find that out very soon.

Antonio looked around and wheeled sharply to face the danger, his listlessness gone in a flash. He was not there because of any orders from Meeker, but for reasons of his own. So when the Bar-20 puncher raised his arm and swept it towards the line he sat in sullen indifference, alert and crafty.

"You've got gall!" cried Hopalong. "Who told you to herd up here!"

Antonio frowned but did not reply.

"Yo're three miles too far north," continued Hopalong, riding slowly forward until their stirrups almost touched.

Antonio shrugged his shoulders.

"I ain't warbling for my health!" cried Hopalong. "You start them cows south right away."

"I can't."

Hopalong stared. "You can't! Well, I reckon you can, an' will."

"I can't. Boss won't let me."

"Oh, he won't! Well, I feel sorry for yore boss but yo're going to push 'em just th' same."

Antonio again shrugged his shoulders and lifted his hands in a gesture of helplessness.

"How long you been here, an' how'd you get in?"

" 'N'our. By de *rio*."

"Oh, yore foreman's goin' to raise hell, ain't he!" Hopalong snorted. "He's going to pasture on us whether we like it or not, is he? He's a land thief, that's what he is!"

"De boss ees all right!" asserted Antonio, heatedly.

"If he is he's lop-sided, but he'll be *left* if he banks on this play going through without a smash-up. You chase them cows home an' keep 'em there. If I find you flittin' around th' ends of th' line or herdin' on this side of it I'll give you something to nurse—an' you'll be lucky if you can nurse it. Come on, get a-going!"

Antonio waved his arm excitedly and was about to expostulate, but Hopalong cut him short by hitting him across the face with his quirt: "Damn you!" he cried, angrily. "Shut yore mouth! Get them cows going! I've a mind to stop you right now. Come on, get a move on!"

Antonio's face grew livid and he tried to back away, swearing. Stung to action by the blow, he jerked at his gun, but found Hopalong's Colt pushing against his neck.

"Drop that gun!" the Bar-20 puncher ordered, his eyes flashing. "Don't you know better'n that? We've put up with yore crowd as long as we're going to, an' th' next thing will be a slaughter if that foreman of yourn don't get some sense, an' get it sudden. Don't talk back! Just start them cows!"

Antonio could do nothing but obey. His triumph at the success of his effort was torn with rabid hatred for the man who had struck him; but he could not fight with the Colt at his neck, and so sullenly cbeyed. As they neared the line Hopalong ceased his personal remarks and, smiling grimly, turned to another topic.

"I let you off easy; but no more. Th' next herd we find in our valley will go sudden an' hard. If anybody is guardin' it they'll never know what hit 'em." He paused for a moment and then continued, cold contempt in his voice: "I reckon you had to obey orders, but you won't do it again if you know what's good for you. If yore boss, as you calls him, don't like what I've done, you tell him I said to drive th' next herd hisself. If he ain't man enough to bring 'em in hisself, tell him that Cassidy says to quit orderin' his men to take risks he's a-scared of."

"He ees brafe; he ain't 'fraid," Antonio rejoined. "He weel keel you ef I tell heem what you say."

"Tell him jus' th' same. I'll be riding th' line mostly, an' if he wants to hunt me up an' talk about it he can find me any time."

Antonio shrugged his shoulders and rode south, filled with elation at his success in stirring up hostility between the two ranches, but his heart seethed with murder for the blow. He would carry a message to Meeker that would call for harsh measures, and the war would be on.

As Antonio departed Lanky Smith rode into sight and cantered forward to meet his friend.

"What's up?" he asked.

"I don't know, yet," replied Hopalong. "He could be lying, I don't know what to think," and he related the matter to his companion.

"Lord, but you sent a stiff message to Meeker!" Lanky exclaimed. "You keep yore eyes plumb open from now on. Meeker'll be wild, an' Antonio won't forget that blow."

"Was anybody on th' east end this morning?"

"Shore; me an' Pete," Lanky replied, frowning. "He couldn't get a cow across without us seein' him—he lied."

"Well, it makes no difference how he got across; he was there, an' that's all I care about."

"There's one of his outfit now," Lanky said.

Hopalong looked around and saw an H2 puncher riding slowly past them, about two hundred yards to the south.

"Who is he?" Lanky asked.

"Doc Riley. Meeker got him an' Curley out of a bad scrape up north an' took them both to punch for him. I hear he is some bad with th' Colt. Sort of reckons he's a whole war-party in breech-cloths an' war-paint just 'cause he's got his man."

"He's gettin' close to th' line," Lanky remarked.

"Yes, because we've been turnin' their cows."

"Reckon he won't stop us none to speak of."

Doc had stopped and was watching them and while he looked a cow blundered out of the brush and started to cross the line. Hopalong spurred forward to stop it, followed by Lanky, and Doc rode to intercept them.

"G'wan back, you bone-yard!" Hopalong shouted, firing his Colt in front of the animal, which now turned and ran back.

Doc slid to a stand, his Colt out. "What do you think you're doing with that cow?"

"None of yore business!" Hopalong retorted.

Doc backed away so he could watch Lanky, his hand

leaping up, and Hopalong fired. Doc dropped the weapon and grabbed at his right arm, cursing wildly.

Hopalong rode closer. "Next time you gets any curious about what I'm doing, you better write. You're a fine specimen to pull a gun on me, you are!"

"You'll stop turnin' our cows, or you'll get a pass to hell!" retorted Doc. "We won't stand for it no more, an' when th' boys hears about this, you'll have all you can take care of."

"I ain't got nothing to do but ride th' line an' answer questions like I did yourn," Hopalong rejoined. "I will have lots of time to take care of any little trouble that blows up from yore way. But *Meeker's* th' man I want to see. Tell him to take a herd across this line, will you?"

"You'll see him!" snapped Doc, wheeling and riding off.

"Things are movin' so fast you better send for Buck," Lanky suggested. "Hell'll be poppin' down here purty soon."

"I'll tell him what's going on, but there ain't no use of bringing him down here till we has to," Hopalong replied. "We can handle 'em. But I reckon Johnny had better go up an' tell him."

"Johnny ought to be riding this way purty quick; he's coming from th' hills."

"We'll meet him an' get him off."

They met Johnny and when he had learned of his mission he protested against being sent away from the line when things were getting crowded. "I don't want to miss th' fun!" he exclaimed. "Send Red, or Lanky."

"Red's too handy with th' Winchester; we might need him," Hopalong replied, smiling.

"Then you go, Lanky," Johnny suggested. "I'm better'n you with th' Colt."

"You're better'n nothing!' retorted Lanky. "You do what you're told, an' quick. Nothing will happen while you're gone, anyhow."

"Then why don't you want to go?"

"I don't want th' ride," Lanky replied. "It's too fur."

"Huh!" snorted Johnny. "Too bad about you an' th' ride! Poor old man, scared of sixty miles. I'll toss up with you."

"One of you has got to ride to Red an' tell him. He mustn't get caught unexpected," Hopalong remarked.

"What do you call?" asked Johnny, flipping a coin and catching it when it came down.

"All right, that's fair enough. Heads," Lanky replied.

"Whoop! It's tails!" cried Johnny, wheeling. "I'm going for Red," and he was gone before Lanky had time to object.

"Blasted Kid!" Lanky snorted. "How'd I know it was tails?"

"That's yore lookout," laughed Hopalong. "You ought to know him by this time. It's yore own fault."

"I'll tan his hide one of these fine days," Lanky promised. "He's too fresh," and he galloped off to cover the thirty miles between him and the bunk house in the least possible time so as to return as soon as he could.

CHAPTER VI

Meeker Is Told

WHEN ANTONIO had covered half of the distance between the line and the H2 bunk house he was hailed from a chaparral and saw Benito ride into view. He told his satellite what had occurred in the valley, gave him a message for Shaw, who was now on the mesa, and cantered on to tell Meeker his version of the morning's happenings.

The H2 foreman was standing by the corral when his broncho-buster rode up, and he stared. "Where'd you get that welt on th' face?" he demanded.

Antonio told him, with many exclamations and angry gestures, that he had ridden through the valley to see if there were any H2 cows grazing on it, that he had found a small herd and was about to return to his own range when he was held up and struck by Hopalong, who accused him of having driven the cattle across the line. When he had denied this he had been called a liar and threatened with death if he was ever again caught on that side of the line.

"By God!" cried the foreman. "That's purty high-handed! I'll give 'em something to beller about when I finds out just what I want to do!"

"He say, 'Tell that boss of yourn to no send you, send heemself nex' time.' He say he weel keel you on sight. I say he can't. He laugh, *so!*" laughing in a blood-curdling manner. "He say he keel nex' man an' cows that cross line. He ees *uno* devil!"

"He will, hey!" Meeker exclaimed, thoroughly angered. "We'll give him all th' chance he wants when we get things fixed. 'Tony, what did you do about getting those two men you spoke of? You went down to Eagle, didn't you?"

"*Si, si,*" assured Antonio. "They come, *pronto*. They can keel heem. They come to-day; *quien sabe?*"

"I'll do my own killin'—but here comes Doc," Meeker replied. "Looks mad, too. Mebby they was going to kill him an' he objected. Hullo, Doc; what's th' matter?"

"That Cassidy damn near blowed my arm off," Doc replied. "Caught him turnin' back one of our cows an' told him not to. When I backed off so I could keep one eye on his friend he up an' plugs me through my gun arm."

"I see; they owns th' earth!" Meeker roared. "Shootin' up my men 'cause they stick up for me! Come in th' house an' get that arm fixed. We can talk in there," he said, glancing at Antonio. "They cut 'Tony across th' face with a quirt 'cause he was ridin' in their valley!"

"Let's get th' gang together an' wipe 'em off th' earth," Doc suggested, following Meeker towards the house.

Mary looked up when they entered: "What's th' matter, Dad? Why, are you hurt, Doc?"

"Don't ask questions, girl," Meeker ordered. "Get us some hot water an' some clean cloth. Sit down, Doc; we'll fix it in no time."

"We better clean 'em up to-morrow," Doc remarked.

"No; there ain't no use of losin' men fighting if there's

any other way. You know there's a good strong line house on th' top of Lookout Peak, don't you?"

"Shore; reg'lar fort. They calls it Number Three."

Mary had returned and was tearing a bandage, listening intently to what was being said.

"What's th' matter with getting in that some day soon an' holdin' it for good?" asked the foreman. "It overlooks a lot of range, an' once we're in it it'll cost 'em a lot of lives to get it back—if they can get it back."

"You're right!" cried Doc, eagerly. "Let me an' Curley get in there to-night an' hold her for you. We can do it."

"You can't do that. Somebody sleeps in it nights. Nope, we've got to work some scheme to get it in th' daylight. They are bound to have it guarded, an' we've got to coax him out somehow. I don't know how, but I will before many hours pass. Hullo, who's this?" he asked, seeing two strangers approach the house.

"The new punchers," grunted Doc.

"Hey, you," cried Meeker through the open door. "You go down to th' corral an' wait for me."

"Sure thing."

"What's th' matter, Dad?" asked Mary. "How did Doc get shot?"

Meeker looked up angrily, but his face softened.

"There's a whole lot th' matter, Mary. That Bar-20 shore is gettin' hot-headed. Cassidy hit 'Tony across th' face with a quirt an' shot Doc. 'Tony was riding through that valley, an' Doc told Cassidy not to drive back a cow of ourn."

She flushed. "There must 'a been more'n that, Dad. He wouldn't 'a shot for that. I know it."

"You know it!" cried Meeker, astonished. "How do you know it?"

"He ain't that kind. I know he ain't."

"I asked how you knew it!"

She looked down and then faced him. "Because I

know him, because he ain't that kind. What did you say to him, Doc?"

Meeker's face was a study and Doc flushed, for she was looking him squarely in the eyes.

"What did you say to him?" she repeated. "Did you make a gun-play?"

"Well, by God!" shouted Meeker, leaping to his feet. "You know him, hey! 'He ain't that kind!' How long have you known him, an' where'd you meet him?"

"This is no time to talk of that," she replied, her spirit aroused. "Ask Doc what he did an' said to get shot. Look at him; he lied when he told you about it."

"I told him to quit driving our cows back," Doc cried. "Of course I had my hand on my gun when I said it. I'd been a fool if I hadn't, wouldn't I?"

"That ain't all," she remarked. "Did you try to use it?"

Meeker was staring first at one and then at the other, not knowing just what to say. Doc looked at him and his mind was made up.

"What'd you do, Doc?" he asked.

"I said: 'What are you doing with that cow?' an' he said it wasn't none of my business. I got mad then an' jerked my gun loose, but he got me first. I wasn't going to shoot. I was only getting ready for him if he tried to."

"How did he know you wasn't going to shoot?" Meeker demanded. "Reckon I can't blame him for that. He must be quick on th' draw."

"Quickest I ever saw. He had his gun out to shoot in front of a cow. At th' time I thought he was going to kill it. That's what made me get in so quick. He slid it back in th' holster an' faced me. I told you what happened then."

"Well, we've got to show them fellers they can't fool with us an' get away with it," Meeker replied. "An' I've got to have th' use of that crick somehow. I'll think of some way to square things."

"Wait, I'll go with you," Doc remarked, following the other towards the door.

"You go in th' bunk house an' wait for me.

"Wonder how much 'Tony didn't tell," mused the foreman, as he went towards the corral. "But I've got to notice plays like that or they'll think I'm scared of 'em. I'll go up an' have it out, an' when I get ready I'll show them swaggerin' bucks what's what."

When he returned he saw Antonio leaning against his shack, for he was not tolerated by the rest of the outfit and so lived alone. He looked at his foreman and leered knowingly, and then went inside the building, where he laughed silently. "That's a joke, all right! Meeker hiring two of my friends to watch his cows an' do his spying! We'll skin this range before we're through."

Meeker frowned when he caught his broncho-buster's look and he growled: "You never did look good, an' that welt shore makes you look more like th' devil than ever." He glanced at the house and the frown deepened. "So you know Cassidy! That's a *nice* thing to tell me! I'll just go up an' see that coyote, right now," and he went for his horse, muttering and scowling.

Antonio knew of a herd of cows and calves which had not been included in the H2 roundup, and which were fattening on an outlying range. There was also a large herd of Bar-20 cattle growing larger every day on the western range far outside the boundaries. Benito was scouting, Shaw and the others were nearly ready for work on the mesa. Added to this was the constantly growing hostility along the line, and this would blaze before he and Benito had finished their work. Everything considered he was very much pleased and even his personal vengeance was provided for. Doc had more cause for animosity against Hopalong than he had, and if the Bar-20 puncher should be killed some day when Doc rode the northern range, Doc would be blamed for it. But Meeker had not acted as he should have done when two of his men had been hurt on the same day, and that must be remedied. The faster things moved towards fighting the less chance there would be of the plot becoming known.

Antonio was the broncho-buster of the H2 because he was a positive genius at the work, and he was a good, all-around cowman; but he was cruel to a degree with both horses and cattle. Because of his fitness Meeker had overlooked his undesirable qualities, which he had in plenty. He was entirely too fond of liquor and gambling, was uncertain in his hours, and used his time as he saw fit when not engaged in breaking horses. A natural liar, vindictive and with a temper dry as tinder, he was shunned by the other members of the outfit. This filled his heart with hatred for them and for Meeker, who did not interfere. He swore many times that he would square up everything some day, and the day was getting closer.

In appearance he was about medium height, but his sloping shoulders and lax carriage gave his arms the appearance of being abnormally long. His face was sharp and narrow, while his thin, wiry body seemed almost devoid of flesh. Like most cowboys he was a poor walker and his toes turned in. Such was Antonio, who longed to gamble with Fortune in a dangerous game for stakes which to him were large, and who had already suggested to Meeker that the line house on Lookout Peak was the key to the situation. It was the germ, which grew slowly in the foreman's brain and became more feasible and insistent day by day, and it accounted for his fits of abstraction; it would not do to fail if the attempt were made.

CHAPTER VII

Hopalong Meets Meeker

WHEN MEEKER was within a mile of the line he met Curley, told him what had occurred and that he was going to find Hopalong. Curley smiled and replied that he had seen that person less than ten minutes ago and that he was riding towards the peak, and alone.

"We'll go after him," Meeker replied. "You come because I want to face him in force so he won't start no gun-play an' make me kill him. That'd set hell to pop."

Hopalong espied Johnny far to the east and he smiled as he remembered the celerity with which that individual had departed after glancing at the coin.

"There ain't no flies on th' Kid, all right," he laughed, riding slowly so Johnny could join him. He saw Curley riding south and looked over the rough plain for other H2 punchers. Some time later as he passed a chaparral he glanced back to see what had become of his friend, but found that he had disappeared. When he wheeled to watch for him he saw Meeker and Curley coming towards him and he shook his holster to be sure his Colt was not jammed in it too tightly.

"Well, here's where th' orchestry tunes up, all right," he muttered grimly. "Licked Antonio, plugged Doc, an' sent word to Meeker to come up if he wasn't scared. He's come, an' now I'll have to lick two more. If they push me I'll shoot to kill!"

The H2 foreman rode ahead of his companion and stopped when fifty yards from the alert line-rider. Pushing his sombrero back on his head, he lost no time in skirmishing. "Did you chase my broncho-buster out of yore valley, cut his face with yore quirt, an' shoot Doc? Did you send word to me that you'd kill me if I showed myself?"

"Was you ever an auctioneer," calmly asked Hopalong, "or a book agent?"

"What's that got to do with it?" Meeker demanded. "You heard what I said."

"I don't know nothing about yore broncho-buster, taking one thing at a time, which is proper."

"What! You didn't drive him out, or cut him?"

"No; why?" asked Hopalong, chuckling.

"He says you did—an' somebody quirted him."

"He's loco—he wasn't in th' valley," Hopalong replied. "Think he could get in that valley? Him, or any other man we didn't want in?"

"You're devilish funny!" retorted Meeker, riding slowly forward, followed by his companion, who began to edge away from his foreman. "Since you are so exact, did you chase him off yore range an' push him over th' line at th' point of yore gun?"

"You've got me. Better not come too close—my cayuse don't like gettin' crowded."

"That's all right," Meeker retorted, not heeding the warning. "Do you mean to tell me you don't know? Yore name's Cassidy, ain't it?" he asked, angrily, his determination to avoid fighting rapidly becoming lost.

"That's my own, shore 'nuf name," Hopalong answered, and then: "Do you mean Antonio, the one I caught stealing our range?"

"Yes!" snapped Meeker, stopping again.

"Why didn't you say so, then, 'stead of calling him yore broncho-buster?" Hopalong demanded. "How do I know who yore broncho-buster is? I don't know what every land pirate does in this country."

"Then you shot Doc—do you know who I mean this time?" sarcastically asked the H2 foreman.

"Oh, shore. He didn't get his gun out quick enough when he went after it, did he? Any more I can tell you before I begins to say things, too?"

Meeker, angered greatly by Hopalong's contemptuous inflection and the reckless assertiveness of his every word and look, began to ride to describe a circle around the Bar-20 puncher, Curley going the other way.

"You said you'd kill me when you saw me, didn't you, you—"

Hopalong was backing away so as to keep both men in front of him, alert, eager, and waiting for the signal to begin his two-handed shooting. "I ain't a whole lot deaf—I can hear you from where you are. You better stop, for I've ridden out of tighter holes than this, an' you'll shore get a pass to hell if you crowd me too much!"

Adown th' road, an' gun in hand,
Comes Whiskey Bill, mad Whiskey Bill—

This fragment of song floated out of a chaparral about twenty yards behind Hopalong, who grinned pleasantly when he heard it. Now he knew where Johnny was, and now he had the whip hand without touching his guns; while the youngster was not in sight he was all the more dangerous, since he presented no target. Johnny knew this and was greatly pleased thereby, and he was more than pleased by the way Hopalong had been talking.

The effect of the singing was instant and marked on Meeker and his companion, for they not only stopped suddenly and swore, but began to back away, glancing around in an endeavor to locate the joker in the deck. This they failed to do because Johnny was far too wise to advertise his exact whereabouts. Meeker looked at Curley and Curley looked at Meeker, both uneasy and angry.

"As I was sayin' before th' concert began," Hopalong remarked, laughing shortly, "it's a pass to hell if you crowd me too much. Now, Meeker, you'll listen to me an' I'll tell you what I didn't have time to say before: I told an Antonio that th' next herd of yourn to cross th' line should be brought in by you, 'less you was scared to run th' risks yore men had to take. He said you'd kill me for that message, an' I told him you knew where you could find me. Now about Doc: When a man pulls a gun on me he wants to be quicker than *he* was or he'll shore get hurt. I could 'a killed him just as easy as to plug his gun arm, an' just as easy as I could 'a plugged both of you if you pulled on me. You came up here looking for my scalp an' if you still wants it I'll go away from th' song bird in the chaparral an' give you th' chance. I'd ruther let things stay as they are, though if you wants, I'll take both you an' Curley, half-mile run together, with Colts."

"No, I didn't come up here after your scalp, but I got mad after I found you. How long is this going to last? I won't stand for it much longer, nohow."

"You'll have to see Buck. I'm obeying orders, which are to hold th' line again you, which I'll do."

"H'm!" replied Meeker, and then: "Do you know my girl?"

Hopalong thought quickly. "Why, I've seen her ridin' around some. But why?"

"She says she knows you," persisted Meeker, frowning.

The frown gave Hopalong his cue, but he hardly knew what to say, not knowing what she had said about it.

"Hey, you!" he suddenly cried to Curley. "Keep yore hand from that gun!"

"I didn't—"

"You're lying! Any more of that an' I'll gimlet you!"

"What in hell are you doing, Curley?" demanded Meeker, the girl question out of his mind instantly. He had been looking closely at Hopalong and didn't know that Curley was innocent of any attempt to use his Colt.

"I tell—"

"Get out of here! I've wasted too much time already. Go home, where that gun won't worry you. You, too, Meeker! Bring an imitation bad-man up here an' sayin' you didn't want my scalp! Flit!"

"I'll go when I'm damn good and ready!" retorted Meeker, angry again. "You're too blasted bossy, you are!" he added, riding towards the man who had shot Doc.

A-looking for some place to land—

floated out of the chaparral and he stiffened in the saddle and stopped.

"Come on, Curley! We can't lick pot-shooters. An' let that gun alone!"

"Damn it! I tell you I wasn't going for my gun!" Curley yelled.

"Get out of here!" blazed Hopalong, riding forward.

They rode away slowly, consulting in low voices. Then the foreman turned and looked back. "You better be careful how you shoot my punchers! They ain't all like Doc."

"Then you're lucky," Hopalong retorted. "You keep yore cows on yore side an' we won't hurt none of yore outfit."

When they had gone Hopalong wheeled to look for Johnny and saw him crawling out of a chaparral, dragging a rifle after him. He capered about, waving the rifle and laughing with joy and Hopalong had to laugh

with him. When they were rid of the surplus of the
merriment Johnny patted the rifle. "Reckon they was
shore up against a marked deck that time! Did you see
'em stiffen when I warbled? Acted like they had roped
a puma an' didn't know what to do with it. Gee, it was
funny!"

"You're all right, Kid," laughed Hopalong. "It was
yore best play—you couldn't 'a done better."

"Shore," replied Johnny. "I had my sights glued to
Curley's shirt pocket, an' he'd been plumb disgusted if
he'd tried to do what you said he did. I couldn't 'a
missed him with a club at that range. I nearly died
when you pushed Meeker's girl question up that blind
canyon. It was a peach of a throw, all right. Bet he ain't
remembered yet that he didn't get no answer to it.
We're going to have some blamed fine times down here
before everything is settled, ain't we?"

"I reckon so, Kid. I'm going to leave you now an' look
around by West Arroyo. You hang around th' line."

"All right—so long."

"Can you catch yore cayuse?"

"Shore I can; he's hobbled," came the reply from behind a spur of the chaparral. "*Stand still, you hen!* All
right, Hoppy."

Johnny cantered away and, feeling happy, began
singing:

> *Adown th' road, an' gun in hand,*
>   *Comes Whiskey Bill, mad Whiskey Bill;*
> *A-looking for some place to land*
>   *Comes Whiskey Bill.*
> *An' everybody'd like to be*
> *Ten miles away behind a tree*
> *When on his joyous, achin' spree*
>   *Starts Whiskey Bill.*
>
> *Th' times have changed since you made love,*
>   *Oh, Whiskey Bill, oh, Whiskey Bill;*

Th' happy sun grinned up above
  At Whiskey Bill.
An' down th' middle of th' street
Th' sheriff comes on toe-in feet,
A-wishing for one fretful peek
  At Whiskey Bill.

Th' cows go grazin o'er th' lea—
  Pore Whiskey Bill, pore Whiskey Bill,
An' aching thoughts pour in on me
  Of Whiskey Bill.
Th' sheriff up an' found his stride,
Bill's soul went shootin' down th' slide—
How are things on th' Great Divide,
  Oh, Whiskey Bill?

CHAPTER VIII

On the Edge of the Desert

THUNDER MESA was surrounded by almost impenetrable chaparrals, impenetrable to horse and rider except along certain alleys, but not too dense for a man on foot. These stretched away on all sides as far as the eye could see and made the desolate prospect all the more forbidding. It rose a sheer hundred feet into the air, its sides smooth rock and affording no footing except a narrow, precarious ledge which slanted up the face of the southern end, too broken and narrow to permit of a horse ascending, but passable to a man.

The top of the mesa was about eight acres in extent and was rocky and uneven, cut by several half-filled fissures which did not show on the walls. Uninviting as the top might be considered it had one feature which was uncommon, for the cataclysm of nature which had caused this mass of rock to tower above the plain had given to it a spring which bubbled out of a crack in the rock and into a basin cut by itself; from there it flowed down the wall and into a shallow depression to the rock below, where it made a small water hole before flowing through the chaparrals, where it sank into the sand and became lost half a mile from its source.

At the point where the slanting ledge met the top of the mesa was a hut built of stones and adobe, its rear wall being part of a projecting wall of rock. Narrow, deep loopholes had been made in the other walls and a rough door, massive and tight fitting, closed the small doorway. The roof, laid across cedar poles which ran from wall to wall, was thick and flat and had a generous layer of adobe to repel the rays of the scorching sun. Placed as it was the hut overlooked the trail leading to it from the plain, and should it be defended by determined men, assault by that path would be foolhardy.

On the plain around the mesa extended a belt of sparse grass, some hundreds of feet wide at the narrowest point and nearly a mile at the widest, over which numerous rocks and bowlders and clumps of chaparral lay scattered. On this pasture were about three score cattle, most of them being yearlings, but all bearing the brand HQQ and a diagonal ear cut. These were being watched by a careless cowboy, although it was belittling their scanty intelligence to suppose that they would leave the water and grass, poor as the latter was, to stray off onto the surrounding desert.

At the base of the east wall of the mesa was a rough corral of cedar poles set on end, held together by rawhide strips, which, put on green, tightened with the strength of steel cables when dried by the sun. In its shadow another man watched the cattle while he worked in a desultory way at repairing a saddle. Within the corral a man was bending over a cow while two others held it down. Its feet were tied and it was panting, wild-eyed and frightened. The man above it stepped to a glowing fire a few paces away and took from it a hot iron, with which he carefully traced over the small brand already borne by the animal. With a final flourish he stepped back, regarding the work with approval, and thrust the iron into the sand. Taking a knife from his pocket he trimmed the V notch in its ear to the same slanting cut seen on the cattle outside on the pasture. He tossed the bit of cartilage from him, stepping back and nodding to his companions, who loosened the ropes and leaped back, allowing the animal to escape.

Shaw, who had altered the H2 brand, turned to one of the others and laughed heartily. "Good job, eh Manuel? Th' H2 won't know their cow now!"

Manuel grinned. "*Si, si;* eet ees!" he cried. He was cook for the gang, a bosom friend of Benito and Antonio. In his claw-like fingers he held a husk cigarette, without which he was seldom seen. He spoke very little but watched always, his eyes usually turned eastward. He seemed to be almost as much afraid of the east as Cavalry was of the west, where the desert lay. He ridiculed Cavalry's terror of the desert and explained why the east was to be feared the more, for the eastern danger rode horses and could come to them.

"Hope 'Tony fixes up that line war purty soon, eh, Cavalry?" remarked Shaw, suddenly turning to the third man in the group.

Cavalry was staring moodily towards the desert and did not hear him.

"Cavalry! Get that desert off yore mind! Do you want to go loco? Who's going to take th' next drive an' bring back th' flour, you or Clausen?"

"It's Clausen's turn next."

Manuel slouched away and began to climb the slanting path up the mesa. Shaw watched him reflectively and laughed. "There he goes again. Beats th' devil how scared he is, spending most of his time on th' lookout. Why, he's blamed near as scared of them punchers as you are of that skillet out yonder."

"We ain't got no kick, have we?" retorted Cavalry. "Ain't he looking out for us at th' same time?"

"I don't know about that," Shaw replied, frowning.

"I ain't got no love for Manuel. If he saw 'em coming an' could get away he'd sneak off without saying a word. It'd give him a chance to get away while we held 'em."

"We'll see him go, then; there's only one way down."

"Oh, the' devil with him!" Shaw exclaimed. "What do you think of th' chances of startin' that range war?"

"From what Antonio says it looks good."

"Yes. But he'll get caught some day, or night, an' pay for it with his life."

Cavalry shrugged his shoulders. "I reckon so. I'd ruther they'd get him out there than to follow him here. If he goes, I hope it's sudden, so he won't have time to squeal."

"He's a malignant devil, an' he hates that H2 outfit like blazes," replied Shaw. "An' now he's got a pizen grudge agin' th' Bar-20. He might let his hate get th' upper hand an' start in to square things; if he does that he'll over-reach, an' get killed."

"I reckon so; but he's clever as th' devil hisself."

"Well, if he gets too big-headed out here Hall will take care of him, all right," Shaw laughed.

"I don't like them saddled us with," Cavalry remarked. "There's Manuel an' Benito. One of 'em is here all th' time an 'close to you, too, if you remember. Then he's going to put two or three on th' range; why?"

"Suspects we'll steal some of his share, I reckon. An' if he gets in trouble with us they'll be on his side. Oh, he's no fool."

"If he 'tends to business an' forgets his grudges it'll be a good thing for us. That Bar-20 has got an awful number of cows. An' there's th' H2, an' th' other two up north."

"We've tackled th' hardest job first—th' Bar-20," replied Shaw, laughing. "I used to know some fellers what said that outfit couldn't be licked. They died trying to prove themselves liars."

"Wonder how much money 'Tony totes around on him?" asked Cavalry.

"Not much; he's too wise. He's cached it somewhere. Was you reckonin' on takin' it away from him at th' end?"

"No, no. I just wondered what he did with it."

The man at the gate looked up. "Here comes 'Tony."

Shaw and his companion rode forward to meet him. "What's up?" cried Shaw.

"I have started th' war," Antonio replied, a cruel smile playing over his sharp face. "They'll be fightin' purty soon."

"That's good," responded Shaw. "Tell us about it."

Antonio, with many gestures and much conceit, told of the trick he had played on Hopalong, and he took care to lose no credit in the telling. He passed lightly over the trouble between Doc and the Bar-20 puncher, but intimated that he had caused it. He finished by saying: "You send to th' same place tomorrow an' Benito'll have some cows for you. They'll soon give us our chance, an' it'll be easy then."

"Mebby it will be easy," replied Shaw, "but that rests with you. You've got to play yore cards plumb cautious. You've done fine so far, but if you ain't careful you'll go to hell in a hurry an' take us with you. You can't fool 'em all th' time, someday they'll get suspicious an' swap ideas. An' when they do that it means fight for us."

Antonio smiled and thought how easy it might be, if the outfits grew suspicious and he learned of it in time, to discover tracks and other things and tell Meeker he was sure there was organized rustling and that all tracks pointed to Thunder Mesa. He could ride across the border before any of his partners had time to confess and implicate him. But he assured Shaw that he would be careful, adding: "No, I won't make no mistakes. I hate 'em all too much to grow careless."

"That's just where you'll miss fire," the other rejoined. "You'll pamper your grouch till you forget everything else. You better be satisfied to get square by taking their cows."

"Don't worry about that."

"All right. Here's yore money for th' last herd," he said digging down into his pocket and handing Antonio some gold coins. "You know how to get more?"

Antonio took the money, considered a moment and then pocketed it, laughing. "Good! But I mus' go back now. I won't be out here again very soon; it's too risky. Send me my share by Benito," he called over his shoulder as he started off.

The two rustlers watched him and Cavalry shook his head slowly. "I'm plumb scairt he'll bungle it. If he does we'll get caught like rats in a trap."

"If we're up there we can hold off a thousand," Shaw replied, looking up the wall.

"Here comes Hall," announced the man at the gate.

The newcomer swept up and leaped from his hot and tired horse. "I found them other ranches are keeping their men ridin' over th' range an' along th' trails—I near got caught once," he reported. "We'll have to be careful how we drives to th' construction camps."

"They'll get tired watchin' after a while," replied the leader. " 'Tony was just here."

"I don't care if he's in hell," retorted Hall. "He'll peach on us to save his mangy skin, one of these days."

"We've got to chance it."

"Where's Frisco?"

"Down to Eagle for grub to tide us over for a few days."

"Huh!" exclaimed Hall. "Everything considered we're goin' to fight like th' devil out here someday. Down to Eagle!"

"We can fight!" retorted Shaw. "An' if we has to run for it, there's th' desert."

"I'd ruther die right here fighting than on that desert," remarked Cavalry, shuddering. "When I go I want to go quick, an' not be tortured for 'most a week." He had an insistent and strong horror of that gray void of sand and alkali so near at hand and so far across. He was nervous and superstitious, and it seemed always to be calling him. Many nights he had awakened in a cold sweat because he had dreamed it had him, and often it was all he could do to resist going out to it.

Shaw laughed gratingly. "You don't like it, do you?"

Hall smiled and walked towards the slanting trail.

"Why, it ain't bad," he called over his shoulder.

"It's an earthly hell!" Cavalry exclaimed. He glanced up the mesa wall. "We can hold that till we starve, or run out of cartridges—then what?"

"You're a calamity howler!" snapped Shaw. "That desert has wore a saddle sore on yore nerves somethin' awful. Don't think about it so much! It can't come to you, an' you ain't going to it," he laughed, trying to wipe out the suggestion of fear that had been awakened in him by the thought of the desert as a place of refuge. He had found a wanderer, denuded of clothes, sweating blood and hopelessly mad one day when he and Cavalry had ridden towards the desert; and the sight of the unfortunate's dying agonies had remained with him ever since. "We ain't going to die out here— they won't look for us where they don't think there's any grass or water."

Fragments of Manuel's song floated down to them as they strode towards the trail, and reassured that all would be well, their momentary depression was banished by the courage of their hearts.

The desert lay beyond, quiet; ominous by its very silence and inertia; a ghastly, malevolent aspect in its every hollow; patient, illimitable, scorching; fascinating in its horrible calm, sinister, forbidding, hellish. It had waited through centuries—and was still waiting, like the gigantic web of the Spider of Thirst.

CHAPTER IX

On the Peak

HOPALONG CASSIDY had the most striking personality of all the men in his outfit; humorous, courageous to the point of foolishness, eager for fight or frolic, nonchalant when one would expect him to be quite otherwise, curious, loyal to a fault, and the best man with a Colt in the Southwest, he was a paradox, and a puzzle even to his most intimate friends. With him life was a humorous recurrence of sensations, a huge pleasant joke instinctively tolerated, but not worth the price cowards pay to keep it. He had come onto the range when a boy and since that time he had laughingly carried his life in his open hand, and although there had been many attempts to snatch it he still carried it there, and just as recklessly.

Quick in decisions and quick to suspect evil designs against him and his ranch, he was different from his foreman, whose temperament was more optimistic. When Buck had made him foreman of the line riders he had no fear that Meeker or his men would take many tricks, for his faith in Hopalong's wits and ability

was absolute. He had such faith that he attended to
what he had to do about the ranch house and did not
appear on the line until he had decided to call on
Meeker and put the question before him once and for
all. If the H2 foreman did not admit the agreement and
promise to abide by it then he would be told to look
for trouble.

While Buck rode towards Lookout Peak, Hopalong
dismounted at the line house perched on its top and
found Red Connors seated on the rough bench by the
door. Red, human firebrand both in hair and temper,
was Hopalong's loyal chum—in the eyes of the other
neither could do wrong. Red was cleaning his rifle, the
pride of his heart, a wicked-shooting Winchester which
used the Government cartridge containing seventy
grains of powder and five hundred grains of lead. With
his rifle he was as expert as his friend was with the
Colt, and up to six hundred yards, its limit with accuracy, he could do about what he wished with it.

"Hullo, you," said Red, pleasantly. "You looks pee-
vish."

"An' you look foolish. What you doing?"

"Minding my business."

"Hard work?" sweetly asked Hopalong, carelessly
seating himself on the small wooden box which lay
close to his friend.

"Hey, you!" cried Red, leaping up and hauling him
away. "You bust them sights an' you'll be sorry! Ain't
you got no sense?"

"Sights? What are you going to do with 'em?"

"Wear 'em 'round my neck for a charm! What'd you
reckon I'd do with 'em!"

"Didn't know. I didn't think you'd put 'em on that
thing," Hopalong replied, looking with contempt at his
friend's rifle. "Honest, you ain't a-goin' to put 'em on
that lead ranch, are you? Yo're like th' Indians—want
a lot of shots to waste without re-loadin'."

"I ain't wasting no shots, an' I'm going to put sights

on that lead ranch, too. These old ones are too coarse," Red replied, carefully placing the box out of danger. "Now you can sit down."

"Thanks; please can I smoke?"

Red grunted, pushed down the lever of the rifle, and began to re-assemble the parts, his friend watching the operation. When Red tried to slip the barrel into its socket Hopalong laughed and told him to first draw out the magazine, if he wanted to have any success.

The line foreman took a cartridge from the pile on the bench and compared it with one which he took from his belt, a huge, 45-caliber Sharps special, shooting five hundred and fifty grains of lead with one hundred and twenty grains of powder out of a shell over three inches long; a cartridge which shot with terrific force and for a great distance, the weight of the large ball assuring accuracy at long ranges. Besides this four-inch cartridge the Government ammunition appeared dwarfed.

"When are you going to wean yoreself from popping these musket caps, Red?" he asked, tossing the smaller cartridge away and putting his own back in his belt.

"Well, you've got gall!" snorted Red, going out for his cartridge. Returning with it he went back to work on his gun, his friend laughing at his clumsy fingers.

"Yore fingers are all thumbs, an' sore at that."

"Never mind my fingers. Have you seen Johnny around?"

"Yes; he was watching one of them new H2 punchers. He'll go off th' handle one of these days. He reminds me a whole lot of a bull-pup chained with a corral-ful of cats."

Red laughed and nodded. "Where's Lanky?"

"Johnny said he was at Number Four fixin' that saddle again. He ain't done nothin' for th' last month but fix it. Purty soon there won't be none of it left to fix."

"There certainly won't!"

"His saddle an' yore gun make a good pair."

"Let up about the gun. You can't say nothin' more about it without repeatin' yoreself."

"It's a sawed-off carbine. I'd ruther have a Spencer any day."

"You remind me a whole lot of a feller I once knowed," Red retorted.

"That so?" asked Hopalong suspiciously. "Was he so nice?"

"No; he was a fool," Red responded, going into the house.

"Then that's where you got it, for they say it's catching."

Red stuck his head out of the door. "On second thought you remind me of another feller."

"You must'a knowed some good people."

"An' he was a liar."

"Hullo, Hop Wah!" came from the edge of the hilltop and Hopalong wheeled to see Skinny Thompson approaching.

"What you doing?" Skinny asked, using his stock question for beginning a conversation.

"Painting white spots on pink elephants!"

"Where's Red?"

"In th' shack, rubbin' 'em off again."

"Johnny chased that Antonio off'n th' ranch," Skinny offered, grinning.

"Good for him!" cried Hopalong.

"Johnny's all right—here comes Buck," Red said, coming out of the house. "Johnny's with him, too. Hullo, Kid!"

"Hullo, Brick-top!" retorted Johnny, who did not like his nickname. No one treated him as anything but a boy and he resented it at times.

"Did he chase you far?" Hopalong queried.

"I'd like to see anybody chase me!"

Buck smiled. "How are things down here?"

Hopalong related what had occurred and the foreman nodded. "I'm going down to see Meeker—he's th'

only man who can tell me what we're to look for. I
don't want to keep so many men down here. Frenchy
has got all he can handle, an' I want somebody up in
Two. So long."

"Let me an' Red go with you, Buck," cried Hopalong.

"Me, too!" exclaimed Johnny, excitedly.

"You stay home, an' don't worry about me," replied
the foreman, riding off.

"I don't like to see him go alone," Hopalong muttered. "He may get a raw deal down there. But if he
does we'll wipe 'em off'n th' earth."

"Mamma! Look there!" softly cried Johnny, staring
towards the other side of the plateau, where Mary
Meeker rode past. Red and Skinny were astonished and
Johnny and Hopalong pretended to be; but all removed
their sombreros while she remained in sight. Johnny
was watching Hopalong's face, but when Red glanced
around he was staring over the Hill.

"Gosh, ain't she a ripper!" he exclaimed softly.

"She is," admitted Skinny. "She shore is."

Hopalong rubbed his nose reflectively and turned to
Red. "Did you ever notice how pretty a freckle is?"

Red stared, and his friend continued:

"Take a purty girl an' stick a freckle on her nose an'
it sort of takes yore breath."

Red grinned. "I ain't never took a purty girl an' stuck
a freckle on her nose, so I can't say."

Hopalong flushed at the laughter and Skinny cried,
joyously: "She's got two of us already! Meeker's got us
licked if he'll let her show herself once in a while. Oh,
these young fellers! Nothing can rope 'em so quick as
a female, an' th' purtier she is th' quicker she can do
it."

A warning light came into Hopalong's eyes. "Nobody
in this outfit'll go back on Buck for all th' purty women
in th' world!"

"Good boy!" thought Johnny.

"We've got to watch th' Kid, just th' same," laughed Skinny.

"I'll knock yore head off!" cried Johnny. "You're sore 'cause you know you ain't got no chance with women while me an' Hoppy are around!"

Red looked critically at Hopalong and snickered. "If we've got to look like him to catch th' women, thank God we don't want 'em!"

"Is that so!" retorted Hopalong.

"Say," drawled Skinny. "Wouldn't th' Kid look nice hobbled with matrimony? That is, after he grows up."

"You go to th' devil!"

"Gee, Kid, you look bloodthirsty," laughed Red.

"You go to," Johnny retorted, swinging into the saddle. "I'm going along th' line to see what's loose."

"I'll lick you when I see you again!" shouted Red, grinning.

Johnny turned and twirled his fingers at his red-haired friend. "Yah, you ain't man enough!"

"Johnny's gettin' more hungry for a fight every day," Hopalong remarked. "He's itching for one."

"So was you a few years back, an' you ain't changed none," replied Red. "You used to ride around looking for fights."

"To hear you talk, anybody'd think you was a Angel of Peace," Hopalong retorted.

"One's as bad as th' other, so shut up," Skinny remarked, going into the house for a drink.

CHAPTER X

Buck Visits Meeker

As BUCK rode south he went over the boundary trouble in all its phases, and the more he thought about it the firmer his resolution grew to hold the line at any cost. He had gone to great expense and labor to improve the water supply in the valley and he saw no reason why the H2 could not do the same; and to him an agreement was an agreement, and ran with the land. What Meeker thought about it was not the question—the point at issue was whether or not the H2 could take the line and use the valley, and if they could they were welcome to it.

But while there was any possibility for a peaceable settlement it would be foolish to start fighting, for one range war had spread to alarming proportions and had been costly to life and property. Then there was the certainty that once war had begun, rustling would develop. But, be the consequences what they might, he would fight to the last to hold that which was rightfully his. He was not going to Meeker to beg a compromise, or to beg him to let the valley alone; he was riding to tell the H2 foreman what he could expect if he forced matters.

When he rode past the H2 corrals he was curiously regarded by a group of punchers who lounged near them, and he went straight up to them without heeding their frowns.

"Is Meeker here?"

"No, he ain't here," replied Curley, who was regarded by his companions as being something of a humorist.

"Where is he?"

"Since you asks, I reckon he's in th' bunk house," Curley replied. "Where he ought to be," he added, pointedly, while his companions grinned.

"That's wise," responded Buck. "He ought to stay there more often. I hope his cows will take after him. Much obliged for th' information," he finished, riding on.

"His cows an' his punchers'll do as they wants," asserted Curley, frowning.

"Excuse me. I reckoned *he* was boss around here," Buck apologized, a grim smile playing about his lips. "But you better change that 'will' to 'won't' when you mean th' valley."

"I mean *will*!" Curley retorted, leaping to his feet. "An' what's more, I ain't through with that game laig puncher of yourn, neither."

Buck laughed and rode forward again. "You have my sympathy, then," he called over his shoulder.

Buck stopped before the bunk house and called out, and in response to his hail Jim Meeker came and stood in the door.

The H2 foreman believed he was right, and he was too obstinate to admit that there was any side but his which should be considered. He wanted water and better grass, and both were close at hand. Where he had been raised there had been no boundaries, for it had been free grass and water, and he would not and could

not see that it was any different on his new range. He
had made no agreement, and if one had been made it
did not concern him; it concerned only those who had
made it. He did not buy the ranch from the old owners,
but from a syndicate, and there had been nothing said
about lines or restrictions. When he made any agree-
ments he lived up to them, but he did not propose to
observe those made by others.

"How'dy, Meeker," said Buck, nodding.

'How'dy, Peters; come in?"

"I reckon it ain't worth while. I won't stay long,"
Buck replied. "I came down to tell you that some of
yore cows are crossing our line. They're gettin' worse
every day."

"That so?" asked Meeker, carelessly.

"Yes."

"Um; well, what's th' reason they shouldn't? An' what
is that 'line,' that we shouldn't go over it?"

"Dawson, th' old foreman of th' Three Triangle, told
you all about that," Buck replied, his whole mind given
to the task of reading what sort of a man he had to
deal with. "It's our boundary; an' yourn."

"Yes? But I don't recognize no boundary. What have
they got to do with me?"

"It has this much, whether you recognize it or not:
It marks th' north limit of yore grazin'. *We* don't cross
it."

"Huh! You don't have to, while you've got that crick."

"We won't have th' crick, nor th' grass, either, if you
drive yore cows on us. That valley is our best grazing,
an' it ain't in th' agreement that you can eat it all off."

"What agreement?"

"I didn't come down here to tell you what you know,"
Buck replied, slowly. "I came to tell you to keep yore
men an' yore cows on yore own side, that's whatever."

"How do you know my cows are over there?"

"How do I know th' sun is shining?"

"What do you want me to do?" Meeker asked, leaning against the house and grinning.

"Hold yore herds where they belong. Of course some are shore to stray over, but strays don't count—I ain't talkin' about them."

"Well, I've punched a lot of cows in my day," replied Meeker, "an' over a lot of range, but I never seen no boundary lines afore. An' nobody ever told me to keep on one range, if they knowed me. I've run up against a wire fence or two in th' last few years, but they didn't last long when I hit 'em."

"If you want to know what a boundary line looks like I can show you. There's a plain trail along it where my men have rode for years."

"So you say; but I've got to have water."

"You've got it; twenty miles of river. An' if you'll put down a well or two th' Jumping Bear won't go dry.'

"I don't know nothing about wells," Meeker replied. "Natural water's good enough for me without fooling with wet holes in th' ground."

"No; but, by God, yo're willin' enough to use them what *I* put down! Do you think I spent good time an' money just to supply *you* with water? Why don't you get yore own, 'stead of hoggin' mine!"

"There's water enough, an' it ain't yourn, neither."

"It's mine till somebody takes it away from me, an' you can gamble on that."

"Oh, I reckon you'll share it."

"I reckon I won't!" Buck retorted. "Look here; my men have held that range for many years against all kinds of propositions an' we didn't get pushed into th' discard once; an' they'll go right on holding it. Hell has busted loose down here purty often during that time, but we've allus roped an' branded it; an' we hain't forgot how!"

"Well, I don't want no trouble, but I've got to use that water, an' my men are some hard to handle."

"You'll find mine worse to handle before you gets

through," Buck rejoined. "They're restless now, an' once they start, all hell can't stop 'em." Meeker started to reply, but Buck gave him no chance. "Do you know why I haven't driven you back by force? It wasn't because I figgered on what *you'd* do. It was on account of th' rustling that'll blossom on this range just as soon as we get too busy to watch things. That's why, but if yo're willing to take a chance with cow thieves, I am."

"I'm willing. I've got to have water on my northwest corner," Meeker replied. "An' I'm going to have it! If my cows get on yore private reservation, it's up to you to drive 'em off; but I wouldn't be none hasty doing it if I was you. You see, my men are plumb touchy."

"That's final, is it?"

"I ain't never swallered nothing I ever said."

"All right. I can draw on forty men to fill up gaps, an' I'll do it before I let any range jumper cheat me out of what's mine. When you buck that line, come ready for trouble."

"Yore line'll burn you before I'm through," retorted Meeker, angrily.

Meeker laughed, stretched, and slipped his thumbs in the armholes of his vest, watching the Bar-20 foreman ride away. Then he frowned and snapped his fingers angrily. "We'll keep you busy on yore 'line' when I get ready to play th' cards I'm looking for!" he exclaimed. "Th' gall of him! Telling me I can't pasture where I wants! By God, I'll be told I'm using his sunlight an' breathing his air!"

He stepped forward. "Curley! Chick! Dan!"

A moment later the three men stood before him.

"What is it, Jim?" asked Curley.

"You fellers drive north to-morrow. Pick up th' stragglers an' herd 'em close to that infernal line. Don't drive 'em over till I tell you, but don't let none stray south again; savy? If they want to stray north it's none of our business."

"Good!"

"Fine!"

"That's th' way to talk!"

"Don't start nothing, but if trouble comes yore way take care of yoreselves," Meeker remarked. "I'm telling you to herd up on our north range, that's all."

"Shore; we'll do it!" laughed Curley.

"Is that house on th' peak guarded?" Meeker asked.

"Somebody's there most of th' time," replied Dan Morgan.

"Yes; it's their bunk house now," explained Chick.

"All right; don't forget to-morrow."

CHAPTER XI

Three Is a Crowd

WHEN BUCK reached the line on his return Hopalong was the first man he met and his orders were to the point: "Hold this line till hell freezes, drive all H2 cows across it, an' don't start a fight; but be shore to finish any that zephyrs up. Keep yore eyes open."

Hopalong grinned and replied that he would hold the line that long and then skate on the ice, that any cow found trying to cross would get indignant, and that he and trouble were old friends. Buck laughed and rode on.

"Red Eagle, old cayuse!" said the line rider, slapping the animal resoundingly. "We're shore ready!" And Red Eagle, to show how ready he was to resent such stinging familiarities, pitched viciously and bit at his rider's leg.

"Hit her up, old devil!" yelled Hopalong, grabbing his sombrero and applying the spurs. Red Eagle settled back to earth and then shot forward at top speed along the line trail, bucking as often as he could.

It was not long before Hopalong saw a small herd of

H2 cows on Bar-20 land and he rode off to head them. When he got in front of the herd he wheeled and dashed straight at it, yelling and firing his Colt, the horse squealing and pitching at every jump.

"Ki-yi, yeow-eow-eow-eow!" he yelled, and the herd, terror-stricken, wheeled and dashed towards their ranch. He followed to the line and saw them meet and terrorize another herd, and he gleefully allowed that it would be a "shore 'nuf stampede."

"Look at 'em go, old Skyrocket," he laughed. The horse began to pitch again but he soon convinced it that play time had passed.

"You old, ugly wart of a cayuse!" he cried, fighting it viciously as it reared and plunged a bit. "Don't you know I can lick four like you an' not touch leather! There, that's better. If you bite me again I'll kick yore corrugations in! But we made 'em hit th' high trail, didn't we, old hinge-back?"

He looked up and stiffened, feeling so foolish that he hardly knew enough to tear off his sombrero, for before him, sitting quietly in her saddle and looking clean through him, was Mary Meeker, a contemptuous firmness about her lips.

"Good-afternoon, Miss Meeker," he said, wondering how much she had seen and heard.

"I'll not spoil yore fun," she icily replied, riding away.

He stared after her until she had ridden around a chaparral and out of his sight, and he slammed his sombrero on the ground and swore.

"Damn th' luck!"

Then he spurred to overtake her and when he saw her again she was talking to Antonio, who was all smiles.

Hopalong muttered, savagely, "I'll spill him all over hisself some day, th' squint-eyed mud-image! Th' devil with him, if he don't like my company he can amble."

He swept up to them, his hair stirred by the breeze and his right hand resting on the butt of his Colt. Antonio was talking when he arrived, but he had no regard for him and interrupted without loss of time.

"Miss Meeker," he began, backing his horse so he could watch Antonio. "I shore hope you ain't mad. Are you?"

She looked at him coldly, and her companion muttered something and found Hopalong's eyes looking into his soul.

"Speak up if you've got anything to say, which you ain't," Hopalong commanded and then turned to the woman. "I'm shore sorry you heard me. I didn't think you was anywhere around."

"Which accounts for you terrorizing our cows an' calves," she retorted. "An' for trying to start a stampede."

Antonio stiffened at this, but did nothing because Hopalong was watching him.

"You ought to be ashamed of yoreself!" she cried, her eyes flashing and deep color surging into her cheeks. "You had no right to treat them calves that way, or to start a stampede!"

"I didn't try to start no stampede, honest," he replied, fascinated by the color playing across her face.

"You did!" she insisted, vehemently. "You may think it's funny to scare calves, but it ain't!"

"I was in a hurry," he replied, apologetically. "I shore didn't think nothing about th' calves. They was over on us an' I had to drive 'em back before I went on."

"You have no right to drive 'em back," she retorted. "They have every right to graze where the grass is good an' where they can get water. They can't live without water."

"They shore can't," he replied in swift accord, as if the needs of cattle had never before crossed his mind. "But they can get it at th' river."

"You have no right to drive 'em away from it!"

"I ain't going to argue none with you, Miss," he responded. "My orders are to drive 'em back, which I'll do."

"Do you mean to tell me that you'll keep them from water?" she demanded, her eyes flashing again.

"It ain't my fault that yore men don't hold 'em closer to th' river," he replied. "There's water a-plenty there. Yore father's keeping 'em on a dry range."

"Don't say anything about my father," she angrily retorted. "He knows his business better'n you can tell it to him."

"I'm sorry if I've gone an' said anything to make you mad," he earnestly replied. "I just wanted to show you that I'm only obeying orders. I don't want to argue with you."

"I didn't come here to argue," she quickly retorted. "I don't want you to drive our calves so hard, that's all."

"I'll be plumb tender with 'em," he assured her, grinning. "An' I didn't try to scare that other herd, honest."

"I saw you trying to scare them just before you saw me."

"Oh!" he exclaimed, chuckling as he recalled his fight with Red Eagle. "That was all th' fault of this ornery cayuse. He got th' idea into his fool head that he could throw me, so me an' him had it out right there."

She had been watching his face while he spoke and she remembered that he had fought with his horse, and believed that he was telling the truth. Then suddenly, the humorous side struck her and brought a smile to her face. "I'm sorry I didn't understand," she replied in a low voice.

"Then you ain't mad no more?" he asked eagerly.

"No; not a bit."

"I'm glad of that," he laughed, leaning forward. "You had me plumb scared to death."

"I didn't know I could scare a puncher so easy, 'specially you," she replied, flushing. "But where's yore sombrero?"

"Back where I throwed it," he grinned.

"Where you threw it?"

"Shore. I got sore when you rode away, an' didn't care much what happened," he replied, coolly. Then he transfixed Antonio with his keen eyes. "If yo're so anxious to get that gun out, say so or do it," he said, slowly. "That's th' second time."

Mary watched them breathlessly, but Hopalong didn't intend to have any fighting in her presence.

"You let it alone before I take it away from you," he said. "An' I reckon you better pull out—you ain't needed around here. Go on, flit!"

Antonio glanced at Mary for orders and she nodded her head. "I don't need you; go."

Hopalong watched him depart and turned to his companion. "What's eating him, anyhow?"

"I don't know. I never saw him act that way before."

"H'm. I reckon I know; but he don't want to act that way again," he said, decisively.

"All men are funny," she replied. "Th' idea of being scared by me when you ain't afraid of a man like him."

"That's a different kind of a scare, an' I never felt like that before. It made me want to kill somebody. I don't want you to get mad at me. I like you too much. You won't will you?"

She smiled. "No."

"Never? No matter what happens?"

"Do you care?"

"Do I care! You know I do. Look at me, Mary!"

"No; don't come any nearer. I must go—good-bye."

"Don't go; let's ride around for a while."

"But 'Tony may tell Dad; an' if he does Dad'll come up here an' make trouble. No, I must go."

"Tell 'Tony I want to see him," he replied. "If he says anything I'll make him pay for it; an' he won't do it again."

"You mustn't do that! It would make things all th' worse."

"Will you come up again to-morrow?"

She laughed. "That'll be too soon, won't it?"

"Not by a blamed sight."

"Well, I don't know. Good-bye."

"Good-bye," he said, holding out his hand.

She gave him her hand and then tried to push him away. "No, no! No, I say! I won't come any more if you do that!"

Despite her struggles he drew her to him and kissed her again and again.

"I hate you! I hate you!" she cried, her face the color of fire. "What made you do it! You've spoiled everything, an' I'll never see you again! I hate you!" and she wheeled and galloped away.

He spurred in pursuit and when he had overtaken her he grasped her horse by the bridle and stopped her. "Mary! Don't be mad—I love you!"

"Will you let me go?" she demanded, her face crimson.

"Not till you say yo're not mad."

"Please let me go," she replied, looking in his eyes. "I'm not mad at you; but you mustn't do that again. Won't you let me go before some one sees us?"

He released her and she impulsively put her hand on his arm. "Look out—an' watch 'Tony," and she was gone.

"Yo're th' best girl ever rode a cayuse," he muttered, joyously. " 'Look out—an' watch 'Tony,' " he cried. "What do I care about him? I can clean out th' whole gang now. Just let 'em start something."

When he neared the place where his sombrero lay he saw Johnny in the act of picking it up, and Johnny might take a notion to make a race out of it before giving it up. "Hey, you!" Hopalong cried, dashing forward, "gimme that cover!"

"Come an' get it; I don't want it," Johnny retorted. "What made you lose it?"

"Fighting."

"Fighting! Fighting who?"

"Just fighting, Kid."

"Ah, come on an' tell me," begged Johnny. Then, like a shot: "Was it Antonio?"

"Nope."

"Who was it?"

"None of yore business," laughed Hopalong, delighted to be able to tease him.

"All right!" Johnny cried. "You wait; th' boys will be glad to learn about you an' her!"

Hopalong's hand shot out and gripped his friend's shoulder. "Don't you say a word about it, do you hear?"

"Shore. I was only fooling," replied Johnny. "Think I tell them kind of things!"

"I was too quick, Kid. I know yo're a thoroughbred. An' now I'll tell you who I was fighting. It was Red Eagle. He got a fit of pitching, an' I had to take it out of him."

"I might 'a knowed it," responded Johnny, eyeing the tracks in the sand. "But I reckoned you might 'a had a run-in with Antonio. I was saving him for myself."

"Why do you hate him so much?"

"Never mind that now. I'll tell you after I get him."

"Have you seen Buck since he came back?"

"No; why?"

Hopalong told him what the foreman had said and his friend grinned. "The good old days are coming back again, Hoppy!" he exulted.

"Shoo, fly! Shoo, fly," laughed Hopalong.

"Where are you going now?" asked Johnny.

"Where I please."

"Shore. I knowed that. That's where you want to go," grinned Johnny. "But where do you want to go?"

"Where I can't go now."

"Ah, shut up! Come on. I'll go with you."

"Well, I'm going east to tell th' fellers what Buck said."

"Go ahead. I'm with you," Johnny said, wheeling.

"I didn't ask you to come.'

"I didn't ask you to go," retorted Johnny. "Here," he said, holding out a cigar and putting another in his mouth. "Have a smoke; they're all right."

"Where the devil did you get 'em?"

"Up in Number Five."

"In Number Five!"

"Shore. Frenchy, th' son-o'-a-gun, had three of 'em hid over th' windy," Johnny explained. "I hooked 'em."

"So I reckoned; did you take 'em all?"

"Was you going up?"

"No; but did you?"

"Well, I looked good, but I didn't see none to leave."

"You wait till he finds it out," Hopalong warned.

"He won't do nothing," assured Johnny, easily. "Anyhow, yo're as guilty as me. He ain't got no right to cache cigars when we can't get to town for any. Besides, he's afraid of me."

"Scared of you! Oh, Lord, that's good!"

"Quit fooling an' get started," Johnny said, kicking his friend's horse.

"You behave, or I'll get that Antonio to lick you good," threatened Hopalong as he quieted Skyrocket.

"Let's get a-going!"

They cantered eastward, driving back Meeker's cows whenever they were found too close to the line or over it, and it was not long before they made out Lanky riding towards them. He had not yet seen them and Johnny eagerly proposed that they prepare an ambush and scare him.

"He don't scare, you fool," replied Hopalong. "A joke is a joke, but there ain't no use getting shot at when you can't shoot back. No use getting killed for a lark."

"He might shoot, mightn't he," Johnny laughed. "I didn't think about that."

Lanky looked around, waved his hand and soon

joined them. "I see yo're taking care of th' Kid, Hopalong. Hullo, Kid."

"Go to blazes!" snorted Johnny.

"Has he been a good boy, Hoppy?"

"No more'n usual. He's looking for Antonio."

"*Again?*" asked Lanky, grinning. "Ain't you found him yet?"

"Ah, go on. I'll find him when I want him," Johnny retorted.

When Lanky had heard Buck's orders he frowned.

"We'll hold it all right. Wait for Billy, he'll be along purty soon. I left him chasing some cows."

"Got yore saddle so it'll stay together for more'n ten minutes at a time?" asked Johnny.

"I bought Billy's old one," Lanky replied. "Got anything to say about it?"

Billy Williams, pessimist by nature and choice, rode up and joined them and, laughing and joking, they rode towards the Peak, to see if Buck had any further orders. But they had not gone far before Hopalong stopped and thought. "You go on. I'll stay out here an' watch things."

"I'm with you, Hoppy," Johnny offered. "You fellers go on; me an' Hopalong'll take care of th' line out here."

"All right," replied Lanky. "So long."

A few minutes later Johnny turned in his saddle. "Hey, Billy!" he shouted.

"What?"

"Has Lanky paid you for that saddle yet?"

"Shore; why?"

"Oh, nothing. But yo're lucky."

Billy turned and said something to Lanky and they cantered on their way.

"Hey, Hoppy; don't you tell Frenchy about them cigars," Johnny suddenly remarked some time later.

CHAPTER XII

Hobble Burns and Sleepers

THE WESTERN part of the Bar-20 ranch was poor range and but few cattle were to be found on it until Big Coulee had been reached. This portion of the ranch fed quite a large number of cattle, many of which were outlaws, but because of the heavy work demanded on the more fertile southern and eastern sections it was the custom with Buck to pay little attention to the Big Coulee herds; if a man rode up there once in a while he was satisfied. This time it was Skinny who was to look over the condition of affairs around Number Two, which was not far from Big Coulee.

Detouring here and there he took his own time and followed the general direction of the western line, and about four hours after he had quitted the Peak he passed line house Number Two and shortly afterward stopped on the rim of the coulee, a brush-grown depression of a score of acres in extent, in which was a pond covering half an acre and fed by springs on the bottom, its outlet being a deep gorge cut in the soft stone. Half a mile from the pond the small stream disappeared in the sand and was lost.

He rode through the coulee without seeing a single cow and an exploration lasting over an hour resulted no better. Beyond a bear track or two among the berry bushes he saw no signs of animal life. This did not disturb him because he took it for granted that the herds had wandered back to where the grass was better. Stopping at the line house to eat, he mounted and rode towards the hills to report to Hopalong.

Suddenly it struck him that he had seen no cow tracks in the mud around the water hole and he began to hunt for cattle. Using Pete's glasses constantly to sweep the plain for the missing herds, it was not until he had reached a point half-way to the Peak that his search was rewarded by seeing a calf far to the east of him. Watching it until it stood out boldly to his sight he followed an impulse and rode towards it to examine it at close range.

Upon getting near it he saw that it bore the V notch of the H2 cut in its ear, and that it was not branded. He thought it strange that an H2 "sleeper" should be so far from home, without a mother to lead it astray, and he roped it to look more closely at the notch. His opinion was that it had been done very recently, for the cartilage had not yet dried on the edges. Releasing the animal he mounted and started for the line, muttering to himself.

As he swung into the line trail he saw a lame cow limping around a thicket and he spurred forward, roped and threw it, this time giving no thought to the ears, for its brand was that of the Bar-20. He looked at the hocks and found them swollen and inflamed, and his experience told him that it had been done by hobbles. This, to him, explained why the calf was alone, and it gave him the choice of two explanations for the hobbling and the newly cut ear notch on the calf. Either the H2 was sleepering Bar-20 calves for their irons later on, or rustlers were at work. It seemed incredible that any H2 puncher should come that distance to make a few sleepers—but the herd had not been to the water hole! He was greatly wrought up and it was none the more pleasant to be unable to say where the blame lay. There was only one thing to do and that was to scout around and try to find a clue to the perpetrators—and, perhaps, catch the thieves at work. This proved to be unfruitful until he came to North Hill, where he found a cow dead from gunshot. He put spurs to his horse and rode straight for the Peak, which he reached as night fell and as Hopalong, Red, Pete, and Lanky were eating supper and debating the line conditions.

Skinny joined them and listened to the conversation, wordless, nodding or shaking his head at the points made. When he had finished eating he leaned back against his saddle and fumbled for tobacco and pipe, gazing reflectively into the fire, at which he spat. Hopalong turned in time to see the act and, knowing Skinny's peculiarities, asked abruptly: "What's on yore mind, Skinny?"

"Little piece of hell," was the slow reply, and it gained the attention of the others at once. "I saw a H2 sleeper, up just above th' Bend and half way between it an' th' line."

"That so!" exclaimed Hopalong.

"Long way from home—starting in young to ramble," Red laughed. "Lazy trick, that sleepering."

"This here calf had a brand new V—hadn't healed yet," Skinny remarked, lighting his pipe. "An' it didn't—*puff*—have no—*puff*—mother," he added, significantly.

"Huh, weaned, you chump—but that fresh V is shore funny."

"Go on, Skinny," ordered Hopalong, eagerly.

"I found its mother an hour later—hobble-burned an' limping; an' it wasn't no H2 cow, neither; it was one of ourn."

"Rustling!" cried Hopalong.

"Th' H2 is doing it," contradicted Red, quickly.

"They wouldn't take a chance like that," replied Hopalong.

"There ain't no rule for taking chances," Red rejoined. "Some men'll gamble with hell itself—you, for instance, in gun-play."

"What else?" demanded Hopalong of Skinny.

"That Big Coulee herd ain't up there, an' hain't been near th' water hole for so long th' mud's smooth around the edges of th' pond; kin savvy?"

"It's rustlers, by God!" cried Hopalong, looking triumphantly at Red.

"An' I found a dead cow—shot—on th' upper end of North Hill," Skinny added.

"H2!" Red shouted. "They're doing it!"

"Yes, likely; it was an H2 cow," Skinny placidly explained.

"Why in hell can't you tell things in a herd, 'stead of stringin' 'em out like a stiff reata trailing to soften!" Red cried. "Yo're the damndest talker that ever opened a mouth!"

Skinny took the pipe from his mouth and looked at Red.

"I allus get it all out, don't I? What are you kicking about?"

"Yes, you do; like a five thousand herd filtering through a two-foot gate!"

"Mebby th' herd drifted to th' valley," Pete offered.

"Mebby nothing!" Red retorted. "Why, we can't *drive* 'em down here without 'em acting loco about it."

"Cows are shore fool animals," Pete suggested in defence.

"There's more than cows that are fool animals," Red snapped, while Skinny laughed to see Pete get his share.

Sixteen miles to the southeast of the Peak, Meeker sat on a soap box and listened, with the rest of his outfit, to what Curley was saying—"an' when I got down a good ways south I found two young calves bellering for their maws. They was sleepers; an' an hour later I found them same maws bellering for them calves—they was limping a-plenty an' their hocks looked burned—hobble burns."

Meeker mused for a moment and then arose. "You ride that range regular, an' be cautious. Watch towards Eagle. If you catch any sons-of-skunks gamboling reckless, an' they can't explain why they are flitting over our range, shoot off yore gun accidental—there won't be no inquest."

CHAPTER XIII

Hopalong Grows Suspicious

THE EASTERN sky grew brighter and the dim morning light showed a group of men at breakfast on the Peak. They already had been given their orders and as soon as each man finished eating he strode off to where his horse was picketed with the others, mounted, and rode away. Pete had ridden in late the night before and was still sleeping in the house, Hopalong not wishing to awaken him until it was absolutely necessary.

Red Connors, riding back to the house from the horse herd, drew rein for a final word. "I'm going out to watch that unholy drift of Meeker's cows, just this side of th' half-way point. They was purty thick last night when I rode in. I told Johnny to keep on that part of th' line, for I reckon things will get too crowded for one man to handle. Th' two of us can take care of 'em, all right. You knows where you can find us if you need us."

"I don't like that drift, but I'll stay here an' give Pete an hour more sleep," Hopalong replied. "Buck didn't know just when he'd be down again, but I'm looking for him before noon, just th' same."

"Well, me an' Johnny'll stop th' drift. So long," and Red cantered away, whistling softly.

Hopalong kicked out the fire and walked restlessly around the plateau, puzzled by the massing of the H2 cows along the line. The play was obvious enough on its face, for it meant that Meeker, tired of inaction, had decided to force the issue by driving into the valley. But Hopalong, suspicious to a degree, was not satisfied with that solution.

On more than one occasion he had searched past the obvious and found deeper motives, and to this ferment of thought he owed his life many times. He, himself, essentially a schemer and trusting no one but the members of his outfit, accused others of scheming and bent his mind to outwit them. Buck often irritated him greatly, for the foreman, optimistic and believing all men honest until they proved to be otherwise, held that Meeker thought himself to be in the right and so was justified in his attempt to use the valley. Hopalong believed that Meeker was not square, that he knew he had no right to the valley and was trying to steal range; he maintained that the wiser way was to believe all men crooked and put the burden on them of proving otherwise; then he was prepared for anything.

A better cow-man than Buck Peters never lived; he knew the cattle industry thoroughly, was honest, fair, and fearless, maintained an even temper and tried to avoid fighting until the last ditch had been reached. But it was an indisputable fact that Hopalong Cassidy had proved himself to be the best man on the ranch when danger threatened. He grasped situations quickly and clearly and his companions looked to him for suggestions when the sky was clouded by impending conflict. Buck realized that his line-foreman was eminently better qualified to handle the skirmish line than himself, that Hopalong could carry out things which would fall flat if any one else attempted them. Back of Buck's confidence was the pleasing knowledge that no man had ever yet got in the first shot against Hopalong on an "even break," and that when his puncher's gun exploded it was all over; this is why Hopalong could, single-handed, win out in any reasonable situation.

While Hopalong turned the matter over in his mind he thought he saw a figure move among the chaparrals far to the south and he whipped out his glasses, peering long and steadily at the place. Then he put them away and laughed softly. "You can't fool me, by God! I'll let you make yore play—an' if Pete don't kill a few of you I'm a liar. Here are th' shells—pick out th' pea."

Returning to the house he shook Pete. "Hey, get up!"

Pete bounded up, wide awake in an instant. "Yes?"

"Put on yore clothes an' come outside a minute," he ordered, going out.

Pete finished buttoning his vest when he joined his friend, who was pointing south. "Pete, they're playing for this house, an' I can't stay—Red an' Johnny may need me any minute. Down there an H2 rider is watching this house. Meeker is massing his cows along th' line for two reasons; he's trying to draw us away from here so he can get in, an' he's going to push over th' line if he falls down here. You stay in that shack. Don't leave it for a second, understand? Stop anybody that comes up here if you have to kill him. But don't leave this house for nothing, savvy?"

"Go ahead. I savvy."

Hopalong vaulted to his saddle and started away. "I'll get somebody to help you as soon as I can," he called.

"Don't need anybody!" Pete shouted, going inside and barring the door.

Hopalong was elated by the way he had forestalled Meeker, and also because it was Pete who guarded the house. He knew his companions only as a man can know friends with whom he has lived for nearly a score of years. Red was too good a fighter to be cooped up while trouble threatened in the open; Johnny, rash and hot-tempered, could be tempted to leave the house to indulge in personal combat if taunted enough, and he, too, was too good a man in a *mêlée* to remain on the Peak. The man for the house was Pete, for he was accurate enough for that short range, he was unemotional and did not do much thinking for himself when it ran counter to his instructions; he had been told to stay in the house and hold it, and that, Hopalong felt certain, he would do.

"Pete'll hold 'em with one leg in th' air if they happen to be taking a step when he sees 'em," he laughed.

But Pete was to be confronted with a situation so unexpected and of such a nature that for once in his life he was going to forget orders—and small blame to him.

CHAPTER XIV

The Compromise

IT WAS night and on the H2 sickly, yellow lights gleamed from the ranch houses. From the bunk house came occasional bursts of song, the swinging choruses thundering out on the night air, deep-toned and strong. In the foreman's quarters the clatter of dishes was soon stilled and shortly afterward the light in the kitchen could be seen no more. A girl stood in the kitchen door for a moment and then, singing, went inside and the door closed. The strumming of a guitar and much laughter came from Antonio's shack, for now he had Juan and Sanchez to help him pass the time.

Meeker emerged from a corral, glanced above him for signs of the morrow's weather, and then stood and gazed at the shack. Turning abruptly on his heel he strode to the bunk house and smiled grimly as the chorus roared out, for he had determined upon measures which might easily change the merriment to mourning before another day passed. He had made up his mind to remain inactive no longer, but to put things to the test—his outfit and himself against the Bar-20.

He entered the building and slamming the door shut behind him, waited until the chorus was finished. When the last note died away he issued his orders for the next day, orders which pleased his men, who had chafed even more than he under the galling inaction, since they did not thoroughly understand the reasons for it.

"I had them cows herded up north for th' last three days so they'd be ready for us when we wanted 'em," he said, and then leaped at the door and jerked it open, peering about outside. Turning, he beckoned Doc Riley to him and the two stepped outside, closing the door behind them. Great noise broke out within the house as his orders were repeated and commented on. Meeker and Doc moved to the corner of the building and consulted earnestly for several minutes, the foreman gesticulating slowly.

"But Juan said they had a man to guard it," Doc replied.

"Yes; he told me," Meeker responded. "I'm going to fix that before I go to bed—we've got to coax him out on some excuse. Once we get him out of th' house we can cover him, an' th' rest'll be easy. I won't be able to be with you—I'll have to stay outside where I can move around an' look out for th' line trouble, an' where they can see me. But you an' Jack can hold it once you get in. By God, you *must* get in, an' you *must* hold it!"

"We'll do it if it's possible."

"That's th' way to talk. Th' boys seem pleased about it," Meeker laughed, listening to the joy loose in the house.

"Pleased! They're tickled plumb to death. They've got so sore about having to keep their guns quiet that when they cut loose—well, something's due to happen."

"I don't want that if there's any other way," Meeker replied earnestly. "If this thing can be done without wholesale slaughter we've got to do it that way. Remember, Doc, this whole country is backing Peters.

He's got thirteen men now, an' he can call on thirty more in two days. Easy is th' way, easy."

"I'll spend th' next hour pounding that into their hot heads," Doc replied. "They're itching for a chance to square up for everything. They're some sore, been so for a couple of days, about that line house being guarded—they get sore plumb easy now, you know."

"Well, good-night, Doc."

"Good-night, Jim."

Meeker went towards his own house and as he neared the kitchen door a deep-throated wolf-hound bayed from the kennels, inciting a clamorous chorus from the others. Meeker shouted and the noise changed to low, deep, rumbling growls which soon became hushed. Chains rattled over wood and the fierce animals returned to their grass beds to snarl at each other. The frightened crickets took up their song again and poured it on the silence of the night.

Meeker opened the door and strode through the kitchen and into the living room, his eyes squinting momentarily because of the light. His daughter was sitting in a rocking chair, sewing industriously, and she looked up, welcoming him. He replied to her and, dexterously tossing his sombrero on a peg in the wall where it caught and hung swinging, walked heavily to the southern window and stood before it, hands clasped behind his back, staring moodily into the star-stabbed darkness. Down the wind came the faint, wailing howl of a wolf, quavering and distant, and the hounds again shattered the peaceful quiet. But he heard neither, so absorbed was he by his thoughts. Mary looked at him for a moment and then took up her work again and resumed sewing, for he had done this before when things had gone wrong, and frequently of late.

He turned suddenly and in response to the movement she looked up, again laying her sewing aside. "What is it?" she asked.

"Trouble, Mary. I want to talk to you."

"I'm always ready to listen, Daddy," she replied. "I wish you wouldn't worry so. That's all you've done since we left Montana."

"I know; but I can't help it," he responded, smiling faintly. "But I don't care much as long as I've got you to talk it over with. Yo're like yore mother that way, Mary; she allus made things easy, somehow. An' she knew more'n most women do about things."

"Yo're my own Daddy," she replied affectionately. "Now tell me all about it."

"Well," he began, sitting on the table, "I'm being cheated out of my rights. I find lines where none exist. I'm hemmed in from water, th' best grazing is held from me, my cows are driven helter-skelter, my pride hurt, an' my men mocked. When I say I must have water I'm told to go to th' river for it, twenty miles from my main range, an' lined with quicksands; an' yet there is water close to me, water enough for double th' number of cows of both ranches! It is good, clean water, unfailing an' over a firm bottom, flowing through thirty miles of th' best grass valley in this whole sun-cursed section. Two hundred miles in any direction won't show another as good. An' yet, I dassn't set my foot in it—I can't drive a cow across that line!"

He paused and then continued: "I'm good an' sick of it all. I ain't going to swaller it no longer, not a day. Peace is all right, but not at th' price I'm paying! I'd ruther die fighting for what's mine than put up with what I have since I came down here."

"What are you going to do?" she asked quietly.

"I'm going to have a force on that line by to-morrow night!" he said, gradually working himself into a temper. "*I'm* going to hold them hills, an' th' springs at th' bottom of 'em. *I'm* going to use that valley an' I'll fight until th' last man goes under!"

"Don't say that, Daddy," she quickly objected. "There ain't no line worth yore life. What good will it do you when yo're dead? You can get along without it if it comes to that. An' what'll happen to me if you get killed?"

"No, girl," he replied. "You've held me back too long. I should 'a struck in th' beginning, before they got so set. It would 'a been easier then. I don't like range wars any more'n anybody, but it's come, an' I've got to hold up my end—an' my head!"

"But th' agreement?" she queried, fearful for his safety. She loved her father with all her heart, for he had been more than a father to her; he had always confided in her and weighed her judgment; they had been companions since her mother died, which was almost beyond her memory; and now he would risk his life in a range war, a vindictive, unmerciful conflict which usually died out when the last opponent died— and perhaps he was in the wrong. She knew the fighting ability of that shaggy, tight-lipped breed of men that mocked Death with derisive, profane words, who jibed whether in *mêlée* or duel with as light hearts as if engaged in nothing more dangerous than dancing. And she had heard, even in Montana, of the fighting qualities of the outfit that rode range for the Bar-20. If they must be fought, then let it be for the right princi- ples and not otherwise. And there was Hopalong!—she knew in her heart that she loved him, and feared it and fought it, but it was true; and he was the active leader of his outfit, the man who was almost the foreman, and who would be in the thickest of the fighting. She didn't purpose to have him killed if he was in the right, or in the wrong, either.

"Agreement!" he cried, hotly. "Agreement! I hear that every time I say anything to that crowd, an' now you give it to me! Agreement be damned! Nason never said nothing about any agreement when he told me he had found a ranch for me. He wouldn't 'a dealt me a hand like that, one that'd give me th' worst of it in a show-down! He found out all about everything before he turned over my check to 'em."

"But they say there is one, an' from th' way they act it looks that way."

"I don't believe anything of th' sort! It's just a trick to hog that grass an' water!"

"Hopalong Cassidy told me there was one—he told me all about it. He was a witness."

"Hopalong hell!" he cried, remembering the day that Doc had been shot, and certain hints which Antonio had let fall.

"Father!" she exclaimed, her eyes flashing.

"Oh, don't mind me," he replied. "I don't know what I'm saying half th' time. I'm all mixed up, now-a-days."

"I believe he was telling the truth—he wouldn't lie to me," she remarked, decisively.

He looked at her sharply. "Well, am I to be tied down by something I don't know about? Am I to swallow everything I hear? *I* don't know about no agreement, except what th' Bar-20 tells me. An' if there was one it was made by th' Three Triangle, wasn't it?—an' not by Nason or me? Am I th' Three Triangle? Am I to walk th' line on something I didn't make? *I* didn't make it!— oh, I'm tired arguing about it."

"Well, even if there wasn't no agreement you can't blame them for trying to keep their land, can you?" she asked, idly fingering her sewing. "The land is theirs, ain't it?"

"Did you ever hear of free grass an' free water?"

"I never heard of nothing else till I came down here," she admitted. "But it may be different here."

"Well, it ain't different!" he retorted. "An' if it is it won't stay so. What goes in Montanny will go down here. Anyhow, I don't want their land—all I want is th' use of it, same as they have. But they're hogs, an' want it all."

"They say it ain't big enough for their herds."

"Thirty-five miles long, and five miles wide, in th' valley alone, an' it ain't big enough! Don't talk to me like that! You know better."

"I'm only trying to show it to you in every light," she responded. "Mebby yo're right, an' mebby you ain't; that's what we've got to find out. I don't want to think of you fightin', 'specially if yo're wrong. Suppose yo're killed—an' you might be. Ain't there some other way to get what you want, if yo're determined to go ahead?"

"Yes, I might be killed, but I won't go alone!" he cried savagely. "Fifty years, man an' boy, I've lived on th' range, taking every kick of fortune, riding hard an' fightin' hard when I had to. I ain't no yearling at any game about cows, girl."

"But can't you think of some other way?" she repeated.

"I've got to get that line house on th' hill," he went on, not heeding her question. "Juan told me three days ago, that they've put a guard in it now—but I'll have it by noon to-morrow, for I've been thinking hard since then. An' once in it, they can't take it from me! With that in my hands I can laugh at 'em, for I can drive my cows over th' line close by it, down th' other side of th' hill, an' into th' valley near th' springs. They'll be under my guns in th' line house, an' let anybody try to drive 'em out again! Two men can hold that house—it was built for defense against Indians. Th' top of th' hill is level as a floor an' only two hundred yards to th' edge. Nobody can cross that space under fire an' live."

"If they can't cross it an' live, how can *you* cross it, when th' house is guarded? An' when th' first shot is fired you'll have th' whole outfit down on you from behind like wild fire. Then what'll you do? You can't fight between two fires."

"By God, yo're right! Yo're th' brains of this ranch," his eyes squinting to hide his elation. He paced back and forth, thinking deeply. Five minutes passed, then ten, and he suddenly turned and faced her, to unfold the plan he had worked out the day before. He had been leading up to it and now he knew how to propose it. "I've got it. I've got it! Not a shot, not a single shot!"

"Tell me," she said smiling.

He slowly unfolded it, telling her of the herds waiting to be driven across the line to draw the Bar-20 men from the Peak, and of the part she was to play. She listened quietly, a troubled frown on her face, and when he had finished and asked her what she thought of it she looked at him earnestly and slowly replied:

"Do you think that's fair? Do you want *me* to do that?"

"What's unfair about it? They're yore enemies as much as they are mine, ain't they? Ain't everything fair in love an' war, as th' books say?"

"In war, perhaps; but not in love," she replied in a low voice, thinking of the man who wore her flower.

"Now look here!" he cried, leaning forward. "Don't you go an' get soft on any of that crowd! Do you hear?"

"We won't mix love an' war, Daddy," she said, decisively. "You take care of yore end, that's war; an' let me run my part. I'll do what I want to when it comes to falling in love; an' I'll help you to-morrow. I don't want to do it, but I will; you've got to have th' line house, an' without getting between two fires. I'll do it, Daddy."

"Good girl! Yo're just like yore mother—all grit!" he cried, going towards the door. "An' I reckon I won't have to take no hand in *yore* courting," he said, grabbing his sombrero. "Yo're shore able to run yore own."

"But *promise* me you won't interfere," she said, calmly, hiding her triumph.

"It's a go. I'll keep away from th' sparking game," he promised. "I'm going out to see th' boys for a minute," and the door slammed, inciting the clamor of the kennels again, which he again hushed. "Damn 'em!" he muttered, exultantly. "They tried to hog th' range, an' then they want my girl! But they *won't* hog th' range no more, an' I'll put a stop to th' courting when she plays her cards to-morrow, an' without having any hand in it. Lord, I win every trick!" he laughed.

CHAPTER XV

Antonio Meets Friends

BEFORE DAYLIGHT the next morning Antonio left the ranch and rode south, bearing slightly to the west, so as not to leave his trail in Curley's path. He was to meet some of Shaw's men who would come for more cattle. When a dozen miles southwest of the ranch house he espied them at work on the edge of an arroyo. They had a fire going and were re-branding a calf. Far out on the plain was a dead cow, the calf's mother, shot because they had become angered by its belligerency when it had gone "on th' prod." They had driven cow and calf hard and when they tried to separate the two the mother had charged viciously, narrowly missing one of them, to die by a shot from the man most concerned. Meanwhile the calf had run back over its trail and they had roped it as it was about to plunge over the bank of the arroyo.

"You fools!" yelled Antonio, galloping towards them. "Don't you know better'n to blot on this range! How many times have I told you that Curley rides south!"

"He never gets this far west—we've watched him," retorted Clausen, angrily.

"Is that any reason why he can't!" demanded Antonio. "How do you know what he'll do?"

"Yes!" rejoined Clausen. "An' I reckon he can find that steep-bank hollow with th' rope gate, can't he? Suppose he finds th' herds you holds in it for us—what then?"

"It's a whole lot farther west than here!" retorted Antonio, hotly. "They never go to Little Muddy, an' if they do, that's a chance we've got to take. But you can wait till you get to th' mesa before you change brands, can't you!"

"Aw, close yore pie-sump!" cried Frisco. "Who th' devil is doing this, anyhow? You make more noise than Cheyenne on th' Fourth of July!"

"What right have you fellers got to take chances an' hobble *me* with trouble?"

"Who's been doing all th' sleepering, hey?" sarcastically demanded Dick Archer. "Let Meeker's gang see the God-forsaken bunch of sleepers running on their range an' you'll be hobbled with trouble, all right."

Through laziness, carelessness, or haste calves might not be branded when found with branded cows. Feeling was strong against the use of the "running iron," a straight iron rod about eighteen inches long which was heated and used as a pencil on the calf's hide, and a man caught with one in his possession could expect to be dealt with harshly; it was a very easy task to light a fire and "run" a brand, and the running iron was easily concealed under the saddle flap. But it was not often that a puncher would carry a stamping iron, for it was cumbersome. With a running iron a brand could be changed, or the wrong mark put on unbranded cattle; but the stamping iron would give only one pattern.

When a puncher came across an unbranded calf with its branded mother, and the number which escaped the roundup was often large, he branded it, if he had an iron; if he did not have the iron he might cut the calf's ear to conform to the notch in its mother's ears. When the calf was again seen it might have attained its full growth. In that case there was no branded mother to show to whom it belonged; but its cut ears would tell.

These unbranded, ear-cut calves were known as "sleepers" and, in localities where cattle stealing was being or had been carried on to any extent, such sleepering was regarded with strong suspicion, and more than one man had paid a dear price for doing the work.

The ear mark of the H2 was a V, while the Bar-20 depended entirely on the brand, and part of its punchers' saddle equipment was a stamping iron.

Cowmen held sleepering in strong disfavor because it was an easy matter for a maverick hunter or a rustler to drive off these sleepers and, after altering the ear cut, to brand them with his own or some strange brand; and it was easy to make sleepers.

In the case of rustling the separation of branded calves and mothers was imperative, for should any one see a cow of one brand with a calf of another, it was very probable that a committee of discretionary powers would look into the matter. Hobbling and laming mothers and then driving away the calves were not the only ways of separating them and of weaning the calves, for a shot was often as good a way as any; but as dead cows, if found, were certain to tell the true story, this was not generally employed.

"Yes," laughed Frisco. "What about th' sleepers?"

They were discreetly silent about the cow they had killed, for they were ashamed of having left such a sign; but they would not stand Antonio's scorn and anger, and that of the other members of the band, and so said nothing about it.

"Where's th' mother of this calf?" demanded Antonio, not heeding the remarks about sleepers.

"Hanged if I know," replied Clausen, easily; "an' hanged if I care—we can leave *one* cow, I reckon."

"Got many for us this time?" asked Archer as they rode west, driving before them the newly branded calf.

"Not many," replied Antonio. "It's risky, with Curley loose. We won't be able to do much till th' fighting starts."

When they reached their destination they came to a deep, steep-walled depression, exit from which was had at only one end where a narrow trail wound up to the plain. Across this trail at its narrowest point was stretched a lariat.

The depression itself was some ten acres in extent and was well covered with grass, while near the southwest corner was a muddy pool providing water for the herd which was now held captive.

Clausen rode down and removed the rope, riding into the basin to hasten the egress of the herd. When the last cow had scrambled out and joined its fellows, Archer and Frisco drove them west, leaving Clausen to say a few final words with Antonio before joining them.

"How's th' range war coming on?"

"Fine!" laughed Antonio. "Meeker's going to attack th' line house on th' Peak, though what good it'll do him is more than I can figure out. I put it in his head because it'll start th' fight. I had to grin when I heard Meeker and Doc planning it last night—they're easy."

"Gee!" laughed Clausen. "It's a stiff play. Who's going to win? Meeker?"

"Meeker's going to get th' licking of his life. I know that Bar-20 gang, every one. I've lived down here for some time, an' I know what they've done. Don't never get in a six-shooter argument with that feller Cassidy; an' if his friend Connors tells you to stop under eight hundred yards, you do it, an' trust to yore tongue, or Colt. He's th' devil hisself with a Winchester."

"Much obliged—but I ain't so bad that way myself. Well, I'm going to ooze west. Got any word for Shaw?"

"I'll sent word by Benito—I'll know more about it tomorrow."

"All right," and Clausen was being jerked over the scenery by his impatient mount.

Antonio wheeled and rode at a gallop, anxious to be found on northern range, and eager to learn the result of his foreman's attack.

"Salem," once a harpooner on a whaling vessel, now cook for the H2, drove home from Eagle in the chuck wagon, which contained food supplies for his ranch. He was in that state hovering between tears and song, which accounted for the winding trail his wagon wheels left, and also for him being late. He had tarried in Eagle longer than he should have, for he was reluctant to quit the society of his several newly made friends, who so pleasantly allowed him to "buy" for them. When he realized how the time had flown and that his outfit would be clamoring for the noonday meal, such clamoring being spicy and personal in its expression, he left the river trail before he should and essayed a shorter way home, chanting a sea song.

A pirate bold, on th' Spanish Main—
Set sail, yo-ho, an' away we go—

"Starboard yore helm, you lubbers!" he shouted when the horses headed towards Mexico. Then he saw a large bulk lying on the sand a short distance ahead and he sat bolt upright.

"There she blows! No, blast me, it's a dead cow!"

He drove closer to it and, stopping the team, staggered over to see what had killed it.

"Damn me, if it ain't shot in th' port eye!" he ejaculated. "If I find the lubber what's sinkin' our cows, I'll send him to Davy Jones' locker!"

He returned to the wagon and steered nor' by nor' east, once more certain of his bearings, for he knew the locality now, and sometime later he saw Curley riding towards him.

"Ahoy!" he yelled. "Ahoy, you wind-jammer!"

"What's eating you? Why are you so late?" demanded Curley, approaching. "You needn't say—I know."

"Foller my wake an' you'll see a dead cow," cried Salem. "Deader'n dead, too! Shot in th' starboard—no, was it starboard? Now, damned if I know—reckon it was in th' port eye, though I didn't see no port light; aye, 'twas in th' port—"

"What in the hell do I care what eye it was!" shouted Curley. "Where is it?"

"Eight knots astern. Shot in th' port eye, an', as I said, deader'n dead. Flew our flag, too."

Curley, believing that the cook had seen what he claimed, wheeled abruptly and galloped away to report it to Meeker.

"Hey! Ain't you going to *see* it?" yelled Salem, and as he received no reply, turned to his team. "Come on, weigh anchor! Think I want to lay out here all night? 'A-sailing out of Salem town—' " he began, and then stopped short and thought. "I *knowed* it!—it *was* th' port eye! Same side th' flag was on!" he exclaimed, triumphantly.

CHAPTER XVI

The Feint

ON THE boundary line alert and eager punchers rode at a canter to and fro, watching the herds to the south of them, and quick to turn back all that strayed across the line. Just east of the middle point of the boundary Red and Johnny met and compared notes, and both reported the same state of affairs, which was that the cattle came constantly nearer.

Johnny removed his field glasses from his eyes.

"There's punchers with that herd, Red. Three of 'em."

"I reckoned so."

"Wonder what they think they're going to do?"

"We'll know purty soon."

"They're coming this way."

"If you had th' brains of a calf you'd know they wouldn't go south."

"Think they're going to rush us?" Johnny asked, eagerly.

"No; course not!" retorted Red. "They're going to make 'em stand on their heads!"

Johnny began to hum—

Joyous Joe got a juniper jag
A-jogging out of Jaytown;
Joyous Joe got a juniper jag—

"We'll show that prickly pear from Montanny some fine points."

"Now, look here, Kid; don't you let 'em get a cow across th' line. Shoot every one, but keep yore eyes on th' gang."

" 'Joyous Joe got a juniper jag—' Come on, you fools!"

"Wonder where Hopalong is?" Red asked.

"Up on th' Peak, I reckon. *Hey*, Billy!" he yelled. "Here comes Billy, Red."

"I guessed as much when you yelled; if you don't yell away from my ear next time I'll kick yore pants over yore hat. Damned idiot, you!"

"Hullo, Billy," cried Johnny, ignoring Red's remarks. "Just in time for th' pie. Where's Hopalong?"

"In th' hills."

"You get along an' tell him what's doing out here," ordered Red. "Go lively!"

"Reckon I'd better stay an' give you a hand; you'll need it before long," Billy replied.

"You know what Hopalong said, don't you?" blazed Red. "What do you think me an' th' Kid are made of, anyhow? You go on, an' quick!"

"Send Johnny," Billy suggested, hopefully.

"Why, you coyote!" cried Johnny, excitedly. "Th' idea! You go on!"

"Yo're a pair of hogs," grumbled Billy, riding off. "I'll get square, someday. Hope they lick you!"

"Run along, little boy," jeered Johnny. "Oh, gee! Here they come!" he cried as Billy rode behind the chaparral. "Look at 'em!"

"*Let* 'em come!" cried Billy, returning. "We'll lick 'em!"

"Get out of here!" shouted Red, drawing his Winchester from its sheath. "For God's sake, do what yo're told! Want to let Meeker win out?"

"Nope; so long," and Billy galloped away.

"That ain't a herd!" cried Johnny, elated. "That's only a handful. It's a scrawny looking bunch, men an' all. Come on, you coyotes!" he yelled, waving his rifle.

"You chump; this ain't the real play—it's a blind, a wedge," Red replied. "They're pushing a big one through somewhere else."

"I'm shore glad Billy went, an' not me," Johnny remarked.

"There's Morgan," Red remarked. "I know his riding."

"Bet you won't know it when th' show's over. An' there's Chick, too. He needs a licking. You won't know his riding, neither."

The herd came rapidly forward and the men who were guarding it waved their sombreros and urged it on. Red, knowing that he would be crowded if he waited until the cows were upon him, threw his rifle to his shoulder and began to shoot rapidly, and cow after cow dropped, and the rush was stopped. Before the H2 men could get free from the panic-stricken herd Red and Johnny were within a hundred yards of them and when they looked up it was to see Red covering them, while Johnny, pleased by the reduced range, was dropping more cows.

"Stop!" Red shouted, angrily.

"Huh!" exclaimed Johnny, looking up. "Oh, I thought you was talking to me," he muttered, and then dropped another cow.

"What in hell do you think yo're doing?" yelled Morgan.

"Just practicing," retorted Johnny. He quickly swung his rifle on Chick. "Hands up! No more of that!"

"You've got gall, shooting our cows!" replied Chick.

"Get 'em up, boy!" snapped Johnny, and Chick slowly raised his arms, speaking rapidly.

"What do you take us for!" shouted Ed Joyce, frantic at his helplessness.

"Coyotes," replied Red. "An' since coyotes don't ride, you get off'n them cayuses, *pronto*."

"Like hell!" retorted Ed.

Johnny's rifle cracked and Ed tumbled off his dead horse, and when he arose the air was blue.

"Nex' gent say 'I,' " called Johnny.

"I'll be damned if I'll stand for that!" yelled Morgan, reaching for his gun. The next thing he knew was that the air was full of comets, and that his horse was dead.

Chick sullenly dismounted and stood watching Red, who was now in vastly better spirits, since the H2 rifles were on the horses and too far away from their owners to be of any use. The range was too great for good revolver shooting even if they could get them into action.

"Watch 'em," said Red, firing. Chick's horse, stung to frenzy by the wound, kicked up its heels and bolted, leaving the three punchers stranded ten miles from home.

"Turn around an' hit th' back trail," ordered Red. "No back talk!"

"I'll bust you wide open, someday, you red-headed wart!" threatened Dan, shaking his fist at the grinning line man. "That's a hell of a thing to do, that is."

"Shut up an' go home. Ain't you got enough?" shouted Red.

"Just wait," yelled Ed Joyce.

"That's two with th' waiting habit," laughed Johnny.

"What do—" began Chick, stepping forward.

"Shut up! Who told you to open yore face!" cried Red, savagely. "Get home! G'wan!"

"Walk, you coyotes, walk!" exulted Johnny.

He and his companions watched the three angry punchers stride off towards the H2 and then Red told Johnny to ride west while he, himself, would go east to help his friends if they should need him. They had just begun to separate when Johnny uttered a shout of joy. Antonio had joined the trio of walkers and they were pulling him from his horse. He waved his arms excitedly, but Chick had him covered. Dan and Ed were already on the animal and they quickly pulled Chick up behind them, narrowly watching Antonio all the while. The horse fought for some time and then started south, the riders shouting while Antonio, still waving his arms, plodded homeward on foot.

Great joy filled Johnny's heart as he gloated over Antonio's predicament. "Hoof it, you snake! Kick up th' dust!"

"They can't get in th' game again for some time, till they get cayuses," remarked Red. "That makes four less to deal with."

"He acts like he had all eternity to get nowhere— look at him! Let's go down an' rope him. He's on th' prod now—we can have a lot of fun."

"If I go down there it'll be to plug him good," Red replied. "You hang around out here for a while. I'm goin' west—Pete's in that house alone—so long, Kid."

Johnny grinned a farewell to Antonio and followed instructions while his friend rode towards the Peak to assist Pete, the lonely, who as it happened, would be very glad to see him.

CHAPTER XVII

Pete Is Tricked

PETE WILSON grumbled, for he was tiring of his monotonous vigil, and almost hoped the H2 would take the house because of the excitement incident to its recapture. At first his assignment had pleased, but as hour after hour passed with growing weariness, he chafed more and more and his temper grew constantly shorter.

With the exception of smoking he had exhausted every means of passing the time; he knew to a certainty how many bushes and large stones were on the plateau, the ranges between him and distant objects, and other things, and now he had to fell back on his pipe.

"Wish some son-of-a-thief would zephyr up an' start something," he muttered. "If I stays in this fly-corral much longer I'll go loco. A couple of years back we wouldn't have waited ten minutes in a case like this—we'd 'a chased that crowd off th' range quick. What's getting into us has got me picking out th' festive pea, all right."

He stopped at the east window and scrutinized the

line as far as he could see the dim, dusty, winding trail,
hoping that some of the outfit would come into sight.
Then he slid the Sharps out of the window and held it
on an imaginary enemy, whom he pretended was going to try to take the house. While he thought of caustic
remarks, with which to greet such a person, he saw the
head of a horse push up into view over the edge of the
hill.

Sudden hope surged through him and shocked him
to action. He cocked the rifle, the metallic clicks sweet
to his ears. Then he saw the rider, and it was—Mary
Meeker.

Astonishment and quick suspicion filled his mind and
he held the weapon ready to use on her escort, should
she have one. Her horse reared and plunged and, deciding that she was alone, and ashamed to be covering
a woman, he slid the gun back into the room, leaning
it against the wall close at his hand, not losing sight of
the rider for a moment.

"Now, what th' devil is she doing up here, anyhow?"
he puzzled, and then a grin flickered across his face as
the possible solution came to him. "Mebby she wants
Hopalong," he muttered, and added quickly, "Purty as
blazes, too!" And she did make a pretty picture even
to his scoffing and woman-hating mind.

She was having trouble with her mount, due to the
spurring it was getting on the side farther from the
water. It reared and plunged, bucking sideways, up-
and-down and fence-cornered, zigzagging over the
ground forward and back, and then began to pitch "stiff-
legged." Pete's eyes glowed with the appreciation of a
master rider and he was filled with admiration, which
soon became enthusiastic, over her saddle-ease and
cool mastery. She seemed to be a part of the horse.

"She'd 'a been gone long ago if she was fool enough
to sit one of them side saddle contraptions," he mused.
"A-straddle is th' only—*Good!* All right! Yo're a stayer!"
he exclaimed as she stepped from one stirrup and stood

up in the other when the animal reared up on its hind legs.

He glanced out of the other windows of the house and fell to watching her again, his face darkening as he saw that she appeared to be tiring, while her mount grew steadily worse. Then she "touched leather," and again and again. Her foot slipped from the stirrup, but found it again, while she frantically clung to the saddle horn.

"Four-legged devil!" Pete exclaimed. "Wish *I* was on you, you ornery dog! Hey! Don't you bite like that! Keep yore teeth away from that leg or I'll blow yore dammed head off!" he cried wrathfully as the animal bit viciously several times at the stirrup leather. "I'll whale th' stuffin' outen you, you wall-eyed claybank! Yo're too bronc for *her* to ride, all right."

Then, during another and more vicious fit of stiff-legged pitching the rider held to the saddle horn with both hands, while her foot, again out of the stirrup, sought for it in vain. She was rapidly losing her grip on the saddle and suddenly she was thrown off, a cry reaching Pete's ears. The victorious animal kicked several times and shook its head vigorously in celebration of its freedom and then buck-jumped across the plateau and out of sight down the hill, Pete strongly tempted to stop its exuberance with a bullet.

Pete glanced at the figure huddled in the dust and then, swearing savagely and fearing the worst, he threw down the bar and jerked open the door and ran as rapidly as his awkward legs would take him to see what he could do for her, his hand still grasping his rifle. As he knelt beside her he remembered that he had been told not to leave the house under any circumstances and he glanced over his shoulder, and just in time to see a chap-covered leg disappear through the doorway. His heart sank as the crash of the bar falling into place told him that he had been unworthy of the trust his best friend had reposed in him. It was plain enough, now, that he had been fooled, to understand it all and to know that as he left the house one or more H2 punchers had sprinted for it from the other side of the plateau.

Red fury filled him in an instant and tearing the revolver from the girl's belt he threw it away and then, grasping her with both hands, he raised her up as though she weighed nothing and threw her over his shoulder, sprinting for the protection of the hillside, which he reached in a few bounds. Throwing her down as he would throw a bag of flour he snarled at her as she arose and brushed her clothes. Years ago in Pete's life a woman had outraged his love and trust and sent him through a very hell of sorrow; and since then he had had no love for the sex—only a bitter, scathing cynicism, which now found its outlet in words. "Yo're a nice one, you are!" he yelled. "You've done yore part! Yo're all alike, every damned one of you—Judas wasn't no man, not by a damned sight! You know a man won't stand by an' see you hurt without trying to help you— an' you play it against him!"

She was about to retort, but smiled instead and went on with her dusting.

"Tickled, hey! Well, you watch an' see what *we* do to coyotes! You'll see what happens to line-thieves down here!"

She looked up quickly and suspected that instead of averting a fight she had precipitated one. Both Hopalong and her father were in as much danger now as if she had taken no part in the trouble.

Pete emptied his revolver into the air as rapidly as he could work the hammer and hurriedly reloaded it, all the time watching his prisoner and the top of the hill. Three quick reports, muffled by distance, replied from Long Hill and he turned to her.

"Now why don't you laugh?" he gritted savagely. He caught sight of her horse grazing calmly further down the hill and his Sharps leaped to his shoulder and crashed. The animal stiffened, erect for a moment, and then sank slowly back on its quivering haunches and dropped.

"*You* won't pitch no more, damn you!" he growled, reloading.

Her eyes snapped with anger and she fought at her holster. "You coward! You coward!" she cried, stamping her foot. "To kill that horse, an' steal my gun— afraid of a woman!" she taunted. "Coward!"

"I'll pull a snake's fangs rather than get bit by one, when I can't shoot 'em!" he retorted, stung by her words. "You'll see how big a coward I am purty soon— an' you'll stay right here an' see it, too!"

"*I* won't run away," she replied, sitting down and tucking her feet under her skirts. "*I'm* not afraid of a coward!"

Another shot rang out just over the top of Stepping Stone Hill and he replied to it. Far to the west a faint report was heard and Pete knew that Skinny was roweling the lathered sides of his straining horse. Yet another sounded flatly from the direction of the dam, the hills multiplying it into a distant fusillade.

"Hear 'em!" he demanded, fierce joy ringing in his voice. "Hear 'em! You've kicked th' dynamite, all right—you'll smell th' smoke of yore little squib clean down to yore ranch house!"

"That's grand—yo're doing it fine," she laughed, strangling the fear which crept slowly through her. "Go on—it's grand!"

"It'll be a whole lot grander when th' boys get here an' find out what's happened," he promised. "There'll be some funerals start out from what's left of yore ranch house purty soon."

"K-i-i-i-e-e-p! Ki-ip ki-ip!" came the hair-raising yell from the top of Stepping Stone Hill, and Pete withheld the rest of his remarks to reply to it in kind. Suddenly Red Connors, his quirt rising and falling, bounded over the top of the hill and shot down the other side at full

speed. Close behind him came Billy Williams, who rode
as recklessly until his horse stepped into a hole and
went down, throwing him forward like a shot out of a
catapult. He rolled down the hill some distance before
he could check his impetus and then, scrambling to his
feet, drew his Colt and put his broken-legged mount
out of its misery before hobbling on again.

Red slid to a stand and leaped to the ground, his eyes
on the woman, but his first thought was for the house.
"What's the matter? Why ain't you in that shack? Didn't
Hopalong tell you to hold it?" he demanded. Turning
to Mary Meeker he frowned. "What are you doing up
here? Don't you know this ain't no place for you to-
day?"

Pete grasped his shoulder and swung him around so
sharply that he nearly lost his balance, crying: "Don't
talk to her, she's a damned snake!"

Red's hand moved towards his holster and then
stopped, for it was a friend who spoke. "What do you
mean, damn you? Who's a snake? What's wrong here,
anyhow?"

Billy limped up and stood amazed at the strange
scene, for besides the presence of the woman, his
friends were quarreling and he had never seen that
before. Seeing Mary look at him he flushed and sneaked
off his sombrero, ashamed because he had forgotten it.

Pete swiftly related all that had occurred, and ended
with another curse flung at his prisoner, who looked
him over with a keen, critical glance and then smiled
contemptuously.

"That's a fine note!" Red cried, his sombrero also
coming off. He looked at Mary and saw no fear in her
face, no sign of any weakness, but rather a grimness
in the firmness of her lips and a battling light in her
eyes, which gained her immunity from his tongue, for
he admired grit. "Here, you, stop that cussing! You
can't cuss no woman while I'm around!" he cried hotly.
"Hopalong'll break you wide open if he hears you. Cuss-

ing won't do no good; what we want is thinking, an' fighting!" Catching sight of Billy, who looked self-conscious and a little uncomfortable, he cried: "An' what's th' matter with you?"

Billy jerked his thumb over his shoulder in the direction of the dead horse and Red, following the motion, knew. "By th' Lord, you got off easy! Pete, you watch yore prisoner; keep her out of danger, an' there'll be lots of it purty soon. We'll get th' house for you."

"Send up to Cowan's saloon; he had some dynamite, an' if we can get any we can blow them sneaks off th' face of th' earth," Pete exclaimed, his anger and shame urging him against his better nature. "Go ahead. I'll take th' chances using th' stuff—I lost th' house."

The pathetic note of self-condemnation in his last words stopped Red's reprimand and he said, instead: "We'll talk about that later. But don't you lose no sleep—they can't hold it, dynamite or no dynamite. We'll have it before sundown."

Dynamite! Mary caught her breath and sudden fear gripped her heart. Dynamite! And two men were in the house, Doc Riley and Jack Curtis, men who would not be there if she had not made it possible for them—she was responsible.

"Here comes Skinny!" cried Billy, waving his arm.

"An' here's Hopalong!" joyously cried Pete, elated, for he pinned his faith in his line-foreman's ability to get out of any kind of a hole, no matter how deep and wide. "Now things'll happen! We're going to get busy *now*, all right!"

The two arrived at the same instant and both asked the same question. Then Hopalong saw Mary and he was at her side in a trice.

"Hullo! What are *you* doing up here?" he cried in astonishment.

"I'm a prisoner—of *that*!" she replied, pointing at Pete.

Hopalong wheeled. "What! What have you been do-

ing to her? Why ain't you in th' house, where you belongs?"

Pete told him, briefly, and he turned to the prisoner,
a smile of admiration struggling to get through his
frown. She looked at him bravely, for now was the
crisis, which she had feared, and welcomed.

"By th' Lord!" he cried, softly. "Yo're a thoroughbred, a fighter from start to finish. But you shouldn't
come up here to-day; there's no telling, sometimes,
where bullets go after they start." Turning, he said,
"Pete, you chump, stay on this side of th' hills an' watch
th' house. Billy, lay so you can watch th' door. Red,
come with me. An' if anybody gets a shot at them range
stealers, shoot to kill. Understand? Shoot to kill—it's
time."

"Dynamite?" queried Pete, hopefully. "I'll use it.
Cowan—"

Hopalong stared. "Dynamite! Dynamite! We ain't
fighting 'em that way, even if they are coyotes. You go
an' do what I told you."

"Yes, but—"

"Shut up!" snapped Hopalong. "I know how you feel
now, but you'll think different to-morrow."

"Let's swap th' girl for th' house," suggested Skinny,
grinning. "It's a shore cinch," he added, winking at
Billy, who laughed.

Hopalong wheeled to retort, caught Skinny's eye
closing, and laughed instead. "I reckon that would work
all right, Skinny. It'd be a good joke on 'em to take th'
house back with th' same card they got it by. But this
ain't no time for joking. Pete, you better stay here an'
watch th' window on this side; Billy, take the window
on th' south side. Skinny can go around west an' Red'll
take th' door. They won't be so joyous after they get
what's coming their way. This ain't no picnic; shoot to
kill. We've been peaceful too blamed long!"

"That's th' way to talk!" cried Pete. "If we'd acted
that way from th' very first day they crossed our line

we wouldn't be fighting to capture our own line house! You know how to handle 'em all right!"

"Pete, how much water is in there?" Hopalong asked.

" 'Bout a hatful—nobody brought me any this morning, th' lazy cusses."

"All right; they won't hold it for long, then. Take yore places as I said, fellers, an' get busy," he replied, and then turned to Mary. "Where's yore father? Is *he* in that house?"

"I don't know—an' I wouldn't tell if I did!"

"Say, yo're a regular hummer! Th' more you talk th' better I like you," he laughed, admiringly. "You've shore stampeded me worse than ever—I'm so loco I can't wait much longer—when are you going to marry me? Of course you know that you've got to someday."

"Indeed I have *not!*" she retorted, her face crimson. "If you wait for me to marry you you will die of old age! An' I'm shore somebody's listening."

"Then *I'll* marry *you*—of course, that's what I meant."

"Indeed you *won't!*"

"Then th' minister will. After this line fighting is over I won't wait. I'll just rope you an' drive you down to Perry's Bend to th' hobbling man, if you won't go any other way. We'll come back a team. I mean what I say," and she knew that he did, and she was glad at heart that he thought none the less of her for the trick she had played on Pete. He seemed to take everything as a matter of course, and as a matter of course he was going to re-take the house.

"You just *dare* try it! Just *dare!*" she cried, hotly.

"Now you have gone an' done it, for I never take a dare, *never*," he laughed. "It's us for th' sky pilot, an' then th' same range for life. Yo're shore purty, an' that fighting spunk doubles it. You can begin to practice calling yourself Mrs. Hopalong Cassidy, of th' Bar-20."

Pete fired, swore, and turned his head. "How th' devil can I hit a house with all that fool talk!" and the two, suddenly realizing that Pete had been ordered to remain close by, looked foolish, and both laughed.

"It gets on my nerves," Pete growled, and then: "Here comes Johnny like a greased coyote."

They looked and saw Johnny tearing down Stepping Stone Hill as if he were afraid that the fighting would be over before he could take a hand in it. When he came within hailing distance he stood up in his stirrups, shouting, "What's up?" and then, seeing Pete, understood. Leaping from the saddle he jerked his rifle out of the sheath and ran to him, jeering. "Oh, Pete! Oh you damned fool!"

"Hey, Johnny! How's things east?" Hopalong demanded.

Johnny stopped and hastily recounted how he and Red had driven back the herd, adding: "Her dad is out there now looking at his dead cows—I saw him when I came back from East Arroyo. An' I saw them three punchers ride over that ridge down south; and they shore made good time. Say, how did they get Pete out?" he asked eagerly.

"I'll tell you that later—Pete, you go an' tell Red to come here, an' take his place. We can't swap Mary for th' house, but we can swap her dad! Mary, you better go home—this won't be no place for you in a little while. Where's yore cayuse?" he asked, looking around.

"It's down there—he shot it," she replied, nodding at Pete.

"Shot it? Lord, but he must 'a been mad! Well, you can get square—Pete, where's yore cayuse?"

"How th' devil do *I* know!" Pete blazed, indignantly. "*I* wasn't keeping track of no cayuse after they got th' house!"

"It's down there on th' hill—see it?" volunteered Johnny. "Shall I get it?" he asked, grinning at the disgruntled Pete.

"Yes; an' strip th' fixings off her cayuse while yo're about it—lively."

Johnny vaulted into his saddle and loped down the hill, shortly returning with Mary's saddle and bridle in front of him and Pete's horse at the end of his rope. Hopalong quickly removed Pete's saddle and put the other in its place, Pete eloquent in his silence, and Johnny manifestly pleased by the proceedings.

"Now you can ride," Hopalong smiled, helping her into the saddle. "Pete don't care at all—he ain't saying a word," whereat Pete said a word, several of them in fact, under his breath and vowed that he would kill the men in the house to get square.

"I'll send it back as soon as I can," she promised, and then, when Hopalong leaned closer and whispered something to her, she flushed and spurred the animal, leaving him standing in a cloud of dust, a smile on his face.

Johnny, grinning until his face threatened to be ruptured, wheeled on Pete. "Yo're a lucky fool, even if you did go an' lose th' house for us—wish she'd ride *my* cayuse!"

Pete replied in keeping with his feelings now that there was no woman present, and walked away to change places with Red, who soon came up. Then the three mounted and cantered east to find the H2 foreman, Johnny mauling "Whiskey Bill" in his exuberance. Suddenly he turned in his saddle and slapped his thigh: "I'll bet four cents to a tooth brush that she's telling her dad to get scarce. She heard what you said, Hoppy!"

"Right! Come on!" exclaimed Hopalong, spurring into a gallop, his companions racing behind, spurring and quirting to catch him.

"Say, Red, she's a straight flush," Johnny shouted to his companion. "Can't be beat—if she turns Hoppy down I'm next in th' line-up!"

"You don't want no wife—you wants a nurse!" Red retorted.

CHAPTER XVIII

The Line House Re-captured

AFTER CHICK, Dan Morgan, and Ed Joyce had comman-deered Antonio's horse and left him on foot they rode as rapidly as they could to the corrals of their ranch, where they saddled fresh mounts and galloped back to try conclusions with the men who had humbled them. They also wished to find their foreman, who they knew was somewhere along the line. Chick rode to the west, Dan to the east, and Ed Joyce straight ahead; intending to search for Meeker and then ride together again.

Meanwhile Antonio, tired of walking, returned to the line and lay in ambush to waylay the first Bar-20 puncher to ride past him, hoping to get a horse and also leave a dead man for the Bar-20 to find and lay the blame on the H2. He knew that his rustler allies had scouts in the chaparrals and were ready to run off a big herd as soon as conditions were propitious, and he was anxious to give them the word to begin.

It chanced, however, that Ed Joyce was the first man to approach Antonio, and he paid dearly for being a party to taking his horse. The dead man would not inflame the Bar-20, but the H2, and the results would be the same in the end. Mounting Ed's horse Antonio galloped north into the valley through West Arroyo so as to leave tracks in the direction of the Bar-20, intending to describe a semi-circle and return to his ranch by way of the river trail, leaving the horse where the trail crossed the Jumping Bear. By going the remainder of the way on foot he would not be seen on the horse of the murdered puncher, which might naturally enough stray in that direction, and so be free from suspicion.

Lanky Smith, wondering why none of his friends had passed him on the line, followed the trail west to see if things were as they should be. He was almost in sight of a point opposite West Arroyo, his view being obstructed by chaparrals, when he heard a faint shot, and spurred forward, his rifle in the hollow of his arm ready for action. It could mean only one thing—one of his friends was shooting H2 cows, and complications might easily follow. When he had turned out of an arroyo which made part of the line for a short distance he saw a body huddled on the sand several hundred feet ahead of him. At that instant Meeker, with Chick and Dan close at his heels, came into view on the other side, saw the body and, drawing their own conclusions, opened a hot fire on the Bar-20 puncher, riding to encircle him. Surprised for an instant, and then filled with rage because they had killed one of his friends, as he thought, he returned their fire and raced at Chick, who was now some distance from his companions. Dan and Meeker wheeled instantly and rode to the aid of their friend, and Lanky's horse dropped from under him. Luckily for him he felt a warning tremor go through the animal and jerked his feet free from the stirrups as it sank down, quickly crawling behind it for protection.

Immediately thereafter Chick lost his hat, then the use of his right arm, followed by being deprived of the services of a very good cow-pony, for Lanky now had a rest for his rifle and while his markmanship was not

equal to that of his friend Red, it was good enough for
his present needs. Dan Morgan started to shout to his
foreman and then swore luridly instead, for Lanky was
pleased to drill him at five hundred yards, the bullet
tearing a disconcerting hole in Dan's thigh.

Meeker had been most zealously engaged all this
time in making his rifle go off at regular intervals, his
bullets kicking up the dust, humming viciously about
Lanky's head, and thudding into the carcass of the dead
horse. Then Lanky swore and shook the blood from his
cheek, telling Meeker what he thought about the matter. Settling down again he determined to husk Meeker's body from its immortal soul, when he found his
magazine empty. Reaching to his belt for the where-
withal for the husking he discovered the lamentable
fact that he had only three cartridges left for the Winchester, and the Colt was more ornamental than useful
at that range. To make matters worse both Chick and
Dan were now sitting up wasting cartridges in his direction, while Meeker seemed to have an unending
supply. Just then the H2 foreman found his mark again
and rendered his enemy's arm useless. At that point
the clouds of misfortune parted and Hopalong, Red, and
Johnny at his heels, whirled into sight from the west,
firing with burning zeal.

Meeker's horse went down, pinning its rider under
it; Dan Morgan threw up his arms as he sat in the saddle, for his rifle was shattered; Chick, propping up his
good arm first, arose from behind his fleshy breastwork
and announced that he could not fight, although he
certainly wanted to; but Meeker said nothing.

Riding first to Lanky, his friends joked him into a
better humor while they attended to his wounds. Then
they divided to extend the wound-dressing courtesy.
First they tried to kill a man, then to save him; but, of
course, they desired mostly to render him incapable of
injuring them and as long as this was accomplished it
was not necessary to deprive him of life.

Hopalong, being in command, went over to look at the H2 foreman and found him unconscious. Dragging him from under the body of his horse Hopalong felt along the pinned leg and found it was not broken. Pouring a generous amount of whiskey down the unconscious man's throat he managed to revive him and then immediately disarmed him. Meeker complained of pains in his groin, not by words but by actions. His left leg seemed paralyzed and would not obey him. Hopalong called Red, who took the injured man up in front of him, where Hopalong bound his hands to the pommel of the saddle.

Meeker preserved a stolid silence until Lanky joined them and then his rage poured out in a torrent of abuse and accusations for the killing of Ed Joyce. Lanky retorted by asking who Ed Joyce was, and wanted to know whose body he had found just before Meeker had come onto the scene. When he found that they were the same he explained that he had not seen it before Meeker had, which the H2 foreman would not believe. Red captured Dan Morgan's horse and led it up. After Chick and Dan had been helped to mount the Bar-20 men's horses, placed before the saddles and bound there, all started towards Lookout Peak, Lanky riding Dan's horse.

When they had arrived at their destination Meeker suddenly realized what he was to be used for and stormed impotently against it. He heard the intermittent firing around the plateau and knew that Doc and Jack still held the house, and believed they could continue to hold it, since the thick adobe walls were impenetrable to rifle fire.

"Well, Meeker, it's you for th' house," Hopalong remarked after he had sent Red to stop the fire of the others. "You got off damned lucky to-day; th' next time you raise heck along our line we'll pay yore ranch houses a visit an' give you something to think about. We handled you to-day with six of us up north, an'

what th' whole crowd can do you can guess. Now walk
up there an' tell them range-jumpers to vamoose th'
house!"

"They'll shoot me before they sees who I am,"
Meeker retorted, sullenly. "If yo're so anxious to get
'em out, do it yoreself—I don't want 'em."

By this time the others were coming up and heard
Meeker's words, and Hopalong, turning to Skinny and
Billy, curtly ordered them to mount. "Take this royal
fool up to th' bunk house to Buck. Tell Buck what's
took place down here, an' also that we're going to shoot
hell out of th' fellers in th' house before he sees us.
After that those of us who can ride are going down to
th' H2 an' clean up that part of th' game, buildings an'
all. Go on, lively! Red, Johnny, Pete; cover th' windows
an' fill that shack plumb full of lead. It's clouding up
now an' when it gets good an' dark we'll bust in th'
door an' end it. Skinny, you come back again, quick,
with all th' grub an' cartridges you can carry. Meeker
started this, but *I'm* going to finish it an' do it right.
There won't be no more line fights down here for a
long time to come."

"I reckon I'll have to order 'em out," Meeker growled.
"What'll you do to 'em if I do?"

"Send 'em home so quick they won't have any time
to say 'good-bye,' " Hopalong rejoined. "We've seen too
much of you fellers now. An' after I send 'em home
you see that they stays away from that line—we'll shoot
on sight if they gets within gunshot of it! You've shore
had a gall, pushing us, you an' yore hatful of men an'
cows! If it wasn't for th' rustling we'd 'a pushed you
into th' discard th' day I found yore man herding on
us."

Meeker, holding his side because of the pain there
from the fall, limped slowly up the hill, waving his sombrero over his head as he advanced.

"What do you want now?—*Meeker!*" cried a voice
from the building. "What's wrong?"

"Everything; come on out—we lose," the foreman cried, shame in his voice.

"Don't you tell us that if you wants us to stay here," came the swift reply. "We're game as long as we last, an' we'll last a long time, too."

"I know it, Doc—" his voice broke—"they've killed Ed an' captured Chick, Dan an' me, I'd say fight it out, an' I'd to th' end, only they'll attack th' ranch house if we do. We're licked, *this time!*"

"First sensible words you've said since you've been on this range," growled Lanky. "You was licked before you began, if you only knowed it. An' you'll get licked *every* time, too!"

"Well, we'll come out an' give up if they'll let us all go, including you," called Doc. "I ain't going to get picked off in th' open while I've got this shack to fight in, not by a blamed sight!"

"It's all right, Doc," Meeker replied. "How's Jack?" he asked, anxiously, not having heard Doc's companion speak.

"Wait an' see," was the reply, and the door opened and the two defenders stepped into sight, bandaged with strips torn from their woollen shirts, the remains of which they did not bother to carry away.

"Who played that gun through th' west window?" asked Doc, angrily.

"Me!" cried Skinny, belligerently. "Why?"

"Muzzle th' talk—you can hold yore pow-wow some other time," interposed Hopalong. "You fellers get off this range, an' do it quick. An' stay off, savvy?"

Meeker, his face flushed by rage and hatred for the men who had so humiliated him, climbed up on Dan's horse and Dan was helped up behind. Then Chick was helped to mount in front of his foreman and they rode down the hill, followed by Doc and Jack. The intention was to let Dan ride to the ranch after they had all got off the Bar-20 range, and send up the cook with spare horses. Just then Doc remembered that he and Jack

had left their mounts below when they walked up the
hill to take the house, and they went after them.

At this instant Curley was seen galloping up and he
soon reported what Salem had seen. Meeker flew into
a rage at this and swore that he would never give in
to either foe. While Curley was learning of the fighting,
Doc and his companion returned on foot, reporting that
their horses had strayed, whereupon Meeker got off the
horse he rode and told Doc and Chick to ride it home,
Curley being despatched for mounts, while the others
sat down on the ground and waited.

When Curley returned with the horses he was very
much excited, crying that during his absence Salem had
seen six men run off a herd of several hundred head
toward Eagle and had tried to overtake them in the
chuck wagon.

"God A'mighty!" cried Meeker, furiously. "Ain't I got
enough, *now*! Rustling, an' on a scale like that! Peters
was right after all about th' rustling, damn him. A whole
herd! Why didn't they take th' rest, an' th' houses, an'
th' whole ranch? An' Salem, th' fool, chasing 'em in th'
chuck wagon! Wonder they didn't take him, too."

"I reckon he wished he had his harpoon with him,"
Chick snorted, the ridiculousness of Salem's action
bringing a faint grin to his face, angry and wounded as
he was. "He's the locoedest thing that wears pants in
this section, or any other!"

"It was a shore fizzle all around," Meeker grumbled.
"But I ain't through with that line yet—no, by th' Lord,
I ain't got started yet! But this rustling has got to be
cleaned up first of all—th' line can wait; an' if we don't
pay no attention to th' valley for a while they'll think
we've given it up an' get off their guard."

"Shore!" cried Dan, whose fury had been aroused
almost to madness by the sting of the bitter defeat, and
who itched to kill, whether puncher or rustler it little
mattered; he only wanted a vent for his rage.

"We'll parade over that south range like buzzards

sighting carrion," Meeker continued, leading the way homeward. "I ain't a-going to get robbed all th' time!"

"Wonder if Smith did shoot Ed?" queried Dan, thoughtfully. "There was quite a spell between th' shot I heard an' us seeing him, an' he acted like he had just seen Ed. But it's tough, all right. Ed was a blamed good feller."

"Who did shoot him, then?" snapped Meeker, savagely. "There's no telling what happened out there before we got there. Here, Curley, you ain't full of holes like us—you ride up there and get him while we go home. He's laying near that S arroyo right close to th' line—th' one we scouted through that time."

"Shore, I'll get him," replied Curley, wheeling. "See you later."

CHAPTER XIX

Antonio Leaves the H2

ON THE H2 Jim Meeker rolled and muttered in his sleep, which had been more or less fitful because of his aching groin and strained leg. Gazing confusedly about him he sat bold upright, swearing softly at the pain and then, realizing that he was where he should be, grumbled at the kaleidoscopic dreams that had beset him during his few hours of sleep, and glanced out of the window. Hastily dressing he strode to the kitchen door, calling his daughter as he passed her room, and looked out. The bunk house and the corrals were beginning to loom up in the early light and the noise in the cook shack told him that Salem was preparing breakfast for the men. He did not like the looks of the low, huge, black cloud east of him and as he figured that it would not pass over the ranch houses unless the wind shifted sharply he suddenly stared at a corral and then hastened back to his room for the Colt which lay on the floor beside his bunk. He had seen a man flit past the further corral, speed across the open, and disappear behind the corral nearest to the bunk house. This ordinarily would have provoked no further thought, but his men were crazy-headed enough to do anything, but while rustling flourished, and so audaciously, and while a line war was on, it would stand prompt investigation.

Peering again from the door, Colt in hand, Meeker slipped out silently and ran to the corral wall as rapidly as his injuries would allow. When he reached it he leaned close to it and waited, his gun levelled at the corner not ten feet from him. Half a minute later and without a sound a man suddenly turned it, crouching and alertly watching the bunk house and cook shack at his left, and then stopped with a jerk and reached to his thigh as he became aware that he was being watched at such close range. Straightening up and smothering an exclamation he faced the foreman and laughed, but to Meeker's suspicious ears it sounded very much forced and strained.

"No *sabe* Anton?" asked the prowler, smiling innocently and raising his hand from the gun.

Meeker stood silent and motionless, the Colt as steady as a rock, and a heavy frown covered his face as he searched the evil eyes of his broncho-buster, whose smile remained fixed.

"No *sabe Anton*?" somewhat hastily repeated the other, a faint trace of anxiety in his voice, but the smile did not waver, and his eyes did not shift. He began to realize that it was about time for him to leave the H2, for he knew that few things grow so rapidly as suspicion.

Meeker slowly lowered his weapon and swore; he did not like the prowling any better than he did the smile and the laugh and the treacherous eyes.

"I no savvy why yo're flitting around th' scenery when you should ought to be in bed," he replied, his words ominously low and distant. "I'm curious as to why yo're prowling around so early before breakfast. It ain't a whole lot like you to be out so early before grub time. What dragged you from th' bunk so damned early, anyhow?"

Antonio rolled a cigarette to gain time, being elaborately exacting, and thought quickly for an excuse. Tossing the match in the air and letting the smoke curl slowly from his nostrils he grinned pleasantly. "I no sleep—have bad dreams. I wake up, *uno, dos* times an' teenk someteeng ees wrong. Then I ride to see. Eet ees soon light after that an' I am hungry, so I come back. Eet ees no more, at all."

"Oh, it ain't!" retorted the foreman, still frowning, for he strongly doubted the truth of what he had heard, so strongly that he almost passed the lie. "It's some peculiar how this ranch has been shedding dreams last night, all right. However, since I had some few myself I won't say I had all there was loose. But you listen to me, an' listen good, too. When I want any scouting done before daylight I'll take care of it myself, savvy? An' if yo're any wise you'll cure yoreself of th' habit of being out nights percolating around when you ought to be asleep. You ain't acted none too wide awake lately an' yore string of cayuses has shore been used hard, so I want it stopped, an' stopped *sudden*; hear me? I ain't paying you to work nights an' loaf days an' use up good cayuses riding hell-bent for nothing. You ain't never around no more when I want you, so you get weaned of flitting around in th' night air like a whip-poor-will; you might go an' catch malaria!"

"I no been out bafo'—Juan, he tell you that ees so, *si*."

"Is that so? I sort of reckon he'd tell me anything you want him to if he thought I'd believe it. Henceforth an' hereafter you mind what *I've* just told *you*. You might run up against some rustler what you don't know very well, an' get shot on suspicion," Meeker hazarded, but he found no change in the other's face, although he had hit Antonio hard, and he limped off to the ranch house to get his breakfast, swearing every time he put his sore leg forward, and at the ranch responsible for his condition.

Antonio leaned against the corral wall and smoked, gazing off into space as the foreman left him, for he had much to think about. He smiled cynically and shrugged his shoulders as he shambled to his shack, making up his mind to leave the H2 and join Shaw on the mesa as soon as he could do so, and the sooner the better. Meeker's remark about meeting strange rustlers, thieves he did not know, was very disquieting, and it was possible that things might happen suddenly to the broncho-buster of the H2. Soon emerging from his hut he walked leisurely to the fartherest corral and returned with his saddle and bridle. After holding a whispered consultation with Juan and Sanchez, who both showed great alarm at what he told them, and who called his attention to the fact that he had lost one of the big brass buttons from the sleeve of his coat, the three walked to the cook shack for their breakfast, where, every morning, they fought with Salem.

"Here comes them Lascars again to fill their holds with grub," the cook growled as he espied them. "If I was th' old man I'd maroon them, or make 'em walk th' plank. Here, *you*! Get away from that bench!" he shouted, running out of the shack. "That's *my* grub! If you ain't good enough to eat longside of th' crew, damned if you can eat with th' cook! Some day I'll slit you open, tail to gills, see if I don't! Here's yore grub—take it out on th' deck an' fight for it," and Salem, mounting guard over the bench, waved a huge butcher knife at them and ordered them off. "Bilgy smelling lubbers! I'll run afoul of 'em some morning an' make shark's food out of th' whole lot!"

Meanwhile Meeker, finding his breakfast not yet ready, went to Antonio's shack and glanced in it. The bunk his broncho-buster used was made up, which struck him as peculiar, since it was well known that Antonio never made up his bunk until after supper. As

he turned to leave he espied the saddle and saw that
the stirrups were streaked with clay. "Now what was
he doing over at th' river last night?" he soliloquized.
Shrugging his shoulders he wheeled and went to the
bunk house, where he stumbled over a box, whacking
his shins soundly. His heartfelt and extemporaneous remarks regarding stiff legs and malicious boxes awakened Curley, who sat up and vigorously rubbed his eyes
with his rough knuckles. Grunts and profanity came
from the other bunks, Dan swearing with exceptional
loquacity and fervor at his wounded thigh.

"Somebody'll shore have to lift me out like a baby,"
he grumbled. "I'll get square for this, all right!"

"Aw, what you cussing about?" demanded Chick,
whose arm throbbed with renewed energy when he sat
up. "How'd you like to have an arm like mine so you
can't use it for grub, hey?"

"You an' yore arm can—"

"What's matter, Jim?" interrupted Curley, dropping
his feet to the floor and groping for his trousers. "You
got my pants?" he asked Dan, whereupon Dan told him
many things, ending with: "In th' name of heaven what
do I want with pants on this leg! I can't get my own
on, let alone yourn. Mebby Chick has put 'em on his
scratched wing!" he added, with great sarcasm, whereupon Curley found them under his bunk and muttered
a profane request to be told why they had crawled so
far back.

"Yo're a hard luck bunch if yo're as sore as me,"
growled Meeker, kicking the offending box out of doors.
"I cuss every time I hobble."

"Oh, I ain't sore, not a bit—I'm feeling fine," exulted
Curley, putting one foot into a twisted trouser leg while
he hopped recklessly about to keep his balance, Dan
watching him enviously. He grabbed Chick's shoulder
to steady himself and then arose from the floor to find
Chick calling him every name in the language and of-

fering to whip him with one hand if he grabbed the wounded arm again.

"Aw, what's th' matter with you!" he demanded, getting the foot through without further trouble. "I didn't stop to think, you chump!"

"Why didn't you?" snapped Chick, aggressively.

"Curley, yo're a plain, damned nuisance—get outside where you'll have plenty of room to get that other leg in," remarked Dan.

"Not satisfied with keeping us all awake by his cussed snoring an' talking, he goes an' *hops* right on my bad arm!" Chick remarked. "He snores something awful, Jim; like a wagon rumbling over a wooden bridge; an' he whistles every lap."

"You keep away from *me*, you cow!" warned Doc, weighing a Colt in his hand by the muzzle. "I'll shore bend this right around yore face if you don't!"

"Aw, go to th' devil! Yo're a bunch of sore-heads, just a bunch of—" Curley snapped, his words becoming inaudible as he went out to the wash bench, where Meeker followed him, glad to get away from the grunting, swearing crowd inside.

"Curley," the foreman began, leaning against the house to ease his thigh and groin, "Antonio is either going *loco*, or he is up to some devilment, an' I a whole lot favors th' devilment. I thought of telling him to clean out, get off th' range an' stay off, but I reckon I'll let him hang around a while longer to see just what his game is. Of course if he is crooked, it's rustling. I'd like an awful lot to ketch him rustling; it'd wipe out a lot of guessing, an' him at th' same time."

"All three of 'em crooked," Curley replied, refilling the basin. "Every blasted one, an' he's worse than th' others—he's a coyote!"

"Yes, I reckon you ain't far from right," replied Meeker. "Well, anyway, I put in a bad night an' rolled out earlier'n usual. I looked out an' saw somebody sneaking around th' corral, an', gettin' my gun, I went after him hot foot. It was Antonio, an' when I asks for whys an' wherefores, he gives me a fool yarn about having a dream. He woke up an' was plumb scared to death somebody was running off with th' ranch, an', being so all-fired worried about th' safety of th' ranch he's too lazy to work for, he just couldn't sleep, but had to get up an' *saddle his cayuse* an' *ride* around th' corrals to see if it was here. Now, what do you think of that?"

"Huh!" snorted Curley. "He don't care a continental cuss about this ranch or anybody on it, an' never did."

"Which same I endorses; it shore was a sudden change," Meeker replied, glancing at his shack. "I looked in his hut an' saw his bunk hadn't been used since night afore last, so he must 'a had his dreams then. There was yaller clay on his stirrups—he must 'a been scared somebody was going to run off with th' river, too. Now he shore was rampaging all over creation last night—he didn't have no dreams nor no sleep in that bunk last night, nohow. Now, th' question is, where was he, an' what th' devil was he doing? I'd give twenty-five dollars if I knowed for shore."

"That's easy!" snorted Curley, trying to get water out of his ear. "Where'd I 'a been last night if I wasn't broke? Why, down in Eagle having a good time—there's lots of good times in that town if you've got th' price of more than a look-in. Or, mebby, he was off seeing his girl. That's a good way to pass th' evening, too." Then, seeing the frown on Meeker's face he swiftly contradicted himself, realizing that it was no time for jesting. "Why, it looks to me like he might be a little interested in some of th' promiscuous cattle lifting that's going on 'round here. I'll pump him easy so he won't know what I'm driving at."

"Yes, you might do that if yo're shore you won't scare him away, but I want you to pass th' horse corral, anyhow, an' see what horse he rode. See how hard he pushed it riding around th' corrals, an' if there's any yellow clay on its legs. Don't let him see you doing it or he'll get gun-shy an' jump th' country. I'm going up to breakfast—Mary's calling me."

Curley looked up. "Shore I'll do it. It's raining some on th' hills, all right. Look yonder!'

"Yes. I saw it this morning early. It passed to th' northeast of us. I'll be back soon," and the foreman limped away. "Hey, Curley," he called over his shoulder for Antonio's benefit, "take a look at them sore yearlings in th' corral," referring to several calves they had quarantined.

"All right, Jim. They was some better last night. I don't think it's anything that's catching."

"O-o-h!" yawned Jack in the doorway. "Seems like I just turned in—gosh, but I'm sleepy."

"Nothing like cold water for that feeling," laughed Curley. "We stayed up too late last night talking it over. Hullo, Chick; still going to lick me one-handed?"

"You get away from that water, so I can wash one-handed," replied Chick. "But you shouldn't ought to 'a done that. No, Jack—go ahead; but I'm next. Hey, Dan!" he cried, laughing, "shall I bring some water in to you?"

"I won't stay here an' listen to such language as Dan's ripping off," Curley grinned, starting away. "I'm going up to look at them sick yearlings in Number Two corral."

True to his word Curley looked the animals over thoroughly and then dodged into the horse corral, where he quickly examined the horses as he passed them, alert for trouble, for a man on foot takes chances when he goes among cow-ponies in a corral. Not one of the animals forming Antonio's *remuda* appeared to have been ridden and it was not until he espied Pete, Doc's favorite horse, that he found any signs. Pete's hair was roughened and still wet from perspiration, there was a streak of yellow clay along its belly on one side but none on its hoofs, and dried lather still clung to its jaws. Pete made no effort to get away, for he was one of the best trained and most intelligent animals on the ranch, a veteran of many roundups and drives, and he knew from experience that he would not be called on to do double duty; he had done his trick while the others rested.

"An' you know I ain't a-going to ride you, hey?" Curley muttered. "You've had yore turn, an' you know you won't be called on to-day, you wise old devil. Pete, some people say cayuses ain't got no sense, that they can't reason—they never knowed you, did they? Well, boy, you'll have yore turn grazing with th' rest purty soon."

He returned to the bunk house and spent a few minutes inside and then sauntered easily towards the ranch house, where the foreman met him.

"So there wasn't no clay on his hoofs, hey?" Meeker exclaimed. "Some on his belly, an' none on his hoofs. Hum! I reckon Pete was left by hisself while Antonio wrastled with th' mud. Must 'a thought he was prospecting. Well, he's a liar, an' a sneak; watch him close, an' tell th' rest to do th' same. Mebby we'll get th' chance soon of stretching his neck some bright morning. I'll be down purty soon to tell you fellers where to ride."

Curley returned to the wash bench and cleansed his hands, and because the cold water felt so good, he dipped his face into it again, blowing like a porpoise. As he squilgeed his face to lessen the duty of the overworked towel, he heard a step and looked up quickly. Antonio was leaning against the house and scowling at him, for he had looked through a crack in the corral wall and had seen Pete being examined.

"Eet ees *bueno* thees mornin'," Antonio offered.

"What's good?" Curley retorted, staring because of Antonio's unusual loquacity.

"*Madre de Dios*, de weatha."

"Oh, salubrious," replied Curley, evading a hole in the towel. "Plumb sumptuous an' highfalutin', so to speak. You had a nice night in Eagle, all right. Who-all was down there?"

"Antone not en Eagle—he no leev de rancho," Antonio replied. He hesitated as if to continue and Curley noticed it.

"What's on yore mind, 'Tony? What's eating you? *Pronto*, I'm hungry."

Antonio hesitated again. "What you do een de corral thees mornin'?"

"Oh, I was looking at them yearlings—they were purty bad, but they're gettin' along all right. What do you think about 'em?"

"No; een de *beeg* corral."

"Oh, you do!" snapped Curley. "Well, I remembered you was riding around this morning before sunup so I reckoned I'd look in an' see if you rid my cayuse, which you didn't, an' which is good for you. I ain't a whole lot intending to go moping about on no tired-out bronc, an' don't you forget it, neither. An' seeing as how it ain't none of your damned business what I do or where I go, that's about all for you."

"You no spik true—*Pah!* eet ees a lie!" cried Antonio excitedly, advancing a step, and running into the wash water and a fist, both of which met him in the face. Curley, reaching for his holster and finding that he had forgotten to buckle it on, snatched the Remington from Antonio's sheath while the fallen man was half dazed. Pointing it at his stomach, he ordered him up and then told him things.

"I reckon you got off easy—th' next time you calls me a liar shoot first, or there'll be one less, shifty-eyed coyote to ride range nights."

Antonio, drenched and seething with fury, his discolored face working with passion and his small, cruel eyes snapping, sprang to the wall and glared at the man who had knocked him down. But for the gun in Curley's hand there would have been the flash of a knife, but the Remington was master of the situation.

Knife throwing is a useful art at times, but it has its limitations. Cursing, he backed away and slunk into his shack as Doc Riley stuck his head out of the bunk house doorway, hoping to be entertained.

"Worth while hanging 'round, Curley? Any chance of seeing a scrap?" Doc asked, eyeing the gun in his friend's hand.

"You could 'a seen th' beginning of a scrap a couple of minutes earlier," Curley replied. "I didn't give him a chance to throw. Why, he was out all night on Pete, yore cayuse—rode him hard, too. He said—"

"My Pete! Out all night on Pete!" yelled Doc, taking a quick step towards Antonio's hut, the door of which slammed shut, whereupon Doc shouted out his opinions of Antonio. "Is that right?" he asked, turning to Curley. "Was he out on Pete?"

"He shore was—used him up, too."

"I'll break every bone in his yaller carcass!" Doc shouted, shaking his fist at the hut. "Every time I see him I want to get my gun going, an' it's getting worse all th' time. I'll fill him full of lead pills surer than anything one of these days."

"If you don't I will," replied Curley. "I just don't know why I didn't then because—"

"Four bells—grub pile!" rang out the stentorian voice of Salem, who could shout louder than any man on the ranch, and the conversation came to an abrupt end, to be renewed at the table.

When Antonio heard the cook's shout he opened the door a trifle and then, seeing that the coast was clear, picked up the bundle which contained his belongings, shouldered his saddle, slipped his rifle under his arm, and ran to the corral. Juan and Sanchez had been there before him and he found that they not only had taken four of the best horses, but that they had also picketed two good ones for him, and had driven off the remainder to graze, which would delay pursuit should it be instituted. Saddling the better of the two, he left the other and cantered northwest until hidden from the sight of any one at the ranch, and then galloped for safety.

Meeker, returning to the bunk house, found his men in far better humor than they were in when he left them, although the death and burial of Ed Joyce and the other misfortunes of the day before had quieted them a little. As he entered the room he heard Salem in the cook shack, droning a mournful dirge-like air as he slammed things about.

"Hey, cook!" shouted the foreman, standing in the door of the gallery. "Cook!"

"Aye, aye, sir!"

"You are shore you didn't recognize none of them thieves that ran off our herd yesterday?"

"Nary a one, sir. They was running with all sails set two points off my port bow, which left me astern of 'em. I was in that water-logged, four-wheeled hunk of a chuck wagon an' I couldn't overhaul 'em, sir, 'though I gave chase. I tried a shot with th' chaser, but I was rolling so hard I couldn't hull 'em. But I'll try again when I'm sober, sir."

"All right, Salem," laughed Meeker. "Curley, you take yore regular range. Doc, suppose you take th' west, next to Curley? Chick an' Dan will have to stay here till they get well enough to ride, an' I'll need somebody on th' ranch after yesterday, anyhow. Jack, how do you feel? Good! Ride between here an' Eagle. I'm going to go down to that town an' see what I can find out."

"But I can ride, Jim," offered Chick, eagerly. "This arm won't bother me much. Let me stick close to Doc, or one of th' boys. Maybe they might need me, Jim."

"You stay right here, like I said. We'll have to wait till we're all right before we can get down to work in earnest. An' every one of you look out for trouble—shoot first an' talk after." He turned again to the gallery. "Salem, kill a cow an' sun cure th' meat; we might want it in a hurry sometime soon. That'll be one cow they don't get, anyway."

"Who's going to ride north, Jim?" asked Doc.

"Nobody; th' Bar-20 has been so damned anxious to turn our cows an' do our herding for us, an' run th' earth, we'll just let 'em for a while. Not much danger of any rustlers buzzing reckless around *that* neighborhood; they'll earn all they steal if they get away with it."

> *I saw her face grow cold in death,*
> *I saw her—*

came Salem's voice in a new wail. Meeker grabbed a quirt and, leaping to the gallery, threw it. The song stopped short and other words, less tuneful, finished the cook's efforts.

"You never mind what you saw!" shouted the foreman. "If you can't sing anything but graveyard howls, you shut up yore singer!"

CHAPTER XX

What the Dam Told

ABOUT THE time Meeker caught Antonio prowling around the corral, Hopalong stepped out of the line house on the Peak and saw the approaching storm, which gladdened him, notwithstanding the fact that he and Red would ride through it to the bunk house. The range was fast drying up, the grass was burning under the fierce heat of the sun, and the reservoir, evaporating as rapidly as it was supplied, sent but little water down the creek through the valley. This storm, if it broke over the valley, promised to be almost a flood, and would not only replenish the water supply, but would fortify the range for quite a while against the merciless sun.

After he had sent Meeker and his men on their homeward journey he ordered all but Red to report to Buck at the bunk house, believing that the line fighting was at an end for a while, at least. But to circumvent any contingency to the contrary, he and Red remained to guard the house and discuss the situation. The rest of the line riders were glad to get away for a day, as there was washing and mending to be done, clothes to be changed, and their supply of cartridges and tobacco to be replenished.

After throwing his saddle on his horse he went back to the house to get his "slicker," a yellow water-proof coat, and saw Red gathering up their few belongings.

"Going to rain like th' devil, Red," he said. "We'll get soaked before we reach th' dam, but it'll give th' grass a chance, all right. It's due us, an' we're going to get it."

Red glanced out of the window and saw the onrushing, low black mass of clouds. "I reckon yes. Going to be some fireworks, too."

Hopalong, slipping into the hideous slicker, followed Red outside and watched him saddle up. "It'll seem good to be in th' house again with all th' boys, an' eat cook's grub once more. I reckon Frenchy an' some of his squad will drift in—Johnny said he was going to ride out that way on his way back an' tell 'em all th' news."

"Yes. Mind yore business, Ginger!" Red added as his horse turned its head and nipped at his arm, half in earnest and half in playful expostulation. Ginger could not accustom himself to the broad, hind cinch which gripped his soft stomach, and he was wont to object to it in his own way. "Yes, it's going to be a shore enough cloud-burst!" Red exclaimed, glancing apprehensively at the storm. "Mebby we better take th' hill trail—we won't have no cinch fording at th' Bend if *that* lets loose before we get there. We should 'a gone home with th' crowd last night, 'stead of staying up here. I knowed they wouldn't try it again—it's all yore fault."

"Oh, yo're a regular old woman!" retorted Hopalong. "A wetting will do us good—an' as for th' ford, I feel like having a swim."

The close, humid air stirred and moaned, and fitful gusts bent the sparse grass and rustled across the plateau, picking up dust and sending it eddying along the ground. A sudden current of air whined around the corners of the line house, slamming the door violently and awakening the embers of the fire into a mass of glowing coals, which crackled and gave off flying sparks. Several larger embers burst into flame and tumbled end over end across the ground, and Hopalong, running them down, stamped them out, returning and kicking dust over the fire, actuated by the plainsman's instinct. Red watched him and grinned.

"Of course that cloud-burst won't put the fire out," he remarked, sarcastically, although he would have done the same thing if his friend had not.

"Never go away an' leave a fire lit," Hopalong replied, sententiously, closing the banging door and fastening it shut. A streak of lightning quivered between earth and clouds and the thunder rolled in many reverberations along the cliffs of the valley's edge, to die out on the flat void to the west. Down the wind came the haunting wail of a coyote, sounding so close at hand that Red instinctively reached for his rifle and looked around.

"Take *mine*!" jeered Hopalong, mounting, having in mind the greater range of his weapon. "You'll shore need it if you want to get that feller. Gee, but it's dark!"

It was dark and the air was so charged with electricity that blue points of flame quivered on the ears of their horses.

"We're going to get hell!" shouted Red above the roar of the storm. "Every time I spits I make a streak in th' air—an' ain't it hot!"

One minute it was dark; another, the lightning showed things in a ghastly light, crackling and booming like a huge fireworks exhibition. The two men could feel the hearts of their horses pounding against their sides, and the animals, nervous as cats, kept their ears moving back and forth, the blue sparks ghostly in the darkness.

"Come on, get out of this," shouted Hopalong. "Damn, there goes my hat!" and he shot after it.

For reply Red spurred forward and they rode down the steep hill at a canter, which soon changed to a gallop, then to a dead run. Suddenly there came a roar that shook them and the storm broke in earnest, the rain pouring down in slanting sheets, drenching them to the skin in a minute, for their slickers were no protection against that deluge. Hopalong stripped his off, to see it torn from his grasp and disappear in the darkness like a frightened thing.

"Go, then!" he snapped. "I was roasting in you, anyhow! I won't have no clothes left by th' time I hits th' Bend—which is all th' better for swimming."

Red slackened pace, rode at his friend's side, their stirrups almost touching, for it was safer to canter than to gallop when they could not see ahead of them. The darkness gradually lessened and when they got close to the dam they could see as well as they could on any dull day, except for a distance—the sheets of water forbade that.

"What's that?" Hopalong suddenly demanded, drawing rein and listening. A dull roar came from the dam and he instinctively felt that something was radically wrong.

"Water, of course," Red replied, impatiently. "This is a *storm*," he explained.

Hopalong rode out along the dam, followed by Red, peering ahead. Suddenly he stopped and swore.

"She's *busted*! Look there!"

A turbulent flood poured through a cut ten feet wide and roared down the other side of the embankment, roiled and yellow.

"Good God! She's a goner shore!" cried Red excitedly.

"It shore is—*No*, Red! It's over th' stone work—see where that ripple runs? We can save it if we hustle," Hopalong replied, wheeling. "Come on! Dead cows'll choke it—get a move on!"

When Buck had decided to build the dam he had

sent for an engineer to come out and look the valley
over and to lay out the lines to be followed. The west
end, which would be built against the bluff, would be
strong; but Buck was advised to build a core of rubble
masonry for a hundred feet east of the centre, where
the embankment must run almost straight to avoid a
quicksand bottom. This had been done at a great increase over the original estimate of the cost of the dam,
but now it more than paid for itself, for Antonio had
dug his trench over the rubble core—had he gone down
a foot deeper he would have struck it and discovered
his mistake.

Hopalong and Red raced along the dam and separated when they struck the plain, soon returning with
a cow apiece dragging from their lariats, which they
released and pushed into the torrent. Their bodies
floated with the stream and both men feared their efforts were in vain. Then Hopalong uttered a shout of
joy, for the carcasses, stranding against the top of the
masonry core, stopped, the water surging over them.
Racing away again they dragged up more cows until
the bodies choked the gap, when they brought up arm-
fuls of brush and threw them before the bodies. Then
Red espied a shovel, swore furiously at what it told
him, and fell to throwing dirt into the breach before
the brush. He had to take it from different places so as
not to weaken the damn, and an hour elapsed before
they stopped work and regarded the results of their
efforts with satisfaction.

"Well, she's there yet, and she'll stay, all right. Good
thing we didn't take th' hill trail," Hopalong remarked.

"Somebody cut it, all right," Red avowed, looking at
the shovel in his hands. "*H2*! Hoppy, see here! This is
their work!"

"Shore enough H2 on th' handle, but Meeker an' his
crowd never did that," Hopalong replied. "I ain't got
no love for any of 'em, but they're too square for this
sort of a thing. Besides, they want to use this water too

much to cheat themselves out of every chance to get it."

"You may be right—but it's damned funny that we find their shovel on th' job," Red rejoined, scowling at the brand burned into the wooden handle.

"What's that yo're treading on?" Hopalong asked, pointing to a bright object on the ground.

Red stooped and then shouted, holding up the object so his friend could see it. "It's a brass button as big as a half-dollar—bet it belonged to th' snake that used this shovel!"

"Yo're safe. I won't bet you—an' Antonio was th' only one I've seen wearing buttons like that in these parts," Hopalong replied. "I'm going to kill him on sight!" and he meant what he said.

"Same here, th' ornery coyote!" Red gritted.

"Antonio had me guessing, but I'm beginning to see a great big light," Hopalong remarked, taking the button and looking it over. "Yep, it's hissn, all right."

"Well, we've filled her," Red remarked after a final inspection.

"She'll hold until to-morrow, anyhow, or till we can bring th' chuck wagon full of tools an' rocks down here," Hopalong replied. "We'll make her solid for keeps. You better take th' evidence with you, Red, an' let Buck look 'em over. It's a good thing Buck spent that extra money putting in that stone core! Besides losing th' reservoir we'd have had plenty of dead cows by this time if it wasn't for that."

"An' that Antonio went an' picked out the weakest spot in th' whole thing, or th' spot what would be th' weakest if that wall wasn't there," Red remarked. "He ain't no fool, but a stacked deck can beat a good head time after time."

When they reached the ford they found a driftwood-dotted flood roaring around the bend, three times as wide as it was ordinarily, for the hills made a watershed that gave quick results in such a rain.

"Now Red Eagle, old cayuse, here's where you swim," Hopalong laughed, riding up stream so he would not be carried past the bottom of the hill trail on the farther side. Plunging in the two horses swam gallantly across, landing within a few feet of the point aimed at, and scrambled up the slippery path, down which poured a stream of water.

When they reached the half-way point between the ford and the ranch houses the storm slackened, evolving into an ordinary rain, which Hopalong remarked would last all day. Red nodded and then pointed to a miserable, rain-soaked calf, which moved away at their approach.

"Do you see that!" he exclaimed. "Our brand, an' Meeker's ear notch!"

"That explains th' shovel being left on th' dam," quickly replied Hopalong. "It would be plumb crazy for th' H2 to make a combination like that ear notch an' our brand, an' you can gamble they don't know nothing bout it. Th' gent that left Meeker's shovel *for us to find* did that, too. You know if any of th' H2 cut th' dam they wouldn't forget to take th' shovel with 'em, Red. It's Antonio, that's who it is. He's trying to make a bigger fight along th' line an' stir things up generally so he can rustle promiscuous. Well, we'll give all our time to th' rustling end from now on, if I have got any voice in th' matter. An' I hope to th' Lord I can get within gun range of that coyote. Why, by th' A'mighty, I'll go down an' plug him on his own ground just as soon as I can get away, which will be to-morrow! That's just what I'll do! I'll stop his plays or know th' reason why."

"An' I'm with you—you'll take a big chance going down there alone," Red replied. "*After* Meeker hears what we've got to say he'll be blamed glad we came."

An hour later they stopped at the ranch house, a squat, square building, flat of roof, its adobe walls three feet thick and impenetrable to heat. Stripping saddles and bridles from their streaming mounts, they drove the animals into a large corral and ran to the bunk house, where laughter greeted their appearance.

"Swimming?" queried Johnny, putting aside his harmonica.

"Hey, you! Get out of here an' lean up against th' corral till you shed some of that water!" yelled Lanky, the wounded, watching the streams from their clothes run over the floor. "We'll be afloat in a minute if you don't get out—we ain't no fishes."

"You shut up," retorted Red. "We'll put you out there to catch what water we missed if you gets funny," he threatened, stripping as rapidly as he could. He hung the saturated garments on pegs in the gallery wall and had Pete rub him down briskly, while Billy did the same for his soaked companion.

Around them were their best friends, all laughing and contented, chaffing and exchanging personal banter with each other, engaged in various occupations, from sewing buttons on shirts to playing cards and mending riding gear. Snatches of songs burst forth at odd intervals, while laughter was continually heard. This was the atmosphere they loved, this repaid them for their hard work, this and the unswerving loyalty, the true, deep affection, and good-natured banter that pricked but left no sting. Here was one of the lures of the range, the perfect fellowship that long acquaintance and the sharing of hard work and ubiquitous danger breeds among the members of a good, square outfit. Not one of them ever counted personal safety before duty to his ranch and his companions, taking his hard life laughingly and without complaint, generous to a fault, truthful and loyal and considerate. There was manhood for you, there was contempt for restricting conventions, for danger; there was a unity of thought and purpose that set the rough-spoken, ready-fighting men of the saddle and rope in a niche by themselves, a niche where fair play, unselfishness, and a rough but sterling honor abides always. Their occupation gave more than it exacted and they loved it and the open, windswept range where they were the dominating living forces.

Buck came in with Frenchy McAllister and Pie Willis and grinned at his crowd of happy "boys," who gave warm welcome. The foreman was not their "boss," their taskmaster, but he was their best friend, and he shared with them the dangers and joys which were their lot, sympathetic in his rough way, kind and trusting.

Hopalong struggling to get his head through a dry shirt, succeeded, and swiftly related to his foreman the occurrences of the morning, pointing to the shovel and button as the total exhibit of his proofs against Antonio. The laughter died out, the banter was hushed, and the atmosphere became that of tense hostility and anger. When he had ceased speaking angry exclamations and threats filled the room, coming from men who always "made good." When Red had told of the H2–Bar-20 calf, an air of finality, of conviction, settled on them; and it behooved Antonio to hunt a new range, for his death would be sudden and merciless if he met any of the Bar-20 outfit, no matter when or where. They never forgot.

After a brief argument they came to the decision that he was connected with the rustling going on around them, and this clenched his fate. Several, from the evidence and from things which they had observed and now understood, were of the opinion that he was the ringleader of the cattle thieves.

"Boys," Buck remarked, "we won't bother about th' line very much for a while. It's been a peaceable sort of a fracas, anyhow, an' I don't expect much further trouble. If H2 cows straggle across an' yo're right handy to 'em an' ain't got nothing pressing to do, drive 'em back; but don't look for 'em particularly. There won't be no more drives against us for a long time. We've got to hunt rustlers from now on, an' hunt hard, or they'll get too numerous to handle very easy. Let th' cows take care of themselves along th' river, Frenchy,

an' put your men up near Big Coulee, staying nights in
Number Two. Pete an' Billy will go with you. That'll
protect th' west, an' there won't be no rustling going
on from the river, nohow. Don't waste no time herding—put it all in hunting. Hopalong, you, Johnny, Red,
an' Skinny take th' hills country an' make yore head-
quarters in Number Three an' Four. Lanky will stay up
here until he can handle hisself good again. I'll ride
promiscuous, but if any of you learn anything you want
me to know, leave it with Lanky or th' cook if you can't
find me. Just as soon as we have anything to go on,
we'll start on th' war path hot foot an' clean things up
right an' proper."

"What'll we do if we catches anybody rustling?"
asked Johnny, assuming an air of ignorance and curiosity, and ducking quickly as Red swung at him.

"Give 'em ten dollars reward an' let 'em go," Buck
grinned.

"Give me ten if I brings Antonio to you?"

"I'll fine you twenty if you waste that much time over
him," Buck replied.

"Whoop!" Johnny exulted. "Th' good old times are
coming back again! Remember Bye-an'-Bye an' Cactus
Springs, Buckskin an' Slippery Trendley? Remember th'
good old scraps? Now we'll have something else to do
besides chasing cows an' wiping th' rust off our guns!"

Lanky, who took keen delight in teasing the youngster, frowned severely. "Yo're just a fool kid, just a
happy idiot!" he snorted, and Johnny looked at him,
surprised but grinning. "Yes, you are! I never seen such
a bloody-minded animal in all my born days as you!
After all th' fighting you've gone an' got mixed up
in, you still yap for more! You makes me plumb disgusted, you do!"

"He *is* awful gory," remarked Hopalong soberly. "Just
a animated massacre in pants."

"Regular Comanche," amended Red, frowning.
"What do you think about him, Frenchy?"

"I'd ruther not say it," Frenchy replied. "You ask Pie—he ain't scared of nothing, massacre *or* Comanche."

Johnny looked around the room and blurted out, "You all think th' same as me, every one of you, even if you are a lot of pussy-cats, an' you know it, too!"

"Crazy as a locoed cow!" Red whispered across the room to Buck, who nodded sorrowfully and went into the cook shack.

"You wait till I sees Antonio an' you'll find out how crazy I am!" promised Johnny.

"I shore hopes he spanks you an' sends you home a-bawling," Lanky snorted. "You needs a good licking, you young cub!"

"Yah, yah!" jibed Johnny. "Needing an' getting are two different tunes, grand-pop!"

"You wasn't down here, was you, Frenchy, when Johnny managed to rope a sleepy gray wolf that was two years old, an' tried to make a pet out of him?" asked Hopalong, grinning at his recollection of the affair.

"No!" exclaimed Frenchy in surprise. "Did he do it?"

"Oh, yes, he did it; with a gun, after th' pet had torn his pants off an' chewed him up real well. He's looking for another, because he says that was too mean a beast to have any luck with."

Buck stepped into the room again. "Who wants to go with me to th' dam in th' wagon?" he asked. "I want to look at that cut an' fix it for keeps if it needs fixing. All right! All right! Anybody'd think I asked you to go to a dance," he laughed. "Pete, you an' Billy an' Pie will be enough."

"Can't we ride alongside?" asked Pie. "Do we have to sit in that thing?"

"You can walk, if you want to. I don't care how you go," Buck replied, stepping into the rain with the three men close behind him. Soon the rattling of the wagon was heard growing fainter on the plain.

The banter and the laughter ran on all the rest of the morning. After dinner Hopalong built a fire in the huge stove and put a ladleful of lead on the coals, while Frenchy and Skinny re-sized and re-capped shells from the boxes on the wall. Hopalong watched the fire and smoked the bullet moulds, while Lanky managed to measure powder and fill the shells after Frenchy and Skinny had finished with them. Hopalong filled the moulds rapidly while Johnny took out the bullets and cooled them by dropping them into cold rain water, being cautioned by Hopalong not to splash any water into the row of moulds. As soon as he found them cool enough, Johnny wiped them dry and passed them on to Red, who crimped them into the charged shells. Soon the piles of cartridges grew to a goodly size, and when the last one had been finished the crowd fell to playing cards until supper was ready. Hopalong, who had kept on running bullets, sorted them, and then dropped them into the boxes made for each size. Finally he stopped and went to the door to look for signs of the morrow's weather.

"Clearing up in th' west an' south—here comes Buck an' th' others," he called over his shoulder. "How was it, Buck?" he shouted, and out of the gathering dusk came the happy reply:

"Bully!"

CHAPTER XXI

Hopalong Rides South

THE MORNING broke clear and showed a clean, freshened plain to the men who rode to the line house on the Peak, there to take up their quarters and from there to ride as scouts. Hopalong sent Red to ride along the line for the purpose of seeing how things were in that vicinity and, leaving the others to go where they wished, struck south down the side of the hill, intending to hunt Antonio on his own ground. Tied to his saddle was the shovel and in his pocket he carried the brass button, his evidence for Meeker. As he rode at an easy lope he kept a constant lookout for signs of rustling. Suddenly he leaned forward and tightened his knee grip, the horse responding by breaking into a gallop, while its rider took up his lariat, shaking it into a long loop, his twisting right wrist imparting enough motion to it to keep it clear of the vegetation and rocks.

A distant cow wheeled sharply and watched him for a moment and then, snorting, its head down and its tail up, galloped away at a speed not to be found among domesticated cattle. It was bent upon only one thing—

to escape that dreaded, whirling loop of rawhide, so
pliant and yet so strong. Hopalong, not as expert as
Lanky, who carried a rope nearly sixty feet long and
who could place it where he wished, used one longer
than the more common lariats.

The cow did its best, but the pony steadily gained,
nimbly executing quick turns and jumping gullies, up
one side of a hill and down the other, threading its way
with precision through the chaparrals and deftly avoid-
ing the holes in its path. Closer and closer together
came the pursued and pursuers, and then the long rope
shot out and sailed through the air, straight for the animal's hind legs. As it settled, a quick upward jerk of
the arm did the rest and there was a snubbing of rope
around the saddle horn, a sudden stopping and dropping back on haunches on the part of the pony, and
the cow went down heavily. The rider did not wait for
the horse to get set, but left the saddle as soon as the
rope had been securely snubbed, and ran to the side of
his victim.

The cow was absolutely helpless, for the rope was
taut, the intelligent pony leaning back and being too
well trained to allow the least amount of slack to bow
the rawhide closer to the earth. Therefore Hopalong
gave no thought to his horse, for while cinches, pommel, and rope held, the small, wiry, wild-eyed bundle
of galvanic cussedness would hold the cow despite all
its efforts to get up.

"Never saw *that* brand before, an' I've rid all over
this country for a good many years, too," he soliloquized. "There sure ain't no HQQ herd down this way,
nor no place close enough for a stray. Somebody is
shore starting a herd on his own hook; from th' cows
on this range, too.

"By th' great horned spoon! I can see Bar-20 in them
marks!" he cried, bending closer. "All he had to do was
to make a H out of th' Bar, close up th' 2, an' put a tail
on th' O! Hum—whoop! There is H2 in it, too! Close th'

2 an' add a Q, an' there you are! I don't mind a hog once in a while, but working both ranches to a common mark is shore too much for me. Stealing from both ranches an' markin' 'em all HQQ!"

He moved up to look at the ears and swore when he saw them. "Damn it! That's all I want to know! Mebby a sheriff wouldn't get busy on th' evidence, but I ain't no sheriff—I'm just a plain cow-punch with good common sense. Meeker's cut is a V in one ear—here I finds a slant like Skinny saw, an' in both ears. If that don't cut under Meeker's notch I'm a liar! All framed up to make a new herd out of our cows. Just let me catch some coyote with a running iron under his saddle flap an' see what happens!"

He quickly slacked the rope and slipped off the noose, running as fast as he could go to his pony, for some cows get "on the prod" very easily, and few cows are afraid of a man on foot; and when a long-horned Texas cow has "its dander up," it is not safe for an unmounted man to take a chance with its horns, unless he is willing to shoot it down. This Hopalong would not do, for he did not want to let the rustlers know that the new brand had been discovered. Vaulting into his saddle he eluded the charge of the indignant cow and loped south, coiling up his rope as he went.

Half an hour after leaving the HQQ cow he saw a horseman ahead of him, threading his way through a chaparral. As Hopalong overtook him the other emerged and stopped, uncertain whether to reach for his gun or not. It was Juan, who had not gone to Mesa overnight, scouting to learn if any new developments had taken place along the boundary. Juan looked at the shovel and then at the puncher, his face expressionless.

Hopalong glanced at the other's cuff, found it was all right, and then forced himself to smile. "Looking for rustlers?" he bantered.

"*Si.*"

"What! There ain't no rustlers loose on this range, is there?" asked Hopalong, surprised.

"Quien sabe?"

"Oh, them sleepers were made by yore own, lazy outfit, an' you might as well own up to it," Hopalong grinned, deprecatingly. "You can fool Meeker, all right, he's easy; but you can't throw dust in my eyes like that. On th' level, now, ain't I right? Didn't you fellers make them sleepers?"

Juan shrugged his shoulders. *"Quien sabe?"*

"That *'Quien sabe'* is th' handiest an' most used pair of words in yore cussed language," replied Hopalong grinning. "Ask one of you fellers something you don't want to tell an' its *'Quien sabe?'* ain't it?"

"Si," laughed Juan.

"I thought so," Hopalong retorted. "You can't tell me that any gang that would cut a dam like they did ourn wouldn't sleeper, an' don't you forget it, neither!"

Juan's face cleared for a moment as he gloated over how Antonio's scheme had worked out, and he laughed. "No can fool you, hey?" Then he pressed his knee tighter against his saddle skirt and a worried look came into his eyes.

Hopalong took no apparent notice of the action, but he saw it, and it sent one word burning through his brain. They were riding at a walk now and Hopalong, not knowing that Juan had left the H2, suggested that they ride to the ranch together. He was watching Juan closely, for it would not be unusual for a man in his position to try to get out of it by shooting. Juan refused to ride south and Hopalong, who was determined to stay with his companion until he found out what he wanted to know, proposed a race to a barranca that cut into the plain several hundred yards ahead. He would let Juan beat him, and all the way, so he could watch the saddle flap, and if this failed he would waste no more time in strategy, but would find out about it quickly. Juan also declined to race, and very hurriedly,

for the less his saddle was jolted the better it would be
for him. He knew Hopalong's reputation as a revolver
fighter and would take no chances.

"That ain't a bad cayuse you got there. I was wondering it it could beat mine, what's purty good itself. Is
it very bronc?" he asked, kicking the animal in the ribs,
whereupon it reared and pranced. Juan's left hand went
to the assistance of his knee, his right grasped the can-
tle of his saddle, where it was nearer the butt of his
Colt, and a look of fear came into his eyes.

Hopalong watched his chance and as the restive animal swung towards him he spurred it viciously, at the
same time crying: "Take yore hand from off that flap,
you damned cowlifter!"

The command was unnecessary, for a thin, straight
rod of iron slipped down and stuck in the sand, having
worked loose from its lashings. Juan had put off until
to-morrow to heat it and bend a loop in one end for
more secure fastening.

At the instant it fell Juan leaned back and dropped
over on the far side of his horse, his right leg coming
up level with his enemy, and reached for his gun, intending to shoot through the end of the holster and
save time. But he went farther than he had intended,
not stopping until he struck the earth, his bullet missing
Hopalong by only a few inches.

The Bar-20 puncher slipped his Colt back into the
sheath and, leaning down, deftly picked up the iron and
fastened it to his saddle. Roping Juan's horse he continued on his way to the H2, leaving Juan where he had
fallen.

When he arrived at the ranch he turned the horse
into the corral and started to ride to the bunk house;
but Salem, enjoying a respite from cooking and washing dishes, saw him and started for him on an awkward
run, crying:

"Where'd you git that hoss? Where'd you clear from,
an' who are you?"

"Th' cayuse belongs to Meeker—Juan was riding it. Is anybody around?"

"I'm around, ain't I, you fog-eyed lubber! Where's th' Lascar? Who are you?"

"Well, Duke, I'm from th' Bar-20, an' my name is Hop—"

"Weigh anchor an' 'bout ship! You can't make this port, you wind-jamming pirate!"

"I want to see yore foreman. This is his shovel, an' I—"

"Then where'd you get it, hey? How'd you get his—"

"Hang it!" interrupted Hopalong, losing his patience. "I tell you I want to see Meeker! I want to see him about some—"

"An' where's th' man that rid that hoss?" demanded the cook, belligerently.

"You won't see that thief no more. That's one of th' things I want to—"

"Hooray!" cried Salem. "Was he drowned, or shanghaied?"

"Was he what? What are you talking about, anyhow? Where did you ever learn how to talk Chinese?"

"What! Chinese! You whale-bellied, barnacle-brained bilge pirate, I've got a good notion—"

"Say, is there anybody around here that ain't loco? Are they all as crazy as you?" Hopalong asked.

Salem grabbed up one of the bars of the corral gate and, roaring strange oaths, ran at the stranger, but Hopalong spurred his horse and kept clear of the pole while Salem grew short winded and more profane. Then the puncher thought of Mary and cantered towards the ranch house intending to ask her where he could find her father, thus combining business with pleasure. Salem shook the pole at him and then espied the saddled horse in the corral. He disliked horses as much as they disliked him, so much, in fact, that he said the only reason he did not get out of the country

and go back to the sea was because he had to ride a
horse to do it. But any way was acceptable under the
present exigencies, so he clambered into the saddle after more or less effort and found it not quite roomy
enough for one of his growing corpulency. Shouting
"Let fall!" he cantered after the invader of his ranch,
waving the pole valiantly. He did not see that the ears
of his mount were flattened or that its eyes were growing murderous in their expression, and he did not know
that the lower end of the pole was pounding lustily
against the horse's legs every time he waved the
weapon. All he thought about was getting his pleasant
duty over with as soon as possible, and he gripped the
pole more firmly.

Hopalong looked around curiously to see what the
cook was doing to make all that noise, and when he
saw he held his sides. "Well, if th' locoed son-of-a-gun
ain't after me! Lord! Hey, stranger," he shouted, "if you
want him to run fast, take hold of his tail an' pull it
three times!"

He was not averse to having a little fun at the ten-
derfoot's expense and he deferred his visit to the house
to circle around the angry cook and shout advice. Instead of laying the reins against his mount's neck to
turn it, Salem jerked on them, which the indignant animal instantly resented. It had felt all along that it was
being made a fool of and imposed upon, but now it
would have a sweet revenge. Leaping forward suddenly it stopped stiff-legged and arched its back several
times with all the force it was capable of; but it could
have stopped immediately after the first pitch, for Salem, still holding to the pole, executed a more or less
graceful parabola and landed in a sitting posture amid
much dust.

"*Whoof!* What'd we strike?" he demanded dazedly.
Then, catching sight of the cause of his flight, which
was at that moment cropping an overlooked tuft of
grass as if it were accustomed to upsetting pole-waving

cooks, Salem scrambled to his feet and ran at it, getting in one good whack before the indignant and groping pony could move.

"There, blast you!" he yelled. "I'll show you what you get for a trick like that!" Turning, and seeing Hopalong laughing until the tears ran down his face, he roared, "What are you laughing at, damn you?"

A rope sailed out and tightened around Salem's feet and he once more sat down, unable to arise this time, because of Hopalong's horse, which backed slowly, step by step, dragging the captive, who was now absolutely helpless.

"Now I want to talk to you for a few minutes, an' I'm going to," Hopalong remarked. "Will you listen quietly or will you risk losing th' seat of yore pants? You've *got* to listen, anyhow."

"Wha—what—go ahead, only stop th' headway of yore craft! Lay tó! I'm on th' rocks!"

Laughing, Hopalong rode closer to him. "Where's Antonio?"

"In hell, I hope, leastwise that's where he ought to be."

"Well, I just sent his friend Juan there—had to; he toted a running iron an'—"

"Did you? Did you?" cried Salem in accents of joy. "Why didn't you say so before! Come in an' splice th' main brace, shipmate! Juan is in Davy Jones' locker, is he? Hey, wait till I get these lashings cast off—yo're a good hand after all. Come in an' have some grog—best stuff this side of Kentucky, where it was made."

"I ain't got time," replied Hopalong, smiling. "Where's that Antonio?"

"Going to send *him* down too? Damn my tops'ls, wish I knowed! He deserted, took shore leave, an' ain't reported since. Yo're clipper-rigged, a regular AB, you are! Spin us th' yarn, matey."

Hopalong told him about the dam and the shooting of Juan and gave him the shovel and button for Meeker,

Salem's mouth wide open at the recital. When he had finished the cook grabbed his stirrup and urged him towards the grog, but Hopalong laughingly declined and, looking towards the ranch house, saw Jim Meeker riding like mad in their direction.

"What do you want?" blazed the foreman, drawing rein, his face dark with anger.

"I want to plug Antonio, an' his friend Sanchez," Hopalong replied calmly. "I just caught Juan with a running iron under his saddle flap an' I drilled him for good. Here's th' iron."

"Good for you!" cried Meeker, taking the rod. "They've jumped, all of 'em. I'm looking for 'em myself, an' we're all looking for coyotes toting these irons. I'm glad you got one of 'em!"

"Antonio scuttled their dike—here's th' shovel he did it with," interrupted Salem eagerly. "An' here's th' button off Antonio's jacket. He left it by th' shovel. My mate, here, is cruising to fall in with 'em, an' when he does there'll be—"

"Why, that's *my* shovel!" cried Meeker. "An' that's his button, all right."

Hopalong told him all about the attempt to cut the dam and when he had ceased Meeker swore angrily. "Antonio and his men are on th' rustle, for shore! They're trying to keep th' fighting going on along th line so we'll be too busy to bother 'em in their stealing. I've been losing cows right an' left—why, they run off a herd of beef right here by th' houses. Salem saw 'em. They killed cows down south an' covered my range with sleepers an' lame mothers. How did you come to guess he had an iron?"

Hopalong told of the HQQ cow he had found and, dismounting, traced the brand in the sand, Meeker bending over eagerly.

"You see this Bar-20?" he asked, pointing it out, and his interested companion interrupted him with a curse.

"Yes, I do; an' do *you* see this H2?" he demanded. "They've merged our brands into one—stealing from both of us!"

"Yes. I figgered that out when I saw th' mark; that's one of th' things I came down to tell you about," Hopalong replied, mounting again. "An' Red an' me found a Bar-20 calf with a V ear notch, too. That proves what th' dam was cut for, don't it?"

"Why didn't I drop that coyote when I caught him skulking th' other morning!" growled Meeker, regretfully. "He had just come back from yore dam then—had yaller mud on his cayuse an' his stirrups. Out all night on a played-out bronc, an' me too thick to guess he was up to some devilment an' shoot him for it! Oh, hell! I thought purty hard of you, Cassidy, but I reckon we all make mistakes. Any man what would stop to think out th' real play when he found that shovel is square."

"Oh, that's all right. I allus did hate Antonio, an' mebby that was why I suspected him, that an' th' button."

Meeker turned to the cook. "Where's Chick an' Dan?" he asked, impatiently. "I ain't seen 'em around."

"Why, Chick rid off down south an' Dan cleared about an hour ago."

"What! With that leg of hissen!"

"Aye, aye, sir; he couldn't leave it behind, you know, sir."

"All right, Cassidy; much obliged. I'll put a stop to th' rustling on *my* range, or know th' reason why. Damn th' day I ever left Montanny!" Meeker swore, riding towards the ranch house.

"Say, I hope you find them Lascars," remarked Salem. "Yo're th' boy that'll give 'em what they needs. Wish you had caught 'em all four instead of only one."

Hopalong smiled. "Then they might 'a got me instead."

"No, no, siree!" exclaimed the cook. "You can lick 'em all, an' I'll gamble on it, too! But you better come in an' have a swig o' grog before you weighs anchor, matey. As I was saying, it's th' best grog west of Kentucky. Come on in!"

CHAPTER XXII

Lucas Visits the Peak

WHEN HOPALONG returned to the line house on the Peak he saw Johnny and Skinny talking with Lucas, the C80 foreman, and he hailed them.

"Hello, Lucas!" he cried. "What are you doing down here?"

"Glad to see you, Hopalong," Lucas replied, shaking hands. "Came down to see Buck, but Lanky, up in th' bunk house, said he was off somewhere scouting. From what Lanky said I reckon you fellers had a little joke down here last week."

"Yes," responded Hopalong, dismounting. "It was a sort of a joke, except that somebody killed one of Meeker's men. I'll be blamed if I know who done it. Lanky says he didn't an' he don't have to deny a thing like that neither. Looks to me like he caught some brand-blotter dead to rights, like I did a little while ago, an' like he got th' worst of th' argument."

"What's that about catching somebody dead to rights?" eagerly asked Johnny.

"Who was it?" asked Skinny.

"Juan. He toted a running iron an' I caught him just after I looked over a cow with a new brand—"

"Did you get him good?" quickly asked Johnny. "Did he put up a fight?"

"Yes; an' what was th' brand?" Skinny interposed.

"Here, here!" laughed Hopalong. "I reckon I'll save time if I tell you th' whole story," and he gave a short account of his ride, interrupted often by the inquisitive and insistent Johnny.

"An' who is Salem?" Johnny asked.

"Meeker's cook."

"What did Meeker say about it when you told him?"

"Gimme a chance to talk an' I'll tell you!" and Johnny remained silent for a moment. Finally the story was told and Johnny, asked one more question, grinning broadly:

"An' what did Mary say?"

"You say Meeker lost a whole herd?" asked Lucas. "Let me tell you there's more people mixed up in this rustling than we think. But I'll tell you one thing; that herd didn't go north, unless they drove ten miles east or west of our range."

"Well, I reckon it's under one man, all right," Hopalong replied. "If it was a lot of separate fellers running it by themselves there'd 'a been a lot of blunders an' some few of 'em would 'a been shot before Juan went. It's a gang, all right. But why th' devil did they turn loose that H2 rebranded cow, that HQQ that I found? They might 'a knowed it would cause some hot thinking when it was found. That cow is just about going to lick 'em."

"Stray," sententiously remarked Skinny.

"Shore, that's what it was," Lucas endorsed.

"An' do you know what that means?" asked Hopalong, looking from face to face. "It means that they can't be holding their heads very far away. It's three to one that I'm right."

"Mebby they're down in Eagle," suggested Johnny

hopefully, for Eagle would be a good, exciting proposition in a fight.

"No, it ain't there," Hopalong replied. "There's too
many people down there. They would all know about
it an' want a share in th' profits; but it ain't a whole lot
foolish to say that Eagle men are in it."

"Look here!" cried Skinny. "Mebby that HQQ is their
road brand—that cow might 'a strayed from their drive.
They've got to have some brand on cows they sell, an'
they can't have ours on an' get back alive."

"You are right, but not necessarily so about th' road
brand," Hopalong rejoined. "But that don't tell us where
they are, does it?"

"We've got to hunt HQQ cows on th' drive," Johnny
interposed as Skinny was about to speak. "I'll go down
to Eagle an' see if I can't get on to a drive. Then I'll
trail th' gang all th' way an' back to where they hangs
out. That'll tell us where to go, all right."

"You keep out of Eagle—you'd be shot before you
reached Quinn's saloon," Hopalong said. "No; it ain't
Eagle, not at all. See here, Lucas; have you watched
them construction camps along that railroad? There
ain't a better market nowhere than them layouts; they
don't ask no questions if th' beef is cheap."

"Yes, I've watched th' trails leading to 'em."

"Why, they wouldn't cross yore range!" Hopalong
cried. "They'd drive around you an' hit th' camp from
above; they ain't fools. Hey! I've got it! They can't go
around th' Double Arrow unless they are willing to
cross th' Staked Plain, an' you can bet they ain't. That
leaves th' west, an' there's a desert out there they
wouldn't want to tackle. They drive between th' desert
an yore range."

"If they drive to th' camps, yo're right without a
doubt," Skinny remarked. "But mebby they are driving
south—mebby they're starting a ranch along th' Grande,
or across it."

"Well, we'll take th' camps first," Hopalong replied.

"Lucas, can you spare a man to look them camps over? Somebody that can live in 'em a month, if he has to?"

"Shore. Wood Wright is just th' man."

"No, he ain't th' man," contradicted Hopalong quickly. "Anybody that wears chaps, or walks like he does would arouse suspicion in no time, an' get piped out in one night. This man had got to have business up there, like looking for a job. Say! Can you get along without yore cook for a while? If you can't we will!"

"You bet yore life I can!" exulted Lucas. "That's good. He can get a job right where th' meat is used, an' where th' hides will be kicking around. He goes tomorrow!"

"That's th' way; th' sooner th' better," Hopalong responded. "But we won't wait for him. We'll scout around lively down here an' if we don't find anything he may. But for th' Lord's sake, don't let him ride a cayuse into that camp that has brands of this section. Cowan will be glad to lend you his cayuse; he got it up north too far to make them suspicious."

"Yes; I reckon that'll be about the thing."

"Here comes Red," Johnny remarked. "Hey, Red, Hoppy got Juan this morning. Caught him toting a straight iron!"

"Johnny, you get away lively an' tell Frenchy to scout west," Hopalong ordered. "You can stay up in Number Two with them to-night, but come down here again in th' morning. Red, to-morrow at daylight we go west an' comb that country.

"That's th' way," remarked Lucas, mounting. "Get right at it. Have you got any word for Buck? I'll go past th' house an' leave it if you have."

"Yes; tell him what we've talked over. An' you might send yore outfit further west, too," Hopalong responded. "I'll bet a month's pay we end this cow-lifting before two weeks roll by.

"Oh, yes; I near forgot it—Bartlett thinks we-all ought to get together after th' rustling is stopped an' shoot that town of Eagle plumb off th' earth," Lucas said. "It's only a hell hole, anyhow, an' it won't do no harm to wipe it out." He looked around the group. "What do you fellers think about it?" he asked.

"Well, we might, then; we've got too many irons in th' fire now, though," Hopalong replied. "Hey, Johnny! Get a-going! We'll talk about Eagle later."

"I'm forgetting lots of things," laughed Lucas. "We had a little fight up our way th' other day. Caught a feller skinning one of Bartlett's cows, what had strayed over on us. Got him dead to rights, too. He put up a fight while he lasted. Said his name was Hawkins."

"Hawkins!" exclaimed Hopalong. "I've heard that name somewhere."

"Why, that's th' name on th' notice of reward posted in Cowan's," Red supplied. "He's wanted for desertion from th' army, an' for other things. They want him bad up at Roswell, an' they'll pay for him, dead or alive."

"Well, they won't get him; he ain't keeping good enough," Lucas replied. "An' we don't want that kind of money. So long," and he was off.

"So you got Juan," Red remarked. "You ought to have took him alive—we could get it all out of him an' find out where his friends are hanging out."

"He went after his gun, an' he had an iron," Hopalong replied. "I didn't know he had left Meeker, an' I didn't stop to think. He was a brand-blotter."

"What's Meeker going to do about th' line?" Red asked.

"Nothing for a while; he's too worried an' busy looking after his sleepers. He ain't so bad, after all."

"Say," remarked Skinny, thoughtfully. "Mebby that gang is over east, like Trendley was. There's lots of water thereabouts, an' good grass, too, in th' Panhandle. Look how close it is to Fort Worth an' th' railroad."

"Too many people over there," Hopalong replied. "An' *they* know all about th' time we killed Trendley an' wiped out his gang. They won't go where they are shore we'll look."

"If I can get sight of one of them I'll find out where they are," Red growled. "I'll put green rawhide around his face if I have to, an' when he savvys what th' sun is going to do to that hide an' him, he'll talk, all right, an' be glad of th' chance."

"To hear you, anybody would think you'd do a thing like that," Hopalong laughed. "I reckon he'd drop at eight hundred, clean an' at th' first shot. But, say, green rawhide wouldn't do a thing to a man's face, would it! When it shrunk he'd know it, all right."

"Crush it to a pulp," Skinny remarked. "But who is going to cook th' supper? I'm starved."

Hopalong awakened suddenly and listened and found Red also awake. Hoofbeats were coming towards the house and Hopalong peered out into the darkness to see who it was, his Colt ready.

"Who's that?" he challenged, sharply, the clicks of his gun ringing clear in the night air.

"Why, me," replied a well-known voice. "Who'd you think it was?"

"Why didn't you stay up in Number Two, like I told you? What's wrong?"

"Nothing," Johnny replied, stripping off his saddle and bridle.

"An' you came all th' way down here in th' dark, just to wake us up?" Hopalong asked, incredulously. "Twenty miles just for that!"

"No. I ain't got here yet—I'm only half way," Johnny retorted. "Can't you see I'm here? An' I didn't care about you waking up. I wanted to get here, an' here I am."

"In the name of heaven, are you drunk, or crazy?" asked Red. "Of all th' damn fools I ever—"

"Oh, shut up, all of you!" growled Skinny, turning over in his bunk. "Lot of locoed cusses that don't know enough to keep still! Let th' Kid alone, why don't you!" he muttered and was sound asleep again.

"No, I ain't drunk or crazy! Think I was going to stay up there when you two fellers are going off scouting to-morrow? Not by a jugful! I ain't letting nothing get past me, all right?" Johnny rejoined.

"Well, you ain't a-going, anyhow," muttered Hopalong, crawling into his bunk again. "You've got to stay with Skinny—" he did not speak very loud, because he knew it would cause an argument, and he wished to sleep instead of talk.

"What'd you say?" demanded Johnny.

"For God's sake!" marvelled Red. "Can't nobody go an' scratch 'emselves unless th' Kid is on th' ground? Come in here an' get to sleep."

> *Adown th' road, his gun in hand,*
> *Comes Whiskey Bill, mad Whiskey—*

Johnny hummed. "Hey! What you doing?" he yelled, leaping back.

"You heave any more guns on my face an' you'll find out!" roared Skinny, sitting up and throwing Johnny's Colt and belt to the floor. "Fool infant!"

"Tumble in an' shut up!" cried Red. "We want some sleep."

"Yo're a lot of tumble-bugs!" retorted Johnny, indignantly. "How did I know Skinny had his face where I threw my gun! He's so cussed thin I can't hardly see him in daylight, th' chalk mark! Why didn't he say so? Think I can see in th' dark?"

"I don't talk in my sleep!" retorted Skinny, "or go flea-hopping around in th' dark like a—"

"*Shut up!*" shouted Hopalong, and silence at last ensued.

CHAPTER XXIII

Hopalong and Red Go Scouting

As HOPALONG and Red rode down the slope of the Peak the rays of the sun flashed over the hills, giving promise of a very hot day. They were prepared to stay several days, if need be, on the semi-arid plain to the west of them, for it would be combed thoroughly before they returned. On they loped, looking keenly over the plain and occasionally using their field glasses to more closely scrutinize distant objects, searching the barrancas and coulees and threading through mesquite and cactus growths. Hopalong momentarily expected to find signs of what they were looking for, while Red, according to his habit, was consistently contradictory in his words and disproportionately pessimistic.

Moving forward at a swinging lope they began to circle to the west and as they advanced Hopalong became eager and hopeful, while his companion grumbled more and more. In his heart he believed as Hopalong did, but there had to be something to talk about to pass the time more pleasantly; so when they

met in some barranca to ride together for a short distance they exchanged pleasantries.

"Yore showing even more than yore usual amount
of pigheaded ignorance to-day," Hopalong grumbled.
"Yore blasted, ingrowing disposition has been shedding
cussedness at every step. I'll own up to being some
curious as to when it's going to peter out."

"As if that's any of yore business," retorted Red. "But
I'll just tell you, since you asks; it's going to stop when
I get good an' ready, savvy?"

"Yo're awful cheerful at times," sarcastically snorted
his companion.

Red's eyes had been roving over the plain and now
he raised his glasses and looked steadily ahead.

"What's that out there? Dead cow?" he asked, calmly.

Hopalong put his glasses on it instantly, "Cow?" he
asked, witheringly. "No; it's an over-grown lizard! Come
on," he cried, spurring forward, Red close behind him.

Riding around it they saw that it bore the brand of
the H2, and Hopalong, dismounting, glanced it over
quickly and swore.

"Shot in th' head—what did I tell you!"

"You didn't have to get off yore cayuse to see that,"
retorted Red. "But get on again, an' come along. There's
more out here. I'll take th' south end of this—don't get
out of hearing."

"Wait! Wonder why they shot it, instead of driving it
off after they got it this far?" Hopalong mused.

"Got on th' prod, I reckon, leaving its calf an' being
run so hard. I've seen many a one I'd like to have shot.
Looks to me like they hang out around that water
hole—they drove it that way."

"You can bet yore head they didn't drive it straight
to their hangout—they ain't doing nothing like that,"
Hopalong replied. "They struck south after they thought
they had throwed off any pursuit. They drove it almost
north, so far; savvy?"

"Well, they've got to have water if they're holding

cows out on this stove," Red rejoined. "An' I just told you where th' water is."

"G'wan! Ten cows would drain that hole in two days!" Hopalong responded. "They've also got to have grass, though mebby you never knew that. An' what about that herd Meeker lost? They wouldn't circle so far to a one-by-nothing water hole like that one is."

"Well, then, where'll they find grass an' water out here?" demanded Red, impatiently. "Th' desert's west, though mebby you never knew that!"

"Red, we've been a pair of fools!" Hopalong cried, slapping his thigh by way of emphasis. "Here we are skating around up here when Thunder Mesa lays south, with plenty of water an' a fair pasture on all sides of it! That's where we'll go."

"Hoppy, once in a great while you do show some intelligence, but we better go up to that water hole first," Red replied. "We can swing south then. We're so close to it now that there ain't nothing to be gained by not taking a look at it. Mebby we'll find a trail, or something."

"Right you are; come on. There ain't no use of us riding separate no more."

Half an hour later Hopalong pointed to one side, to a few half-burned greasewood and mesquite sticks which radiated like the spokes of a wheel.

"Yes, I saw 'em," Red remarked. "They couldn't wait till they got home before they changed th' brand, blamed fools."

"Yes, an' that explains th' HQQ cow I discovered," Hopalong quickly replied. "They got too blamed hasty to blot it an' it got away from 'em."

"Well, it shore beats th' devil how Meeker had to go an' stir up this nest of rattlers," Red grumbled, angrily.

"If these fellers hang out at Thunder Mesa an' drive to th' railroad camps we ought to strike their trail purty close to th' water hole," Hopalong remarked. "It's right in their path."

Red nodded his head. "Yes, we ought to."

An hour later they rode around a chaparral and came within sight of the water hole, which lay a few hundred yards away. As they did so a man rode up out of the depression and started north, unconscious of his danger.

The two men spurred to overtake him, both drawing their rifles and getting ready for action. He turned in his saddle, saw them, and heading westward, quirted and spurred his horse into a dead run, both of his pursuers shouting for him to stop as they followed at top speed. He glanced around again and, seeing that they were slowly but surely gaining, whipped up his rifle and fired at them several times, both replying. He kept bearing more and more to the west and Red rode away at an angle to intercept him. Ten minutes later the fleeing man turned and rode north again, but Red had gained fifty yards over Hopalong and suddenly stopping his horse to permit better shooting, he took quick aim and fired. The pursued man found that his horse was useful only as a breastwork as Red's report died away, and hastily picked himself up and crawled behind it.

"Look out, Red!" warned Hopalong as he flung himself off his horse and led it down into a deep coulee for protection. "That's Dick Archer, an' he can shoot like th' very devil!"

Red, already in a gully, laughed. "An' so can I."

"Hey, I'm going around on th' other side—look out for him," Hopalong called, starting away. "We can't waste no more time up here than we has to."

"All right; go ahead," Red replied, pushing his sombrero over the edge of the gully where the rustler could see it; and he laughed softly when he saw the new hole in it. "He shore can shoot, all right," he muttered. Working down the gully until he came to a clump of greasewood he crawled up the bank and looked out at the man behind the dead horse, who was intently watching the place where he had seen Red's sombrero. "I knowed Eagle was holding cards in this game," Red remarked, smiling grimly. "Wonder how many are in it, anyhow?"

Hearing the crack of a gun he squinted along the sights of his Winchester and waited patiently for a chance to shoot. Then he heard another shot and saw the rustler raise himself to change his position, and Red fired. "I knowed, too, that Hoppy would drive him into range for me, even if he didn't hit him. Wonder what Mr. Dick Archer thinks about *my* shooting about now? Ah!" he cried as the smoke from his second shot drifted away. "Got you again!" he grunted. Then he dropped below the edge of the gully and grinned as he listened to the bullets whining overhead, for the rustler, wounded twice inside of a minute by one man, was greatly incensed thereby and petulantly bombarded the greasewood clump. He knew that he was done for, but that was no reason why he shouldn't do as much damage as he could while he was able.

"Bet he's mad," grinned Red. "An' there goes that Sharps—I could tell Hoppy's gun in a fusillade."

Crawling back up the gully to his first position Red peered out between some gramma grass tufts and again slid his rifle to his shoulder, laughing softly at the regular reports of the Sharps.

A puff of smoke enveloped his head and drifted behind him as he worked the lever of his rifle and, arising, he walked out towards the prostrate man and waved for his friend to join him. As he drew near the rustler struggled up on one elbow, and Red, running forward with his gun raised half-way to his shoulder, cried: "Don't make no gun-play, or I'll blow you apart! Where's th' rest of yore gang?"

"Go to hell!" coughed the other, trying to get his Colt out, for his rifle was empty. He stiffened and fell flat.

Ten minutes later Hopalong and Red were riding southwest along a plain and well beaten trail, both si-

lent and thoughtful. And at the end of an hour they
saw the ragged top of Thunder Mesa towering against
the horizon. They went forward cautiously now and
took advantage of the unevenness of the plain, riding
through barrancas and keeping close to chaparrals.

"Well, Red, I reckon we better stop," Hopalong remarked at last, his glasses glued to his eyes. "No use
letting them see us."

"Is that smoke up there?" asked Red.

"Yes; an' there's somebody moving around near th'
edge."

"I see him now."

"I reckon we know all that's necessary," Hopalong
remarked. "That trail is enough, anyhow. Now we've
got to get back to th' ranch without letting them fellers
see us."

"We can lead th' cayuses till we can get in that barranca back there," Red replied. "We won't stick up so
prominent if we do that. After we make it we'll find it
easy to keep from being seen if we've any caution."

Hopalong threw himself out of the saddle. "Dis-
mount!" he cried. "That feller up there is coming towards this end. He's their lookout, I bet."

They remained hidden and quiet for an hour while
the lookout gazed around the plain, both impatient and
angry at the time he gave to his examination. When he
turned and disappeared they waited for a few minutes
to see if he was coming back, and satisfied that the way
was clear, led their horses to the barranca and rode
through it until far enough away to be safe from observation.

Darkness caught them before they had covered half
of the distance between the mesa and the ranch, and
there being no moon to light the way, they picketed
their mounts, had supper, and rolling up in their blankets, spent the night on the open plain.

CHAPTER XXIV

Red's Discomfiture

ON THEIR return they separated and Red, coming to an arroyo, rode along its edge for a mile and then turned north. Ten minutes after he had changed his course he espied an indistinct black speck moving among a clump of cottonwoods over half a mile ahead of him, and as he swung his glasses on it a cloud of smoke spurted out. His horse reared, plunged, and then sank to earth where it kicked spasmodically and lay quiet. As the horse died Red, who had dismounted at the first tremor, threw himself down behind it and shoved his rifle across the body, swearing at the range, for at that distance his Winchester was useless. A small handful of sand flew into the air close beside him with a vicious spat, and the bullet hummed away into the brush as a small pebble struck him sharply on the cheek. A few seconds later he heard the faint, flat report.

"It's a clean thousand, an' more," he growled. "Wish I had Hopalong's gun. I'd make that feller jump!"

He looked around to see how close he was to cover and when he glanced again at the cottonwoods they

seemed to be free of an enemy. Then a shot came from
a point to the north of the trees and thudded into the
carcass of the horse. Red suddenly gave way to his
accumulated anger which now seethed at a white heat
and, scrambling to his feet, ran to the brush behind
him. When he gained it he plunged forward to top
speed, leaping from cover to cover as he zig-zagged
towards the man who had killed Ginger, and who had
tried his best to kill him.

He ran on and on, his rifle balanced in his right hand
and ready for instant use, his breath coming sharply
now. Red was in no way at home out of the saddle. His
high-heeled, tight-fitting boots cramped his toes and the
sand made running doubly hard. He was not far from
the cottonwoods; they lay before him and to his right.

Turning quickly he went north, so as to go around
the plot of ground on which he hoped to find his accurate, long-range assailant, and as he came to a break
in the hitherto close-growing brush he stopped short
and dropped to one knee behind a hillock of sand, the
rifle going to his shoulder as part of the movement.

Several hundred yards east of him he saw two men,
who were hastily mounting, and running from them
was a frightened calf. One of the pair waved an arm
towards the place where Ginger lay and as he did so a
puff of smoke lazily arose from behind the hillock of
sand to the west and he jumped up in his saddle, his
left arm falling to his side. Another puff of smoke arose
and his companion fought his wounded and frightened
horse, and then suddenly grasped his side and groaned.
The puffs were rising rapidly behind the hillock and
bullets sang sharply about them; the horse of the first
man hit leaped forward with a bullet-stung rump. Spurring madly the two rustlers dashed into the brush, lying
close along the necks of their mounts, and soon were
lost to the sight of the angry marksman.

Red leaped up, mechanically re-filling the magazine
of his rifle, and watched them out of sight, helpless

either to stop or pursue them. He shook his rifle, almost blind with rage, crying: "I hope you get to Thunder Mesa before *we* do, an' stay there; or run into Frenchy an' his men on yore way back! If I could get to Number Two ahead of you you'd never cross that boundary."

As he returned to his horse his rage cooled and left him, a quiet, deep animosity taking its place, and he even smiled with savage elation when he thought how he had shot at eight hundred yards—they had not escaped entirely free from punishment and his accuracy had impressed them so much that they had not lingered to have it out with him, even as they were two to one, mounted, and armed with long-range rifles. And he could well allow them to escape, for he would find them again at the mesa, if they managed to cross the line unseen by his friends, and he could pay the debt there.

He swore when he came to the body of his horse and anger again took possession of him. Ginger had been the peer of any animal on the range and, contrary to custom, he had felt no little affection for it. At cutting out it had been unequalled and made the work a pleasure to its rider; at stopping when the rope went home and turning short when on the dead run it had not been excelled by any horse on the ranch. He had taught it several tricks, such as coming to him in response to a whistle, lying down quickly at a slap on the shoulder, and bucking with whole-hearted zeal and viciousness when mounted by a stranger. Now he slapped the carcass and removed the saddle and bridle which had so often displeased it.

"Ginger, old boy," he said, slinging the forty-pound saddle to his shoulder and turning to begin his long tramp toward the dam, "I shore hate to hoof it, but I'd do it with a lot better temper if I knowed you was munching grass with th' rest of the cavvieyh. You've been a good old friend, an' I hates to leave you; but if

I get any kind of a chance at th' thief that plugged you I'll square up for you good an' plenty."

To the most zealous for exercise, carrying a forty-pound double-cinch saddle for over five miles across a hot, sandy plain and under a blazing, scorching sun, with the cinches all the time working loose and falling to drag behind and catch in the vegetation, was no pleasant task; and add to that a bridle, full magazine rifle, field glasses, canteen, and a three-pound Colt revolver swinging from a belt heavily weighted with cartridges, and it becomes decidedly irksome, to say the least. Red's temper can be excused when it is remembered that for years his walking had been restricted to getting to his horse, that his footwear was unsuited for walking, that he had been shot at and had lost his best horse. Each mile added greatly to his weariness and temper and by the time he caught sight of Hopalong, who rode recklessly over the range blazing at a panic-stricken coyote, he was near the point of spontaneous combustion.

He heaved the saddle from him, kicked savagely at it as it dropped, for which he was instantly sorry, and straightened his back slowly for fear that any sudden exertion would break it. His rifle exploded, twice, thrice; and Hopalong sat bolt upright and turned, his rifle going instinctively to his shoulder before he saw his friend's waving sombrero.

The coyote-chaser slid the smoking Sharps into its sheath and galloped to meet his friend who, filling the air with sulphurous remarks, now seated himself on the roundly cursed saddle.

Hopalong swept up and stopped, grinning expectantly and, to Red, exasperatingly. "Where's yore cayuse?" he asked. "Why are you toting yore possessions on th' hoof? Are you emigrating?"

Red's reply was a look wonderfully expressive of all the evils in human nature; it was fairly crowded with murder and torture, and Hopalong held his head on one side while he weighed it.

"Phew!" he exclaimed in wondering awe. "Yo're shore mad! You'd freeze old Geronimo's blood if he saw that look!"

"An' I'll freeze yourn; I'll let it soak into th' sand if you don't change yore front!" blazed Red.

"What's the matter? Where's Ginger?"

A rapid-fire string of expletives replied and then Hopalong began to hear sensible words, which more and more interspersed the profanity, and it was not long before he learned of Red's ride along the arroyo's rim.

"When I turned north," Red continued, wrathfully, "I saw something in them dozen cottonwoods around that come-an'-go spring; an' then what do you think happened?" he cried. Not waiting for any reply he continued hastily: "Why, some murdering squaw's dog went an' squibbed at me at long range! With me on my own ranch, too! An' he killed Ginger first shot. He missed me three straight an' *I* couldn't do nothing at a thousand an' over with this gun."

"Th' damn pirate!" exclaimed Hopalong, hotly.

"I was a whole lot mad by that time, so I jumped back into th' brush an' ran for th' grove, hoping to get square when I got in range. After I'd run about a thousand miles I came to th' edge of th' clearing west of th' trees an' damned if I didn't see two fellers climbing on their cayuses, an' some hasty, too. Reckon they didn't know how many friends I might have behind me. Well, I was some shaky from running like I did, an' they was a good eight hundred away, but I let drive just th' same an' got one in th' arm, th' other somewhere else, an' hit both of their cayuses. I wish I'd 'a filled 'em so full of holes they couldn't hang together, th' thieves!"

"I'd shore like to go after them, Red," Hopalong remarked. "We could ride west an' get 'em when they pass that water hole if you had a cayuse."

"Oh, we'll get 'em, all right—at th' mesa," Red rejoined. "I'm so tired I wouldn't go now if I could. Walking all th' way down here with that saddle! You get off that cayuse an' let me ride him," he suggested, mopping his face with his sleeve.

"What! Me? *Me* get off an' walk! I reckon not!" replied Hopalong, and then his face softened. "You pore, unfortunate cowpunch," he said, sympathetically. "You toss up yore belongings an' climb up here behind me. I'll take you to th' dam, where Johnny has picketed his cayuse. Th' Kid's going in for a swim; said he didn't know how soon he'd get a chance to take a bath. We can rustle his cayuse for a joke—come on."

"Oh, wait a minute, can't you?" Red replied, wearily. "I can't lift my legs high enough to get up there—they're like lead. That trail was hell strung out."

"You should 'a cached yore saddle an' everything but th' gun an' come down light," Hopalong remarked. "Or you could 'a gone to th' line an' waited for somebody to come along. Why didn't you do that?"

"I ain't leaving that saddle nowhere," Red responded. "Besides I was too blamed mad to stop an' think."

"Well, don't wait very long—Johnny may skin out if you do," Hopalong replied, and then, suddenly: "Just where was it you shot at them snakes?"

Red told him and Hopalong wheeled as if to ride after them.

"Here, you!" cried Red, the horseless. "Where th' devil are you going so sudden?"

"Up to get them cow-lifters that you couldn't, of course," his companion replied. "I'm shore going to show you how easy it is when you know how."

"Like hell you are!" Red cried, springing up, his lariat in his hand. "Yo're going to stay right here with me, that's what yo're going to do! I've got something for you to do, you compact bundle of gall! You try to get away without me and I'll make you look like an interrupted spasm, you wart-head!"

"Do you want 'em to get plumb away?" cried the man in the saddle, concealing his mirth.

"I want you to stick right here an' tote me to a cayuse!" Red retorted, swinging the rope. "*I'm* going to be around when anybody goes after them Si-washes, an' don't you forget it. There ain't no hurry—we'll get 'em quick enough when we starts west. An' if you try any get-away play an' leave me out here on my two feet with all these contraptions, I'll pick you off'n that pie-bald like hell greased with calamity!"

Hopalong laughed heartily. "Why, I was only a-fooling, Red. Do you reckon I'd go away an' leave you standing out here like a busted-down pack mule?"

"I hoped you was only fooling, but I wasn't taking no chances with a cuss like you," Red replied, grinning. "Not with this load of woe, you bet."

"Say, it's too bad you didn't have my gun up there," Hopalong said, regretfully. "You could 'a got 'em both then, an' had two cayuses to ride home on."

"Well, *I* could 'a got 'em with it," Red replied, grinning, his good nature returning under the chaffing. "But you can't hit th' mesa with it over six hundred. They'd 'a got away from you without getting hit."

Hopalong laughed derisively and then sobered. "Yo're right, Red, yo're right. Now you get right up here behind me an' I'll take you to th' dam where th' Kid is. Pore feller," he sighed. "Well, I ain't a-wondering after all you've been through. It was enough to make a *strong*-minded man loco." He smiled reassuringly. "Now climb right up behind me, Reddie. Gimme yore little saddle an' yore no-account gun—Ouch!"

"I'll give you th' butt of it again if you don't act like you've made th' best of them gravy brains!" Red snorted. "Here, you lop-eared cow-wrastler—catch this!" throwing the saddle so sudden and hard that Hopalong almost lost his balance from the impact. "Now you gimme a little room in front of th' tail—I ain't no blasted fly."

Hopalong gave his friend a hand and Red landed across the horse's back, to the instant and strong dislike of that animal, which showed its displeasure by bucking mildly.

"Glory be!" cried Hopalong, laughing. "Riding double on a bucking hinge ain't no play, is it? Suppose he felt like pitching real strong—where would you be with that tail holt?"

"You bump my nose again with th' back of yore head an' you'll see how much play it is!" Red retorted. "Come on—pull out. We ain't glued fast. Th' world moves, all right, but if yo're counting on it sliding under you till th' dam comes around yo're way off; it ain't moving that way. Hey! Stop that spurring!"

"I'll hook 'em in you again if you don't shut up!" Hopalong promised, jabbing them into the horse, which gave one farewell kick, to Red's disgust, and cantered south with ears flattened.

"Whoop! I'm riding again!" Red exulted.

"I'm glad it wasn't Red Eagle they went an' killed," Hopalong remarked.

"Red Eagle!" snorted Red, indignantly. "What good is this cayuse, anyhow? Ginger was worth three like this."

"Well, if you don't like this cayuse you can get off an' hoof it, you know," Hopalong retorted. "But I'll tell you what you know a'ready; there ain't no cayuse in this part of th' country that can lose him in long-distance running. He ain't no fancy parlor animal like Ginger was; he don't know how to smoke a cig or wash dishes, or do any of th' fool things yore cayuse did, but he's right on th' job when it comes to going hard an' long. An' it's them two things that tell how much a cayuse is worth, down here in this country. If I could 'a jumped on him up there when they made their get-away from you, me an' th' Sharps would 'a fixed 'em. They wouldn't be laughing now at how easy you was."

"They ain't laughing, not a bit of it—an' they won't

even be able to swear after I get out to th' mesa," Red asserted. "Have you seen Buck, or anybody 'cept th' Kid?"

"Yes. I told Buck an' Frenchy about it, an' Skinny, too," Hopalong replied. "Buck an' Frenchy went north along th' west line to get th' boys from Number Two. Buck says we'll go after 'em just as soon as we can get ready, which most of us are now. Pore Lanky; he's got to stay home an' pet his wounds—Buck said he couldn't go."

"Did Buck say who was going an' who was going to stay home?"

"Yes; you, Johnny, Billy, Pete, Skinny, Frenchy, me, Buck, an' Pie Willis are going—th' rest will have to watch th' ranch. That makes nine of us. Wonder how many are up at the mesa?"

"There'll be plenty, don't you worry," Red replied. "When we go after anybody we generally has to mix up with a whole company. I wouldn't be a whole lot surprised if they give us an awful fight before they peter out. They'll be up in th' air a hundred feet. We'll have plenty to do, all right."

"Well, two won't be there, anyhow—Archer an' Juan. I bet we'll find most of th' people of Eagle up there waiting for us."

"Lord, I hope they are!" cried Red. "Then we can clean up everything at once, town an' all."

"There's th' Kid—see th' splash?" Hopalong laughed. "He shore is stuck on swimming. He don't care if there's cottonmouths in there with him. One of them snakes will get him some day, an' if one does, then we'll plant him, quick."

"Oh, I dunno. I ain't seen none at th' dam," Red replied. "They don't like th' sand there as much as they do th' mud up at th' other end, an' along th' sides. Gee! There's his cayuse!"

Johnny dove out of sight, turned over and came up again, happy as a lark, and saw his friends riding towards him, and he trod water and grinned. "Hullo, fellers. Coming in?—it's fine! Hey, Red. We're all going out to Thunder Mesa as soon as we can! But what are you riding double for? Where's yore cayuse?" Something in Red's expression made him suspicious of his friends' intentions and, fearing that he might have to do some walking, he made a few quick strokes and climbed out, dressing as rapidly as his wet skin would permit.

Red briefly related his experience and Johnny swore as he struggled through his shirt. "What are you going to do?" he asked, poking his head out into sight.

"I'm going to ride yore cayuse to th' line house—you ain't as tired as me," replied Red.

"Not while I'm alive, you ain't!" cried Johnny, running to his horse. Then he grinned and went back to his clothes. "You take him an' rope th' cayuse I saw down in that barranca—there's two of 'em there, both belonging to Meeker. But you be shore to come back!"

"Shore, Kid," Red replied, vaulting into the saddle and riding away.

Johnny fastened his belt around him and looked up. "Say, Hoppy," he laughed, "Buck said Cowan sent my new gun down to th' bunk house yesterday. He's going to bring it with him when he comes down to-morrow. But I only got fifty cartridges for it—will you lend me some of yourn if I run short?"

"Where did Cowan get it?"

"Why, don't you remember he said he'd get me one like yourn th' next time he went north? He got back yesterday—bought it off some feller up on th' XS. Cost me twenty-five dollars without th' cartridges. But I've got fifty empties I can load when I get time, so I'll be all right later on. Will you lend me some?"

"Fifty is enough, you chump," laughed Hopalong. "You won't get that many good chances out there."

"I know; but I want to practice a little. It'll shoot flatter than my Winchester," Johnny grinned, hardly able to keep from riding to the bunk house to get his new gun.

Red rode up leading a horse. "That's a good rope, Kid, 'though th' hondo is purty heavy," he said, saddling the captured animal. "Is Buck going to bring down any food an' cartridges when he comes?" he asked.

"Yes; three cayuses will pack 'em. We can send back for more if we stay out there long enough to need more. Buck says that freak spring up on top flows about half a mile through th' chaparral before it peters out. What do you know about it, Red?" Hopalong asked.

"Seems to me that he's right. I think it flows through a twisting arroyo. But there'll be water enough for us, all right."

"I got a .45-120 Sharps just like Hopalong's, Red," Johnny grinned. "He said he'd lend me fifty cartridges for it, didn't you, Hoppy?"

"Well, I'll be blamed!" exclaimed Hopalong. "First thing *I* knowed about it, if I did. I tell you you won't need 'em.

"Where'd you get it?" asked Red.

"Cowan got it. I told you all about it three weeks ago."

"Well, you better give it back an' use yore Winchester," replied Red. "It ain't no good, an' you'll shoot some of us with it, too. What do *you* want with a gun that'll shoot eighteen hundred? You can't hit anything now above three hundred."

"Yo're another—I can, an' you know it, too. Three hundred!" he snorted. "Huh! Here comes Skinny!"

Skinny rode up and joined them, all going to the Peak. Finally he turned and winked at Johnny.

"Hey, Kid. Hopalong ought to go right down to th' H2 while he's got time. He hadn't ought to go off fighting without saying good-bye to his girl, had he?"

"She'd keep him home—wouldn't let him take no chances of getting shot," Red asserted. "Anyhow, if he went down there he'd forget to come back."

"Ow-wow!" cried Johnny. "You hit him! You hit him! Look at his face!"

"He shore can't do no courting while he's away," Skinny remarked. "He wouldn't let Red go with him when he went to give Meeker th' shovel, an' I didn't know why till just now."

"You go to blazes, all of you!" exclaimed Hopalong, red and uncomfortable. "I ain't doing no courting, you chump! An' Red knows why I went down there alone.

"Yes; you gave me a fool reason, an' went alone," Red retorted. "An' if that ain't courting, for th' Lords sake what is it? Or is she doing all of it, you being bashful?"

"Yes, Hoppy; tell us what it is," asked Skinny.

"Oh, don't mind them, Hoppy; they're jealous," Johnny interposed. Don't you make no excuses, not one. Admit that yo're courting an' tell 'em that yo're going to keep right on a-doing it an' get all th' honey you can."

Red and Skinny grinned and Hopalong, swearing at Johnny, made a quick grab for him, but missed, for Johnny knew the strength of that grip. "I ain't courting! I'm only trying to—trying to be—sociable; that's all!"

"Sociable!" yelled Red. "Oh, Lord!"

"It must be nice to be sociable," replied Johnny. "Since you ain't courting, an' are only trying to be sociable, then you won't care if we go down an' try it!"

"You bet; an' I'm going down, too," asserted Red, who was very much afraid of women, and who wouldn't have called on Mary Meeker for a hundred dollars.

Hopalong knew his friend's weakness and he quickly replied: "Red, I dare you to do that. I dare you to go down there an' talk to her for five minutes. When I say talk, I don't mean stammer. I dare you!"

"Do you dare *me*?" asked Johnny, quickly, glancing at the sun to see how much time he had.

"Oh, I ain't got time," replied Red, grinning.

"You ain't got th' nerve, you mean," jeered Skinny.

"I dare you, Red," Hopalong repeated, grimly.

"I asked you if you dared *me*?" hastily repeated Johnny.

"*You*! Not on yore life, Kid. But you stay away from there!" Hopalong warned.

"Gee—wish you'd lend me them cartridges," sighed Johnny. "Mebbe Meeker has got some he ain't so stingy with," he added, thoughtfully.

"I'll lend you th' cartridges, Kid," Hopalong offered. "But you stay away from th' H2. D'y hear?"

CHAPTER XXV

Antonio's Revenge

WHILE RED had been trudging southward under his saddle and other possessions a scene was being enacted on a remote part of the H2 range which showed how completely a cowboy leased his very life to the man who paid him his monthly wage, one which serves to illustrate in a way how a ranchman was almost a feudal lord. There are songs of men who gave up their lives to save their fellows, one life for many, and they are well sung; but what of him who risks his life to save one small, insignificantly small portion of his employer's possessions, risks it without hesitation or fear, as a part of his daily work? What of the man who, not content with taking his share of danger in blizzard, fire, and stampede, on drive, roundup, and range-riding, leaps fearlessly at the risk of his life to save a paltry head or two of cattle to his ranch's tally sheet? Such men were the rule, and such a one was Curley, who, with all his faults, was a man as a man should be.

Following out his orders he rode his part of the range with alertness, and decided to explore the more remote southwestern angle of the ranch. Doc had left him an hour before to search the range nearer Eagle and would not be back again until time to return to the ranch house for the night. This was against Meeker's order, for they had been told to keep together for their own protection, but they had agreed that there was little risk and that it would be better to separate and cover more ground.

The day was bright and, with the exception of the heat, all he could desire. His spirits bubbled over in snatches of song, but all the time moving in the general direction of the little-ridden territory. On all sides stretched the same monotonous view, sage brush, mesquite, cactus, scattered tufts of grass, and the brown plain, endless, flat, wearying.

The surroundings did not depress him, but only gradually slowed the exultant surge of his blood and, as he hummed at random, an old favorite came to him out of the past, and he sung it joyously:

> *My taste is that of an aristocrat,*
> > *My purse that of a pauper:*
> *I scorn the gold her parents hold—*
> > *But shore I love their daughter.*
> *Hey de diddle de, hey de dee,*
> > *But shore I love their daughter.*

> *When silvery nights my courting light*
> > *An' souls of flowers wander,*
> *Then who's to blame if I loved th' game*
> > *An' did not pause to ponder?*
> *Hey de diddle de, hey de dee,*
> > *An' did not pause to ponder.*

> *Her eyes are blue, an' oh, so true—*
> > *Th' words were said ere thought, Lad.*
> *Her father swore we'd meet no more—*
> > *But I am not distraught, Lad.*

Hey de diddle de, hey de de—
But I am not distraught, Lad.

He ceased abruptly, rigidly erect, staring straight
ahead as the significance of the well trodden trail impressed itself on his mind. He was close to the edge of
a steep-walled basin; and leading to it was a narrow,
steep gully, down which the beaten trail went. Riding
closer he saw that two poles were set close to the wall
of the gully, and from one of them dangled a short,
frayed hempen rope. There was a water hole in the
basin, surrounded by a muddy flat, and everywhere
were the tracks of cattle.

As he hesitated to decide whether or not it would be
worth while to ride through the depression he chanced
to look south, and the question decided itself. Spurring
savagely, he leaned forward in the saddle, the wind
playing a stern song in his ears, a call to battle for his
ranch, his pride, and his hatred for foul work. He felt
the peculiar, compelling delight, the surging, irresistible
intoxication of his kind for fighting, the ecstasy of the
blood lust, handed down from his Saxon forefathers.

A mile ahead of him was a small herd of cattle, being
driven west by two men. Did he stop to return to the
ranch for assistance? Did he count the odds? Not he,
for he saw the perpetrators of the insults he and his
companions had chafed under—the way was clear, the
quarry plain, and he asked naught else.

They saw him coming—one of them raised a pair of
glasses to his eyes and looked closely at him and from
him all around the plain. All the time they were driving
the cattle harder, shouting and whipping about them
with their rawhide quirts; and constantly nearer came
the cowboy, now standing up in his stirrups and lashing
his straining mount without mercy. Soon he thought he
recognized one of the herders, and he flung the name
on the whistling wind in one contemptuous shout: "*An-*

tonio! Damn his soul!" and fell to beating the horse all the harder.

It was Antonio, and a puff of smoke arose from the Mexican's shoulder, and streaked behind, soon followed by another. Curley knew the rifle, a .40–90 Sharps, and did not waste a shot, for he must be on equal terms before he could hope to cope with it. Another puff, then another and another, but still he was not hit. Now he drew his own rifle from his holster and hazarded a shot, but to no avail. Then the second herder, who had not as yet fired, snatching the rifle from Antonio's hands and, checking his horse, leaped off and rested the weapon across the saddle. Taking deliberate aim, he fired, and Curley pitched out of the saddle as his horse stumbled and fell. The rider scrambled to his feet, dazed and hurt, and ran to his horse, but one look told the story and he ended the animal's misery with a shot from his Colt.

The herder and the cattle were rapidly growing smaller in the distance but the Mexican rode slowly around the man on foot, following the circumference of a large circle and shooting with calm deliberation. The bullets hummed and whined viciously past the H2 puncher, kicking up the dust in little spurts, and cold ferocity filled his heart as he realized the rustler's purpose. He raised his own rifle and fired—and leaded the barrel. When he had fallen the barrel had become choked with sand and dust and he was at the mercy of his gloating enemy, who would now wipe out the insult put upon him at the bunk house. Slowly Antonio rode and carefully he fired and then, seeing that there was something wrong with Curley's rifle, which the puncher threw aside, he drew closer, determined to shoot him to pieces.

Curley was stung with rage now. He knew that it was only a question of waiting until the right bullet came, and scorning to hug the sand for the man he held in such contempt, and vaguely realizing that such an act would not change the result, he put all his faith in a dash. He ran swiftly towards his astonished enemy, who expected him to seek what cover the dead horse would give him, Colt in hand, cursing at every jump and hoping to be spared long enough to get within range with his six-shooter, if only for one shot. Antonio did not like this close work and cantered away, glancing back from time to time. When Curley finally was forced to stop because of exhaustion the rider also stopped and slipped off his horse to have a rest for the rifle. Curley emptied the Colt in a futile, enraged effort to make a lucky hit while his enemy had now aimed from across the saddle. Hastily reloading the Colt as he ran, the puncher dashed forward again, zig-zagging to avoid being hit. There was a puff of gray smoke, but Curley did not hear the report. He threw one arm half up as if to ward off the shot and pitched forward, face down in the dust, free from all pain and strife.

Antonio fired again and then cautiously drew nearer to his victim, the rifle at the ready. Turning shortly he made a quick grab at his horse, fearing that it might leave him on foot to be caught by some wandering H2 puncher. Springing into the saddle he rode forward warily to get a closer look at the man he had murdered, proud of his work, but fearful that Curley was playing dead.

When assured that he had nothing to fear from the prostrate form, he rode close. "Knock me down, will you!" he gritted, urging the horse to trample on the body, which the animal refused to do. "Come out looking for us, did you? Well, you found us, all right, but a hell of a lot of good it did you. You ain't saying a word, are you, you carrion? You ain't got no smart come-back now, an' you ain't throwing no wash water on me, are you?"

He started and looked around nervously, fearful that he might be caught and left lying on the sand as he had left Curley. One or two of the H2 outfit carried single-shot rifles which shot as far if not farther than his own, and the owners of them knew how to shoot. Wheeling abruptly he galloped after the herd, looking back constantly and thinking only of putting as great a distance as possible between himself and the scene of the killing.

A lizard crawled out of a hillock and stared steadily at the quiet figure and then, making a tentative sortie, disappeared under the sand; but the man who had sung so buoyantly did not mind it, he lay wrapped in the Sleep Eternal. He had died as he had lived, fearlessly and without a whimper.

Late in the afternoon Doc Riley, sweeping on a circling course, rode through chaparrals, alert even after his fruitless search, looking around on all sides, and wondered if Curley and he would meet before they reached the ranch proper. Suddenly something caught his eye and he stood up in the stirrups to see it better, a ready curse leaping from his lips. He could not make out who it was, but he had fears and he spurred forward as hard as he could go. Then he saw the horse and knew.

Riding close to the figure so as to be absolutely sure, he knew beyond a hope of mistake and looked around the plain, his expression malevolent and murderous.

"Curley! Curley!" he cried, leaping off his horse and placing a heavy, kindly hand on the broad, sloping shoulder of the man who had been his best friend for years. "So they got you, lad! They got you! In God's name, why did I leave you?" he cried in bitter self-condemnation. "It's my fault, it's my fault, lad!" He straightened up suddenly and glared around through tear-dimmed eyes. "*But by th' living God I'll pay them for this*, I'll pay them for this! Damn their murdering souls!"

He caught sight of an empty cartridge shell and snatched it up eagerly. ".40–90, by God! That's Antonio's! Curley, my lad, I'll get him for you—an' when I *do!* I'll send his soul to th' blackest pit in hell, an' send it *slow!*"

He noticed and followed the tracks in the sand, reading them easily. He found the Winchester and quickly learned its story, which told him the whole thing. Returning to the body of his friend he sat by it quietly, looking down at it for several minutes, his sombrero in his hand.

"Well, wishing won't do no good," he muttered, dismounting. "I'll take you home, lad, an' see you put down too deep for coyotes to bother you. An' I'll square yore scores or join you trying."

He lifted the body across the withers of his horse and picked up the Colt. Mounting, he rode at a walk toward the bunk house, afire with rage and sorrow.

For the third time Meeker strode to the door of the bunk house and looked out into the darkness, uneasy and anxious. Chick sauntered over to him and leaned against the frame of the door. "They'll show up purty soon, Jim," he remarked.

"Yes. I reckon so—Salem!" the foreman called. "Put their grub where it'll keep warm."

"Aye, aye, sir. I was just thinking I ought to. They're late, ain't they, sir?" he asked. "An' it's dark, too," he added, gratis.

"Why, is it, Salem?" queried Dan, winking at Jack Curtis, but Salem disappeared into the gallery.

"Listen!—I hear 'em!" exclaimed Chick.

"You hear one of 'em," corrected Meeker, turning to the table to finish drinking his coffee. "Hey, Salem! Never mind warming that grub—rustle it in here. One of 'em's here, an' he'll be starved, too."

Suddenly Chick started back with an exclamation as Doc Riley loomed up in the light of the door, carrying a body over his shoulder. Stepping into the room while his friends leaped to their feet in amazement and incredulity, he lowered his burden to a bench and faced them, bloody and furious.

"What's th' matter?" exclaimed Meeker, the first to find his voice, leaping forward and dropping the cup to the floor. "Who did that?"

Doc placed his sombrero over the upturned face and ripped out a savage reply. "Antonio! Yore broncho-buster! Th' snake that's raising all th' devil on this range! Here—see for yoreself!" tossing the cartridge shell to his foreman, who caught it clumsily, looked at it, and then handed it to Dan. Exclamations and short, fierce questions burst from the others, who crowded up to see the shell.

"Tell me about it, Doc," requested Meeker, pacing from wall to wall.

"He was shot down like a dog!" Doc cried, his rage sweeping over him anew in all its savagery. "I saw th' whole thing in th' sand, plain as day. Antonio got his cayuse first an' then rode rings around him, keeping out of range of Curley's Colt, for Curley had leaded his rifle. It was Colt against Sharps at five hundred, that was what it was! He didn't have a show, not a measly show for his life! Shot down like a *dog!*"

"Where'd it happen?" asked Chick, breathlessly, while the low-voiced threats and imprecations swelled to an angry, humming chorus.

"Away down in th' southwest corner," replied Doc, and he continued almost inaudibly, speaking to himself and forgetful of the others. "Me an' him went to school together an' I used to lick every kid that bullied him till he got big enough to do it hisself. We run away together an' shared th' same hard luck. We went through that Sioux campaign together, side by side, an' to think that after he pulled out of *that* alive he had to be murdered by a yaller coward. If he'd been killed in fair fight it would be all right; but by that coyote—it don't seem possible, not noway. I licked th' feller that hurt him on his first day at school—I'm going to kill th' last!

"Meeker," he said, coming to himself and facing the angry foreman, "I'm quitting to-night. I won't punch no more till I get that murderer. I take up that trail at daylight an' push it to a finish. It's got to be him or me, now."

"You don't have to quit to do that, an' you *know* it!" "I don't care if yore gone for six months—yore pay goes on just th' same. He went down fighting for me, an' I'll be everlastingly condemned if I don't have a hand in squaring up for it. Yo're going on special duty for th' H2, Doc, an' yore orders are to get Antonio. Why, by th' Lord, I'll take up th' trail with you, Doc, an' with th' rest of th' boys behind me. This ranch can go galley-west an' crooked till we get that snake. Dan an' Salem stays with my girl an' to watch th' ranch— th' rest of us are with you—we're as anxious as you to push him Yonder, Doc."

"If I can get him alive, get my two hands on his skinny neck," Doc muttered, his fingers twitching. "I'll kill him slow, so he'll feel it longer, so he'll be shore to know why he's going. I want to *feel* his murdering soul dribble hell-wards, an' let him come back a couple of times so I can laugh in his yaller face when he begs! I want to get him—*so!*" and Chick shuddered as the knotted, steel-like fingers opened and shut, for Doc was half devil now. While Chick stared, the transformed man walked over to the bench and picked up the body in his brawny arms and strode into the blackness—Curley was going to lie in the open, with the stars and the sky and the sighing wind.

"God!" breathed Chick, looking around, "I never saw a man like *that* before!"

"I hope he gets what he wants!" exclaimed Dan, fiercely.

"You fellers get yore traps ready for a chase," Meeker ordered as he strode to the door of the gallery. "Fifty rounds for six-shooters an' fifty for rifle, an' plenty of grub. It's a whole lot likely that killer's headed for his gang, an' we've got to be ready to handle everything that comes up. Hey, Salem!" he shouted.

"Aye, aye, sir!" replied Salem, who had just come in from one of the corrals and knew nothing of what had occurred.

"Did you cure that beef I told you to?" demanded the foreman.

"Yes, sir; but it ain't had time to cure—th' weather's not been right. Howsomever, I smoked some. That'll be ship-shape."

"Well, have it on our cayuses at daylight. Did you cut this beef in strips, or in twenty-pound chunks, like you did th' last?"

"Strips, *little* strips—I ain't trying to sun-cure no more big hunks, not me, sir."

Meeker turned and went towards the outer door.

"Don't waste no time, boys," he said. "Get all th' sleep you can to-night—you'll need it if I reckon right. Good-night," and he stepped out into the darkness. "Damn them dogs!" he muttered, disappearing in the direction of the kennels, from which came quavering, long-drawn howls.

CHAPTER XXVI

Frisco Visits Eagle

EAGLE DID not thoroughly awaken until the sun began to set, for it was not until dark that its inhabitants, largely transient, cared to venture forth. Then it was that the town seethed, boldly, openly, restrained by nothing save the might of the individual.

Prosperity had blessed the town, for there had been an abrupt and pleasing change in local conditions since the disagreement between th two ranches north of the town had assumed warlike aspect. Men who heretofore had no standing with the proprietors of the town's places of amusement and who had seldom been able to pay for as much liquor as they were capable of drinking, now swaggered importantly where they pleased, and found welcome where formerly it had been denied them; for their hands were thrust deep into pockets from which came the cheerful and open-sesame clinking of gold. Even Big Sandy, who had earned his food by sweeping out the saloons and doing odd jobs about them, and was popularly believed to be too lazy to earn a better living by real work, now drank his fill and failed to recognize a broom when he saw it. While the inhabitants could not "get in" on the big plums which they were certain were being shaken down on the range, they could and did take care of the windfalls, and thrived well. They would stay in town until their money was gone and then disappear for a week, and return to spend recklessly. It is not out of place to state, in passing, that numerous small herds bearing strange brands frequently passed around the town at a speed greater than that common to drives, and left clouds of dust on the southeastern horizon.

The town debated the probable whereabouts of ten men who had suddenly disappeared in a body, along with Antonio of the H2. It was obvious what they were doing and the conjectures were limited as to their whereabouts and success. For a while after they had left one or two had ridden in occasionally to buy flour and other necessities, and at that time they had caused no particular thought. But now even these visits had ceased. It was common belief that Quinn knew all about them, but Quinn for good reasons was not urged to talk about the matter. Big Sandy acted as though he knew, which increased his importance for a time, and discredited him thereafter.

While the citizens had been able to rustle as they pleased they had given but little thought to the ten men, being too busy to trail. But now that the H2 punchers rode range with rifles across their arms rustling had become very risky and had fallen off. Then it was that the idlers renewed their conjectures about Shaw and his men and thrashed that matter over and over again. The majority being, as we have said, transients, knew nothing about Thunder Mesa, and those who did know of it were silent, for Shaw and some of his companions knew only one way to close a man's mouth, and were very capable.

So it happened that about noon of the day Curley lost his life six men met in the shadow cast by the front

of the "Rawhide" a hundred yards from Quinn's, and
exercised squatter sovereignty on the bench just outside the door, while inside the saloon Big Sandy and
Nevada played cards close to the bar and talked in low
tones. When they were aware of the presence of those
on the bench they played silently and listened. The six
men outside made up one of the groups of the town's
society, having ridden in together and stuck together
ever since they had arrived, which was wise.

Big Sandy and Nevada made a team more feared
than any other combination. The former, while fair
with weapons, was endowed with prodigious strength;
by some it was hailed as being greater than that of
Pete Wilson, the squat giant of the Bar-20, whose
strength was proverbial, as it had good right to be.
Nevada was the opposite type, short, wiry, and soft-
spoken, but the quickest man in the draw and of uncertain temper.

Chet Bates, on the bench, replied to a companion
and gave vent to his soft, Southern laugh. "Yuh still
wondering 'bout thet man Shaw, an' th' othas?"

"Nothing else to do, is there?" retorted Dal Gilbert.
"We can't run no more cattle, can we?"

"I reckon we can't."

"They're running a big game an' I want to get in it,"
remarked John Elder. "Frisco was allus friendly. We've
got to go trailing for 'em."

"Yes; an' get shot," interposed George Lewis.
"They're ten to our six. An' that ain't all of our troubles,
neither. We'll find ourselves in a big fight some
day, an' right here. Them ranches will wake up, patch
up their troubles, an' come down here. You remember
what Quinn said about th' time Peters led a lot of mad
punchers agin Trendley an' his crowd, don't you? In a
day he can raise men enough to wipe this town off th'
map."

"Yuh forget, suh, that they are fighting foh princi-

ples, an' men who fight foh principles don't call truces,"
said Chet Bates.

"You've said that till it's old," laughed Sam Austin.

"*I* say we've got to keep our eyes open," warned
Lewis.

"Th' devil with that!" broke in Con Irwin. "What *I*
want to know is how we're going to get some of th'
easy money Shaw's getting."

"We'll have to wait for one of his men to come to
town an' trail him back," replied Gilbert.

"What do you say that we try to run one more good
herd an' then scout for them, or their trails?" asked
Irwin.

"Heah comes somebody," remarked Chet, listening.

The sound of galloping grew rapidly louder and
soon they saw Frisco turn into the street and ride towards them. As they saw him a quiet voice was heard
behind them and looking up, they saw Nevada smiling
at them. "Get him drunk an' keep him away from
Quinn's," he counselled.

They exchanged looks and then Elder stepped out
into the street and held up his hand. "Hullo, Frisco!" he
cried.

"Where yuh been keeping yuhself foh so long?"
asked Chet, affably. "Holed up som'ers?"

"Hullo, fellers," grinned Frisco, drawing rein.

"Everybody have a drink on me," laughed Chet.
"Ah'm pow'ful thirsty."

Frisco was escorted inside to the bar, where Chet did
the honors, and where such a spirit of hospitality and
joviality surrounded him that he forgot how many
drinks he had taken. He dug up a handful of gold and
silver and spread it out on the bar and waved at the
bartender. "Bes' you got—ver' bes'," he grinned. "Me
an' my fren's want th' ver' bes'; don't we, fellers? I got
money—helluva lot of money—an' thersh more where
it came from, ain't that so, boys?"

When the noise had subsided he turned around and

levelled an unsteady finger at the bartender. "I never go—back onsh fren', never. An' we're all frensh—ain't we, fellers? Tha's right. I got s'more frensh—good fellesh, an' lots of money cached in sand."

"Ah'll bet yuh have!" cried Chet.

"You allus could find pay-dirt," marvelled Nevada, glancing warningly around him. "Yo're a fine prospector, all right."

Frisco stared for a moment and then laughed loudly and leaned against the bar for support. "Proshpector! Proshpector! W'y, we earned tha's money—run a helluva lot of risks. Mebbe tha's Bar-20 outfit'll jump us an' make us fight 'em. No; they can't jump us—they can't get up at us!"

"On a mesa, shore!" whispered Elder to Lewis.

"Wha's you shay?"

"Said they couldn't lick you."

"Who couldn't—lick us?"

"Th' Bar-20," explained Elder.

Frisco rubbed his head and drew himself up, suspicion percolating through his muddled brain. "Never shaid nozzing 'bout no Bar-Twensh!" he asserted, angrily. "Nozzing 'tall. I'm going out of here—don't like you! Gotta get some flour an' ozzer stuff. Never shaid nozzing 'bout—" he muttered, staggering out.

Nevada turned to Elder. "You go with him an' quiet his suspicions. Keep him away from Quinn, for that coyote'll hold him till he gets sober if you don't. This is the chance we've been wanting. Don't try to pump him—his trail will be all we need."

"Wonder what mesa they're on?" asked Lewis.

"Don't know, an' don't care," Nevada replied. "We'll find out quick enough. There's eight of us an' we can put up a stiff argument if they won't take us in. You know they ain't going to welcome us, don't you?"

"Hey, go out th' back way," growled Big Sandy interposing his huge hulk between Bates and the door.

"An' don't let Frisco see you near a cayuse, neither," he added.

Nevada walked quickly over to his friend and said a few hurried words in a low voice and Big Sandy nodded. "Shore, Nevada; he might try that, but I'll watch him. If he tries to speak I'll let you know hasty. We're in this to stay," and he followed the others to the door.

Nevada turned and faced the bartender. "Mike, you keep quiet about what you saw an' heard to-day; understand? If you don't, me an' you won't fit in this town at th' same time."

Mike grinned. "I forgot how to talk after one exciting day up in Cheyenne, an' I ain't been drunk since, neither."

"Yo're a wise man," replied the other, stepping out by the back door and hastening up the street where he could keep watch over Quinn's saloon. It was an hour before he caught sight of Frisco, and he was riding west, singing at the top of his lungs. Then Quinn slipped into his corral and threw a saddle on a horse.

"Drop it!" said a quiet voice behind him and he turned to see Nevada watching him.

"What do you mean?" demanded Quinn, ominously.

"Let loose of that cayuse an' go back inside," was the reply.

"You get th' hell out of here an mind yore own—" Quinn leaped aside and jerked at his Colt; but was too late, and he fell, badly wounded. Nevada sprang forward and disarmed him and then, mounting, galloped off to join his friends.

CHAPTER XXVII

Shaw Has Visitors

WHEN FRISCO reached the edge of the clearing around the mesa he saw Antonio and Shaw toiling cautiously up the steep, precarious trail leading to the top, and he hailed vociferously. Both looked around, Antonio scowling and his companion swearing at their friend's condition. Frisco's pack horse, which he had sense enough to bring back, was loaded down with bags and packages which had been put on recklessly, inasmuch as a slab of bacon hung from the animal's neck and swayed to and fro with each step; and the animal he rode had a bartender's apron hanging down before its shoulders.

"Had a rip-snorting time—rip-snorting time," he announced pleasantly, in a roar. "Salubrious—rip-snorting—helluva time!"

"Nobody'd guess it!" retorted Shaw. "Look at them bundles! An' him an expert pack-horse man, too. An' that cayuse with a shirt! For anybody that can throw as neat a diamond hitch as him, that pack horse is a howling disgrace!"

"Hang th' pack horse!" growled Antonio. "I bet th' whole town knows our business now! He ought to be shot. Where you going?"

"Down to help him up," Shaw replied. "He'll bust his fool neck if he wrestles with that trail alone. You go on up an' send a couple of th' boys down to bring up th' grub," he ordered, starting down the path.

"Let him bust his fool neck!" replied Antonio. "He should 'a done that before he left."

"What's th' ruction?" asked Clausen, looking down over the edge.

"Oh, Frisco's come back howling drunk. Go down an' help him tote th' grub up. Shaw said for somebody else to help you."

"Hey, Cavalry," cried Clausen. "Come on an' gimme a hand," and the two disappeared down the trail.

The leader returned, heralded by singing and swearing, and pushed Frisco over the mesa top to sprawl full-length on the ground. Shaw looked down at him with an expression of anger and anxiety and then turned abruptly on his heel as a quavering snore floated up from the other.

"Here, Manuel!" he called, sharply. "Take my glasses an' go out to yore lookout rock. Look towards Eagle an' call me if you see anybody."

Manuel moved away as Cavalry and Clausen, loaded down, appeared over the edge of the mesa wall and dropped their loads at Shaw's feet.

"What did you tell him to get?" asked Clausen, marvelling.

"What do you think I told him to get?" snapped Shaw.

"I don't know, seeing what he brought back," was the reply.

Shaw examined the pile. "God's name, what's all this stuff?" he roared. "Bacon! An' all th' meat we want is down below. Canned milk! Two bottles XXX Cough Syrup, four bottles of whiskey, bottle vaniller extract, plug tobacco, an' three harmonicas! Is *that* flour!" he yelled, glaring at a small bag. "Twenty pounds! Five pounds of salt!"

"I reckon he bought all th' cartridges in town," Cavalry announced, staggering into sight with a box on his shoulder. "Lord, but it's heavy!"

"Twenty pounds of flour to last nine men a month!" Shaw shouted, kicking at the bag. "An' look at this coffee—two pounds! I'll teach him a lesson when he gets sober."

"Well, he made up th' weight in th' cartridges," Cavalry grinned. He grasped Shaw's arm. "What's got into Manuel?"

The leader looked and sprinted to the lookout rock, where Manuel was gesticulating, and took the glasses. Half a minute later he returned them and rejoined his companions near the pile of supplies.

"What is it?" asked Cavalry.

"Some of our Eagle friends. Mebby they want cards in this game, but we'll waste little time with 'em. Post th' fellers along th' edge, Clausen, an' you watch th' trail up. Keep 'em covered while I talks with 'em. Don't be slow to burn powder if they gets to pushing things."

"They trailed Frisco," growled Cavalry.

"Shore; oh, he was a great success!" snapped Shaw, going to the edge of the mesa to await the eight newcomers, his men finding convenient places along the top of the wall, their rifles ready for action.

They did not have long to wait for soon Nevada and Chet Bates rode into the clearing and made for the trail.

"That's far enough, Nevada!" shouted Shaw, holding up his hand.

"Why, hullo, Shaw!" cried the man below. "Yo're up a good tree, all right," he laughed.

"Yes."

"Can we ride up, or do we have to take shank's mare?"

"Neither."

"Well, we want some water after that ride," replied Nevada.

"Plenty of it below. Nobody asked you to take that ride. What do you want, anyhow?"

"Why, when Frisco said you was out here we thought we'd drop in on you an' pay you a little visit."

"You have paid us a little visit. Call again next summer."

"Running many cows?" asked Nevada.

"Nope; educating coyotes. Didn't see none, did you?"

Nevada exchanged a few words with his companion and then looked up again. "I reckon you need us, Shaw. Eight more men means twice as many cows; an' we can all fight a little if th' ranches get busy out here."

"We're crowded now. Better water up an' hit th' back trail. It's hard riding in th' dark."

"We didn't come out here for a drink," replied Nevada. "We came out to help you rustle, which same we'll do. I tell you that you need us, man!"

"When I need you I'll send for you. *Adios.*"

"You ain't going to let us come up?"

"Not a little bit. Pull yore stakes an' hit th' back trail. *Adios!*"

"Well, we'll hang around to-night an' talk it over again tomorrow. Mebby you'll change yore mind. So long," and the two wheeled and disappeared into the chaparrals, Nevada chuckling. "I didn't spring that little joker, Chet, because it's a good card to play last. When we tell him that we won't let nobody come down off'n th' mesa it'll be after we can't do nothing else. No use making him mad."

Up on the mesa Shaw wheeled, scowling. "I knowed that fool would fire off something big! Why can't he get drunk out here, where it's all right?"

"That Nevada is a shore bad proposition," Clausen remarked.

"So'm I!" snapped Shaw. "He can't come up, an' pur-

sooant to that idee I reckon you an' Hall better arrange
to watch th' trail to-night."

He walked away and paced slowly along the edge of
the wall, studying every yard of it. He had done this
thing before and had decided that no man set a saddle
who could scale the sheer hundred feet of rock which
dropped so straight below him. But somehow he felt
oppressed, and the sinking sun threw into bold relief
the furrows of his weather-beaten, leathery face and
showed the trouble marks which sat above his eyes. At
one part of the wall he stopped and peered over, mar-
shalling imaginative forces in attack after attack against
it. But at the end he smiled and moved on—that was
the weakest point in his defense, but he would consider
himself fortunate if he should find no weaker defense
in future conflicts. As he returned to the hut he glanced
at the lookout rock and saw Manuel in his characteris-
tic pose, unmoving, silent, watchful.

"I'm getting as bad as Cavalry and his desert," he
grumbled. "Still, they can't lick us while we stay up
here."

CHAPTER XXVIII

Nevada Joins Shaw

LATE IN the forenoon of the day after Nevada had argued with Shaw, Manuel shifted his position on the lookout rock and turned to face the hut. "Señor! Señor Shaw! He ees here."

Shaw strode to the edge of the mesa and looked down, seeing Nevada sitting quietly on a horse and looking up at him. Manuel, his duty performed, turned and looked eastward, shrinking back as Shaw stepped close to him. Lying prone along the edge half a dozen men idly fingered rifles as they covered the man below, Antonio's face in particular showing intense aversion to any more recruits.

"Morning, Shaw," shouted Nevada. "Going to let us come up?"

The leader was about to reply when he felt a tug at his ankle and saw Manuel's lips moving. "What is it"

"Look, Señor, look!" whispered the frightened Mexican, pointing eastward. "Eet ees de Bar-20! They be here *poco tiempo!*"

"Shut up!" retorted Shaw in a whisper, glancing east, and

what he saw changed his reply to the man below. "Well, Nevada, we are purty crowded up here as it is, but I'll ask th' boys about it. They ain't quite decided. Be back in a minute," and he stepped back out of sight of those below and waved his companions to him. Briefly stating the facts he asked that Nevada and his force be allowed up to help repulse the Bar-20, and the men who only a short time before had sworn that they would take in no partners nodded assent and talked over the new conditions while their leader again went to the edge.

"We can get along without you fellers," he called down, "but we don't reckon you'll cut any hole in our profits as long as you do yore share of work. If yo're willin' to share an' share alike, in work, grub, profits, an' fighting, why I reckon you can come up. But I'm leader here an' what I says goes: are you agreeable?"

"That's fair," Nevada replied. "Th' harder you work th' bigger th' pay—come on, boys," he cried, turning and waving his arm. "We're in!"

While the newcomers put their horses in the corral and toiled carefully up the steep trail Manuel stared steadily into the east and again saw the force that had filled him with fear. Hall, who was now watching with him, abruptly arose and returned to the hut, reporting: "Seven men out there—it's th' Bar-20, all right, I reckon;" and almost immediately afterward Manuel found a moving speck far to the east which Shaw's powerful glasses soon showed to be three pack horses driven by two men.

Nevada looked curiously about him as he gained his goal and then sought a place in the hut for his bunk. This, however, was full, and he cast around outside to find the best place for his blankets. Finding it, he stepped to the spring and had just quenched his thirst when he saw Shaw standing on a ledge of rock above him, looking down. "What is it, Shaw?" he asked.

"Well, you fellers shore enough raised hell, now

didn't you!" demanded the leader, a rising anger in his voice. "Yo're a fine collection of fools, you are—"

"What do—"

"—Leading that Bar-20 gang out here by th' nice, plain trail you left," Shaw continued, sarcastically, not heeding the other's explosive interjection. "That's a nice thing to saddle us with! Damn it, don't you know you've queered th' game for good?"

"Yo're drunk!" retorted Nevada, heatedly. "We came up from th' south! How th' devil could that crowd hit *our* trail?"

"They must 'a hit southwest on a circle," lied Shaw. "Manuel just now saw 'em pass a clearing an' heading this way—nine of 'em!"

"Th' devil!" exclaimed Nevada. "How many are up here now?" he asked quickly.

"Sixteen."

"All right! Let 'em come!" cried the other. "Sixteen to nine—it's easy!" he laughed. "Look here; we can clean up them fellers an' then raid their ranch, for there's only four left at home. We can run off a whopping big herd, sell 'em, an' divvy even. Then we separates, savvy? Why, it couldn't be better!"

Shaw showed his astonishment and his companion continued. "Th' H2 is shy men, an' th' C8o and th' Double Arrow is too far away to bother us. As soon as we lick this aggregation of trouble hunters, what's left will ride hell-bent for that valley. Then th' biggest herd ever rustled in these parts, a trip to a new range, an' plenty of money to spend there."

"That sounds good—but this pleasing cleaning-up is due to be full of knots," Shaw rejoined. "Them nine men come from th' craggiest outfit of high-toned gun-artists in these parts, an' you can bet that they are th' pick of th' crowd! Cassidy, Connors, Peters—an' they've got forty friends purty nigh as bad, an' eager to join in. I ain't no ways a quitter, but this looks to me like Custer's last stand, us being th' Custers."

"Ah, yo're loco!" retorted Nevada. "Look here! Send a dozen picked men down quick an' let 'em lose 'emselves in th' chaparral, far back. When th' terrible man-killers of th' great Bar-20 get plugging this way, our trouble-gang slips up from behind an' it's all over! Go on, before it's too late! Or one of us will ride like th' devil to Eagle for help—but it's got to be quick! You say I got you in this, which I know well I didn't, but now I'll get you out an' put you in th' way of a barrel of money."

The crack of a rifle sounded from the plain and the next instant Clausen dashed up, crying, "Manuel tried to cut an' run, but somebody down below dropped him off'n th' trail. They're all around us!"

"Good for th' somebody!" cried Shaw. "I'll kill th' next man that tries to leave us—that goes, so pass it along." Then he turned to Nevada, a sneer on his face. "That means anybody riding for help, too!" and he backed away.

Hall turned the corner, looking Nevada squarely in the eyes. "Say, Shaw, wonder what's got into Archer? He's been gone a long time for that trip."

"Reckon he's got tired an' quit," replied Shaw.

"You know he ain't that kind!" Hall cried, angrily.

"All right, all right. If he comes back an' finds out what's up he'll probably hustle to Eagle for some of th' boys," Shaw responded. Neither would ever see Dick Archer again—his bones were whitening near a small water hole miles to the north, as Hopalong and Red could testify.

"As long as one of us is outside we've got a chance," Nevada remarked. "How're we fixed for grub, Hall?"

"Got enough jerked beef to last us a month," and Hall departed.

A shot hummed over Nevada's head and, ducking quickly, he followed Hall. Close behind him went Shaw, muttering. "Well, it had to come sometime—an' we're better fixed than I ever reckoned we'd be. Now we'll see who gets wiped out!"

CHAPTER XXIX

Surrounded

ABOVE, A pale, hot sky with only a wisp of cloud; below, a semi-arid "pasture," scant in grass, seamed by tortuous gullies and studded with small, compact thickets and bulky boulders. A wall of chaparral, appearing solid when viewed from a distance, fenced the pasture, and rising boldly from the southwest end of the clearing a towering mass of rock flung its rugged ramparts skyward. Nature had been in a sullen mood when this scene had been perpetrated and there was no need of men trying to heighten the gloomy aspect by killing each other. Yet they were trying and had been for a week, and they could have found no surroundings more in keeping with their occupation.

Minute clouds of smoke spurted from the top of the wall and from the many points of vantage on the pasture to hang wavering for an instant before lazily dissipating in the hot, close air. In such a sombre setting men had elected to joke and curse and kill, perhaps to die; men hot with passion and blood-lust plied rifles with deliberate intent to kill. On one side there was

fierce, deep joy, an exultation in forcing the issue, much
as if they had tugged vainly at a leash and suddenly
found themselves free. They had been baited, tricked,
robbed, and fired upon and now, their tormentors
penned before them, there would be no cessation in
their efforts to wipe out the indignities under which
they had chafed for so long a time.

On the other side, high up on a natural fortress which
was considered impregnable, lay those who had
brought this angry pack about them. There was no joy
there, no glad eagerness to force the battle, no jokes
nor laughter, but only a grim desperation, a tenacious
holding to that which the others would try to take. On
one side aggression; on the other, defense. Fighters all,
they now were inspired by the merciless end always in
their minds; they were trapped like rats and would fight
while mind could lay a plan or move a muscle. Of the
type which had out-roughed, out-fought for so long
even the sturdy, rough men who had laid the foundation for an inland empire amid dangers superlative,
they knew nothing of yielding; and to yield was to die.
It was survivor against survivor in an even game.

"Ah, God!" moaned a man on the mesa's lofty rim,
staggering back aimlessly before he fell, never to rise
again. His companions regarded him curiously, stolidly,
without sympathy, as is often the case where death is
constantly expected. Dal Gilbert turned back to his rifle
and the problems before him. "So you've gone, too. An'
I reckon we'll follow"—such was Chet Bates' obituary.

In a thicket two hundred yards south of the mesa
Red Connors worked the lever of his rifle, a frown on
his face. "I got him, all right. Do you know who he is?"

"No; but I've seen him in Eagle," replied Hopalong,
lowering the glasses. "What's worrying me is water—
my throat's drying awful."

"You shouldn't 'a forgot it," chided Red. "Now we've
got to go without it all day."

Hopalong ducked and swore as he felt of his bleeding face. "Purty close, that!"

"Mind what yo're doing!" replied Red. "Get off my hand."

"This scrap is shore slow," Hopalong growled. "Here we've been doing this for a whole week, all of us shot up, an' only got two of them fellers."

"Well, yo're right; but there ain't a man up there that ain't got a few bullet holes in him," Red replied. "But it is slow, that's shore."

"I've got to get a drink, an' that's all about it," Hopalong asserted. "I can crawl in that gully most of th' way, an' then trust a side-hopping dash. Anyhow, I'm tired of this place. Johnny's got th' place for *me*."

"You better stay here till it's dark, you fool."

"Aw, stay nothing—so long," and Hopalong, rifle in hand, crawled towards the gully. Red watched the mesa intently, hoping to be able to stop some of the firing his rash friend was sure to call forth.

Twenty minutes passed and then two puffs of smoke sailed against the sky, Red replying. Then half a dozen puffs burst into sight. A faint shout came to Red's ears and he smiled, for his friend was safe.

As Hopalong gained the chaparral he felt himself heartily kicked and, wheeling pugnaciously, looked into Buck Peters' scowling face. "Yo're a healthy fool!" growled the foreman. "Ain't you got no sense at all? Hereafter you flit over that pasture after dark, d'y hear!"

"He's th' biggest fool I ever saw, an' th' coolest," said a voice in the chaparral at the left.

"Why, hullo, Meeker," Hopalong laughed, turning from Buck. "How do you like our little party now?"

"I'm getting tired of it, an' it's some costly for me," grumbled the H2 foreman. "Bet them skunks in Eagle have cleaned out every head I owned." Then he added as an afterthought: "But I don't care a whole lot if I can see this gang wiped out—*Antonio* is th' coyote *I'm* itching to stop."

"He'll be stopped," replied Hopalong. "Hey, Buck, Red's shore thirsty."

"He can stay thirsty, then. An' don't you try to take no water to him. You stay off that pasture during daylight."

"But it was all my fault—" Hopalong began, and then he was off like a shot across the open, leaping gullies and dodging around bowlders.

"Here you!" roared Buck, and started to stare, Meeker at his side. A man was staggering in circles near a thicket which lay a hundred yards from them. He dropped and began to crawl aimlessly about, a good target for the eager rifles on the mesa. Bullets whined and shrilled and kicked up the dust on the plain, but still the rushing Bar-20 puncher was unhit. From the mesa came the faint cracking of rifle fire and clouds of smoke hovered over the cover sheltering Red Connors. Here and there over the pasture and along the chaparral's rim rifles cracked in hot endeavor to drive the rustlers from their positions long enough to save the reckless puncher. Buck and Meeker both were firing now, rapidly but carefully, muttering words of hope and anxiety as they worked the levers of their spurting guns. Then they saw Hopalong gain the prostrate man's side, drag him back to cover, and wave his arm. The fire from the mesa was growing weaker and as it stopped Hopalong, with the wounded man on his back, ran to the shelter of a gully and called for water.

"He's th' best man in this whole country!" cried Meeker, grabbing up a canteen and starting to go through the chaparral to give them water. "To do that for one of *my* men!"

"I've knowed that for nigh onto fifteen years," replied Buck.

Near the Eagle trail Billy Williams and Doc Riley lay side by side, friendly now.

"I tell you we've been shooting high," Doc grumbled. "It's no cinch picking range against that skyline."

"Hey! Look at Hopalong!" cried Billy, excited. "Blamed idiot—why, he's going out to that feller. Lord. Get busy!"

"That's Curtis out there!" ejaculated Doc, angrily. "They've got him, damn 'em!"

"My gun's jammed!" cursed Billy, in his excitement and anger standing up to tear at the cartridge. "I allus go an'—" he pitched sideways to the sand, where he lay quiet."

Doc dropped his rifle and leaped to drag his companion back to the shelter of the cover. As he did so his left arm was hit, but he accomplished his purpose and as he reached for his canteen the Bar-20 pessimist saved him the trouble by opening his eyes and staring around. "Oh, my head! It's shore burning up, Doc!" he groaned. "What th' devil happened that time, anyhow?"

"Here; swaller this," Doc replied, handing him the canteen.

"Who got me?" asked Billy, laying the vessel aside.

"How do I know? Whoever he was he creased you nice. His friends got me in th' arm, too. You can help me fix it soon."

"Shore I will! We can lick them thieves, Doc," Billy expounded without much interest. "Yessir," he added.

"You make me tired," Doc retorted. "You talking about being careful when you stand up in plain sight of them fellers like you just did."

"Yes, I know. I was mad, an' sort of forgot about 'em being able to shoot me—but what happened out there, anyhow?"

Doc craned his neck. "There's Cassidy now, in that gully—Meeker's just joined him. Good men, both of 'em."

"You bet," replied Billy, satisfied. "Yessir, we can lick 'em—we've got to."

On the west side of the mesa, and out of sight of the

rustlers, Pie Willis lay face down in the sand, quiet.
Near him lay Frenchy McAllister, firing at intervals,
aflame with anger and a desire to kill. Opposite him on
the mesa, a scant three hundred yards away, two rustlers gloated and fired, eager to kill the other puncher,
who shot so well.

"That other feller knows his business, Elder," remarked Nevada as a slug ricochetted past his head.
"Wonder who he is."

"Wonder *where* he is," growled Elder, firing at a new
place.

"He's been shifting a lot. Anyhow, we got one.
There's so much smoke down there I can't seem to
place him. Mebby—" he fell back, limp, his rifle clattering down a hundred feet of rock.

Nevada looked at him closely and now drew back to
a more secure position. "We're even, stranger, but we
ain't quits, by a good deal!" He swore. *Zing-ing-ing!* "Oh,
you know I moved, do you!" he gritted. "Well, how's
that!" *Spat!* a new, bright leaden splotch showed on the
rock above his head and hot lead stung his neck and
face as the bullets spattered. "I'll get you yet, you coyote!" he muttered, changing his position again. "Ah,
hell!" he sobbed and dropped his rifle to grasp his right
elbow, shattered by a Winchester .45. Pain shot through
every fibre of his body and weakened him so he could
not crawl for shelter or assistance. He swayed, lost his
balance and swayed further, and as his side showed
beyond the edge of his rocky rampart he quivered and
sank back, helpless, pain-racked, and bleeding to death
from two desperate wounds.

"We was—tricked—up here!" he moaned. "That
must—be Red—Connors out there. Ah!" *Spat! Chug!
Spat!* But Nevada did not hear them now.

Down in the chaparral, Frenchy, getting no response
to his shots, picked up his glasses and examined the
mesa. A moment later he put them back in the case,
picked up his rifle and crawled towards his companion.

"Pie!" he called, touching the body. "Pie, old feller! I got 'em both for you, Pie—got 'em—" Screened by the surrounding chaparral he stood up and shook a clenched fist at the sombre, smoke-wreathed pile of rock and shouted: "An' they won't be all! Do you hear, you thieves? *They won't be all!*"

Lying in a crack on the apex of a pinnacle of rock a hundred yards northwest of the mesa Johnny Nelson cursed the sun and squirmed around on the hot stone, vainly trying to find a spot comparatively cool, while two panic-stricken lizards huddled miserably as far back in the crack as they could force themselves. Long bright splotches marked the stone all around the youthful puncher and shrill whinings came to him out of the air, to hurtle away in the distance ten times as loud and high-pitched. For an hour he had not dared to raise his head to aim, and his sombrero, which he had used as a dummy, was shot full of holes. Johnny, at first elated because of his aerial position, now cursed it fervently and was filled with disgust. When he had begun firing at sunrise he had only one man to face. But the news went around among the rustlers that a fool had volunteered to be a target and now three good shots vied with each other to get the work over with quickly, and return to their former positions.

"I reckon I can squirm over th' edge an' drop down that split," Johnny soliloquized, eying a ragged, sharp edge in the rock close at hand. "Don't know where it goes to, or how far down, but it's cool, that's shore."

He wriggled over to it, flattened as much as possible, and looked over the edge, seeing a four-inch ledge ten feet below him. From the ledge it was ten feet more to the bottom, but the ledge was what interested him.

"Shore I can—just land on that shelf, hug th' wall an' they can't touch me," he grinned, slipping over and hanging for an instant until he stopped swinging. The rock bulged out between him and the ledge, but he did not give that any thought. Letting go he dropped down

the face of the rock, shot out along the bulge and over
his cherished ledge, and landed with a grunt on a mass
of sand and debris twenty feet below. As he pitched
forward to his hands he heard the metallic warning of
a rattlesnake and all his fears of being shot were
knocked out of his head by the sound. When he landed
from his jump he was on the wrong side of the crevice
and among hot lead. Ducking and dodging he worked
back to the right side and then blew off the offending
rattler's head with his Colt. Other rattlers now became
prominent and Johnny, realizing that he was an un-
welcome guest in a rattlesnake den, made good use of
his eyes and Colt as he edged towards the mouth of
the crevice. Behind him were rattlers; before him, rustlers who could and would shoot. To say that he was
disgusted is to put it mildly.

"Cussed joint!" he grunted. "This is a measly place
for me. If I stay I get bit to death; if I leave I get shot.
Wonder if I can get to that ledge—ugh!" he cried as the
tip of a rattler's tail hung down from it for an instant.
"Come on! Bring 'em all out! Trot cut th' tarantulas,
copper heads, an' Gilas! Th' more th' merrier! Blasted
snake hangout!"

He glanced about him rapidly, apprehensively, and
shivered. "No more of this for Little Johnny! I'll chance
th' sharp-shooters," he yelled, and dashed out and
around the pile so quickly as to be unhit. But he was
not hit for another reason, also. Skinny Thompson and
Pete Wilson, having grown restless, were encircling the
mesa by keeping inside the chaparral and came opposite the pinnacle about the time Johnny discovered his
reptilian neighbors. Hearing the noise they both
stopped and threw their rifles to their shoulders. Here
was a fine opportunity to lessen the numbers of the
enemy, for the rustlers, careless for the moment, were
peering over their breastwork to see what all the noise
was about, not dreaming that two pairs of eyes three
hundred yards away were calculating the range. Two

puffs of smoke burst from the chaparral and the rustlers ducked out of sight, one of them hard hit. At that moment Johnny made his dash and caused smiles to flit across the faces of his friends.

"We might 'a knowed it was him!" laughed Skinny. "Nobody else would be loco enough to pick out that thing."

"Yes; but now what's he doing?" asked Pete, seeing Johnny poking around among the rocks, Colt in hand.

"Hunting rustlers, I reckon," Skinny replied. "Thinks they are tunnelling an' coming up under him. I suppose. Hey! Johnny!"

Johnny turned, peering at the chaparral.

"What are you doing?" yelled Skinny.

"Hunting snakes."

Skinny laughed and turned to watch the mesa, from which lead was coming.

"Can you cover me if I make a break?" shouted Johnny, hopefully.

"No; stay where you are!" shouted Pete, and then ducked.

"Stop yelling and move about some or you'll get us both hit," ordered Skinny. "Them fellers can *shoot!*"

"Come on; let's go ahead. Johnny can stay out there till dark an' hunt snakes," Pete was getting sarcastic. "Wonder if he reckons we came here to get shot at just to hunt snakes!"

"No; we'll help him in," Skinny replied. "You'll find th' rattlers made it too hot for him up there. Start shooting."

Johnny, hearing the rapid firing of his friends, ran backwards, keeping the pinnacle between him and his enemies as long as he could. Then, once out of its shelter, he leaped erratically over the plain and gained a clump of chaparral. He now had only about a hundred yards to go, and Johnny could sprint when need was. He sprinted. Joining his friends the three disappeared in the chaparral and two disgusted rustlers helped a badly wounded companion to the rough hospital in the hut at the top of the mesa trail.

Johnny and his friends had not gone far before Johnny, eager to find a rustler to shoot at, left them to go to the edge of the chaparral and while he was away his friends stumbled on the body of Pie Willis. Johnny, moving cautiously along the edge of the chaparral, soon met Buck and Hopalong, who were examining every square foot of the mesa wall for a way up.

"Hullo, Johnny!" cried Hopalong. "What you doing here? Thought you were plumb stuck on that freak rock up north."

"I was—an' *stuck*, for shore," grinned Johnny. "That rock is a nest of snakes, besides being a fine place to get plugged by them fellers. An' hot!"

"How'd you get away?"

"Pete an' Skinny drove 'em back an' I made my getaway. They're in th' chaparral somewhere close," Johnny replied. "But why are you telescoping at th' joker? Think you see money out there?"

"Looking for a place to climb it," Hopalong responded. "We're disgusted with this long-range squibbing. You didn't see no breaks in th' wall up where you was, did you?"

"Lemme see," and Johnny cogitated for a moment. Then his face cleared. "Shore I did; there's lots of cracks in it, running up an' down, an' a couple of ledges. I ain't so shore about th' ledges, though—you see I was too busy to look for ledges during th' first part of th' seance, and I dassn't look during th' last of it. There was three of 'em a-popping at me!"

"Hey, Johnny!" came a hail; "Johnny!"

"That's Pete an' Skinny—Hullo!" Johnny shouted.

"Come here—Pie Willis is done for!"

"What?"

"Pie—Willis—is—done—for!"

The three turned and hastened towards the voice, shouting questions. They found Skinny and Pete stand-

ing over the body and sombreros came off as the foreman knelt to examine it. Pie had been greatly liked by
the members of the outfit he had lately joined, having
been known to them for years.

"Clean temple shot," Buck remarked, covering the
face and arising. "There's some fine shots up on that
rock. Well, here's another reason why we've got to get
up there an' wipe 'em out quick. Pie was square as a
die and a good puncher—I wouldn't have asked for a
better pardner. You fellers take him to camp—we're
going to find a way to square things if there is one. No,
Pete, you an' Johnny carry him in—Skinny is going with
us."

Buck, Hopalong, and Skinny returned to the edge of
the pasture and the foreman again swept the wall
through his glasses. "Hey! What's that? A body?"

Hopalong looked. "Yes, two of 'em! I reckon Pie died
game, all right."

"Well, come on—we've got to move along," and Buck
led the way north, Skinny bringing up the rear. Next
to Lanky Smith, at present nursing wounds at the ranch,
Skinny was the best man with a rope in the Bar-20
outfit and the lariat he used so deftly was one hundred
and fifty feet in length, much longer than any used by
those around the mesa. Buck had asked him to go with
them because he wished to have his opinion as to the
possibility of getting a rope up the mesa wall.

When they came opposite the rock which had shel-
tered Johnny they sortied to see if that part of the mesa
was guarded, but there was no sign of life upon it. Then,
separating, they dashed to the midway cover, the
thicket, which they reached without incident. From
there they continued to the pinnacle and now could see
every rock and seam of the wall with their naked eyes.
But they used the glasses and after a few minutes' examination of the ledges Hopalong turned to his companions. "Just as Johnny said. Skinny, do you reckon

if you was under them tonight that you could get yore
rope fast to th' bottom one?"

"Shore; that's easy. But it won't be no cinch roping
th' other," Skinny replied. "She sticks out over th' first
by two feet. It'll be hard to jerk a rope from that narrow foothold."

"Somebody can hang onto you so you can lean out,"
Buck replied. "Pete can hold you easy."

"But what'll he hold on to?"

Hopalong pointed. "See that spur up there, close to
th' first ledge? He can hitch a rope around that an' hang
on th' rope. I tell you it's *got* to be done. We can't lose
no more men in this everlasting pot-shooting game.
We've got to get close an' clean up!"

"Well, I ain't saying nothing different, am I?" snapped
Skinny. "I'm saying it'll be hard, an' it will. Now suppose one of them fellers goes on sentry duty along this
end; what then?"

"We'll solve that when we come to it," Hopalong replied. "I reckon if Red lays on this rock in th' moonlight
that he can drop any sentry that stands up against th'
sky at a hundred yards. We're got to try it, anyhow."

"*Down!*" whispered Buck, warningly. "Don't let 'em
know we're here. Drop that gun, Hoppy!"

They dropped down behind the loose boulders while
the rustler passed along the edge, his face turned towards the pinnacle. Then, deciding that Johnny had
not returned, he swept the chaparral with a pair of
glasses. Satisfied at length that all was well he turned
and disappeared over a rocky ledge ten feet from the
edge of the wall.

"I could 'a dropped him easy," grumbled Hopalong,
regretfully, and Skinny backed him up.

"Shore you could; but I don't want them to think we
are looking at this end," Buck replied. "We'll have th'
boys raise th' devil down south till dark an' keep that
gang away from this end."

"I reckon they read yore mind—hear th' shooting?" Skinny queried.

"That must be Red out there—I can see half of him from here," Hopalong remarked, lowering his glasses. "Look at th' smoke he's making! Wonder what's up? Hear th' others, too!"

"Come on—we'll get out of this," Buck responded. "We'll go to camp an' plan for to-night, an' talk it over with th' rest. I want to hear what Meeker's going to do about it an' how we can place his men."

"By thunder! If we *can* get up there, half a dozen of us with Colts, an' sneak up on 'em, we'll have this fight tied up in a bag so quick they won't know what's up," Skinny remarked. "You can bet yore life that if there's any way to get a rope up that wall I'll do it!"

CHAPTER XXX

Up the Wall

PIPES WERE glowing in the shadows away from the fire, where men lay in various attitudes of ease. A few were examining wounds while others cleaned rifles and saw that their revolvers were in good condition. Around the fire but well back from it four men sat cross-legged, two others stretched out on their elbows and stomachs near them.

"You say everything is all right on th' ranch?" asked Buck of a man who, covered with alkali, had just come from the Bar-20. "No trouble, hey?"

"Nope; no trouble at all," replied Cross, tossing his sombrero aside. "Lucas an' Bartlett each sent us four men to help out when they learned you had come out here. We shipped four of 'em right on to th' H2, which is too short-handed to do any damage to rustlers."

"Much obliged for that," spoke up Meeker, relief in his voice. "I'm blamed glad to hear things are quiet back home—but I don't know how long they'll stay that way with Eagle so close."

"Well, Eagle ain't a whole lot anxious to dip in no

more," laughed Cross, looking at the H2 foreman. "Leastawise, that's what Lucas said. He sent a delegation down there which made a good impression. There was ten men in it an' they let it be known that if they came back again there would be ten more with 'em. In that case Eagle wouldn't be no more than a charred memory. Since Quinn died, being shot hard by Nevada, who I reckons is out here, th' town ain't got nobody to tell it how to do things right, which is shore pleasant."

"You bring blamed good news—I'm glad Lucas went down there," Buck replied. "I can't tell of good news about us out here, yet. We've had a hard time for a week. They got Pie to-day, an' most of us are shot up plentiful. Yo're just in time for th' festival, Cross—we're going to try to rush 'em to-night an' get it over. We reckon Skinny an' Pete can get us a way up that wall before dawn."

"Me for th' rush," laughed Cross. "I'm fresh as a daisy, which most of you fellers ain't. How many of 'em have you got so far? Are there many still up there?"

"We've got four of 'em that I knows of, an' how many of 'em died from their wounds I can't say," replied Hopalong. "But a whole lot of 'em have been plugged, an' plugged hard."

"But how many are up there still able to fight?"

"I should say about nine," Hopalong remarked, thoughtfully.

"Ten," corrected Red. "I've been watching th' positions an' I know."

"About nine or ten—they shift so nobody can really tell," Buck replied. "I reckon we've seen 'em all in Eagle, too."

"Frenchy got Nevada an' another to-day, on th' west side," Johnny interposed.

"I'm glad Nevada is gone—he's a terror in a mixup," Cross rejoined. "Best two-handed gun man in Eagle, he was."

"Huh!" snorted Johnny. "Stack him up against Hoppy an' see how long he'd last!"

"I said in Eagle!" retorted Cross.

Buck suddenly stood up and stretched. "You fellers all turn in now an' snatch some sleep. I'm going out to see how things are with Billy. I'll call you in time. Doc, you an' Curtis are too shot up to do any climbing—you turn in too. When I come back I'll wake you an' send you out to help Billy watch th' trail. Where's Red?"

"Over here—what do you want?" came from the shadows.

"Nothing, only get to sleep. I reckoned you might be off somewheres scouting. Skinny, where's yore rope? Got that manilla one? Good! Put three more hemp lariats out here where I can find 'em when I come back. Now don't none of you waste no time; turn in right now!" He started to walk away and then hesitated, turning around. "Doc, you an' Curtis better come with me now so you won't lose no time hunting Billy in th' dark when yore eyes are sleepy—it's hard enough to find him now in th' dark, when I'm wide awake. You can get yore sleep out there—he'll wake you when yo're needed."

The two punchers arose and joined him, Doc with his left arm bandaged and his companion with three bandages on him. When they joined Buck Doc protested. "Let me go with you an' th' rest of th' boys, Peters, when you go up that wall. I came out here to get th' man that murdered Curley, an' I hate to miss him now. If I can't climb th' boys will be glad to pull me up, an' it won't take no time to speak of. My gun arm is sound as a dollar—*I* want that murderer!"

Buck glanced at Meeker, who refused to give any sign of his thoughts on the matter. "Well, all right, Doc. But if we should have to fight as soon as we get up an' don't have no time to pull you after us, you'll miss everything. But you can do what you want."

"I'll just gamble on that. I ain't hurt much, an' if I

can't climb I'll manage to get in th' scrap someway, even if I has to hunt up Billy," replied Doc, contentedly, returning to the fire.

Buck and his companion moved away into the darkness while those around the fire lay down to get a few hours' rest, which they needed badly. George Cross, who was not sleepy, remained awake in a shadow and kept guard, although none was needed.

Buck and Curtis found Billy by whistling and the wounded H2 puncher found a place to lie down and was soon asleep, while the foreman and his friend sat up, watching the faint glow on the mesa, the camp-fire of the besieged. Once they heard the clatter of a rifle from the head of the trail and later they saw a dim figure pass quickly across the lighted space. They were content to watch on such a night, for the air had cooled rapidly after the sun went down and the sky was one twinkling mass of stars.

Twice during the wait Buck disappeared into the black chaparral close at hand and struck a match under his coat to see the time, and on the last occasion he returned to Billy, remarking: "Got half an hour yet before I leave you. Are you sleepy?"

"No, not very; my head hurts too much to sleep," Billy replied, re-crossing his legs and settling himself in a more comfortable position. "When you leave I'll get up on my hoofs so I won't feel like dosing off. I won't wake Curtis unless I have to—he's about played out."

"You wake him when you think I've been gone half an hour," Buck ordered. "It'll take him some time to get his eyes open—we mustn't let any get away. They've got friends in Eagle, you know."

"Wish I could smoke," Billy remarked, wistfully.

"Why, you can," replied Buck, quickly. "Go back there in th' chaparral an' get away with a pipeful. I'll watch things till you come back an' if I need you quick I can call. You've got near half an hour—make th' best of it."

"Here's th' gun—much obliged, Buck," and Billy disappeared, leaving the foreman to plan and watch. Buck glanced at the sleeping man occasionally when he heard him toss or mutter and wished he could let him sleep on undisturbed.

Suddenly a flash lighted up the top of the trail for an instant and the sharp report of a rifle rang out loudly on the still, night air. Buck, grabbing the Winchester, sprang to his feet as an excited chorus came from the rustlers' stronghold. Then he heard laughter and a few curses and quiet again ensued.

"What was that, Buck?" came a low, anxious hail from behind.

The foreman laughed softly and said: "Nothing, Billy, except that th' guard up there reckoned he saw something to shoot at. It's funny how staring at th' dark will get a feller seeing things that ain't. Why, had yore smoke so soon?" he asked in surprise as Billy sat down beside him.

"Shore," replied Billy. "Two of 'em. I reckon yore time is about up. Gimme th' gun now."

"Well, good luck, Billy. Better move up closer to th' trail if you can find any cover. You don't want to miss none. So long," and Billy was alone with his sleeping companion.

When the foreman returned to the camp he was challenged, and stopped, surprised. "It's Peters," he called.

"Oh, all right. Time to go yet?" asked Cross, emerging from the darkness.

"Purty near; but I thought I told you to go to sleep?"

"I know, but I ain't sleepy, not a bit. So I reckoned I'd keep watch over th' rest of th' gang."

"Well, since yo're wide awake, you help me knot these ropes an' let th' others have a few minutes more," Buck responded, picking up Skinny's fifty-foot lariat and placing it to one side. He picked up the three shorter ropes and threw one to his companion. "Put a knot every foot an' a half—make 'em tight an' big."

In a few minutes the work was finished and Buck
awakened the sleeping men, who groped their way to
the little stream close by and washed the sleep out of
their tired eyes, grabbing a bit of food on their return
to the fire.

"Now, fellers," said the foreman, "leave yore rifles
here—it's Colts this trip, except in Red's case. Got plenty
of cartridges? Everybody had a drink an' some grub?
All right; single file after me an' don't make no noise."

When the moon came up an hour later Red Connors,
lying full length on the apex of the pinnacle which
Johnny had tried and found wanting, watched an indistinct blur of men in the shadow of the mesa wall. He
saw one of them step out into the moonlight, lean back
and then straighten up suddenly, his arm going above
his head. The silence was so intense that Red could
faintly hear the falling rope as it struck the ground.
Another cast, and yet another, both unsuccessful, and
then the fourth, which held. The puncher stepped back
into the shadow again and another figure appeared, to
go jerking himself up the face of the wall. While he
watched the scaling operations Red was not missing
anything on top of the mesa, where the moon bathed
everything in a silvery light.

Then he saw another figure follow the first and kick
energetically as it clambered over onto the ledge. Soon
a rope fell to the plain and the last man up, who was
Skinny, leaned far out and cast at the second ledge,
Pete holding him. After some time he was successful
and again he and his companion went up the wall. Pete
climbed rapidly, his heavy body but small weight for
the huge, muscular arms which rose and fell so rapidly.
On the second ledge the same casting was gone through
with, but it was not until the eighth attempt that the
rope stayed up. Then Red, rising on his elbows, put his
head closer to the stock of his rifle and peered into the
shadows back of the lighted space on the rocky pile.
He saw Pete pull his companion back to safety and

then, leaping forward, grasp the rope and climb to the top. Already one of the others was part way up the second rope while another was squirming over the lower ledge, and below him a third kicked and hauled, half way up the first lariat.

"String of monkeys," chuckled Red. "But they can't none of 'em touch Pete in that sort of a game. Wonder what Pete's doing?" he queried as he saw the man on the top of the mesa bend, fumble around for a moment, and then toss his arm out over the edge. "Oh, it's a knotted rope—he's throwing it down for th' others. Well, Pete, old feller, you was th' first man to get—*Lord*!"

He saw Pete wheel, leap forward into a shadow, and then a heaving, twisting, bending bulk emerged into the moonlight. It swayed back and forth, separated into two figures and then became one again.

"They're fighting, rough an' tumble!" Red exclaimed. "Lord have mercy on th' man who's closing with that Pete of ourn!"

He could hear the scuffling and he knew that the others had heard it, too, for Skinny was desperately anxious to wriggle over the edge, while down the line of ropes the others acted like men crazed. Still the pair on the mesa top swayed back and forth, this way and that, bending, twisting, and Red imagined he could hear their labored breathing. Then Skinny managed to pull himself to the top of the wall and sprang forward, to sink down from a kick in the stomach.

"God A'mighty!" cried Red excitedly. "Who is it that can give Pete a fight like that? Well, I'm glad he's so busy he can't use his gun!"

Skinny was crawling around on his hands and knees as Buck's head arose over the edge. The foreman, well along in years, and heavy, was too tired to draw himself over the rim without a moment's rest. He had no fear for Pete, but he was worried lest some rustler might sound an alarm. Skinny now sat up and felt for his Colt, but the foreman's voice stopped him. "No shooting, yet! Want to tell 'em what's up! You let them fellers alone for a minute, an' give me a hand here."

Pete, his steel-like fingers darting in for hold after hold, managed to jerk his opponent's gun from its sheath and throw it aside, where Skinny quickly picked it up. He was astonished by the skill and strength of his adversary, who blocked every move, every attempt to get a dangerous hold. Pete, for a man reputed as being slow, which he was in some things, was darting his arms in and out with remarkable quickness, but without avail. Then, realizing that his cleaner living was standing him in good stead, and hearing the labored breathing of the rustler, he leaped in and clinched. By this time Hopalong and three more of the attacking force had gained the mesa top and were sent forward by the foreman, who was now intent upon the struggle at hand.

"It's Big Sandy!" Hopalong whispered to Skinny, pausing to watch for a moment before he disappeared into the shadows.

He was right, and Big Sandy, breathless and tired, was fighting a splendid fight for his life against a younger, fresher, and stronger man. The rustler tried several times for a throat hold but in vain, and in a fury of rage threw his weight against his opponent to bear him to the ground, incautiously bringing his feet close together as he felt the other yield. In that instant Pete dropped to a crouch, his vice-like hands tightened about Big Sandy's ankles, and with a sudden, great surge of his powerful back and shoulders he straightened up and Sandy plunged forward to a crashing fall on the very edge of the mesa, scrambled to his feet, staggered, lost his balance, and fell backwards a hundred feet to the rocks below.

The victor would have followed him but for Buck, who grasped him in time. Pete, steady on his feet again, threw Buck from him by one sweep of his arms and wheeled to renew the fight, surprise flashing across his face at not seeing his opponent.

"He's down below, Pete," Buck cried as Johnny, white-faced, crawled over the edge.

"What was that?" exclaimed the Kid. "Who fell?"

"Big Sandy," replied the foreman. "He—" the report of a shot cut him short. "Come on!" he called. "They're at it!" and he dashed away, closely followed by Johnny and Pete as Jim Meeker came into view. The H2 foreman slid over the mesa rim, leaped to his feet and sprinted forward, Colt in hand, to be quickly lost in the shadows, and after him came Red Connors, the last.

Down below Doc, hearing a thud not far from him, hurried around a spur of rock in the wall, sick at heart when he saw the body. Bending over quickly he recognized the mass as once having been Big Sandy, and he forthwith returned to the rope to be pulled up. When he at last realized that his friends had forgotten him there was loud, lurid cursing and he stamped around like a wild man, waving a Colt in his right hand. Finally he dropped heavily on a rock, too enraged to think, and called the attacking force, collectively and individually, every name that sprang to his lips. As he grew calmer he arose from the rock, intending to join Billy and Curtis at the other end of the pasture, and as he took a step in that direction he heard a sharp click and a pebble bounced past him. He stepped backwards quickly and looked up, seeing a figure sliding rapidly down the highest rope. He was immediately filled with satisfaction and easily forgave his companions for the anxiety they had caused him, and as he was about to call out he heard something spoken in Spanish. Slipping quickly and noiselessly into the deeper shadow at the base of the wall he flattened himself behind the spur of rock close to the rope, where he waited tensely, a grim smile transforming his face. He knew that voice.

CHAPTER XXXI

Fortune Snickers at Doc

ANTONIO WAS restless and could not sleep. He turned from side to side on the ground near the fire before the hut and was one of the first to run to the top of the trail when the guard there discharged his rifle at nothing. Returning to his blanket he tried to compose himself to rest, but was unsuccessful. Finally, he arose, picked up his rifle, and slouched off into the shadows to wander about from point to point.

Cavalry, coming in from his post to get a drink, caught sight of Antonio before he was swallowed up by the darkness and, suspicious as ever of Antonio, forgot the drink and followed.

After wandering about all unconscious of espionage Antonio finally drifted to the western edge and seated himself comfortably against a boulder, Cavalry not fifty feet away in a shadow. Time passed slowly and as Antonio was about to return to the fire he chanced to glance across the mesa along a moon-lighted path and stiffened at what he saw. A figure ran across the lighted space, silently, cautiously, Colt in hand, and then another, then two together, and he knew that the enemy had found a way up the wall and were hurrying forward to fight at close quarters, to effect a surprise on the unsuspecting men about the fire and in the hut. There remained, perhaps, time enough for him to escape and he arose and ran north, crouching as he zigzagged from cover to cover, cautious and alert.

Cavalry, because of his position, had not seen the flitting punchers and, his suspicions now fully aroused, he slipped after Antonio to find out just what he was going to do. When the firing burst out behind him he paused and stood up, amazed. As he struggled to understand what it meant he saw three men run past a boulder at his left and then he knew, and still hesitated. He was not a man who thought quickly and his first natural impulse, due to his army training, was to join his friends, but gradually the true situation came to him. How many men there were in the attacking force he did not know, but he had seen three after the fighting had begun; and it was evident that the cowmen would not rush into the lion's jaws unless they were strong enough to batter down all resistance. Four of his friends were dead, another had evidently deserted, and the remainder were all more or less severely wounded— there could be no hope of driving the ranchmen back, and small chance of him being able to work through their line to join his friends. There remained only one thing to be done, to save himself while he might.

As he moved forward slowly and cautiously to find a way down the wall he remembered Antonio's peculiar actions and wondered if he had a hand in helping the cowmen up.

Meanwhile Antonio, reaching the edge of the open space where Pete and Big Sandy had fought, saw Red Connors appear over the rim and dash away to join in the fighting. Waiting long enough to assure himself that there were none following Red he ran to the edge and knelt by the rope. Leaving his rifle behind and seeing that the flap of his holster was fastened securely, he lowered himself over, sliding rapidly down to the first ledge. Here he spent a minute, a minute that seemed an eternity, hunting for the second rope in the shadows, found it and went on.

Sliding and bumping down the rough wall he at last reached the plain and, with a sigh of relief, turned to run. At that instant a figure leaped upon him from behind and a hand gripped his throat and jerked him over backwards. Antonio instinctively reached for his Colt with one hand while he tore at the gripping fingers with the other, but he found himself pinned down between two rocks in such a manner that his whole weight and that of his enemy was on the holster and made his effort useless. Then, terrified and choking for breath, he dug wildly at the vise-like fingers which not for a moment relaxed, but in vain, for he was growing weaker with each passing second.

Doc leaned forward, peering into the face before him, his fingers gripping with all their power, gripping with a force which made the muscles of the brawny forearm stand out like cords, his face malevolent and his heart full of savage joy. Here was the end of his hunt, here was the man who had murdered Curley in cold blood, cowardly, deliberately. The face, already dark, was turning black and the eyes were growing wide open and bulging out. He felt the surge of Antonio's pulse, steadily growing weaker. But he said no word as he watched and gloated, he was too intent to speak, too centered upon the man under him, too busy keeping his fingers tight-gripped. He would make good his threat, he would keep his word and kill the murderer of his best friend with his naked hands, as he had sworn.

Up above the two Cavalry, working along the edge, had come across Antonio's rifle and then as he glanced about, saw the rope. Here was where the cowmen had come up and here was where he could go down. From the way the shooting continued he knew that the fight was desperate and he believed himself to be cut off from his friends. He hated to desert in the face of the enemy, to leave his companions of a dangerous business to fight for their lives without him, but there was only one thing to do since he could not help them—he must save himself.

Dropping his rifle beside the other he lowered himself over the edge and slid rapidly down. When halfway down the last rope his burning hands slipped and he fell head over heels, and landed on Doc, knocking him over and partially stunning him. Cavalry's only idea now was to get from the men who, as he thought, were guarding the rope and, hastily picking himself up, he dashed towards the chaparral to the west as fast as he could run, every moment expecting to feel the hot sting of a bullet. At last, when the chaparral closed about him he plunged through it recklessly and ran until sheer exhaustion made him drop insensible to the sand. He had run far, much farther than he could have gone were it not for the stimulus of the fear which gripped him; and had he noticed where he was going he would have known that he was running up a slope, a slope which eventually reached a level higher than the top of the mesa. And when he dropped if he had been capable of observation he would have found himself in a chaparral which arose above his head, and seen the narrow lane through it which led to a great expanse of sand, tawney and blotched with ash-colored alkali, an expanse which stretched away to the desolate horizon.

Shortly after Cavalry's descent Antonio stirred, opened his eyes, stared vaguely about him and, feeling his bruised and aching throat, staggered to his feet and stumbled to the east, hardly conscious of what he was doing. As he proceeded his breath came easier and he began to remember having seen Doc lying quiet against a rock. He hesitated a moment as he wondered if Doc was dead and if so, who had killed him. Then he swore because he had not given him a shot to make sure that he would not rejoin his friends. Hesitating a moment he suddenly decided that he would be better off if he put a good distance between himself and the mesa, and ran on again, eager to gain the shelter of the chaparral.

When Doc opened his eyes and groped around he slowly remembered what had occurred and his first conscious act was to look to see if his expected victim were dead or alive. It did not take him long to realize that he was alone and his hand leaped for his Colt as he peered around. Limping out on the plain he caught sight of Antonio running, rapidly growing indistinct, and hazarded two shots after him. Antonio leaped into a new speed as though struck with a whip and cursed himself for not having killed the H2 puncher when he had the chance. A moment more and he was lost in the thickets. Doc tried to follow, but his leg, hurt by Cavalry's meteoric descent, was not equal to any great demand for speed and so, turning, he made his way towards the camp to get a horse and return to take up Antonio's trail.

He lost an hour in this, a feverishly impatient hour, punctuated with curses as he limped along and with an unsparing quirt once he was astride. What devilish Humpty Dumpty had cheated him this time? "All the king's horses and all the king's men couldn't put Humpty Dumpty together again." He laughed grimly and swore again as the cranky beast beneath him shied a pain into his sore leg. "Go on, you!" he yelled, as he swept up to where the ropes still dangled against the wall. The world was not big enough to hide the murderer of Curley, to save him from his just deserts. The two trails lay plain before him in the brilliant moonlight and his pony sprang forward toward the spot where Antonio had disappeared in the chaparral.

CHAPTER XXXII

Nature Takes a Hand

WHEN HOPALONG caught up with his four companions he was astonished by the conditions on the mesa. Instead of a boulder-strewn, rocky plain as he had believed it to be he found himself on a table-land cut and barred by fissures which ran in all directions. At one time these had been open almost to the level of the surrounding pasture but the winds had swept sand and debris into the gashes until now none were much more than ten feet deep. Narrow alleyways which led in every direction, twisting and turning, now blocked and now open for many feet in depth, their walls sand-beaten to a smoothness baffling the grip of one who would scale them, were not the same in a fight as a comparatively flat plain broken only by miscellaneous bowlders and hummocks. There could be no concerted dash for the reason that one group of the attacking force might be delayed until after another had begun to fight. And it was possible, even probable, that the turns in the alleyways might be guarded; and once separated in the heat of battle it would be easy enough to shoot each other. Instead of a dashing fight soon to be over, it looked as though it would be a deadly game of hide and seek to wear out the players and which might last for an indefinite length of time. It was disconcerting to find that what had been regarded as the hardest part of the whole affair, the gaining of the mesa top, was the easiest.

"Here, fellows!" Hopalong growled. "We'll stick together till we get right close, an' then if we have time an' these infernal gorges don't stop us, we may be able to spread out. We've got to move easy, too. If we go galloping reckless we'll run into some guard an' there won't be no surprise party on Thunder Mesa. We can count on having light, though not as much as we might have, for th' moon won't go back on us till th' sun fades it."

"It's light enough," growled Skinny. "Come on— we've got to go ahead an' every minute counts. *I* don't think we'd lose so much time roping them knobs an' getting up."

They moved forward cautiously in single file, alert and straining eyes and ears, and had covered half of the distance when a shot was heard ahead and they listened, expecting an uproar. Waiting a minute and hearing nothing further, they moved on again, angry and disgruntled. Then another shot rang out and they heard Billy and Curtis reply.

"Shooting before daylight, before they get their morning's grub," grumbled George Cross.

"Yes; sort of eye-opener, I reckon," softly laughed Chick Travers, who was nervous and impatient. "Get a move on an' let's start something," he added.

As they separated to take advantage of a spoke-like radiation of several intersecting fissures another shot rang out ahead and there was an angry *spat*! close to Hopalong's head. Another shot and then a rattling volley sent the punchers hunting cover on the run, but they were moving forward all the time. It was a case

of getting close or be killed at a range too great for
Colts, and their rifles were in the camp. Had the light
been better the invaders might have paid dearly right
there for the attack.

Confusion was rife among the defenders and the
noise of the shouts and firing made one jumble of
sound. Bullets whistled along the fissures in the dim
light and hummed and whizzed as they ricochetted
from wall to wall. As yet the attacking force had made
no reply, being too busily occupied in getting close to
lose time in wasting lead at that range, and being only
five against an unknown number protected by a stone
hut and who knew every boulder, crevice, and other
points of vantage.

Hopalong slid over a bowlder which choked his particular and personal fissure and saw Jim Meeker sliding
down the wall in front of it. And as Meeker picked
himself up Skinny Thompson slid down the other wall.

"Well, I'm hanged!" grunted Hopalong in astonishment.

"Same here," retorted Skinny. "What you doing 'way
over here?"

"Thought you was going to lead th' other end of th'
line!" rejoined Hopalong.

"This is it—yo're off yore range."

"Well, I reckon not!" Hopalong responded, indignantly.

"An' say, Meeker, how'd you get over here so quick?"
Skinny asked, turning to the other. "You was down
below when I saw you last."

"*Me*? Why, I just follered my nose, that's all," Meeker
replied, surprised.

"You've got a blamed crooked nose, then," Skinny
snorted, and turned to Hopalong. "Why don't you un-
tangle yoreself an' go where you belong, you carrot-
headed blunderer!"

"Hang it! I tell you—" Hopalong began, and then

ducked quickly. "Lord, but somebody's got us mapped out good!"

"Well, some of our fellers have started up—hear 'em over there?" exclaimed Skinny as firing broke out on the east. "Them's Colts, all right. Mebby it's plumb lucky for us it *ain't* so blamed light, after all; we'll have time to pick our places before they can see us real good."

"Pick our places!" snorted Hopalong. "Get tangled up, you mean!" he added.

"Hullo! What you doing, fellers?" asked a pained and surprised voice above them. "Why ain't you in it?"

"For th' love of heaven—it's Frenchy!" cried Hopalong. "Skinny, I reckon them Colts you heard belonged to th' rustlers. *We're* all here but a couple."

"Didn't I leave you over east five minutes ago, Frenchy?" demanded Skinny, his mouth almost refusing to shut.

"Shore. I'm east—what's eating at you?" asked Frenchy.

"Come on—get out of this!" ordered Hopalong, scrambling ahead. "You foller me an' you'll be all right."

"We'll be back to th' ropes if we foller you," growled Skinny. "Of all th' locoed layouts I ever run up against this here mesa top takes th' prize," he finished in disgust.

Bullets whined and droned above them and frequently hummed down the fissure to search them out, the high, falsetto whine changing quickly to an angry *spang!* as they struck the wall a slanting blow. They seemed to spring away again with renewed strength as they sang the loud, whirring hum of the ricochette, not the almost musical, sad note of the uninterrupted bullet, but venomous, assertive, insistent. The shots could be distinguished now, for on one side were the sharp cracks of rifles; on the other a different note, the roar of Colts.

"This ain't no fit society for six-shooters," Meeker

remarked in a low voice as they slid over a ridge, and dropped ten feet before they knew it.

"For th' Lord's sake!" ejaculated Hopalong as he arose to his feet. "Step over a rock an' you need wings! Foller a nice trail an you can't get out of th' cussed thing! Go west an' you land east, say 'solong' to a friend an' you meet him a minute later!"

"We ought to have rifles in this game," Meeker remarked, rubbing his knee-cap ruefully.

"Yes; an' ladders, ropes, an' balloons," snorted Skinny.

"Send somebody back for th' guns," suggested Frenchy.

"Who?" demanded Hopalong. "Will *you* go?"

"Me? Why, I don't want no rifle."

"Huh! Neither do I," remarked Skinny. "Here, Frenchy, give me a boost up this wall—take my hand."

"Well, don't wiggle so, you!"

"That's right! Walk backwards. I ain't no folding stepladder! How do you think I'm going to grab that edge if you takes me ten feet away from it?"

Spang! Spang! Zing-ing-ing!

"Here, you! Lemme down! Want me to get plugged!" yelled Skinny, executing ungraceful and rapid contortions. "Lower me, you fool!"

"Let go that ridge, then!" retorted Frenchy.

During the comedy Hopalong had been crawling up a rough part of the wall and he fired before he lost his balance. As he landed on Meeker a yell rang out and the sound of a rifle clattering on rock came to them. "I got him, Skinny—go ahead now," he grunted, picking himself up.

It was not long until they were out of the fissure and crawling down a boulder-strewn slope. As they came to the bottom they saw a rustler trying to drag himself to cover and Meeker fired instantly, stopping the other short.

"Why, I thought *I* stopped him!" exclaimed Hopalong.

"Reckon you won't rustle no more cows, you thief," growled Meeker, rising to his knees.

Hopalong pulled him down again as a bullet whizzed through the space just occupied by his head. "Don't you get so curious," he warned. "Come on—I see Red. He's got his rifle, lucky cuss."

"Good for him! Wish I had mine," replied Meeker, grinning at Red, who wriggled an elbow as a salutation. In his position Red could hardly be expected to do much more, since two men were waiting for a shot at him.

"Well, you can get that gun down there an' have a rifle," Hopalong suggested, pointing to the Winchester lying close to its former owner. "You can do it, all right."

"Good idea—shoot 'em with their own lead," and the H2 foreman departed on his hands and knees for the weapon.

"I hit one—he's trying to put his shoulder together," hollered Red, grinning. "What makes you so late—I was th' last one up, an' I've been here a couple of hours."

"You're a sinful liar!" retorted Hopalong. "We stopped to pick blackberries back at that farm house," he finished with withering sarcasm.

"You fellers had time to get married an' raise a family," Red replied. He ducked and looked around. "Ah, you coyote—hit him, but not very hard, I reckon."

It was daylight when Pete, on the other end of the line, turned and scourged Johnny. "Ain't you got no sense in yore fool head? How can I see to shoot when you kick around like that an' fill my eyes with dirt! Come down from up there or I'll lick you!"

"Ah, shut up!" retorted Johnny with a curse. "You'd kick around if somebody nicked *yore* ear!"

"Well, it serves you right for being so unholy curious!" Pete replied. "You come down before he nicks yore eye!"

"Not before I get square—*Wow!*" and Johnny came down rapidly.

"Where'd he get you that time?"

"None of yore business!" growled Johnny.

"I told you to come—"

"Shut up!" roared Johnny, glaring at him. "Wish I had that new Sharps of mine!"

"Go an' get it, Kid. Yo're nimble," Pete responded. "An' bring up some of th' others, too, while yo're about it."

"But how long will this fight last, do you reckon?" the other asked, with an air of weighing something.

"All day with rifles—a week without 'em."

"Shore yo're right?"

"Yes; go ahead. There'll be some of th' scrap left for you when you get back."

"All right—but don't you get that feller. I want him for what he did to me," and Johnny hastened away. He returned in fifteen minutes with two rifles and gave one of them to his companion.

"They're .45–70's—an' full, too," he remarked. "But I ain't got no more cartridges for 'em."

"How'd you get 'em so quick?"

"Found 'em by th' rope where we came up—didn't have to stop; just picked 'em up an' came right back," Johnny laughed. "But I wonder how they got there?"

"Bet four dollars an' a tooth-pick they means that two thieves got away down them ropes. Where's Doc?"

"Don't know—but I don't think anybody pulled him up here."

"Then he might 'a stopped them two what owned th' rifles—he would be mad enough to stay there a month if Red forgot him."

"Yes; waiting to lick Red when he came down," and Johnny crawled up again to his former position. "Now, you cow-stealing coyote, watch out!" As he settled down he caught sight of his foreman. "Hullo, Buck! What yo doing?"

"Stringing beads for my night shirt," retorted Buck. "You get down from up there, you fool!"

"Can't. I got to pay for—" He ducked, and then fired twice. "Just missed th' other ear, Pete. But I made him jump a foot—plugged him where he sits down. He was moving away.

"Yes; an' you took two shots to do it, when cartridges are so scarce," Pete grumbled.

At first several of the rustlers had defended the hut but the concentrated fire of the attacking force had poured through its north window from so many angles that evacuation became necessary. This was accomplished through the south window, which opened behind the natural breastwork, and at a great cost, for Con Irwin and Sam Austin were killed in the move.

The high, steep ridge which formed the rear wall of the hut and overlooked the roof of the building ran at right angles to the low breastwork and extended from the north end of the hut to the edge of the mesa, a distance of perhaps fifty feet. On the side farthest from the breastwork it sloped to the stream made by the spring and its surface was covered with bowlders. The rustlers, if they attempted to scale its steep face, would be picked off at short range, but they realized that once the enemy gained its top their position would be untenable except around the turn in the breastwork at the other side of the mesa. In order to keep the punchers from gaining this position they covered the wide cut which separated the ridge from the enemy's line and so long as they could command this they were safe.

After wandering from point to point Hopalong finally came to the edge of the cut and found Red Connors ensconced in a narrow, shallow depression on a comparatively high hummock. While they talked his eyes rested on the ridge across the cut and took in the possibilities that holding it would give.

"Say, Red, if we could get up on that hill behind th'

shack we'd have this fight over in no time—see how it overlooks everything?"

"Yes," slowly replied Red. "But we can't cross this barranca—they sweep it from end to end. I tried to get over there, an' I know."

"But we can try again," Hopalong replied. "You cover me."

"Now don't be a fool, Hoppy!" his friend retorted. "We can't afford to lose you for no gang of rustlers. It's shore death to try it."

"Well, you can bet I ain't going to be fool enough to run twenty yards in th' open," Hopalong replied, starting away. "But I'm going to look for a way across, just th' same. Keep me covered."

"All right, I'll do my best—but don't you try no dash!"

But the rustlers had not given up the idea of holding the ridge themselves, and there was another and just as important reason why they must have it; their only water was in the hut and the spring. To enter the building was certain death, but if they could command the ridge it would be possible to get water, for the spring and rivulet lay on the other side at its base. Hall, well knowing the folly of trying to scale the steep bank under fire, set about finding another way to gain the coveted position. He found a narrow ledge on the face of the mesa wall, at no place more than eight inches wide, and he believed that it led to the rear of the ridge. Finding that the wall above the narrow foothold was rough and offered precarious finger holds, he began to edge along it, a hundred feet above the plain. When he had almost reached the end of his trying labors he was discovered by Billy and Curtis, who lay four hundred yards away in the chaparral, and at once became the target for their rifles. Were it not for the fact that they could not shoot at their best because of their wounds Hall would never have finished his attempt, and as it was the bullets flattened against the wall so close to him that on two occasions he was struck by spattering lead and flecks of stone. Then he moved around the turn and was free from that danger, but found that he must get fifty yards north before he could gain the plateau again. To make matters worse the ledge he was on began to grow narrower and at one place disappeared altogether. When he got to the gap he had to cling to the rough wall and move forward inch by inch, twice narrowly missing a drop to the plain below. But he managed to get across it and strike the ledge again and in a few minutes more he stepped into a crevice and sat down to rest before he pushed on. When he looked around he found that the crevice led northeast and did not run to the ridge, and he swore as he realized that he must go through the enemy's line to gain the position. He would not risk going back the way he had come, for he was pretty well tired out. He thought of trying to get to the other end of the mesa so as to escape by the way the attacking force had come up, but immediately put it out of his mind as being too contemptible for further consideration. He arose and moved forward, seeking a way up the wall of the crevice—and turning a corner, bumped into Jim Meeker.

There was no time for weapons and they clinched. Meeker scorned to call for help and Hall dared make no unnecessary noise while in the enemy's line and so they fought silently. Both tried to draw their Colts, Meeker to use his either as a gun or a club, Hall as a club only, and neither succeeded. Both were getting tired when Hall slipped and fell, the H2 foreman on top of him. At that instant Buck Peters peered down at them from the edge of the fissure and then dropped lightly. He struck Hall over the head with the butt of his Colt and stepped back, grinning.

"There'll be a lot more of these duets if this fight drags out very long," Buck said. "This layout is shore loco with all its hidden trails. Have you got a rope, Jim? We'll tie this gent so he won't hurt hisself if you can find one."

"No. Much obliged, Peters," Meeker replied. "Why, yes I have, too. Here, use this," and he quickly untied his neck-kerchief and gave it to his friend. Buck took the one from around Hall's neck and the two foremen gave a deft and practical exhibition of how to tie a man so he cannot get loose. Meeker took the Winchester from Hall's back, the Colt and the cartridge belt, and gave them to Buck, laughing.

"Seventy-three model; .44 caliber," he explained. "You'll find it better than th' six-shooter, an' you'll have plenty of cartridges for it, too."

"But don't you want it?" asked Buck, hesitating.

"Nope. I left one around th' corner here. I can get along with it till I get my own from th' camp."

"All right, Jim. I'll be glad to keep this—it'll come in handy."

"Tough luck, finding them fellers in such a strong layout," Meeker growled, glancing around at the prisoner. "Ah, got yore eyes open, hey?" he ejaculated as Hall glared at him. "How many of you fellers are up here, anyhow?"

"Five thousand!" snapped Hall. "It took two of you to get me!" he blazed. "Got my guns, too, ain't you? Hope they bust an' blow yore cussed heads off!"

"Thanks, stranger, thanks," Buck replied, turning to leave. "But Meeker had you licked good—I only hurried it to save time. Coming, Jim?"

"Shore. But do you think this thief can get loose?"

Buck paused, searching his pockets, and smiled as he brought to light a small, tight roll of rawhide thongs. "Here, this'll keep him down," and when they had finished their prisoner could move neither hands nor feet. They looked at him critically and then went away towards the firing, the rustler cursing them heartily.

"What's the matter, Meeker?" asked Buck suddenly, noticing a drawn look on his companion's face.

"Oh, I can't help worrying about my girl. She ain't scared of nothing an' she likes to ride. She's too pretty to go breezing over a range that's covered with rustling skunks. I told her to stay in th' house, but—"

"Well, why in thunder don't you go back where you can take care of her?" Buck demanded, sharply. "She's worth more than all th' cows an' rustlers on earth. You ain't needed bad out here, for we can clean this up, all right. You know as long as there are fellers like us to handle a thing like this no man with a girl depending on him has really got any right to take chances. I never thought of it before, or I'd 'a told you so. You cut loose for home to-day, an' leave us to finish this."

"Well, I'll see how things go to-morrow, then. I can pull out th' next morning if everything is all right out here." He hesitated a moment, looking Buck steadily in the eyes, a peculiar expression on his face. "Peters, yo're a good man, one of th' best I ever met, an' you've got a good outfit. I don't reckon we'll have no more trouble about that line of yourn, not nohow. When we settle down to peace an' punching again I'm going to let you show me how to put down some wells at th' southern base of yore hills, like you said one day. If I can get water, a half as much as you got in th' Jumping Bear, I'll be fixed all right. But I want to ask you a fair question, man to man. I ain't no real fool an' I've seen more than I'm supposed to, but I want to be shore about this, dead shore. What kind of a man is Hopalong Cassidy when it comes to women?"

Buck looked at him frankly. "If I had a daughter I wouldn't want a better man for her."

CHAPTER XXXIII

Doc Trails

DOC HAD not gone far into the chaparral before he realized that his work was going to be hard. The trail was much fainter than it would have been if the man he followed were mounted; the moonlight failed to penetrate the chaparral except in irregular patches which made the surrounding shadows all the deeper by contrast; what little he saw of the trail led through places far too small and turning too sharply to permit being followed by a man on horseback, and lastly, he expected every minute to be fired upon, and at close range. He paused and thought a while—Antonio would head for Eagle, that being the only place where he could get assistance, and there he would find friends. Doc picked his way out of the labyrinth of tortuous alleys and finally came to a comparatively wide lane leading southeast. He rode at a canter now and planned how he would strike the fugitive's trail further down, and after he had ridden a few miles he was struck by a thought that stopped him at once.

"Hang it all, he might 'a headed for them construc-

tion camps or for one of th' north ranches, to steal a
cayuse," he muttered. "Th' only safe thing for me to do
is to jump his trail an' stop guessing, an' even then
mebby he'll get me before I get him. That's a clean
gamble, an' so here goes," wheeling and retracing his
course. When he again found the trail at the place he
had quit in, he dismounted and crawled along on his
hands and knees in order to follow the foot-prints
among the shadows. Then some animal bounded up in
front of him and leaped away, and as he turned to look
after it he caught sight of his horse standing on its hind
legs, and the next instant it was crashing through the
chaparral. Drawing his Colt and cursing he ran back in
time to see the horse gain an alleyway and gallop off.
Angered thoroughly he sent a shot after it and then
followed it, finally capturing it in a blind alley. Roundly
cursing the frightened beast he led it back to where he
had left the trail and, keeping one hand on the reins,
continued to follow the foot-prints. Day broke when he
had reached the edge of the chaparral and he mounted
with a sigh of relief and rode forward along the now
plainly marked trail.

As he cantered along he kept his eyes searching
every possible cover ahead of and on both sides of him,
watching the trail as far ahead as he could see it, for
Antonio might have doubled back to get a pursuer as
he rode past. After an hour of this caution he slapped
his thigh and grinned at his foolishness.

"Now ain't I a cussed fool!" he exclaimed. "A regular,
old-woman of a cow-puncher! He won't do no doubling
back or ambushing. He'll shore reckon on being trailed
by a bunch an' not by a locoed, prize-winning idiot.
Why, he's making th' best time he can, an' that's a-
plenty, too. Besides he ain't got no rifle. Lift yore feet,
you four-legged sage hen," he cried, spurring his horse
into a lope. He mechanically felt at the long rifle holster
at the saddle flap and then looked at it quickly. "An'
no rifle for *me*, neither! Oh, well, that's all right, too. I

don't need any better gun than he's got, th' coyote.
Canteen full of water an' saddle flaps stuffed with grub.
Why, old cayuse, if you can do without drinking till we
get back to th' mesa we'll be plumb happy. Wonder
when you was watered last?"

The trail had been swinging to the north more and
more and when Doc noted this fact he grinned again.

"Nice fool I'd 'a been hunting for these tracks down
towards Eagle, wouldn't I? But I wonder where he reckons he's going, anyhow?"

Sometime later he had his answers for he found himself riding towards a water hole and then he knew the
reason for the trail swinging north. He let his mare
drink its fill and while he waited he noticed a torn sombrero, then a spur, and further away the skeleton of a
horse. Looking further he saw the skeleton of a man,
all that the coyotes had left of the body of Dick Archer,
the man killed by Red on the day when he and Hopalong had discovered that Thunder Mesa was inhab-
ited. He pushed around the water hole and then caught
sight of something in the sand. Edging his mount over
to it he leaned down from the saddle and picked up a
Colt's revolver, fully leaded and as good as the day
Archer died. That air contained no moisture. As he
slipped it in a saddle bag he spurred forward at top
speed, for on the other side of a hummock he saw the
head and then the full figure of a man plodding away
from him, and it was Antonio.

The fugitive, hearing hoof-beats, looked back and
then dropped to one knee, his rifle going to his shoulder with the movement.

"Where in the hell did *he* get a rifle?" ejaculated Doc,
forcing his horse to buck-jump and pitch so as to be an
erratic target. "He didn't have none when *I* grabbed
him! Th' devil! That cussed skeleton back there gave
me a six-shooter, an' *him* a rifle!"

There was a dull smothered report and he saw Antonio drop the gun and rock back and forth, apparently

in agony, and he rode forward at top speed. Jerking his horse to its haunches he leaped off it just as Antonio wiped the blood from his eyes and jerked loose his Remington six-shooter. But his first shot missed and before he could fire again Doc grappled with him.

This time it was nearly an even break and Doc found that the slim figure of his enemy was made up of muscles of steel, that the lazy rider of the H2 ranch was, when necessary, quick as a cat and filled with the courage of desperation. It required all of Doc's attention and skill to keep himself from being shot by the other's gun and when he finally managed to wrest the weapon loose he was forced to drop it quickly and grab the same hand, which by some miracle of speed and dexterity now held a knife, a weapon far more deadly in hand-to-hand fighting. Once when believing himself to be gone the buckle of his belt stayed the slashing thrust and he again fought until the knife was above his head. Then, suddenly, two fingers flashed at his eyes and missed by so close a margin that Doc's eyebrows were torn open and his eyes blinded with blood. Instinct stronger than the effect of the disconcerting blindness made him hold his grip on the knife hand, else he would have been missing when his foreman looked for him at the mesa. He dug the fingers of his left hand, that had gripped around the waist, into his enemy's side and squeezed the writhing man tighter to him, wiping the blood from his eyes on the shirt of the other. As he did so he felt Antonio's teeth sink into his shoulder and a sudden great burst of rage swept over him and turned a man already desperate into a berserker, a mad man.

The grip tightened and then the brawny, bandaged left arm quickly slipped up and around Antonio's neck, pressing against the back of it with all the power of the swelling, knotted muscles. A smothered cry sobbed into his chest and he bent the knife hand back until the muscles were handicapped by their unnatural position and then, suddenly releasing both neck and hand, leaped back a step and the next instant his heavy boot thudded into the other's stomach and he watched the gasping, ghastly-faced rustler sink down in a nerveless heap, fighting desperately for the breath that almost refused to return.

Doc wiped his eyes free of blood and hastily bound his neck-kerchief around the bleeding eyebrows. As he knotted the bandage he stepped forward and picked up both the revolver and knife and threw them far from him. Glancing at the rifle he saw that it had burst and knew that the greased, dirty barrel had been choked with sand. He remembered how Curley's rifle had been leaded by the same cause and fierce joy surged through him at this act of retributive justice. He waited patiently, sneering and taunting him until the desperate man had gained his feet.

Doc stepped back a pace, tossing the burst rifle from him, and grinned malignantly. "Take yore own time. Get all yore wind an' strength. *I* ain't no murderer—I don't ride circles around a man an' potshoot him. I'm going to kill you fair, with my hands, like I said. Th' stronger you are th' better I'll feel when I leave you. An' if you should leave me out here on th' sand, all right—but it's got to be fair."

When fully recovered Antonio began the struggle by leaping forward, thinking his enemy unprepared. Doc faced him like a flash and bent low, barely escaping the other's kick. They clinched and swayed to and fro, panting, straining, every ounce of strength called into play. Then Doc got the throat hold again and took a shower of blows unflinchingly. His eyebrows, bleeding again, blinded him, but he could feel if he could not see. Slowly the resistance weakened and finally Doc wrestled Antonio to his knees, bending, and slowly tightening his grip; and the man who had murdered Curley went through all he had felt at the base of the mesa wall, at last paying with his life for his career of murder, theft, fear, and hypocrisy.

Doc arose and went to his horse. Leading the animal back to the scene of the struggle he stood a while, quietly watching for any sign of life, although he knew there would be none.

"Well, bronc, Curley's squared," he muttered, swinging into the saddle and turning the animal's head. "Come on, get out of this!" he exclaimed, quirting hard. As he passed the water hole he bowed to the broken skeleton. "Much obliged, stranger, whoever you was. Yore last play was a good one."

CHAPTER XXXIV

Discoveries

WHEN THE two foremen entered the firing line again they saw Red Connors and they cautiously went towards him. As they came within twenty feet of him Buck chanced to glance across the cut and what he saw brought a sudden smile to his face.

"Meeker, Red has got that spring under his gun!" he exclaimed in a low voice. "They can't get within ten feet of it or within ten feet of th' water at any point along its course. This is too good to bungle—wait for me," and he ran out of sight around a bend in the crevice, Meeker staring across at the spring, his eyes following the rivulet until it flowed into the deep, narrow cut it had worn in the side of the mesa.

Red looked around. "Why, hullo, Meeker! Where's Buck? Thought I heard him a minute ago. If you have any water to spare I can use some of it. Some thief drilled my canteen when I went fooling along this barranca, an' I ain't got a drop left."

Meeker began to move closer to him, Red warning him to be careful, and adding, "Three of them fellers ain't doing nothing but watch this cut. Scared we'll get across it an' flank 'em, I reckon."

"Do you know that yo're covering their water supply?" Meeker asked, handing his canteen to his thirsty companion. "They can't get to it as long as you stay here. That's why they're after you so hard."

Red wiped his lips on his sleeve and sighed contentedly. "It's blamed hot, but it's wet. But is that right? Am I keeping 'em thirsty? Where's th' water?"

"Shore you are! it's right over there—see that little ditch?" Meeker replied, pointing.

Bing! Spat!

The H2 foreman dropped his arm and grinned. "They're watching us purty close, ain't they? Didn't miss me far, at that," showing his companion a torn sleeve and a lead splotch on the rock behind him.

"Not a whole lot. Two of them fellers can shoot like blazes. Yo're plumb lucky," Red responded. "If you'd showed more'n your sleeve that time they'd 'a hit you." He looked across the cut and puckered his brow. "Well, if that's where their water is they don't get none. Mebby we can force 'em out if we watches that spring right smart."

"Here comes Buck now, with Skinny."

"It's too good a card to lose, Skinny," the Bar-20 foreman was saying as he approached. "You settle some place near there where you can pot anybody that tries for a drink. Mebby this little trick wins th' game for us—*quien sabe*? Hullo, Red; where's yore side pardner?"

"Oh, he went prospecting along this barranca to see if he could get across," Red replied. "He wants to get up on top of that ridge behind th' shack. Says if he can do it th' fight won't last long. See how it overlooks their layout?"

Buck looked and his eyes glistened. "An' he's right, too, like he is generally. That's th' key, an' it lies between them an' th' spring. Beats all how quick that

feller can size up a hand. If he could play poker as well
as he can fight he could quit working for a living."

"Yes; yo're shore right," Red replied.

Several shots rang out from the breastwork and the
bullets hummed past them down the cut. A burst of
derisive laughter replied fifty yards to their right and a
taunt followed it. More shots were fired and answered
by another laugh and taunt, inducing profanity from
the marksman, and then Hopalong called to Red. "Six
out of seven went plumb through my sombrero, Red,
when I poked it out to find out if they was looking.
They was. Purty good for 'em, eh?"

"Too blamed good to suit me—lucky yore head
wasn't in it," Red replied.

Hopalong, singing in stentorian voice an original version of "Mary and Her Little Lamb" in which it seemed
he aspired to be the lamb, finally came into view with
a perforated sombrero in his hand, which he eyed ruefully. "A good roof gone up, but I didn't reckon everybody was looking my way," he grumbled. "Somebody
shore has got to pay for that lid, too," then he glanced
up, saw Meeker, and looked foolish. "Howd'y, Meeker;
what's new, Buck?"

"Hey, Hoppy! Did you know I was covering their
drinking water?" asked Red, triumphantly.

"I knowed you was covering some of it, but you
needn't take on no airs about it, for you didn't know
it," Hopalong retorted. "What *I* want to know is why
you wasn't covering *me*, like you said you would! It's
all yore fault that my Stetson's bust wide open, an' that
being so, we'll just swap, right now, too!" suiting the
action to the words.

"Hey! Gimme that war-bonnet, you bunch of gall!"
yelled Red kicking at his tormentor and missing.
"Gimme that, d'y hear!"

"Give you a punch in th' eye, you sheep!" retorted
Hopalong, backing away. "Think you can get away with

a play like that after saying you was going to cover me? *I* ain't no papoose, you animated carrot!"

"Gimme that Stetson!" Red commanded, starting to rise. There was a sharp hum and he dropped back again, blood flowing from his cheek, that being the extent of his person he had so inadvertently exposed. "There, blank you! See what you made me do! Going to drop that hat?"

"Why don't you give 'em a good shot at you? That ain't no way to treat 'em—but honest, Red, you shouldn't get so excited over a little thing like that," Hopalong replied. "Now, I'll leave it to Meeker, here— hadn't I ought to take his roof?"

Meeker laughed. "Th' Court reserves its decision, but possession is nine points in law."

"Huh! Possession is everything. Since I can keep it, why, then, according to th' Court, th' hat belongs to me. Hear that, Red?"

"Yes, I hear it! An' if I wasn't so cussed busy I'd show you how long you'd keep it," Red rejoined. "I'll bet you a hat you don't keep it a day after we get this off'n our hands. Bow-legged cuss, you!"

"Done—then I'll have two hats; one for work an' one to wear when I'm visiting." Hopalong laughed. "But you've got th' best of th' swap, anyhow. That new lid of yourn, holes an' all, is worth twice as much as this wool thing I'm getting for it. My old one is a *hat*!"

Red refused to lower his dignity by replying and soon fired. "Huh! Reckon that feller won't shoot no more with his right hand."

"Say, I near forgot to tell you Meeker captured one of them fellers out back; got him tied up now," Buck remarked, relating the incident, Meeker interrupting to give the Bar-20 foreman all the credit.

"Good!" exclaimed Red. "It's a rope necktie for him. An' one less to shoot at me."

"An' *you* here, Buck!" cried Hopalong in surprise.

"Come on, lead th' way! How do you know he was th' only one to get behind us! Good Lord!"

"Gosh, yo're right!" Buck exclaimed, running off. "Come on, Jim. We're a pair of fools, after all!"

At the other end of the line Chick Travers and George Cross did as well as they could with their Colts, but found their efforts unavailing. Their positions were marked by the rustlers and they had several narrow escapes, both being wounded, Cross twice. Ten yards west of them Frenchy McAllister was crawling forward a foot at a time from cover to cover and so far he had not been hit. His position also had been marked and he was now trying to find a new one unobserved, where he could have a chance to shoot once without instantly being fired upon. Pete and Johnny had separated, the latter having given up his attempt to make the rustler pay for his wounded ear. He had emptied the magazine of the rifle he had found and now only used his Colt. As he worked along the firing line he saw Frenchy ten yards in front of him, covered nicely by a steep rise in the ground.

"How are you doing out there, Frenchy?" he asked in a low voice.

"Not very good; wish I had my rifle," came the soft-spoken reply.

"I had one that I found, but I used up all th' cartridges there was in th' magazine."

"What kind an' caliber?"

"45–70 Winchester. I found it by th' ropes. Pete says he reckoned some rustler must have left it behind an' got away down th'—"

"Get it for me, Kid, will you?" interrupted Frenchy, eagerly. "I plumb forgot to leave my belt of rifle cartridges back in th' camp. Got it on now, an' it's chock full, too. Hurry up, an' I'll work back to you for it."

"What luck! In a second," Johnny exulted, disappearing. Returning with the rifle he handed it to his friend and gazed longingly at the beltful of rifle cartridges. "Say, Frenchy," he began. "You know we'll all have our rifles to-night, an' you've got more cartridges for that than you can use before then. It won't be more than three hours before we send for ours. Suppose you gimme some of them for Pete—he's got th' mate to that gun, an' can't use it no more because it's empty."

"Shore, Kid," and Frenchy slipped a handful of cartridges out of his belt and gave them to Johnny. "With my compliments to Pete. What was that you was saying about rustlers an' th' ropes?"

Johnny told of Pete's deductions regarding the finding of the rifles and Frenchy agreed with them, and also that Doc had taken care of the owners of the weapons when they had reached the plain.

"Well, I'm going further away from them thieves now that I've got something to shoot with," Frenchy asserted. "They won't be looking for any of us a hundred yards or more farther back. Mebbe I can catch some of 'em unawares."

"I'll chase off an' give Pete these pills," Johnny replied. "He'll be tickled plumb to death. He was cussing bad when I left him."

George Cross, crawling along a steep, smooth rock barely under the shelter of a bowlder, endeavored to grasp the top, but under-reached and slipped, rolling down to the bottom and in plain sight of the rustlers. As his companion, Chick Travers, tried to help him two shots rang out and Cross, sitting up with his hands to his head, toppled back to arise no more. Chick leaped up and fired twice at one of the marksmen, and missed. His actions had been so sudden and unexpected that he escaped the return shot which passed over him by a foot as he dropped back to cover. Somehow the whole line seemed to feel that there had been a death among them, as evidenced by the burst of firing along it. And the whole line felt another thing; that the cartridges of the rustlers were getting low, for they seemed to be saving their shots. But it was Hopalong who found the cause of the diminishing fire. After hunting fruitlessly with the two foremen and finding that Hall was the only man to get back of the firing line he left his two companions in order to learn the condition of his friends. As he made his way along the line he chanced to look towards the hut and saw four rifles on the floor of it, and back of them, piled against the wall, was the rustlers' main supply of ammunition. Calling out, he was answered by Pete, who soon joined him.

"Pete, you lucky devil, turn that rifle through th' door of th' shack an' keep it on them cartridges," he ordered. "They ain't been shooting as fast as they was at first, an' there's th' reason for it. Oh, just wait till daylight to-morrow! They won't last long after that!"

"They won't get them cartridges, anyhow," Pete replied with conviction.

"Hey, fellers," cried a voice, and they looked around to see Chick Travers coming towards them. "Yore man Cross has passed. He rolled off his ledge an' couldn't stop. They got him when he hit th' bottom of it."

"Damn 'em!" growled Hopalong. "We'll square our accounts to-morrow morning. Pete, you watch them cartridges."

"Shore—" *Bang!* "Did you see that?" Pete asked, frantically pumping the lever of his rifle.

"Yes!" cried Chick. "Some feller tried to get in that south window! Bet he won't try again after that hint. Hear him cuss? There—Red must 'a fired then, too!"

"Good boy, Pete!—keep 'em out. We'll have somebody in there after dark," Hopalong responded. "They've got th' best covers now, but we'll turn th' table on 'em when th' sun comes up to-morrow."

"Here comes Buck an' Meeker," remarked Chick. "Them two are getting a whole lot chummy lately, all right. They're allus together."

"That's good, too. They're both of 'em all right," Hopalong replied, running to meet them. Chick saw the three engage in a consultation and look towards the hut and the ridge behind it, Buck and Meeker nodding slowly at what Hopalong was saying. Then they moved off towards the west where they could examine the building at closer range.

CHAPTER XXXV

Johnny Takes the Hut

AS THE day waned the dropping shots became less and less frequent and the increasing darkness began to work its magic. The unsightly plain with its crevices and boulders and scrawny vegetation would soon be changed into one smooth blot, to be lighted with the lurid flashes of rifles as Red and Pete fired at irregular intervals through the south windows of the hut to keep back any rustler who tried to get the ammunition within its walls. Two were trying and had approached the window just as a bullet hummed through it. They stopped and looked at each other and moved forward again. Then a bullet from Pete's rifle, entering through the open door, hummed out the window and struck against the rocky ridge.

"Say! Them coyotes can see us through that windy," remarked Clausen. 'Th' sky at our backs is too light yet."

"They can't see us standing here," objected Shaw.

"Then what are they shooting at?"

"Cuss me if I know. Looks like they was using th'

winder for a target. Reckon we better wait till it gets darker."

"If we wait till it's dark we can sneak in through th' door," suggested Clausen. "If we go in crawling we ain't likely to stop no shot high enough to go through that windy."

"You can if you wants, but I ain't taking no chances like that, none whatever."

Another shot whined through the window and stopped with an angry spat against the ridge. Shaw scratched his head reflectively. "It shore beats me why they keeps that up. There ain't no sense to it," he declared in aggrieved tones. "They don't know nothing about them cartridges in there."

"That's it!" exclaimed Clausen, excitedly. "I bet a stack of blues they do know. An' they're covering somebody going in to steal 'em. Oh, hell!" and he slammed his hat to the ground in bitter anger. "An' us a-standing here like a couple of mired cows! I'm going to risk it."

"Wait," advised Shaw. "Let's try a hat an' see if they plug it."

"Wait be damned! My feet are growing roots right now. I'm going in," and Clausen broke away from his friend and ran towards the hut, a crouching run, comical to look at but effective because it kept his head below the level of the window; without pausing in his stride his body lengthened into a supple curve as he plunged head foremost through the window, landing on the cabin floor with hands and feet bunched under him, his passing seen only as a fleeting puzzling shadow, by the watchful eyes outside.

Across the cut Johnny was giving Red instructions and turned to leave. "Th' cut is full of shadows an' th' moon ain't up yet. Now, remember, one more shot through that window—I'm going to foller it right in. Get word to Pete as soon as you can, though I won't pass

th' door. He's only got three cartridges left an' he'll be
getting some anxious about now. So long."

"So long, an' good luck, Kid," Red replied.

Johnny wriggled across the cut on his stomach, picking out the shadows and gaining the shelter of the opposite bank, stood up, and ran to the hut. Red fired and
then Johnny cautiously climbed through the window
and dropped to the floor.

He had anticipated Clausen by the fraction of a second. As his feet touched the floor the noise of Clausen's
arrival saluted him and the startled Johnny jerked his
gun loose and sent a shot in the other's direction, leaping aside on the instant. The flash of the discharge was
gone too quickly for him to distinguish anything and
the scrambling sound that followed mystified him further. That there had been no return shot did not cause
him to dance with joy, far otherwise; it made him drop
silently to his stomach and hunt the darkest part of the
hut, the west wall. He lay still for a minute, eyes and
ears strained for a sound to tell him where to shoot.
Then Red called to him and wanted an answer, whereupon Johnny thought of things he ached to call Red.
Then he heard a low voice outside the south window,
and it called: "Clausen, Clausen—what happened? Why
don't you answer?"

"Oh, so my guest is Clausen, hey?" Johnny thought.
"Wonder if Clausen can see in th' dark?' Nother damned
fool wanting an answer! I'll bet Clausen is hugging th'
dark spots, too. Wonder if I scared him as much as he
scared me?"

The suspense was becoming too much of a strain
and, poking his Colt out in front of him, he began to
move forward, his eyes staring ahead of him at the
place where Clausen ought to be.

Inch by inch he advanced, holding his breath as well
as he could, every moment expecting to have Clausen
salute him in the face with a hot .45. Johnny was
scared, and well scared, but in only proves courage to

go on when scared stiff, and Johnny went on and along
the wall he thought Clausen was using for a highway.

"Wonder how it feels to have yore brains blowed
out," he shivered. "For God's sake, Clausen, make a
noise—sneeze, cough, choke, yell, anything!" he
prayed, but Clausen remained ominously silent. Johnny
pushed his Colt out farther and poked it all around.
Touching the wall it made a slight scraping sound and
Johnny's blood froze. Still no move from Clausen, and
his fright went down a notch—Clausen was evidently
even more scared than he was. That was consoling.
Perhaps he was so scared that he couldn't pull a trigger,
which would be more consoling.

"Johnny! Johnny! Answer, can't you!" came Red's
stentorian voice, causing Johnny to jump a few inches
off the floor.

"Clausen! Clausen!" came another voice.

"For God sake, answer, Clausen! Tell 'em yo're here!"
prayed Johnny. "Yo're damned unpolite, anyhow."

By this time he was opposite the door and he wondered if Pete had been told not to bombard it. He
stopped and looked, and stared. What was that thing
on the floor? Or was it anything at all? He blinked and
moved closer. It looked like a head, but Johnny was
taking no chances. He stared steadily into the blackest
part of the hut for a moment and then looked again at
the object. He could see it a little plainer now, for it
was not quite as dark outside as it was in the building;
but he was not sure about it.

"Can't fool me, you coyote," he thought. "Yo're hugging this wall as tight as a tick on a cow, a blamed sight
tighter than I am, an' in about a minute I'm going to
shoot along it about four inches from th' floor. I'd just
as soon get shot as be scared to death, anyhow. Mebby
we've passed each other! An' Holy Medicine! Mebby
there's two of 'em!"

He regarded the object again. "That shore looks like
a head, all right." He felt a pebble under his hand and

drawing back a little he covered the questionable object and then tossed the pebble at it. "Huh, if it's a head, why in thunder didn't it move?"

There were footsteps outside the south window and he listened, the Colt ready to stop any one rash enough to look in, Clausen or no Clausen.

"Where's Clausen, Shaw?" said a voice, and the reply was so low Johnny could not make it out.

"Yes; that's just what I want to know," and Johnny stared in frowning intentness at the supposed head. He moved closer to the object and by dint of staring thought he saw the head and shoulders of a man face down in a black, shallow pool. Then his hand became wet and he jerked it back and wiped it on his sleeve; he could hardly believe his senses. As he grasped the significance of his discovery he grinned sheepishly and moved back to the north wall, where no rustler's bullet could find him. "Lord! An' I got him th' first crack! Got him shooting by ear!"

"Johnny! Johnny!" came Red's roar, anxious and querulous.

Johnny wheeled and shook his Colt out of the window, for the moment forgetting the peril of losing sight of the opening in the other wall. "I'll Johnny *you*, you blankety-blank fool!" he shouted. Then he heard a curse at the south window and turned quickly, his Colt covering the opening. "An' I'll Johnny you too, you cow-stealing coyotes! Stick yore thieving heads in that windy an' holler for yore Clausen! *I* can show you where he is, an' send you after him if you'll just take a look! Want them cartridges, hey? Well, come an' get 'em!"

A bullet, fired at an angle through the window, was the reply and several hummed through the open door and glanced off the steep sides of the ridge. Waiting until they stopped coming he dropped and wriggled forward along the west wall, feeling in front of him until he touched a box. Grasping it he dragged the important cartridges to him and then backed to the north window with them.

He fell to stuffing his pockets with the captured ammunition and then stopped short and grinned happily. "Might as well *hold* this shack an' wait for somebody to look in that windy. They can't get me."

He dropped the box and walked to the heavy plank door, slamming it shut. He heard the thud of bullets in it as he propped it, and laughed. "Can't shoot through them planks, they're double thick." He smelled his sticky fingers. "An' they're full of resin, besides."

He stopped suddenly and frowned as a fear entered his mind; and then smiled, reassured. "Nope; no rustling snake can climb up that ridge—not with Red an' Pete watching it."

CHAPTER XXXVI

The Last Night

FIFTY YARDS behind the firing line of the besiegers a small fire burned brightly in a steep-walled basin, casting grotesque shadows on the rock walls as men passed and re-passed. Overhead a silvery moon looked down at the cheerful blaze and from the cracks and crevices of the plain came the tuneful chorus of Nature's tiny musicians, sounding startlingly out of place where men were killing and dying. A little aside from the others three men in consultation reached a mutual understanding and turned to face their waiting friends just as Pete Wilson ran into the lighted circle.

"Hey, Johnny is in th' hut with th' cartridges," he exclaimed, telling the story in a few words.

"Good for th' Kid!"

"It's easy now, thanks to him."

"Why didn't he tell us he was going to try that?" demanded Buck. "Taking a chance like that on his own hook!"

"Scared you wouldn't let him," Pete laughed. "Red an' me backed him up with our rifles th' best we could.

He had a fight in there, too, judging from th' shot. He had me an' Red worried, thinking he might 'a been hit, but he was cussing Red when I left."

"Well, that helps us a lot," Buck replied. "Now I want three of you to go to camp an' bring back grub, rifles, an' cartridges. Pete, Skinny, Chick—yo're th' ones. Leave yore canteens here an' hustle! Hopalong, you an' Meeker go off somewhere an' get some sleep. I'll call you before it gets light. Frenchy, me an' you will take all th' canteens at hand an' fill 'em while we've got time. They won't be able to see us now. We'll pass Red an' get his, too. Come on."

When they returned they dropped the dripping vessels and began cleaning their Colts. That done they filled their pipes and sat cross-legged, staring into the fire. A snatch of Johnny's exultant song floated to them and Buck smiled, laying his pipe aside and rising. "Well, Frenchy, things'll happen in chunks when th' sun comes up. Something like old times, eh? There ain't no Deacon Rankin or Slippery Trendley here—" He stopped, having mentioned a name he had promised himself never to say in Frenchy's presence, and then continued in a subdued voice, bitterly scourging himself for his blunder. "They're stronger than I thought, an' they've shot us up purty well, killed Willis an' Cross, an' made fools of us for weeks on th' range; but this is th' end of it all. *We* deal to-morrow, an' we cut th' cards to-night."

Frenchy was strangely silent, staring fixedly at the fire. Buck glanced at him in strong sympathy, for he knew what his slip of the tongue had awakened in his friend's heart. Frenchy had adored his young wife and since the day he had found her murdered in his cabin on the Double Y he had been another man. When the moment of his vengeance had come, when he had her murderer in his power and saw his friends ride away to leave him alone with Trendley that day over in the Panhandle, to exact what payment he wished, then he had become his old self for a while, but it was not long before he again sank into his habitual carelessness, waiting patiently for death to remove his burden and make him free. His vengeance did not bring him back his wife.

Buck shook his head slowly and affectionately placed a heavy hand on his friend's shoulder. "Frenchy, won't you ever forget it? It hurts me to see you this way so much. It's over twenty years now an' day after day I've grieved to see you so unhappy. You paid him for it in yore own way. Can't you forget it now?"

"Yes; I killed him, an' slow. He never thought a man could make th' payment so hard, not even his black heart could realize it till he felt it," Frenchy replied, slowly and calmly. "He took th' heart out of me; he killed my wife and made my life a living hell. All I had worth living for went that day, an' if I could kill him over again every day for a year it wouldn't square th' score. I reckon I ain't built like other men. You never heard me whimper. I kept my poison to myself an' tried to do the best that was in me. An' you ain't never heard me say what I'm going to tell you now. I never believed in hunches, but something tells me that I'll leave all this behind me before another day passes. I felt it somehow when we left th' ranch an' it's been growing stronger every hour since. If I do pass out to-morrow, I want you to be glad of it, same as I would be if I could know. I'm going back to th' line now an' watch them fellers. So long."

The two men, bosom friends for thirty years, looked in each other's eyes as they grasped hands, and it was Buck's eyes that grew moist and dropped first. "So long, Frenchy—an' good luck, as you see it."

The foreman watched his friend until lost in the darkness and he thought he heard him singing, but of this he was not sure. He turned and stared at the fire for a minute, silent, immovable, and then breathed heavily.

"I never saw anybody carry a grief so long, never. I reckon it sort of turned his brain, coming so sudden an' in such a damnable way. I know it made me see red for a week. If I had only stayed there that day! When he got Trendley in th' Panhandle I hoped he would change, an' he did for a while, but that was all. He lived for that alone, an' since then I reckon he's felt he hadn't nothing to do with his life. He has been mixed up in a bunch of gun-arguments since then; but he didn't have no luck. Well, Frenchy, I hate to lose a friend like you, but here's better luck to-morrow, luck as you see it, friend!"

He kicked the fire together and was about to add fuel when he heard two quick shots and raised his head to listen. Then a ringing whoop came from the front and he recognized Johnny's voice. He heard Red call out and Johnny reply and he smiled grimly as he went towards the sounds. "Reckon somebody tried to get in that shack, like a fool. He must 'a been disgusted. How that Kid shore does love to fight!"

> *Joyous Joe got a juniper jag,*
> *A jogging out of Jaytown,*

came down the wind.

"Did you get him, Kid?" cried Buck from the firing line.

"Nope; got his hat, thought—but I shore got Clausen an' all of their cartridges!"

"Can you keep them shells alone?"

"*Can I? Wow,* ask th' other fellers! An' I'm eating jerked beef—sorry I can't give you some."

"Shut up about eating, you pig!" blazed Red, who was hungry.

"You'll eat hot lead to-morrow, all of you!" jeered a rustler's voice.

Red fired at the sound. "Take yourn now!" he shouted.

"You can't hit a cow!" came the taunt, while other strange voices joined in.

Buck found Red and ordered him to camp to get some sleep before Pete and the others returned, feeling that he and Frenchy were enough to watch. Red demurred sleepily and finally compromised by lying down at Buck's side, where he would be handy in case of trouble. Buck waited patiently, too heavily laden with responsibility to feel the need of rest, and when he judged that three hours had passed began to worry about the men he had sent to camp. Drawing back into a crevice he struck a match and looked at him.

"Twelve o'clock!" he muttered. "I'll wake Red an' see how Frenchy is getting on. Time them fellers were back too."

Frenchy changed his position uneasily and peered at the distant breastwork, hearing the low murmur of voices behind it. All night he had heard their curses, but a new note made him sit up and watch more closely. The moon was coming up now and he could see better. Suddenly he caught the soft flash of a silver sombrero buckle and fired instantly. Curses and a few shots replied and a new, querulous voice was added to the murmur, a voice expressing pain.

"I reckon you got him," remarked a quiet voice at his side as Buck lay down beside him. The foreman had lost some time in wandering along the whole line of defense and was later than he had expected.

"Yes; I reckon so," Frenchy replied without interest, and they lapsed into silence, the eloquent silence of men who understand each other. They heard a shot from below and knew that Billy or Curtis was about and smiled grimly at the rising murmur it caused among the rustlers. Buck glanced at the sky and frowned. "There can't be more'n five or six left by now, an' if it wasn't for th' moon I'd get th' boys together an' rush that bunch." He was silent for a moment and then added, half to himself, "but it won't be long now, an' we can wait."

Distant voices heralded the return of Pete and his companions and the foreman arose. "Frenchy, I'm going to place th' boys an' start things right away. We've been quiet too long."

"Might as well," Frenchy replied, "I'm getting sleepy—straining my eyes too much, I reckon, trying to see a little better than I can."

"Here's th' stuff, Buck," Skinny remarked as the foreman entered the circle of light. "Two day's fighting rations, fifty rounds for th' rifles an' fifty for th' Colts. Chick is coming back there with th' rifles."

"Good. Had yore grub yet?" Buck asked. "All right—didn't reckon you'd wait for it. What kept you so long? You've been gone over three hours."

"We was talking to Bill an' Curtis," Skinny remarked. "They're anxious to have it over. They've been spelling each other an' getting some sleep. We saw Doc's saddle piled on top of th' grub when we got to camp. It wasn't there when we all left th' other night. Billy says Doc came running past last night, saddled up an' rode off. He got back this afternoon wearing a bandage around his head. He didn't say where he had been, but now he is at th' bottom of th' trail waiting for a shot, so Billy says. Pete reckons he went after somebody that got down last night, one of them fellers that left their rifles up here by th' ropes."

"Mebby yo're right," replied Buck, hurriedly. "Get ready to fight. I ain't going to wait for daylight when this moonlight will answer. Pete, Skinny, Chick—you get settled out on th' east end, where me an' Frenchy will join you. We'll have this game over before long."

He strode away and returned with Hopalong and Meeker, who hastily ate and drank and, filling their belts with cartridges and taking their own rifles from the pile Chick had brought, departed toward the cut with orders for Red to come in.

Pete and his companions moved away as Frenchy, shortly followed by Red, came in and reported.

"Eat an' drink, lively. Red, you get back to yore place an' take care of th' cut," Buck ordered. "Frenchy, you come out east with th' rest. There's cartridges for you both an' there's yore own rifle, Frenchy."

"Glad yo're going to start things," chewed Red through a mouthful of food. "It's about time we show them fellers we can live up to our reputation. Any of 'em coming my way won't go far."

Frenchy filled his pipe and lighted it from a stick he took out of the fire and as it began to draw well he stepped quickly forward and held out his hand. "Good luck, Red. They can't fight long."

"Same to you, Frenchy. You look plumb wide awake, like Buck—how'd you do it?"

Frenchy laughed and strode after his foreman, Red watching him. "He's acting funny—reckon it's th' sleep he's missed. Well, here goes," and he, too, went off to the firing line.

> —An' aching thoughts pour in on me,
>   Of Whiskey Bill,

came Johnny's song from the hut—and the fight began again.

CHAPTER XXXVII

Their Last Fight

A FIGURE suddenly appeared on the top of the flanking ridge, outlined against the sky, and flashes of flame spurted from its hands, while kneeling beside it was another, rapidly working a rifle, the roar of the guns deafening because of the silence which preceded it. Shouts, curses, and a few random, futile shots replied from the breastworks, its defenders, panic-stricken by the surprise and the deadly accuracy of the two marksmen, scurrying around the bend in their fortifications, so busy in seeking shelter that they failed to make their shots tell. Two men, riddled by bullets, lay where they had fallen and the remaining three, each of them wounded more than once, crouched under cover and turned their weapons against the new factors; but these had already slid down the face of the ridge and were crawling along the breastwork, alert and cautious.

In front of the rustlers heavy firing burst out along the cowmen's line and Red Connors, from his old position above the cut, swung part way around and turned his rifle against the remnant of the defenders at an-

other angle, and fired at every mark, whether it was
hand, foot, or head; while Johnny, tumbling out of
the south window of the hut, followed in the wake of
Hopalong and Meeker. The east end of the line was
wrapped in smoke, where Buck and his companions
labored zealously.

Along the narrow trail up the mesa's face a man
toiled heavily and it was not long before Doc Riley
opened fire from the rear. The three rustlers, besieged
from all sides, found their positions to be most desperate and knew then that only a few minutes intervened
between them and eternity. They had three choices—
to surrender, to die fighting, or to leap from the mesa
to instant death below.

Shaw, to his credit, chose the second and like a cornered
wolf goaded to despair leaped up and forward to take a
gambler's chance of gaining the hut. Before him were Hopalong, Meeker, Johnny, and Doc. Doc was hastily reloading
his Colt, Johnny was temporarily out of sight as he crawled
around a boulder, and Hopalong was greatly worried by
ricochettes and wild shots from the rifles of his friends which
threatened to end his career. Meeker alone was watching
at that moment but his attention was held by the rustler
near the edge of the mesa who was trying to shrink himself
to fit the small rock in front of him and to use his gun at
the same time.

Shaw sprang from his cover and straight at the H2
foreman, his foot slipping slightly as he fired. The bullet
grazed Meeker's waist, but the second, fired as the rustler was recovering his balance, bored through Meeker's shoulder. The H2 foreman, bending forward for a
shot at the man behind the small rock, was caught unawares and his balance, already strained, was de-
stroyed by the shock of the second bullet, and he
flopped down to all fours. Shaw sprang over him just
as Hopalong and Johnny caught sight of him and he
swung his revolver on Hopalong at the moment when
the latter's bullet crashed through his brain.

Buck Peters, trying for a better position, slipped on the rock which had been the cause of the death of George Cross and before he could gain his feet a figure leaped down in front of him and raised a Colt in his defense, but spun half way around and fell, shot through the head. A cry of rage went up at this and a rush was made against the breast works from front and side. Frenchy McAllister's forebodings had come true.

Sanchez, finding his revolver empty and no time to reload, held up his hands. Frisco, blinded by blood, wounded in half a dozen places, desperate, snarling, and still unbeaten, wheeled viciously, but before he could pull his trigger, Hopalong grasped him and hurled him down, Johnny going with them. Doc, a second too late, waved his sombrero. "Come on, it's all over!"

In another second the rushing punchers from the front slid and rolled and plunged over the breastwork and eyed the results of their fire.

Meeker staggered around the corner and leaned against Buck for support. "My God! This is awful! I didn't think we were doing so much damage."

"I did!" retorted Buck. "I know what happens when my outfit burns powder. Where's Red?" he asked anxiously.

"Here I am," replied a voice behind him.

"All right; take that feller to the hut," the foreman ordered. "Johnny, you an Pete take the other," pointing to Frisco. "He's th' one that killed Frenchy. Hopalong, take Red, an' bring in that feller me an' Meeker tied up in that crevice, if he ain't got away."

Hopalong and Red went off to bring in Hall and Buck turned to the others. "You fellers doctor yore wounds. Meeker, yo're hard hit," he remarked, more closely looking at the H2 foreman.

"Yes. I know it—loss of blood, mostly," Meeker replied. "An' if it hadn't been for Cassidy I'd been hit a damned sight harder. Where's Doc? He knows what to do—*Doc!*"

"Coming," replied a voice and Doc turned the corner. He had a limited knowledge of the work he was called upon to do, and practice, though infrequent, had kept it more or less fresh.

"Reckon yo're named about right, Doc," Buck remarked as he passed the busy man. "You got me beat an' I ain't no slouch."

"I'd 'a been a real Doc if I hadn't left college like a fool—you've got to keep still, Jim," he chided.

"Hey, Buck," remarked Hopalong, joining the crowd and grinning at the injured, "we've got that feller in th' shack. When th' feller I grabbed out here saw him he called him Hall. Th' other is Frisco. How you feeling, Meeker? That was Shaw plugged you."

"Feeling better'n him," Meeker growled. "Yo're a good man to work with, Cassidy."

"Well, Cassidy, got any slugs in you?" affably asked Doc, the man Hopalong had wounded on the line a few weeks before. Doc brandished a knife and cleaning rod and appeared to be anxious to use them on somebody else.

"No; but what do you do with them things?" Hopalong rejoined, feeling of his bandage.

"Take out bullets," Doc grinned.

"Oh, I see; you cut a hole in th' back an' then push 'em right through," Hopalong laughed. "Reckon I'd rather have 'em go right through without stopping. Who's that calling?"

"Billy an' Curtis. Tell 'em to come up," Buck replied, walking towards the place where Frenchy's body lay.

Hopalong went to the edge and replied to the shouts and it was not long before they appeared. When Doc saw them he grinned pleasantly and drew them aside, trying to coax them to let him repair them. But Billy, eyeing the implements, side-stepped and declined with alacrity; Curtis was the victim.

"After *him* th' undertaker," Billy growled, going towards the hut.

CHAPTER XXXVIII

A Disagreeable Task

TWO MEN, Hall and Frisco, sat with their backs against the wall of the hut, weaponless, wounded, nervous, one sullen and enraged, the other growling querulously to himself about his numerous wounds. The third prisoner, was pacing to and fro with restless strides, vicious and defiant, his burning eyes quick, searching, calculating. It seemed as though he was filled with a tremendous amount of energy which would not let him remain quiet. When his companions spoke to him he flashed them a quick glance but did not answer; thinking, scheming, plotting, he missed not the slightest movement of those about him. Wounded as he was he did not appear to know it, so intent was he upon his thoughts.

Hall, saved from the dangers of the last night's fight, loosed his cumulative rage frequently in caustic and profane verbal abuse of his captors, his defeat, his companions, and the guard. Frisco, courageous as any under fire, was dejected because of the wait; merely a difference of temperament.

The guard, seated carelessly on a nearby rock, kept watch over the three and cogitated upon the whole affair, his Colt swinging from a hand between his knees. Twenty paces to his right was a stack of rifles and Sanchez, lengthening his panther stride with barely perceptible effort, drew nearer to them on each northward lap. He typified the class of men who never give up hope, and as he gained each yard he glanced furtively at the guard and then estimated the number of leaps necessary to reach the coveted rifles. His rippling muscles were bunching up for the desperate attempt when the guard interfered, the sharp clicks of his Colt bringing the Mexican to an abrupt stop. Sanchez shrugged his shoulders and wheeling, resumed his restless walk, being careful to keep it within safe limits.

Hall, lighting his pipe, blew a cloud of smoke into the air and looked at the guard, who was still cogitating.

"How did you fools finally figger we was out here?"

Hopalong looked up and smiled. "Oh, we just figgered you fools would be here, and would stay up here. Yore friend Antonio worked too hard."

Hall carefully packed his pipe and puffed quietly. "I knowed he'd bungle it."

"What happened to Cavalry an' Antonio?" asked Hall. "Did you get 'em when you came up?"

"They got down th' way we came up—Doc trailed Antonio an' got him at that water hole up north," Hopalong replied. "Don't know nothing about th' other feller. Reckon he got away, but one don't make much difference, anyhow. He'll never come back to this country."

"Say, how much longer will it take yore friends to do th' buryin' act?" asked Frisco irritably. "I'm plumb tired of waiting—these wounds hurt like blazes, too."

"Reckon they're coming now," was the reply. "I hear—yes, here they are."

"I owe you ten dollars, Hall," Frisco remarked, trivial

thing now entering his mind. "Reckon you won't get it, neither."

"Oh, pay me in hell!" Hall snapped.

"Yes," Buck was saying, "He knowed he was going an' he went like th' man he was—saving a friend. 'Tain't th' first time Frenchy McAllister's saved my life, neither."

Frisco glanced around and his face flashed with a look of recognition, but he held his tongue; not so with Curtis, who stared at him in surprise and stepped forward.

"Good God! It's Davis! What ever got you into this?"

"Easy money an' a gun fight," Davis, alias Frisco, replied.

"Tough luck, tough luck," Curtis muttered slowly.

"Damn tough, if you asks me," Frisco growled.

"What happened to th' others?" Curtis asked, referring to three men with whom he and Frisco had punched and prospected several years before.

"Little Dan went out in that same gun fight, Joe Baird was got by th' posse next day, an' George Wild an' I got into th' mountains an' was separated. I got free after a sixty-mile chase, but I don't know how George made out. We had stuck up a gold caravan an' killed two men what was with it. They was th' only fellers to pull their guns against us."

"Well, I'm damned!" ejaculated Curtis. "An' so that crowd went bad!"

"Say, for th' Lord's sake, get things moving," cried Hall, angrily. "If we've got to die make it quick. Wish I'd a' gone with Shaw 'stead of waiting for my own funeral."

Buck surveyed them. "Got anything to say?"

"Not me—I've had mine," replied Frisco, toying with a bandage. Then he started to say something but changed his mind. "Oh, well what's th' use! Go ahead."

"Don't drag it out," growled Hall. "Say, you got *my*

rope there?" he demanded suddenly, eyeing the coils slung over Skinny's shoulder. "No, you ain't, I want my own, savvy?"

"Oh, we ain't got time to hunt for no ropes," rejoined Skinny. "One's as good as another, ain't it."

"Yes, I reckon so—hustle it through," Hall replied, sullenly.

"Go ahead, you fellers," ordered Hopalong as some of his friends went first down the trail after the two sent to the camp for the horses. "Come, on, Sanchez! Fall in there!"

When the procession reached the bottom of the trail Buck halted it to wait for the horses and his prisoners took one more look around.

"Say, Peters, where's th' cayuses we had in that corral?" asked Hall, surprised.

"Oh, we got them out th' first night—we wasn't taking no chances," replied the foreman. "They're somewhere near th' camp now."

As the horse herd was driven up Sanchez made his last play. All were intent upon tightening cinches, the more intent because of the impending and disagreeable task, when he slipped like a shadow through the group and throwing himself across a pinto, headed in a circular track for the not too distant chaparral.

"*Take* him, Red!" shouted Buck, who was the first to recover.

Red's rifle leaped to his shoulder and steadied; in three more jumps the speedy pinto would have shielded Sanchez, clinging like a burr to the further side; but the rifle spoke once and he dropped and lay quiet on the sand.

Hopalong rode out to him and glancing at the still form, wheeled and returned. "Got him clean, Red."

A group of horsemen rode eastward towards the chaparral and as it was about to enclose them one of the riders bringing up the rear turned in his saddle and looked back at two dangling forms outlined against the darker background of the frowning mesa, two where he had expected to see three.

"Well, th' rustling is over," he remarked.

CHAPTER XXXIX

Thirst

THE STARS grow dim and a streak of color paints the eastern sky, sweeping through the upper reaches of the darkness and tingeing the earth's curtain until the dim gray light outlines spectral yuccas and twisted, grotesque cacti leaning in the hushed air like drunken sentries of some monstrous army. The dark carpet which stretched away on all sides begins to show its characteristics and soon develops into greasewood brush. As if curtains were drawn aside objects which a moment before were lost to sight in the darkness emerge out of the light like ghosts, bulky, indistinct, grotesque, and array themselves to complete the scene.

The silence seems to deepen and become strained, as if in fear of what is to come; the dark ground is now gray and tawny in places and the vegetation is plain to the eye. Then out of the east comes a flash and a red, coppery sun flares above the horizon, molten, quivering, blinding; the cool of the night swiftly departs and a caldron-like heat bursts upon the plain. The silence seems almost to shrink and become portentous with evil, the air is hushed, the plants stand without the movement of a leaf, and nowhere is seen any living creature. The whole is unreal, a panorama, with vegetation of wax and a painted, faded blue sky, the only movement being the shortening shadows and the rising sun.

Across the sand is an erratic trail of shoe prints, coming from the east. For a dozen yards it runs evenly and straight, then a few close prints straggle to and fro, zigzagging for a distance, finally going on straight again. But the erratic prints grow more frequent and become more pronounced as they go on, circling and weaving, crossing, recrossing and doubling back as their maker staggered hopelessly on his way, urged only by the instinct of thirst, to find water, if it were only a mouthful. The trail is here blurred, for he fell, and the prints of his hands and knees and shoe-tips tell how he went on for some distance. He gained his feet here and threw away his Colt, and later his holster and belt.

The sun is overhead now and the sand shimmers, the heated air quivering and glistening, and the desolate void takes on an air of mystery and fear, and death. No living thing moves across the heat-cursed sand, but here is a tangled mass of sand and clay and greasewood twigs, in the heart of which mice sleep and wait for night, and over there is a hillock sheltering lizards. Stay! Under that greasewood bush a foolish gray wolf is waiting for night—but he has little to fear, for he can cover forty miles between dark and dawn, and his instinct is infallible; no wandering trail will mark his passing, but one as straight as the flight of a bullet. The shadows shrink close to the stems of the plants and the thin air dances with heat.

Behind that clump of greasewood, back beyond those crippled cacti, a man staggers on and on. His hair is matted, his fingers bleeding from digging frantically in the sand for water; his lips, cracked and bleeding and swollen, hide the shrivelled, stiff tongue which clicks against his teeth at every painful step. His eyelids are stiff and the staring, unblinking eyes are set and swollen. He clutches at his throat time and time again—a drowning sensation is there. Ha! He drops to his knees and digs frantically again, for the sand is moist! A few days ago a water hole lay there. He throws off his shirt and finally staggers on again.

His tongue begins to swell and forces itself beyond the swollen, festering lips; the eyelids split and the protruding eyeballs weep tears of blood. His skin cracked and curls up, the clefts going constantly deeper into the flesh, and the exuding blood quickly dries and leaves a tough coating over the wounds. Wherever the exudation touches it stings and burns, and the cracks and clefts, irritated more and more each minute, deepen and widen and lengthen, smarting and nerve-racking with their pain.

There! A grove of beautiful green trees is before him, and in it a fountain splashes with musical babbling. He yells and dances and then, casting aside the rest of his clothes, staggers towards it. Water, water, at last! Water and shade! It grows indistinct, wavers—and is gone! But it must be there. It was there only a moment ago—and on and on he runs, hands tearing at his choking, drowning throat. Here is water—close at hand—a purling, cold brook, whispering and tinkling over its rocky bed—he jumps into it—it moved! It's over there, ten paces to his right. On and on he staggers, the stream just ahead. He falls more frequently and wavers now. Oh, for just a canteen of water, just a swallow, just a drop! The gold of the world would not buy it from him— just a drop of water!

He is dying from within, from the inside out. The liquids of his body exude through the clefts and evaporate. His brain burns and bands of white-hot steel crush his throbbing head and his burning lungs. No amount of water will save him now—only death, merciful death can end his sufferings.

Water at last! Real water, a pool of stagnant liquid lies at the bottom of a slight depression, the dregs of a larger pool concentrated by evaporation. Around it are the prints of many kinds of feet. It is water, water!—he plunges forward into it and lies motionless, half submerged. A grayback lizard darts out of the greasewood near at hand, blinks rapidly and darts back again, glad to escape the intolerable heat.

Cavalry had escaped.

CHAPTER XL

Changes

WITH THE passing of the weeks the two ranches had settled down to routine duty. On the H2 conditions were changed greatly for the better and Meeker gloated over his gushing wells and the dam which gave him a reservoir on his north range, the early completion of which he owed largely to the experience and willing assistance of Buck and the Bar-20 outfit.

It was getting along towards fall when a letter came to the Bar-20 addressed to John McAllister. Buck looked at it long and curiously. "Wonder who's writing to Frenchy?" he mused. "Well, I've got to find out," and he opened the envelope and looked at the signature; it made him stare still more and he read the letter carefully. George McAllister, through the aid of the courts, had gained possession of the old Double Y in the name of its owners and was going to put an outfit on the ground to evict and hold off those who had jumped it. He knew nothing about ranching and wanted Frenchy McAllister, who owned half of it, to take charge of it and to give him the address of Buck Peters the other half-owner. He advised that Peters' share be bought because the range was near a railroad and was growing more valuable every day.

Buck's decision was taken instantly. Much as he disliked to leave the old outfit here was the chance he had been waiting for without knowing it. He would never have set foot on the Double Y during Frenchy's lifetime because of loyalty to his old friend. Had he at any time desired possession of the property he and his friends could have taken it and left court actions to the other side. But Frenchy was gone, and he still owned half of a valuable piece of property and one that he could make pay well. He was getting on in years and it would be pleasant to have his cherished dream come true, to be the over-lord and half-owner of a good cattle ranch and to know that when he became too old to work with any degree of pleasure he need not worry about his remaining years. If he left the Bar-20 one of his friends would take his place and he was sure it would be Hopalong. The advancement in pay and authority would please the man whom he had looked upon as his son. And perhaps it would bring to Hopalong that which now kept his eyes turned towards the H2. Yes, it was time to go to his own and let another man come into *his* own; to move along and give a younger man a chance.

He replied to George McAllister at length, covering everything, and took the letter to the bunk house to have it mailed.

"Billy," he said, "here's a letter to go to Cowan's first thing to-morrow. Don't forget."

Buck started the fall work early and pushed it harder than usual for he wished to have everything done before the new foreman took charge. The beef roundup and drives were over with quickly, considering the time and labor involved, and when the chill blasts of early winter swept across the range and whined around the ranch buildings Buck smiled with the satisfaction which comes with work well done. George McAllister, failing to buy Buck's interest, now implored him to go to the Double Y at once and take charge, which he had promised to do in time to become familiar with conditions on the winterbound northern range before the new herds were driven to it.

As yet he had told his men nothing of his plans for fear they would persuade him to stay where he was, but he could tell Meeker, and one crisp morning he called at the H2 and led its foreman aside. When he had finished Meeker grasped his hand, told him how sorry he was to lose so good a friend and neighbor, and how glad he was at the friend's good fortune.

"I hope Cassidy *is* th' man to take yore place, Peters," he remarked, thoughtfully. "He's a good man, th' best in th'country, strong, square, and nervy. I've had my eyes on him for some time an' I'll back him to bust anything he throws his rope on. He can handle that ranch easy an' well."

"Yo're right," replied Buck, slowly. "He ain't never failed to make good yet. Whoever th' boys pick out to be foreman will be foreman, for th' owners have left that question with me. But Meeker, it's like pulling teeth for me to go up to Montana without him. I can't take him 'less I take 'em all, an' I've got reasons why I can't do that. An' I ain't quite shore he'd go with me now— yore ranch holds something that ties him tight to this range. He'll be lonely up in our ranch house, an' it's plenty big enough for two," he finished, smiling interrogatively at his companion.

"Well, I reckon it'll not be lonely if he wants to change it," laughed Meeker. "Leastawise, them's th' symptoms plentiful enough down here. I was dead set agin it at first, but now I don't want nothing else but to see my girl fixed for life. An' when I pass out, all I have is hers."

CHAPTER XLI

Hopalong's Reward

SEVEN MEN loitered about the line house on Lookout Peak, wondering why they, the old outfit, had been told to await their foreman there. Why were the others, all good fellows, excluded? What could it mean? Foreboding grew upon them as they talked the matter over and when Buck approached they waited eagerly for him to speak.

He dismounted and looked at them with pride and affection and a trace of sorrow showed in his voice and face when he began to talk.

"Boys," he said, slowly, "We've got things ready for snow when it comes. Th' cattle are strong an' fat, there's plenty of grass curing on th' range, an' th' biggest drive ever sent north from this ranch has been taken care of. There's seven of you here, two on th' north range, an' four more good men coming next week; an' thirteen men can handle this ranch with some time to spare.

"I've been with you for a long time now. Some of you I've had for over twelve years, an' no man ever had a better outfit. You've never turned back on any

game, an' you've never had no trouble among yoreselves. You've seen me sending an' getting letters purty
regular for some time, an' you've been surprised at how
I've pushed you to get ready for winter. I'm going to
tell you all about it now, an' when I've finished I want
you to vote on something," and they listened in dumb
surprise and sorrow while he told them of his decision.
When he had finished they crowded about him and
begged him to stay with them, telling them they would
not allow him to leave. But if he must go, then they,
too, must go and help him whip a wild and lawless
range into submission. He would need them badly in
Montana, and nowhere could he get men who would
work and fight so hard and cheerfully for him as his
old outfit. They would not let him talk and he could
not if they would, for there was something in his throat
which choked and pained him. Johnny Nelson and Hopalong were tugging at his shoulders and the others
stormed and pleaded and swore, tears in the eyes of
all. He wavered and would have thrown away all his
resolutions, when he thought of Hopalong and the girl.
Pushing them back he told them he could not stay and
begged them, as they loved him to consider his future.
They looked at one another strangely and then realized
how selfish they were, and said so profanely.

"*Now* yo're my old outfit," he cried, striking while
the iron was hot. "I've told you why I must go, an' why
I can't take *all* of you with me, an' why I won't take a
few an' leave th' rest. Don't think I don't want you!
Why, with you at my back I'd buck that range into
shape in no time, an' chase th' festive gunfighters off
th' earth. Mebby some day you can come up to me, but
not now. Now I want th' new foreman to th' Bar-20 to
be one of th' men who worked so hard an' loyally an'
long for me an' th' ranch. I want one of you to take my
place. Th' owners have left th' choice to me, an' say th'
man I appoint will be their choice; an' I ain't a-going to
do it—I can't do it. One last favor, boys; go in that

house an' pick yore foreman. Go now, an' I'll wait for you here."

"We'll do it right here—Red Connors!" cried Hopalong.

"Hopalong!" yelled Red and Johnny in the same voice, and only a breath ahead of the others. "Hopalong! Hopalong!" was the cry, his own voice lost, buried, swept under. He tried to argue, but he could make no headway, for his exploits were shouted to convince him. As fast as he tried to speak someone remembered something else he had done—they ranged over a period of ten years and from Mexico to Cheyenne; from Dodge City and Leavenworth to the Rockies.

Buck laughed and clapped his hands on Hopalong's shoulders. "I appoint you foreman, an' you can't get out of it, nohow! Lemme shake hands with th' new foreman of th' Bar-20—I'm one of th' boys now, an' glad to get rid of th' responsibility for a while. Good luck, son!"

"No you ain't going to get rid of 'em," laughed Hopalong, but serious withal. "Yo're th' foreman of this ranch till you leave us—ain't he, boys?" he appealed.

Buck put his hands to his ears and yelled for less noise. "All right, I'll play at breaking you in—'though th' Lord knows I can't show you nothing you don't know now. My first order under these conditions is that you ride south, Hopalong, an' tell th' news to Meeker, an' to his girl. An' tell 'em separate, too. An' don't forget I want to see you hobbled before I leave next month—tell her to make it soon!"

Hopalong reddened and grinned under the rapid-fire advice and chaffing of his friends and tried to retort.

Johnny sprang forward. "Come on, fellers! Put him on his cayuse an' start him south! We've got to have *some* hand in his courting, anyhow!"

"Right!"

"Good idea!"

"Look out! *Grab* him, Red!"

"Up with him!"

"We ought to escort him on his first love trail," yelled Skinny above the uproar. "Come on! *Saddles*, boys!"

"Like hell!" cried Hopalong, spurring forward his nettlesome mount. "You've got to grow wings to catch me an' Red Eagle! *Go, bronc!*" and he shot forward, cheers and good wishes thundering after him.

Buck moved about restlessly in his sleep and then awakened suddenly and lay quiet as a hand touched his shoulder. "What is it? Who are you?" he demanded, ominously.

"I reckoned you'd like to know that yo're going to be best man in two weeks, Buck," said a happy voice. "She said a month, but I told her you was going away before then, an' you *might*, you know. I shore feel joyous!"

The huge hand of the elder man closed over his in a grip which made him wince. "Good boy, an' good luck, Hoppy! It was due you. Good luck, an' happiness, son!"